"Perhaps this *was* a magic day."

When Marigold turned to look down the other road there was the wished-for little girl standing by her very elbow and grinning at her.

Marigold stared in amazement. She had never seen the girl before or any one just like her. The stranger was about her own age—possibly a year older. She wore an odd, smart green dress with touches of scarlet embroidery and she had wonderful slim white hands—very beautiful and very white. But—the stranger had *bare knees*.

Who could this girl be? She had appeared so suddenly, so uncannily. She looked different in every way from the Harmony little girls.

"Who are you?" she asked abruptly.

The stranger grinned.

"I'm Princess Varvara," she said.

Marigold turned haughtily away. A Lesley of Cloud of Spruce was not going to be made fun of by any little nobody from nowhere.

But the girl in green whirled about on tip-toes till she was in front of Marigold once more.

Varvara laughed. There was some trick about her laugh. It made you want to laugh too. Marigold had hard work to keep from laughing. But she wouldn't laugh. She would show this young Yankee, who thought her soft enough to believe any old yarn, just what it was to be Marigold Lesley of Cloud of Spruce.

Lucy Maud Montgomery fans will also enjoy these other
Bantam Books by the author

Chronicles of Avonlea
The Story Girl
The Golden Road
The Blue Castle

The Anne of Green Gables series
Anne of Green Gables
Anne of Avonlea
Anne of the Island
Anne of Windy Poplars
Anne's House of Dreams
Anne of Ingleside
Rainbow Valley
Rilla of Ingleside

The Emily Books
Emily of New Moon
Emily Climbs
Emily's Quest

Magic for Marigold

L. M. Montgomery

BANTAM BOOKS
NEW YORK • TORONTO • LONDON • SYDNEY • AUCKLAND

RL 6, IL age 10 and up

MAGIC FOR MARIGOLD
A Bantam Book / published by arrangement with
the author's estate

PRINTING HISTORY
Copyright 1929 by McClelland and Stewart Limited
Canadian Favourites Edition (McClelland and Stewart) 1977
Bantam edition / May 1989

ISBN 0-553-28046-5

PRINTED IN CANADA
COVER PRINTED IN U.S.A.

U   0 9 8 7 6 5 4 3 2 1

To
NORA

IN MEMORY OF A WORLD
THAT HAS PASSED AWAY

Contents

CHAPTER I

What's in a Name?

1

Once upon a time—which, when you come to think of it, is really the only proper way to begin a story—the only way that really smacks of romance and fairyland—all the Harmony members of the Lesley clan had assembled at Cloud of Spruce to celebrate Old Grandmother's birthday as usual. Also to name Lorraine's baby. It was a crying shame, as Aunt Nina pathetically said, that the little darling had been in the world four whole months without a name. But what could you do, with poor dear Leander dying in that terribly sudden way just two weeks before his daughter was born and poor Lorraine being so desperately ill for weeks and weeks afterwards? Not very strong yet, for that matter. And there was tuberculosis in her family, you know.

Aunt Nina was not really an aunt at all—at least, not of any Lesley. She was just a cousin. It was the custom of the Lesley caste to call every one "Uncle" or "Aunt" as soon as he or she had become too old to be fitly called by a first name among the young fry. There will be no end of these "aunts" and "uncles" bobbing in and out of this story—as well as several genuine ones. I shall not stop to explain which kind they were. It doesn't matter. They were all Lesleys or married to Lesleys. *That* was all that mattered. You were born to the purple if you were a Lesley. Even the pedigrees of their cats were known.

All the Lesleys adored Lorraine's baby. They had all agreed in loving Leander—about the only thing they had ever been known to agree on. And it was thirty years since there had been a baby at Cloud of Spruce. Old Grandmother had more than once said gloomily that the good old stock was running out. So this small lady's advent would have been hailed with delirious delight if it hadn't been for

1

Leander's death and Lorraine's long illness. Now that Old Grandmother's birthday had come, the Lesleys had an excuse for their long-deferred jollification. As for the name, no Lesley baby was ever named until every relative within get-at-able distance had had his or her say in the matter. The selection of a suitable name was, in their eyes, a much more important thing than the mere christening. And how much more in the case of a fatherless baby whose mother was a sweet soul enough—but—you know—a Winthrop!

Cloud of Spruce, the original Lesley homestead, where Old Grandmother and Young Grandmother and Mrs. Leander and the baby and Salome Silversides lived, was on the harbour shore, far enough out of Harmony village to be in the real country; a cream brick house—a nice chubby old house—so covered with vines that it looked more like a heap of ivy than a house; a house that had folded its hands and said, "I will rest." Before it was the beautiful Harmony Harbour; with its purring waves, so close that in autumnal storms the spray dashed over the very doorsteps and encrusted the windows. Behind it was an orchard that climbed the slope. And about it always the soft sighing of the big spruce wood on the hill.

The birthday dinner was eaten in Old Grandmother's room—which had been the "orchard room" until Old Grandmother, two years back, had cheerfully and calmly announced that she was tired of getting up before breakfast and working between meals.

"I'm going to spend the rest of my life being waited on," she said. "I've had ninety years of slaving for other people— and bossing them, the Lesleys said in their hearts. But not out loud, for it did really seem at times as if Old Grandmother's ears could hear for miles. Uncle Ebenezer said something once about Old Grandmother, to himself, in his cellar at midnight, when he knew he was the only human being in the house. Next Sunday afternoon Old Grandmother cast it up to him. She said Lucifer had told her. Lucifer was her cat. And Uncle Ebenezer suddenly remembered that *his* cat had been sitting on the edge of the potato bin when he said that.

It was safest not to say things about Old Grandmother.

Old Grandmother's room was a long, dim-green apartment running across the south end of the house, with a glass door opening right into the orchard. Its walls were hung with photographs of Lesley brides for sixty years back, most of them with enormous bouquets and wonderful veils and trains. Clementine's photograph was among them— Clementine, Leander's first wife, who had died six years ago with *her* little unnamed daughter. Old Grandmother had it hanging on the wall at the foot of her bed so that she could see it all the time. Old Grandmother had been very fond of Clementine. At least, she always gave Lorraine that impression.

The picture was good to look at—Clementine Lesley had been very beautiful. She was not dressed as a bride—in fact the picture had been taken just before her marriage and had a clan fame as "Clementine with the lily." She was posed standing with her beautiful arms resting on a pedestal and in one slender, perfect hand—Clementine's hands had become a tradition of loveliness—she held a lily, at which she was gazing earnestly. Old Grandmother had told Lorraine once that a distinguished guest at Cloud of Spruce, an artist of international fame, had exclaimed on seeing that picture,

"Exquisite hands! Hands into which a man might fearlessly put his soul!"

Lorraine had sighed and looked at her rather thin little hands. Not beautiful—scarcely even pretty; yet Leander had onced kissed their finger-tips and said—but Lorraine did not tell Old Grandmother what Leander had said. Perhaps Old Grandmother might have liked her better if she had.

Old Grandmother had her clock in the corner by the bed—a clock that had struck for the funerals and weddings and goings and comings and meetings and partings of five generations; the grandfather clock her husband's father had brought out from Scotland a hundred and forty years ago; the Lesleys plumed themselves on being Prince Edward Island pioneer stock. It was still keeping excellent time and Old Grandmother got out of bed every night to wind it. She would have done that if she had been dying.

Her other great treasure was in the opposite corner. A big glass case with Alicia, the famous Skinner doll, in it. Old Grandmother's mother had been a Skinner and the doll had no part in Lesley traditions, but every Lesley child had been brought up in the fear and awe of it and knew its story. Old Grandmother's mother's sister had lost her only little daughter of three years and had never been "quite right" afterwards. She had had a waxen image of her baby made and kept it beside her always and talked to it as if it had been alive. It was dressed in a wonderful embroidered dress that had belonged to the dead baby, and wore one of her slippers. The other slipper was held in one waxen hand ready for the small bare foot that peeped out under the muslin flounces. The doll was so lifelike that Lorraine always shuddered when she passed it, and Salome Silversides was very doubtful of the propriety of having such a thing in the house at all, especially as she knew that Lazarre, the French hired man, thought and told that it was the Old Lady's "Saint" and believed she prayed before it regularly. But all the Lesleys had a certain pride in it. No other Prince Edward Island family could boast a doll like that. It conferred a certain distinction upon them and tourists wrote it up in their local papers when they went back home.

Of course the cats were present at the festivity also. Lucifer and the Witch of Endor. Both of black velvet with great round eyes. Cloud of Spruce was noted for its breed of black cats with topaz-hued eyes. Its kittens were not scattered broadcast but given away with due discrimination.

Lucifer was Old Grandmother's favourite. A remote, subtle cat. An inscrutable cat so full of mystery that it fairly oozed out of him. The Witch of Endor became her name but compared to Lucifer she was commonplace. Salome wondered secretly that Old Grandmother wasn't afraid of a judgment for calling a cat after the Old Harry. Salome "liked cats in their place" but she was furious when Uncle Klon said to her once,

"Salome Silversides! Why, you ought to be a cat yourself with a name like that. A sleek, purring plushy Maltese."

"I'm sure I don't look like a cat," said Salome, highly insulted. And Uncle Klon agreed that she did not.

Old Grandmother was a gnomish dame of ninety-two who meant to live to be a hundred. A tiny, shrunken, wrinkled thing with flashing black eyes. There was a Puckish hint of malice in most things she said or did. She ruled the whole Lesley clan and knew everything that was said and done in it. If she had given up "slaving" she certainly had not given up "bossing." To-day she was propped up on crimson cushions, with a fresh, frilled, white cap tied around her face, eating her dinner heartily and thinking things not lawful to be uttered about her daughters-in-law and her granddaughters-in-law and her great-grand-daughters-in-law.

2

Young Grandmother, a mere lass of sixty-five, sat at the head of the long table—a tall, handsome lady with bright, steel-blue eyes and white hair, whom Old Grandmother thought a somewhat pert young thing. There was nothing of the traditional grandmother of caps and knitting about *her*. She was like a stately old princess in her purple velvet gown with its wonderful lace collar. The gown had been made eight years before, but when Young Grandmother wore anything it seemed at once in the height of the fashion. Most of the Lesleys present thought she should not have laid aside her black even for a birthday dinner. But Young Grandmother did not care what they thought any more than Old Grandmother did. She had been a Blaisdell—one of "the stubborn Blaisdells"—and the Blaisdell traditions were as good as the Lesley traditions any day.

Lorraine sat on the right of Young Grandmother at the table, with the baby in her cradle beside her. Because of the baby she had a certain undeniable importance never before conceded her. All the Lesleys had been more or less opposed to Leander's "second choice." Only the fact that she was a minister's daughter appeased them. She was a shy, timid, pretty creature—quite insignificant except for her enormous masses of lustrous, pale gold hair. Her small face was sweet and flower-like and she had peculiarly soft grey-blue eyes with long lashes. She looked very young and fragile in her black dress. But she was beginning to be a little happy once more. Her arms, that had reached out so emptily in the silence of the night, were filled again. The fields and hills around Cloud of Spruce that had been so stark and bare and chill when her little lady came were green and golden now, spilled over with blossoms, and the orchard was an exquisite perfumed world by itself. One could not be altogether unhappy, in springtime, with such a wonderful, unbelievable baby.

The baby lay in the old Heppelwhite cradle where her father and grandfather had lain before her—a quite adorable baby, with a saucy little chin, tiny hands as exquisite as the apple-blossoms, eyes of fairy blue, and the arrogant, superior smile of babies before they have forgotten all the marvellous things they know at first. Lorraine could hardly eat her dinner for gazing at her baby—and wondering. Would this tiny thing ever be a dancing, starry-eyed girl— a white bride—a mother? Lorraine shivered. It did not do to look so far ahead. Aunt Anne got up, brought a shawl, and tenderly put it around Lorraine's shoulders. Lorraine was almost melted, for the June day was hot, but she wore the shawl all through dinner rather than hurt Aunt Anne's feelings. That one fact described Lorraine.

On Young Grandmother's left sat Uncle Klondike, the one handsome, mysterious, unaccountable member of the Lesley clan, with his straight, heavy eyebrows, his flashing blue eyes, his mane of tawny hair and the red-gold beard which had caused a sentimental Harmony lady of uncertain years to say that he made her think of those splendid old Vikings.

Uncle Klondike's real name was Horace, but ever since he had come back from the Yukon with gold dropping out of his pockets he had been known as Klondike Lesley. His deity was the God of All Wanderers and in his service Horace Lesley had spent wild, splendid, adventurous years.

When Klondike had been a boy at school he had a habit of looking at certain places on the map and saying, "I'll go there." Go he did. He had stood on the southernmost boulder of Ceylon and sat on Buddhist cairns at the edge of

Thibet. The Southern Cross was a pal and he had heard the songs of nightingales in the gardens of the Alhambra. India and the China seas were to him as a tale that is told, and he had walked alone in great Arctic spaces under northern lights. He had lived in many places but he had never thought of any of them as home. That name had all unconsciously been kept sacred to the long, green, seaward-looking glen where he had been born.

And finally he had come home, sated, to live the rest of his life a decent law-abiding clansman, whereof the conclusive sign and token was that he had trimmed his moustache and beard into decency. The moustache had been particularly atrocious. Its ends hung down nearly as far as his beard did. When Aunt Anne asked him despairingly why upon earth he wore a moustache like that he retorted that he wrapped it round his ears to keep them warm. The clan were horribly afraid he meant to go on wearing them—for Uncle Klon was both Lesley *and* Blaisdell. He finally had them clipped, though he could never be induced to go the length of a clean-shaven face, fashion or no fashion. But, though he went to bed early at least once a week, he still savoured life with gusto and the clan were always secretly much afraid of him and his satiric winks and cynical speeches. Aunt Nina, in particular, had held him in terror ever since the day she had told him proudly that her husband had *never* lied to her.

"Oh, you poor woman," said Uncle Klon, with real sympathy in his tone.

Nina supposed there was a joke somewhere but she could never find it. She was a W. C. T. U. and an I. O. D. E. and most of the other letters of the alphabet—but somehow she found it hard to get the hang of Klondike's jokes.

Klondike Lesley was known to be a woman-hater. He scoffed openly at all love, more especially the supreme absurdity of love at first sight. This did not prevent his clan from trying for years to marry him off. It would be the making of Klondike if he had a good wife who would stand no nonsense. They were very obvious about it, and with the renowned Lesley frankness, recommended several excellent brides to him. But Klondike Lesley was notoriously hard to please.

"Katherine Nichols?"

"But look at the thick ankles of her."

"Emma Goodfellow?"

"Her mother used to call out 'meow' in church whenever the minister said something she didn't like. Can't risk heredity."

"Rose Osborn?"

"I can't stand a woman with pudgy hands."

"Sara Jennet?"

"An egg without salt."

"Lottie Parks?"

"I'd like her as a flavouring, not as a dish."

"Ruth Russell?"—triumphantly, as having at last hit on a woman with whom no reasonable man could find fault.

"Too peculiar. When she has nothing to say she doesn't talk. That's really too uncanny in a woman, you know."

"Dorothy Porter?"

"Ornamental by candlelight. But I don't believe she'd look so well at breakfast."

"Amy Ray?"

"Always purring, blinking, sidling, clawing. Nice small pussy-cat but I'm no mouse."

"Agnes Barr?"

"A woman who says Coué's formula instead of her prayers!"

"Olive Purdy?"

"Tongue—temper—and tears. Go sparingly, thank you."

Even Old Grandmother took a hand and met with no better success. She was wiser than to throw any one girl at his head—the men of the Lesley clan never had married the women picked out for them. But she had her own way of managing things.

"'He travels the fastest who travels alone,'" was all she could get out of Klondike.

"Very clever of you," said Old Grandmother, "if travelling fast is all there is to life."

"Not clever of *me*. Don't you know your Kipling, Grandmother?"

"What is a Kipling?" said Old Grandmother.

Uncle Klondike did not tell her. He merely said he was doomed to die a bachelor—and could not escape his kismet.

Old Grandmother was not a stupid woman even if she didn't know what a Kipling was.

"You've waited too long—you've lost your appetite," she said shrewdly.

The Lesleys gave it up. No use trying to fit this exasperating relative with a wife. A bachelor Klon remained, with an awful habit of wiring "sincere sympathy" when any of his friends got married. Perhaps it was just as well. His nephews and nieces might benefit, especially Lorraine's baby whom he evidently worshipped. So here he was, unwedded, light-hearted and content, watching them all with his amused smile.

Lucifer had leaped on his knee as soon as he had sat down. Lucifer condescended to very few but, as he told the Witch of Endor, Klondike Lesley had a way with him. Uncle Klon fed Lucifer with bits from his own plate and Salome, who ate with the family because she was a fourth cousin of Jane Lyle, who had married the stepbrother of a Lesley, thought it ghastly.

3

The baby had to be talked all over again and Uncle William-over-the-bay covered himself with indelible disgrace by saying dubiously,

"She is not—ahem—really a pretty child, do you think?"

"All the better for her future looks," said Old Grandmother tartly. She had been biding her moment, like a watchful cat, to give a timely dig. "*You*," she added maliciously, "were a very pretty baby—though you did not have any more hair on your head than you have now."

"Beauty is a fatal gift. She will be better without it," sighed Aunt Nina.

"Then why do you cold-cream your face every night and eat raw carrots for your complexion and dye your hair?" asked Old Grandmother.

Aunt Nina couldn't imagine how Old Grandmother knew about the carrots. *She* had no cat to tattle to Lucifer.

"We are all as God made us," said Uncle Ebenezer piously.

"Then God botched some of us," snapped Old Grandmother, looking significantly at Uncle Ebenezer's enormous ears and the frill of white whisker around his throat that made him look oddly like a sheep. But then, reflected Old Grandmother, whoever might be responsible for the nose, it was hardly fair to blame God for Ebenezer's whiskers.

"She has a peculiarly shaped hand, hasn't she?" persisted Uncle William-over-the-bay.

Aunt Anne bent over and kissed one of the little hands. "The hand of an artist," she said.

Lorriane looked at her gratefully and hated Uncle William-over-the-bay bitterly for ten minutes under her golden hair.

"Handsome is as handsome does," said Uncle Archibald, who rarely opened his mouth save to emit a proverb.

"Would you mind telling me, Archibald," said Old Grandmother pleasantly, "if you really look that solemn when you're asleep."

No one answered her. Aunt Mary Martha-over-the-bay, the only one who could have answered, had been dead for ten years.

"Whether she's pretty or not, she's going to have very long lashes," said Aunt Anne, reverting to the baby as a safer subject of conversation. There was no sense in letting Old Grandmother start a family row for her own amusement so soon after poor Leander's passing away.

"God help the men then," said Uncle Klon gravely.

Aunt Anne wondered why Old Grandmother was laughing to herself until the bed shook. Aunt Anne reflected that it would have been just as well if Klondike with his untimely sense of humour had not been present in a serious assemblage like this.

"Well, we must give her a pretty name, anyhow," said Aunt Flora briskly. "It's simply a shame that it's been left as long as this. No Lesley ever was before. Come, Grandmother, you ought to name her. What do you suggest?"

Old Grandmother affected the indifferent. She had three namesakes already so she knew Leander's baby wouldn't be named after *her*.

"Call it what you like," she said. "I'm too old to bother about it. Fight it out among yourselves."

"But we'd like your advice, Grandmother," unfortunately said Aunt Leah, whom Old Grandmother was just detesting because she had noticed the minute Leah shook hands with her that she had had her nails manicured.

"I have no advice to give. I have nothing but a little wisdom and I cannot give you *that*. Neither can I help it if a woman has a bargain-counter nose."

"Are you referring to *my* nose," inquired Aunt Leah with spirit. She often said she was the only one in the clan who wasn't afraid of Old Grandmother.

"The pig that's bit squeals," retorted Old Grandmother. She leaned back on her pillows disdainfully and sipped her tea with a vengeance. She had got square with Leah for manicuring her nails.

She had insisted on having her dinner first so that she might watch the others eating theirs. She knew it made them all more or less uncomfortable. Oh, but it was fine to be able to be disagreeable again. She had had to be so good and considerate for four months. Four months was long enough to mourn for anybody. Four months of not daring to give anybody a wigging. They had seemed like four centuries.

Lorraine sighed. She knew what *she* wanted to call her baby. But she knew that she would never have the courage to say it. And if she did she knew they would never consent to it. When you married into a family like the Lesleys you had to take the consequences. It was very hard when you couldn't name your own baby—when you were not even asked what you'd *like* it named. If Lee had only lived it would have been different. Lee, who was not a bit like the other Lesleys—except Uncle Klon, a little—Lee, who loved wonder and beauty and laughter—laughter that had been hushed so suddenly. Surely the jests of Heaven must have had more spice since he had joined in them. How he would have howled at this august conclave over the naming of his baby! How he would have brushed them aside! Lorraine felt sure he would have let her call her baby——

"*I* think," said Mrs. David Lesley, throwing her bombshell gravely and sadly, "that it would only be graceful and fitting that she should be called after Leander's first wife."

Mrs. David and Clementine had been very intimate friends. But Clementine! Lorraine shivered again and wished she hadn't, for Aunt Anne's eye looked like another shawl.

Everybody looked at Clementine's picture.

"Poor little Clementine," sighed Aunt Stasia in a tone that made Lorraine feel she should never have taken poor little Clementine's place.

"Do you remember what lovely jet black hair she had?" asked Aunt Marcia.

"And what lovely hands?" said Great-Aunt Matilda.

"She was so young to die," sighed Aunt Josephine.

"She was *such* a sweet girl," said Great-Aunt Elizabeth.

"A sweet girl all right," agreed Uncle Klon, "but why condemn an innocent child to carry a name like that all her life? That would really be a sin."

The clan, with the exception of Mrs. David, felt grateful to him and looked it, especially Young Grandmother. The name simply wouldn't have done, no matter how sweet Clementine was. That horrid old song, for instance—*Oh, my darling Clementine*, that boys used to howl along the road at nights. No, no, not for a Lesley. But Mrs. David was furious. Not only because Klondike disagreed with her but because he was imitating her old lisp, so long outgrown that it really was mean of him to drag it up again like this.

"Will you have some more dressing?" inquired Young Grandmother graciously.

"No, thank you." Mrs. David was not going to have any more, by way of signifying displeasure. Later on she took a still more terrible revenge by leaving two-thirds of her pudding uneaten, knowing that Young Grandmother had concocted it. Young Grandmother woke up in the night and wondered if anything could really have been the matter with the pudding. The others *might* have eaten it out of politeness.

"If Leander's name had been almost anything else she might have been named for her father," said Great-Uncle Walter. "Roberta—Georgina—Johanna—Andrea—Stephanie—Wilhelmina——"

"Or Davidena," said Uncle Klon. But Great-Uncle Walter ignored him.

"You can't make anything out of a name like *Leander*. Whatever did you call him that for, Marian?"

"His grandfather named him after him who swam the Hellespont," said Young Grandmother as rebukingly as if she had not, thirty-five years before, cried all one night because Old Grandfather had given her baby such a horrid name.

"She might be called Hero," said Uncle Klon.

"We had a dog called that once," said Old Grandmother.

"Leander didn't tell you before he died that he wanted any special name, did he, Lorraine?" inquired Aunt Nina.

"No," faltered Lorraine. "He—he had so little time to tell me—anything."

The clan frowned at Nina as a unit. They thought she was very tactless. But what could you expect of a woman who wrote poetry and peddled it about the country? *Writing* it might have been condoned—and concealed. After all, the Lesleys were not intolerant and everybody had some short-comings. But *selling* it openly!

"I should like baby to be called Gabriella," persisted Nina.

"There has never been such a name among the Lesleys," said Old Grandmother. And that was *that*.

"I think it's time we had some new names," said the poetess rebelliously. But every one looked stony, and Nina began to cry. She cried upon the slightest provocation. Lorraine remembered that Leander had always called her Mrs. Gummidge.

"Come, come," said Old Grandmother, "surely we can name this baby as well comfortably as uncomfortably. Don't make the mistake, Nina, of thinking that you are helping things along by making a martyr of yourself."

"What do *you* think, Miss Silversides?" inquired Uncle Charlie, who thought Salome was being entirely ignored and didn't like it.

"Oh, it doesn't matter what *I* think. *I* am of no consequence," said Salome, ostentatiously helping herself to the pickles.

"Come, come, now, you're one of the family," coaxed Uncle Charlie, who knew—so he said—how to handle women.

"Well"—Salome relaxed because she was really dying to have her say in it—"I've always thought names that ended in 'ine' were so elegant. *My* choice would be Rosaline."

"Or Evangeline," said Great-Uncle Walter.

"Or Eglantine," said Aunt Marcia eagerly.

"Or Gelatine," said Uncle Klon.

There was a pause.

"Juno would be such a nice name," said Cousin Teresa.

"But we are Presbyterians," said Old Grandmother.

"Or Robinette," suggested Uncle Charlie.

"We are English," said Young Grandmother.

"I think Yvonne is such a romantic name," said Aunt Flora.

"Names have really nothing to do with romance," said Uncle Klon. "The most thrilling and tragic love affair I ever knew was between a man named Silas Twingletoe and a woman named Kezia Birtwhistle. It's my opinion children shouldn't be named at all. They should be numbered until they're grown up, then choose their own names."

"But then you are not a mother, my dear Horace," said Young Grandmother tolerantly.

"Besides, there's an Yvonne Clubine keeping a lingerie shop in Charlottetown," said Aunt Josephine.

"Lingerie? If you mean underclothes for heaven's sake say so," snapped Old Grandmother.

"Juanita is a rather nice uncommon name," suggested John Eddy Lesley-over-the-bay. "J-u-a-n-i-t-a."

"Nobody would know how to spell it or pronounce it," said Aunt Marcia.

"I think," began Uncle Klon—but Aunt Josephine took the road.

"*I* think——"

"*Place aux dames*," murmured Uncle Klon. Aunt Josephine thought he was swearing but ignored him.

"*I* think the baby should be called after one of our missionaries. It's a shame that we have three foreign missionaries in the connection and not one of them has a namesake—even if they are only fourth cousins. *I* suggest we call her Harriet after the oldest one."

"But," said Aunt Anne, "that would be slighting Ellen and Louise."

"Well," said Young Grandmother haughtily—Young Grandmother was haughty because nobody had suggested naming the baby after *her*—"call her the whole three names, Harriet Ellen Louise Lesley. Then no fourth cousin need feel slighted."

The suggestion seemed to find favour. Lorraine caught her breath anxiously and looked at Uncle Klon. But rescue came from another quarter.

"Have you ever," said Old Grandmother with a wicked chuckle, "thought what the initials spell?"

They hadn't. They did. Nothing more was said about missionaries.

4

"Sylvia is a beautiful name," ventured Uncle Howard, whose first sweetheart had been a Sylvia.

"You couldn't call her that," said Aunt Millicent in a shocked tone. "Don't you remember Great-Uncle Marshall's Sylvia went insane? She died filling the air with shrieks. *I* think Bertha would be more suitable."

"Why, there's a Bertha in John C. Lesley's family-over-the-bay," said Young Grandmother.

John C. was a distant relative who was "at outs" with his clan. So Bertha would never do.

"Wouldn't it be nice to name her Adela?" said Aunt Anne. "You know Adela is the only really distinguished person the connection has ever produced. A famous authoress——"

"*I* should like the mystery of her husband's death to be cleared up before any grandchild of mine is called after her," said Young Grandmother austerely.

"Nonsense, Mother! You surely don't suspect Adela."

"There *was* arsenic in the porridge," said Young Grandmother darkly.

"I'll tell you what the child should be called," said Aunt Sybilla, who had been waiting for the psychic moment. "Theodora! It was revealed to me in a vision of the night. I was awakened by a feeling of icy coldness on my face. I came all out in goose flesh. And I heard a voice distinctly pronounce the name—*Theodora*. I wrote it down in my diary as soon as I arose."

John Eddy Lesley-over-the-bay laughed. Sybilla hated him for weeks for it.

"I wish," said sweet old Great-Aunt Matilda, "that she could be called after my little girl who died."

Aunt Matilda's voice trembled. Her little girl had been dead for fifty years but she was still unforgotten. Lorraine loved Aunt Matilda. She wanted to please her. But she couldn't—she *couldn't*—call her dear baby Emmalinza.

"It's unlucky to call a child after a dead person," said Aunt Anne positively.

"Why not call the baby Jane," said Uncle Peter briskly. "My mother's name—a good, plain, sensible name that'll wear. Nickname it to suit any age. Jenny—Janie—Janet—Jeannette—Jean—and Jane for the seventies."

"Oh, wait till I'm dead—*please*," wailed Old Grandmother. "It would always make me think of Jane Putkammer."

Nobody knew who Jane Putkammer was or why Old Grandmother didn't want to think of her. As nobody asked why—the dessert having just been begun—Old Grandmother told them.

"When my husband died she sent me a letter of condolence written in red ink. Jane, indeed!"

So the baby escaped being Jane. Lorraine felt really grateful to Old Grandmother. She had been afraid Jane might carry the day. And how fortunate there was such a thing as red ink in the world.

"Funny about nicknames," said Uncle Klon. "I wonder did they have nicknames in Biblical times. Was Jonathan ever shortened into Jo? Was King David ever called Dave? And fancy Melchizedek's mother always calling him that."

"Melchizedek hadn't a mother," said Mrs. David triumphantly—and forgave Uncle Klon. But not Young Grandmother. The pudding remained uneaten.

"Twenty years ago Jonathan Lesley gave me a book on 'The Hereafter,'" said Old Grandmother reminiscently. "And he's been in the Hereafter eighteen years and I am still in the Here."

"Any one would think you expected to live forever," said Uncle Jarvis, speaking for the first time. He had been sitting in silence, hoping gloomily that Leander's baby was an elect infant. What mattered a name compared to that?

"I do," said Old Grandmother, chuckling. That was one for Jarvis, the solemn old ass.

"We're not really getting anywhere about the baby's name, you know," said Uncle Paul desperately.

"Why not let Lorraine name her own baby?" said Uncle Klon suddenly. "Have you any name you'd like her called, dear?"

Again Lorraine caught her breath. Oh, hadn't she! She wanted to call her baby Marigold. In her girlhood she had had a dear friend named Marigold. The only girl-friend she ever had. Such a dear, wonderful, bewitching, lovable creature. She had filled Lorraine's starved childhood with beauty and mystery and affection. And she had died. If only she might call her baby Marigold! But she knew the horror of the clan over such a silly, fanciful, outlandish name. Old Grandmother—Young Grandmother—no, they would never consent. She knew it. All her courage exhaled from her in a sigh of surrender.

"No-o-o," she said in a small, hopeless voice. Oh, if she were only not such a miserable coward.

And that terrible Old Grandmother knew it.

"She's fibbing," she thought. "She has a name but she's too scared to tell it. Clementine, now—she would have stood on her own feet and told them what was what."

Old Grandmother looked at Clementine, forever gazing at her lily, and forgot that the said Clementine's ability to stand on her own feet and tell people—even Old Grandmother—what was what had not especially commended her to Old Grandmother at one time. But Old Grandmother liked people with a mind of their own—when they were dead.

Old Grandmother was beginning to feel bored with the whole matter. What a fuss over a name. As if it really mattered what that mite in the cradle, with the golden fuzz on her head, was called. Old Grandmother looked at the tiny sleeping face curiously. Lorraine's hair but Leander's chin and brow and nose. A fatherless baby with only that foolish Winthrop girl for a mother.

"I *must* live long enough for her to remember me," thought Old Grandmother. "It's only a question of keeping on at it. Marian has no imagination and Lorraine has too much. Somebody must give that child a few hints to live by, whether she's to be minx or madonna."

"If it was only a boy it would be so easy to name it," said Uncle Paul.

Then for ten minutes they wrangled over what they would have called it if it had been a boy. They were beginning to get quite warm over it when Aunt Myra took a throbbing in the back of her neck.

"I'm afraid one of my terrible headaches is coming on," she said faintly.

"What would women do if headaches had never been invented?" asked Old Grandmother. "It's the most convenient disease in the world. It can come on so suddenly—go so conveniently. And nobody can prove we haven't got it."

"I'm sure no one has ever suffered as I do," sighed Myra.

"We all think that," said Old Grandmother, seeing a chance to shoot another poisoned arrow. "I'll tell you what's the matter with you. Eye strain. You should really wear glasses at your age, Myra."

"Why can't those headaches be cured?" said Uncle Paul. "Why don't you try a new doctor?"

"Who is there to try now that poor Leander is in his grave?" wailed Myra. "I don't know what we Lesleys are ever going to do without him. We'll just have to *die*. Dr. Moorhouse drinks and Dr. Stackley is an evolutionist. And you wouldn't have me go to that woman-doctor, would you?"

No, of course not. No Lesley would go to that woman-doctor. Dr. M. Woodruff Richards had been practising in Harmony for two years, but no Lesley would have called in a woman-doctor if he had been dying. One might as well commit suicide. Besides, a woman-doctor was an outrageous portent, not to be tolerated or recognised at all. As Great-Uncle Robert said indignantly, "The weemen are gittin' entirely too intelligent."

Klondike Lesley was especially sarcastic about her. "An unsexed creature," he called her. Klondike had no use for

unfeminine women who aped men. "Neither fish nor flesh
nor good red herring," as Young Grandfather had been wont
to say. But they talked of her through their coffee and did
not again revert to the subject of the baby's name. They
were all feeling a trifle sore over *that*. It seemed to them all
that neither Old Grandmother nor Young Grandmother nor
Lorraine had backed them up properly. With the result that
all the guests went home with the great question yet unset-
tled.

"Just as I expected. All squawks—nothing but squawks as
usual," said Old Grandmother.

"We might have known what would happen when we had
this on Friday," said Salome, as she washed up the dishes.

"Well, the great affair is over," said Lucifer to the Witch of
Endor as they discussed a plate of chicken bones and Pope's
noses on the back veranda, "and that baby hasn't got a name
yet. But these celebrations are red-letter days for *us*. Listen
to me purr."

CHAPTER II

Sealed of the Tribe

1

Things were rather edgy in the Lesley clan for a few weeks. As Uncle Charlie said, they had their tails up. Cousin Sybilla was reported to have gone on a hunger strike—which she called a fast—about it. Stasia and Teresa, two affectionate sisters, quarrelled over it and wouldn't speak to each other. There was a connubial rupture between Uncle Thomas and Aunt Katherine because she wanted to consult Ouija about a name. Obadiah Lesley, who in thirty years had never spoken a cross word to his wife, rated her so bitterly for wanting to call the baby Consuela that she went home to her mother for three days. An engagement trembled in the balance. Myra's throbbings in the neck became more frequent than ever. Uncle William-over-the-bay vowed he wouldn't play checkers until the child was named. Aunt Josephine was known to be praying about it at a particular hour every day. Nina cried almost ceaselessly over it and gave up peddling poetry for the time being, which led Uncle Paul to remark that it was an ill wind which blew no good. Young Grandmother preserved an offended silence. Old Grandmother laughed to herself until the bed shook. Salome and the cats held their peace, though Lucifer carefully kept his tail at half-mast. Everybody was more or less cool to Lorraine because she had not taken his or her choice. It really looked as if Leander's baby was never going to get a name.

Then—the shadow fell. One day the little lady of Cloud of Spruce seemed fretful and feverish. The next day more so. The third day Dr. Moorhouse was called—the first time for years that a Lesley had to call in an outside doctor. For three generations there had been a Dr. Lesley at Cloud of Spruce. Now that Leander was gone they were all at sea.

Dr. Moorhouse was brisk and cheerful. Pooh—pooh! No need to worry—not the slightest. The child would be all right in a day or two.

She wasn't. At the end of a week the Lesley clan were thoroughly alarmed. Dr. Moorhouse had ceased to pooh-pooh. He came anxiously twice a day. And day by day the shadow deepened. The baby was wasting away to skin and bone. Anguished Lorraine hung over the cradle with eyes that nobody could bear to look at. Everybody proposed a different remedy but nobody was offended if it wasn't used. Things were too serious for that. Only Nina was almost sent to Coventry because she asked Lorraine one day if infantile paralysis began like that, and Aunt Marcia was frozen out because she heard a dog howling one night. Also, when Flora said she had found a diamond-shaped crease in a clean tablecloth—a sure sign of death in the year—Klondike insulted her. But Klondike was forgiven because he was nearly beside himself over the baby's condition.

Dr. Moorhouse called in Dr. Stackley, who might be an evolutionist but had a reputation of being good with children. After a long consultation they changed the treatment; but there was no change in the little patient. Klondike brought a specialist from Charlottetown who looked wise and rubbed his hands and said Dr. Moorhouse was doing all that could be done and that while there was life there was always hope, especially in the case of children.

"Whose vitality is sometimes quite extraordinary," he said gravely, as if enunciating some profound discovery of his own.

It was at this juncture that Great-Uncle Walter, who hadn't gone to church for thirty years, made a bargain with God that he would go if the child's life was spared, and that Great-Uncle William-over-the-bay recklessly began playing checkers again. Better break a vow before a death than after it. Teresa and Stasia had made up as soon as the baby took ill, but it was only now that the coolness between Thomas and Katherine totally vanished. Thomas told her for goodness' sake to try Ouija or any darned thing that might help. Even Old Cousin James T., who was a black sheep and never called "Uncle" even by the most tolerant, came to Salome one evening.

"Do you believe in prayer?" he asked fiercely.

"Of course I do," said Salome indignantly.

"Then *pray. I* don't—so it's no use for me to pray. But you pray your darnedest."

2

A terrible day came when Dr. Moorhouse told Lorraine gently that he could do nothing more. After he had gone Young Grandmother looked at Old Grandmother.

"I suppose," she said in a low voice, "we had better take the cradle into the spare room."

Lorraine gave a bitter cry. This was equivalent to a death sentence. At Cloud of Spruce, just as with the Murrays down at Blair Water, it was a tradition that dying people must be taken into the spare room.

"You'll do one thing before you take her into the spare room," said Old Grandmother fiercely. "Moorhouse and Stackley have given up the case. They've only half a brain between them anyhow. Send for that woman-doctor."

Young Grandmother looked thunderstruck. She turned to Uncle Klon, who was sitting by the baby's cradle, his haggard face buried in his hands.

"Do you suppose—I've *heard* she was very clever—they say she was offered a splendid post in a children's hospital in Montreal but preferred general practice——"

"Oh, get her, get her," said Klondike—savage from the bitter business of hoping against hope. "Any port in a storm. She can't do any harm now."

"Will *you* go for her, Horace," said Young Grandmother quite humbly.

Klondike Lesley uncoiled himself and went. He had never seen Dr. Richards before—save at a distance, or spinning past him in her smart little runabout. She was in her office and came forward to meet him gravely sweet.

She had a little, square, wide-lipped, straight-browed face like a boy's. Not pretty but haunting. Wavy brown hair with one teasing, unruly little curl that *would* fall down on her forehead, giving her a youthful look in spite of her thirty-five years. What a dear face! So wide at the cheek-bones—so deep grey-eyed. With such a lovely, smiling, generous mouth. Some old text of Sunday-school days suddenly flitted through Klondike Lesley's dazed brain:

"She will do him good and not evil all the days of her life."

For just a second their eyes met and locked. Only a second. But it did the work of years. The irresistible woman had met the immovable man and the inevitable had happened. She might have had thick ankles—only she hadn't; her mother might have meowed all over the church. Nothing would have mattered to Klondike Lesley. She made him think of all sorts of lovely things, such as sympathy, kindness, generosity, and women who were not afraid to grow old. He had the most extraordinary feeling that he would like to lay his head on her breast and cry, like a little boy who had got hurt, and have her stroke his head and say, "Never mind—be brave—you'll soon feel better, dear."

"Will you come to see my little niece?" he heard himself pleading. "Dr. Moorhouse has given her up. We are all very fond of her. Her mother will die if she cannot be saved. Won't you come?"

"Of course I will," said Dr. Richards.

She came. She said little, but she did some drastic things about diet and sleeping. Old and Young Grandmothers gasped when she ordered the child's cradle moved out on the veranda. Every day for two weeks her light, steady footsteps came and went about Cloud of Spruce. Lorraine and Salome and Young Grandmother hung breathlessly on her briefest word.

Old Grandmother saw her once. She had told Salome to bring "the woman-doctor in," and they had looked at each other for a few minutes in silence. The steady, sweet, grey eyes had gazed unquailingly into the piercing black ones.

"If a son of mine had met you I would have ordered him to marry you," Old Grandmother said at last with a chuckle.

The little humorous quirk in Dr. Richards's mouth widened to a smile. She looked around her at all the laughing brides of long ago in their billows of tulle.

"But I would not have married him unless I wanted to," she said.

Old Grandmother chuckled again.

"Trust you for that." But she never called her "the woman-doctor" again. She spoke with her own dignity of "Dr. Richards"—for a short time.

Klondike brought Dr. Richards to Cloud of Spruce and took her away. Her own car was laid up for repairs. But nobody was paying much attention to Klondike just then.

At the end of the two weeks it seemed to Lorraine that the shadow had ceased to deepen on the little wasted face.

A few more days—was it not lightening—lifting? At the end of three more weeks Dr. Richards told them that the baby was out of danger. Lorraine fainted and Young Grandmother shook and Klondike broke down and cried unashamedly like a schoolboy.

3

A few days later the clan had another conclave—a smaller and informal one. The aunts and uncles present were all genuine ones. And it was not, as Salome thankfully reflected, on a Friday.

"This child must be named at once," said Young Grandmother authoritatively. "Do you realize that she might have died without a name?"

The horror of this kept the Lesleys silent for a few minutes. Besides, every one dreaded starting up another argument so soon after those dreadful weeks. Who knew but what it had been a judgment on them for quarrelling over it?

"But *what* shall we call her?" said Aunt Anne timidly.

"There is only one name you can give her," said Old Grandmother, "and it would be the blackest ingratitude if you didn't. Call her after the woman who has saved her life, of course."

The Lesleys looked at each other. A simple, graceful, natural solution of the problem—if only——

"But *Woodruff*!" sighed Aunt Marcia.

"She's got another name, hasn't she?" snapped Old Grandmother. "Ask Horace there what M stands for? *He* can tell you, or I'm much mistaken."

Every one looked at Klondike. In the anxiety of the past weeks everybody in the clan had been blind to Klondike's goings-on—except perhaps Old Grandmother.

Klondike straightened his shoulders and tossed back his mane. It was as good a time as any to tell something that would soon have to be told.

"Her full name," he said, "is now Marigold Woodruff Richards, but in a few weeks' time it will be Marigold Woodruff Lesley."

"And that," remarked Lucifer to the Witch of Endor under the milk bench at sunset, with the air of a cat making up his mind to the inevitable, "is that."

"What do you think of her?" asked the Witch, a little superciliously.

"Oh, she has points," conceded Lucifer. "Kissable enough."

The Witch of Endor, being wise in her generation, licked her black paws and said no more, but continued to have her own opinion.

CHAPTER III

April Promise

1

On the evening of Old Grandmother's ninety-eighth birthday there was a sound of laughter on the dark staircase—which meant that Marigold Lesley, who had lived six years and thought the world a very charming place, was dancing downstairs. You generally heard Marigold before you saw her. She seldom walked. A creature of joy, she ran or danced. "The child of the singing heart," Aunt Marigold called her. Her laughter always seemed to go before her. Both Young Grandmother and Mother, to say nothing of Salome and Lazarre, thought that golden trill of laughter echoing through the somewhat prim and stately rooms of Cloud of Spruce the loveliest sound in the world. Mother often said this. Young Grandmother never said it. That was the difference between Young Grandmother and Mother.

Marigold squatted down on the broad, shallow, uneven sandstone steps at the front door and proceeded to think things over—or, as Aunt Marigold, who was a very dear, delightful woman, phrased it, "make magic for herself." Marigold was always making magic of some kind.

Already, even at six, Marigold found this an entrancing occupation—"int'resting," to use her own pet word. She had picked it up from Aunt Marigold and from then to the end of life things would be for Marigold interesting or uninteresting. Some people might demand of life that it be happy or untroubled or successful. Marigold Lesley would only ask that it be interesting. Already she was looking with avid eyes on all the exits and entrances of the drama of life.

There had been a birthday party for Old Grandmother that day, and Marigold had enjoyed it—especially that part in the pantry about which nobody save she and Salome knew. Young Grandmother would have died of horror if she

26

had known how many of the whipped cream tarts Marigold had actually eaten.

But she was glad to be alone now and think things over. In Young Grandmother's opinion Marigold did entirely too much thinking for so small a creature. Even Mother, who generally understood, sometimes thought so too. It couldn't be good for a child to have its mind prowling in all sorts of corners. But everybody was too tired after the party to bother about Marigold and her thoughts just now, so she was free to indulge in a long delightful reverie. Marigold was, she would have solemnly told you, "thinking over the past." Surely a most fitting thing to do on a birthday, even if it wasn't your own. Whether all her thoughts would have pleased Young Grandmother, or even Mother, if they had known them, there is no saying. But then they did not know them. Long, long ago—when she was only five and a half— Marigold had horrified her family—at least the Grandmotherly part of it—by saying in her nightly prayer, "Thank you, dear God, for 'ranging it so that nobody knows what I think." Since then Marigold had learned worldly wisdom and did not say things like that out loud—in her prayers. But she continued to think privately that God was very wise and good in making thoughts exclusively your own. Marigold hated to have people barging in, as Uncle Klon would have said, on her little soul.

But then, as Young Grandmother would have said and did say, Marigold always had ways no orthodox Lesley baby ever thought of having—"the Winthrop coming out in her," Young Grandmother muttered to herself. All that was good in Marigold was Lesley and Blaisdell. All that was bad or puzzling was Winthrop. For instance, that habit of hers of staring into space with a look of rapture. *What* did she see? And what right had she to see it? And when you asked her what she was thinking of she stared at you and said, "Nothing." Or else propounded some weird, unanswerable problem such as, "Where was I before I was me?"

The sky above her was a wonderful soft deep violet. A wind that had lately blown over clover-meadows came around the ivied shoulder of the house in the little purring puffs that Marigold loved. To her every wind in the world was a friend—even those wild winter ones that blew so

fiercely up the harbour. The row of lightning-rod balls along
the top of Mr. Donkin's barn across the road seemed like silver
fairy worlds floating in the afterlight against the dark trees
behind them. The lights across the harbour were twinkling
out along the shadowy shore. Marigold loved to watch the
harbour lights. They fed some secret spring of delight in her
being. The big spireas that flanked the steps—Old Grandmother always called them Bridal Wreaths, with a sniff for
meaningless catalogue names—were like twin snowdrifts in
the dusk. The old thorn hedge back of the apple-barn, the
roots of which had been brought out from Scotland in some
past that was to Marigold of immemorial antiquity, was as
white as the spireas, and scented the air all around it. Cloud
of Spruce was such a place always inside and out for sweet,
wholesome smells. People found out there that there was
such a thing as honeysuckle left in the world. There was the
entrancing pale gold of lemon lilies in the shadows under
the lilac-trees, and the proud white iris was blooming all
along the old brick walk worn smooth by the passing of
many feet. Away far down Marigold knew the misty sea was
lapping gladly on the windy sands of the dunes. Mr. Donkin's dear little pasture-field, full of blue-eyed grass, with
the birches all around it, was such a *contented* field. She
had always envied Mr. Donkin that field. It looked, thought
Marigold, as if it just loved being a field and wouldn't be
anything else for the world. Right over it was the dearest
little grey cloud that was slowly turning to rose like a
Quaker lady blushing. And all the trees in sight were whispering in the dusk like old friends—all but the lonely, un-
sociable Lombardies.

Salome was singing lustily in the pantry, where she was
washing dishes. Salome couldn't sing, but she always sang
and Marigold liked to hear her, especially at twilight. "Shall
we ga-a-a-ther at the ri-ver. The *bew*-tiful-the *bew*-tiful
river?" warbled Salome. And Marigold *saw* the beautiful
river, looking like the harbour below Cloud of Spruce.
Lazarre was playing his fiddle behind the copse of young
spruces back of the apple-barn—the old brown fiddle that
his great-great-great-grandfather had brought from Grand
Pré. Perhaps Evangeline had danced to it. Aunt Marigold
had told Marigold the story of Evangeline. Young Grand-

mother and Mother and Aunt Marigold and Uncle Klon
were in Old Grandmother's room talking over clan chit-chat
together. A bit of gossip, Old Grandmother always averred,
was an aid to digestion. Everybody Marigold loved was near
her. She hugged her brown knees with delight, and thought
with a vengeance.

2

Marigold had lived her six years, knowing no world but
Harmony Harbour and Cloud of Spruce. All her clan loved
her and petted her, though some of them occasionally
squashed her for her own good. And Marigold loved them
all—even those she hated she loved as part of her clan. And
she loved Cloud of Spruce. How lucky she had happened to
be born there. She loved everything and everybody about
it. To-night everything seemed to drift through her con-
sciousness in a dreamy, jumbled procession of delight, big
and little things, past and present, all tangled up together.

The pigeons circling over the old apple-barn; the apple-
barn itself—such an odd old barn with a tower and oriel
window like a church—and the row of funny little hemlocks
beyond it. "Look at those hemlocks," Uncle Klon had said
once. "Don't they look like a row of old-maid school-
teachers with their fingers up admonishing a class of
naughty little boys." Marigold always thought of them so
after that and walked past them in real half-delicious fear.
What if they should suddenly shake their fingers so at *her*?
She would die of it, she knew. But it *would* be int'resting.

The hemlocks were not the only mysterious trees about
Cloud of Spruce. That lilac-bush behind the well, for example. Sometimes it was just lilac-bush. And sometimes, especially in the twilight or early dawn, it was a nodding old
woman knitting. It *was*. And the spruce-tree down at the
shore which in twilight or on stormy winter days looked just
like a witch leaning out from the bank, her hair streaming
wildly behind her. Then there were trees that talked—
Marigold heard them. "Come, come," the pines at the right
of the orchard were always calling. "We have something to
tell you," whispered the maples at the gate. "Isn't it enough

to look at us?" crooned the white birches along the road side of the garden, which Young Grandmother had planted when she came to Cloud of Spruce as a bride. And those Lombardies that kept such stately watch about the old house. At night the wind wandered through them like a grieving spirit. Elfin laughter and fitful moans sounded in their boughs. You might say what you liked but Marigold would never believe that those Lombardies were just *trees*.

The old garden that faced the fair blue harbour, with its white gate set midway, where darling flowers grew and kittens ran beautiful brief little pilgrimages before they were given away—or vanished mysteriously. It had all the beauty of old gardens where sweet women have aforetime laughed and wept. Some bit of old clan history was bound up with almost every clump and walk in it, and already Marigold knew most of it. The things that Young Grandmother and Mother would not tell her Salome would, and the things that Salome would not Lazarre would.

The road outside the gate—one of the pleasant red roads of "the Island." To Marigold, a long red road of mystery. On the right hand it ran down to the windy seafields at the harbour's mouth and stopped there—as if, thought Marigold, the sea had bitten it off. On the left it ran through a fern valley, up to the shadowy crest of a steep hill with eager little spruce-trees running up the side of it as if trying to catch up with the big ones at the top. And over it to a new world beyond where there was a church and a school and the village of Harmony. Marigold loved that hill road because it was full of rabbits. You could never go up it without seeing some of the darlings. There was room in Marigold's heart for all the rabbits of the world. She had horrible suspicions that Lucifer caught baby rabbits—and *ate them*. Lazarre had as good as given that dark secret away in his rage over some ruined cabbages in the kitchen-garden. "Dem devil rabbit," he had stormed. "I wish dat Lucifer, he eat dem *all*." Marigold *couldn't* feel the same to Lucifer after that, though she kept on loving him, of course. Marigold always kept on loving—and hating—when she had once begun. "She's got *that* much Lesley in her anyhow," said Uncle Klon.

The harbour, with its silent mysterious ships that came and went; Marigold loved it the best of all the outward facts of her life—better, as yet, than even the wonderful green cloud of spruce on the hill eastward that gave her home its name. She loved it when it was covered with little dancing ripples like songs. She loved it when its water was smooth as blue silk; she loved it when summer showers spun shining threads of rain below its western clouds; she loved it when its lights blossomed out in the blue of summer dusks and the bell of the Anglican Church over the bay rang faint and sweet. She loved it when the mist mirages changed it to some strange enchanted haven of "fairylands forlorn"; she loved it when it was ruffled in rich dark crimson under autumn sunsets; she loved it when silver sails went out of it in the strange white wonder of dawn; but she loved it best on late still afternoons, when it lay like a great gleaming mirror, all faint, prismatic colours like the world in a soap-bubble. It was so nice and thrilly to stand down on the wharf and see the trees upside down in the water and a great blue sky underneath you. And what if you couldn't stick on but fell down into that sky? *Would you fall through it?*

And she loved the purple-hooded hills that cradled it— those long dark hills that laughed to you and beckoned— but always kept some secret they would never tell.

"What is over the hills, Mother?" she had asked Mother once.

"Many things—wonderful things—heart-breaking things," Mother had answered with a sigh.

"I'll go and find them all sometime," Marigold had said confidently.

And then Mother had sighed again.

But the other side of the harbour—"over the bay"—continued to told a lure for Marigold. Everything, she felt sure, would be different over there. Even the people who lived there had a fascinating name—"over-the-bay-ers"—which when Marigold had been *very* young, she thought was "over-the-bears."

Marigold had been down to the gulf shore on the other side of the dreamy dunes once, with Uncle Klon and Aunt Marigold. They had lingered there until the sunken sun had sucked all the rosy light out of the great blue bowl of the sky and twilight came down over the crash and the white turmoil of the breakers. For the tide was high and the winds were out and the sea was thundering its mighty march of victory. Marigold would have been terrified if she had not had Uncle Klon's lean brown hand to hold. But with him to take the edge off those terrible thrills it had been all pure rapture.

Next to the harbour Marigold loved the big spruce wood on the hill—though she had been up there only twice in her life.

As far back as she could remember that spruce hill had held an irresistible charm for her. She would sit on the steps of Old Grandmother's room and look up it by the hour so long and so steadily that Young Grandmother would wonder uneasily if the child were just "right." There had been a half-wit two generations back in the Winthrops.

The hill was so high. Long ago she had used to think that if she could get up on that hill she could touch the sky. Even yet she thought if she were there and gave a little spring she *might* land right in heaven. Nothing lived there except rabbits and squirrels—and perhaps "de leetle green folk," of whom Lazarre had told her. But beyond it—ah, beyond it—was the *Hidden Land*. It seemed to Marigold she had always called it that—always known about it. The beautiful, wonderful Hidden Land. Oh, to see it, just to climb up that hill to the very top and gaze upon it. And yet when Mother asked her one day if she would like a walk up the hill Marigold had shrunk back and exclaimed,

"Oh, Mother, the hill is so high. If we got to the top we'd be above *everything*. I'd rather stay down here with things."

Mother had laughed and humoured her. But one evening, only two months later, Marigold had daringly done it alone. The lure suddenly proved stronger than the dread. Nobody was around to forbid her or call her back. She walked boldly up the long flight of flat sandstone steps that led right up the middle of the orchard, set into the grass. She paused at the first step to kiss a young daffodil goodnight—for there were daffodils all about that orchard. Away beyond, the loveliest rose-hued clouds were hanging over

the spruces. They had caught the reflection of the west, but
Marigold thought they shone so because they looked on
the Hidden Land—the land she would see in a moment if
her courage only held out. She could be brave so long as it
was not dark. She must get up the hill—and back—before
it was dark. The gallant small figure ran up the steps to the
old lichen-covered fence and sagging green gate where
seven slim poplars grew. But she did not open it. Somehow
she could not go right into that spruce wood. Lazarre had
told her a story of that spruce wood—or some other spruce
wood. Old Fidèle the caulker had been cutting down a tree
there and his axe was dull and he swore, "Devil take me,"
he said, "if I don't t'row dis dam axe in de pond." "An' de
devil took heem." Lazarre was dreadfully in earnest.

"Did any one see it?" asked Marigold, round-eyed.

"No; but dey see de hoof-prints," said Lazarre conclusively. "And stomp in de groun' roun' de tree. An' you
leesten now—where did Fidèle go if dè devil didn't take
heem? Nobody never see heem again roun' dese parts."

So no spruce wood for Marigold. In daylight she never
really believed the devil had carried off Fidèle, but one is
not so incredulous after the sun goes down. And Marigold
did not really want to see the devil, though she thought to
herself that it *would* be int'resting.

She ran along the fence to the corner of the orchard
where the spruces stopped. How cool and velvety the
young grass felt. It *felt* green. But in the Hidden Land it
would be ever so much greener—"living green," as one of
Salome's hymns said. She scrambled through a lucky hole
in the fence, ran out into Mr. Donkin's wheat-stubble and
looked eagerly—confidently for the Hidden Land.

For a moment she looked—tears welled up in her eyes—
her lips trembled—she almost cried aloud in bitterness of
soul.

There was no Hidden Land!

Nothing before her but fields and farmhouses and barns
and groves—just the same as along the road to Harmony.
Nothing of the wonderful secret land of her dreams. Marigold turned; she must rush home and find Mother and
cry—cry—cry! But she stopped, gazing with a suddenly
transfigured face at the sunset over Harmony Harbour.

She had never seen the whole harbour at one time before; and the sunset was a rare one even in that island of wonderful sunsets. Marigold plunged her eyes into those lakes of living gold and supernal crimson and heavenly apple-green—into those rose-coloured waters—those far-off purple seas—and felt as if she were drowning ecstatically in loveliness. Oh, *there* was the Hidden Land—there beyond those shining hills—beyond that great headland that cut the radiant sea at the harbour's mouth—there in that dream city of towers and spires whose gates were of pearl. It was not lost to her. How foolish she had been to fancy it just over the hill. Of course it couldn't be there—so near home. But she knew where it was now. The horrible disappointment and the sense of bitter loss that was far worse than the disappointment, had all vanished in that moment of sheer ecstasy above the world. She *knew*.

It was growing dark. She could see the lights of Cloud of Spruce blooming out in the dusk below her. And the night was creeping out of the spruces at her. She looked once timidly in that direction—and there, just over a little bay of bracken at the edge of the wood, beckoning to her from a copse—a Little White Girl. Marigold waved back before she saw it was only a branch of wild, white plum-blossom, wind-shaken. She ran back to the orchard and down the steps to meet Mother at the door of Old Grandmother's room.

"Oh, Mother, it's so nice to come home at bedtime," she whispered, clutching the dear warm hand.

"Where have you been, child?" ask Young Grandmother rather sternly.

"Up on the hill."

"You must not go there alone at this time of night," said Young Grandmother.

Oh, but she had been there once. And she had seen the Hidden Land.

Then she had gone up the hill with Mother this spring—only a few weeks ago—to pick arbutus. They had had a lovely time and found a spring there, with ferns thick around its untrampled edges—a delicate dim thing, half shadow, all loveliness. Marigold had pulled the ferns aside and peeped into it—had seen her own face looking up at her. No, not her own face. The Little Girl who lived in the spring, of course, and came out on moonlit nights to dance around it. Marigold knew naught of Grecian myth or Anglo-Saxon folk-lore but the heart of childhood has its own lovely interpretation of nature in every age and clime, and Marigold was born knowing those things that are hidden forever from the wise and prudent and sceptical.

She and Mother had wandered along dear little paths over gnarled roots. They had found a beautiful smooth-trunked beech or two. They had walked on sheets of green moss velvety enough for the feet of queens. Later on, Mother told her, there would be June-bells and trilliums and wild orchids and lady's slippers there for the seeking. Later still, strawberries out in the clearings at the back.

"When I get big I'm coming here every day," said Marigold. She thought of the evening so long ago—a whole year—when she had seen for a moment the Little White Girl. It *couldn't* have been a plum-bough. Perhaps some day she would see her again.

3

Lucifer was prowling about the bed of striped ribbon-grass, giving occasional mysterious pounces into it. The Witch of Endor was making some dark magic of her own on the white gate-post. They were both older than Marigold, who felt therefore that they were uncannily aged. Lazarre had confided to her his belief that they would live as long as the Old Lady did. "Dey tells her everyt'ing—everyt'ing," Lazarre had said. "Haven' I seen dem, sittin' dare on her bed, wi' deir tail hangin' down, a-talkin' to her lak dey was Chreestian? An' every tam dat Weetch she catch a mouse, don' she go for carry it to de Old Lady to see? You take care what you do 'fore dose cats. I wouldn't lak to be de chap dat would hurt one of dem. What dem fellers don' know ain't wort' knowin'." Marigold loved them but held them in awe. Their unfailing progeny gave her more delight. Little furry creatures were always lying asleep on the sunwarm grasses or frisking in yard and orchard. Ebon balls of fluff. Though not all ebon, alas. The number of spotted and striped kit-

tens around led Uncle Klon to have his serious doubts about
the Witch's morals. But he had the decency to keep his
doubts to himself, and Marigold liked the striped kittens
best—undisturbed by any thought of bends sinister. Creatures with such sweet little faces could have no dealings
with the devil she felt quiet sure, whatever their parents
might be up to.

Lazarre had given over fiddling and was going home—his
little cottage down in "the hollow," where he had a black-
eyed wife and half a dozen black-eyed children. Marigold
watched him crossing the field, carrying something tied up
in a red hanky, whistling gaily, as he was always doing when
not fiddling, his head and shoulders stooped because he
was continually in such a hurry that they were always several inches in advance of his feet. Marigold was very fond of
Lazarre, who had been choreman at Cloud of Spruce before
she was born and so was part of the things that always had
been and always would be. She liked the quick, cordial
twinkle in his black eyes and the gleam of his white teeth in
his brown face. He was very different from Phidime
Gautier, the big blacksmith in the Hollow, of whom Marigold went in positive dread, with his fierce black
moustaches you could hang your hat on. There was an un-
proved legend that he ate a baby every other day. But
Lazarre wasn't like that. He was kind and gentle and gay.

She was sure Lazarre couldn't hurt anything. To be sure
there was that horrible tale of his killing pigs. But Marigold
never believed it. She knew Lazarre couldn't kill pigs—at
least, not pigs he was acquainted with.

He could carve wonderful baskets out of plum-stones and
make fairy horns out of birch-bark, and he always knew the
right time of the moon to do anything. She loved to talk
with him, though if Mother and the Grandmothers had
known what they talked about sometimes they would have
put a sharp and sudden stop to it. For Lazarre, who firmly
believed in fairies and witches and "ghostises" of all kinds,
lived therefore in a world of romance, and made Marigold's
flesh creep deliciously with his yarns. She didn't believe
them all, but you *had* to believe what had happened to
Lazarre himself. He had seen his grandmother in the middle of the night standing by his bed when she was forty

miles away. And next day word had come that the old lady had "gone daid."

That night Marigold had cried out in terror, when Mother was taking the lamp out of her room, "Oh, Mother, don't let the dark in—don't let the dark in. Oh, Mother, I'm so afraid of the big dark."

She had never been afraid to go to sleep in the dark before, and Mother and Young Grandmother could not understand what had got into her. Finally they compromised by leaving the light in Mother's room with the door open. You had to go through Mother's room to get to Marigold's. The dusky, golden half-light was a comfort. If people came and stood by your bed in the middle of the night—people who were forty miles away—you could at least *see* them.

Sometimes Lazarre played his fiddle in the orchard on moonlight nights and Marigold danced to it. Nobody could play the fiddle like Lazarre. Even Salome grudgingly admitted that.

"It's angelic, ma'am, that's what it is," she said with solemn reluctance as she listened to the bewitching lilts of the unseen musician up in the orchard. "And to think that easygoing French boy can make it. My good, hardworking brother tried all his life to learn to play the fiddle and never could. And this Lazarre can do it without trying. Why he can almost make *me* dance."

"That would be a miracle indeed," said Uncle Klon.

And Young Grandmother did tell Marigold she spent too much time with Lazarre.

"But I like him so much, and I want to see as much of him as I can in this world," explained Marigold. "Salome says he can't go to heaven because he's a Frenchman."

"Salome is very wicked and foolish to say such a thing," said Young Grandmother sternly. "Of course, Frenchmen go to heaven if they behave themselves"—not as if she were any too sure of it herself, however.

4

Salome went through the hall and into the orchard room with a cup of tea for Old Grandmother. As the door opened Marigold heard Aunt Marigold say,

"We'd better go to the graveyard next Sunday."

Marigold hugged herself with delight. One Sunday in every spring the Cloud of Spruce folks made a special visit to the little burying-ground on a western hill with flowers for their graves. Nobody went with them except Uncle Klon and Aunt Marigold. And Marigold loved a visit to the graveyard and particularly to Father's grave. She had an uneasy conviction that she ought to feel sad, as Mother and Young Grandmother did, but she never could manage it.

It was really such a charming spot. That smooth grey stone between the two dear young firs all greened over with their new spring tips, and the big spirea-bush almost hiding the grave and waving a hundred white hands to you in the wind that rippled the long grasses. The graveyard was full of spirea. Salome liked this. "Makes it more cheerful-like," she was wont to say. Marigold didn't know whether the graveyard was cheerful or not, but she knew she loved it. Especially when Uncle Klon was with her. Marigold was very fond of Uncle Klon. There was such fun in him. His sayings were so int'resting. He had such a delightful way of saying, "When I was in Ceylon," or "When I was in Borneo," as another might say, "When I was in Charlottetown" or "When I was over the bay." And he occasionally swore such fascinating oaths—at least Salome said they were oaths, though they didn't sound like it. "By the three wise monkeys," was one of them. *So* mysterious. *What* were the three wise monkeys? Nobody ever talked to her as he did. He told her splendid stories of the brave days of old, and wonderful yarns of his own adventures. For instance, that thrilling tale of the night he was lost on the divide between Gold Run and Sulphur Valleys in the Klondike. And that one about the ivory island in the far northern seas—an island covered with walrus tusks heaped like driftwood, as if all the walruses went there to die. He told her jokes. He always made her laugh—even in the graveyard, because he told her such funny stories about the names on the tombstones and altogether made her feel that these folks were really all alive somewhere. Father and all, just as nice and funny as they were in the world. So why grieve about them? Why sigh as Salome always did when she paused by Mrs. Amos Reekie's grave and said,

"Ah, many's the cup of tea I've drunk with *her*!"

"Won't you drink lots more with her in heaven?" demanded Marigold once, rather recklessly, after some of Uncle Klon's yarns.

"Good gracious, no, child." Salome was dreadfully shocked. Though in her secret soul she thought heaven would be a much more cheerful place if one *could* have a good cup of tea with an old crony.

"They drink wine there, don't they?" persisted Marigold. "The Bible says so. Don't you think a cup of tea would be more *respectable* than wine?"

Salome *did* think so, but she would have died the death before she would have corrupted Marigold's youthful mind by saying so.

"There are mysteries too deep for us poor mortals to understand," she said solemnly.

Uncle Klon was third in Marigold's young affections. Mother of course came first; and then Aunt Marigold, with her dear wide mouth quirked up at the corners, so that she always seemed to be laughing even when very sad. These three were in the inner sanctum of Marigold's heart, a very exclusive little sanctum out of which were shut many who thought they had a perfect right to be there.

Marigold sometimes wondered whom she wanted to be like when she grew up. In some moods she wanted to be like Mother. But Mother was "put upon." Generally she thought she wanted to be like Aunt Marigold—who had a little way of saying things. Nobody else could have said them. Marigold always felt she would recognise one of Aunt Marigold's sayings if she met it in her porridge. And when she said only, "It's a fine day," her voice had a nice confidential tone that made you feel nobody else knew it was a fine day—that it was a lovely secret shared between you. And when you had supper at Aunt Marigold's she *made* you take a third helping.

5

Marigold hardly knew where the grandmothers came in. She knew she ought to love them, but did she? Even at six

Marigold had discovered that you cannot love by rule o' thumb.

Young Grandmother was not so bad. She was old, of course, with that frost-fine, serene old age that is in its way as beautiful as youth. Marigold felt this long before she could define it, and was disposed to admire Young Grandmother.

But Old Grandmother. To Marigold, Old Grandmother, so incredibly old, had never seemed like anything human. She could never have been born; it was equally unthinkable that she could ever die. Marigold was thankful she did not have to go into Old Grandmother's room very often. Old Grandmother could not be bothered with children—"unspanked nuisances," she called them.

But she had to go sometimes. When she had been naughty she was occasionally sent to sit on a little stool on the floor of Old Grandmother's room as a punishment. And a very dreadful punishment it was—much worse than Mother and Young Grandmother, who thought they were being lenient, realised. There she sat for what seemed like hours, and Old Grandmother sat up against her pillows and stared at her unwinkingly. Never speaking. *That* was what made it so ghastly.

Though when she did speak it was not very pleasant, either. How contemptuous Old Grandmother could be. Once when she had made Marigold angry, "Hoity toity, a little pot is soon hot!" Marigold winched under the humiliation of it for days. A little pot indeed!

It was no use trying to keep anything from this terrible old lady who saw through everything. Once Marigold had tried to hoodwink her with a small half-fib.

"You are not a true Lesley. The Lesleys never lie," said Old Grandmother.

"Oh, don't they!" cried Marigold, who already knew better.

Suddenly Old Grandmother laughed. Old Grandmother was surprising sometimes. After Marigold had gone into the spare room one day and tried on the hats of several guests, there was a council in the orchard room that evening. Mother and Young Grandmother were horrified. But Old Grandmother would not allow Marigold to be punished.

"I did that myself once," she said. "But I wasn't found out," she whispered to Marigold with a chuckle. She chuckled again on the day when Young Grandmother had asked Marigold a foolish, unanswerable question. "*Why* are you so bad?" But Marigold had answered it—sulkily. "It's more int'resting than being good."

Old Grandmother called her back as she was following outraged Young Grandmother out of the room, and put a tiny blue-veined hand on her shoulder.

"It may be more interesting," she whispered, "but *you* can't keep it up because you're a Lesley. The Lesleys never *could* be bad with any comfort to themselves. Too much conscience. No use making yourself miserable just for the sake of being bad."

Marigold always went into the orchard room on Sunday mornings to recite her golden text and catechism questions to Old Grandmother. Woe betide her if she missed a word. And in her nervousness she always did miss, no matter how perfectly she could say them before she went in. And she always was sent in there to take pills. Nobody at Cloud of Spruce could make Marigold take pills except Old Grandmother. *She* had no trouble. "Don't screw up your face like that. I hate ugly children. Open your mouth." Marigold opened it. "Pop it in." Popped in it was. "Swallow it." It was swallowed—somehow. And then Old Grandmother would put her hand somewhere about the bed and produce a handful of big fat juicy blue raisins.

For she was not always unamiable. And sometimes she showed Marigold the big family Bible—a sort of Golden Book where all the clan names were written, and where all sorts of yellowed old clippings were kept. And sometimes she told her stories about the brides on the walls and the hair wreaths where the brown and gold and black locks of innumerable dead and gone Lesleys bloomed in weird, unfading buds and blossoms.

Old Grandmother was always saying things, too—queer, odd speeches with a tang in them Marigold somehow liked. They generally shocked Young Grandmother and Mother, but Marigold remembered and pondered over them though she seldom understood them fully. They did not seem related to anything in her small experience. In after life they

were to come back to her. In many a crsis some speech of
Old Grandmother's suddenly popped into mind and saved
her from making a mistake.

But on the whole Marigold always breathed a sigh of relief when the door of the orchard room closed behind her.

6

Marigold at six had already experienced most of the pas-
sions that make life vivid and dreadful and wonderful—
none the less vivid and dreadful at six than at sixteen or
sixty. Probably she was born knowing that you were born to
the purple if you were a Lesley. But pride of race blossomed
to full stature in her the day she talked with little May
Kemp from the Hollow.

"Do you wash your face *every* day?" asked May in-
credulously.

"Yes," said Marigold.

"Whether it needs it or not?"

"Of course. Don't you?"

"Not me," said May contemptuously. "I just wash mine
when it's dirty."

Then Marigold realised the difference between the
Lesley caste and outsiders as all Young Grandmother's
homilies had not been able to make her.

Shame? Oh, she had known it to the full—drunk its cup
to the dregs. Would she ever forget that terrible supper-
table when she had slipped, red and breathless, into her
seat, apologising for being late? An inexcusable thing when
there were company to tea—two ministers and two ministers' wives.

"I couldn't help it, Mother. I went to help Kate Blac-
quierre drive Mr. Donkin's cows to water and we had such a
time chasing that bloody heifer."

At once Marigold knew she had said something dreadful.
The frozen horror on the faces of her family told her that.
One minister looked aghast, one hid a grin.

What had she said?

"Marigold, you may leave the table and go to your room,"
said Mother, who seemed almost on the point of tears.

Marigold obeyed wretchedly, having no idea in the world what it was all about. Later on she found out.

"But Kate said it," she wailed. "Kate said she'd like to break every bloody bone in that bloody heifer's body. I never thought 'bloody' was swearing, though it's an ugly word."

She had *sworn* before the minister—before two ministers. And their wives! Marigold did not think she could ever live it down. A hot wave of shame ran over her whenever she thought about it. It did not matter that she was never allowed to go with Kate again; she had not cared much for Kate anyhow. But to have disgraced herself and Mother and the Lesley name! She had thought it bad enough when she had asked Mr. Lord of Charlottetown, with awe and reverence, "Please, *are you God?*" She had been laughed at so for that and had suffered keen humiliation. But this! And yet she could not understand why "bloody" was swearing. Even Old Grandmother—who had laughed herself sick over the incident—couldn't explain that.

The spirit of jealousy had claimed her, too. She was secretly jealous of Clementine, the girl who had once been Father's wife—whose grave was beside his on the hill under the spireas—jealous for her mother. Father had belonged to Clementine once. Perhaps he belonged to her again now. There were times when Marigold was absolutely possessed with this absurd jealousy. When she went into Old Grandmother's room and saw Clementine's beautiful picture on the wall, she hated it. She wanted to go up and tear it down and trample on it. Lorraine would have been horrified if she had dreamed of Marigold's feelings in this respect. But Marigold kept her secret fiercely and went on hating Clementine—especially her beautiful hands. Marigold thought her mother quite as beautiful as Clementine. She always felt so sorry for little girls whose mothers were not beautiful. And Mother had the loveliest feet. Uncle Klon had said more than once that Lorraine had the daintiest little foot and ankle he had ever seen in a woman. This did not count for much among the Lesleys. Ankles were better not spoken of, even if the present-day fashion of skirts did show them shamelessly. But Mother's hands weren't pretty; they were too thin—too small; and Marigold felt sometimes she just couldn't *bear* Clementine's hands. Especially when some of the clan praised them. Old Grandmother referred to them constantly; it really did seem as if Old Grandmother sensed Marigold's jealousy and liked to tease her.

"I don't think she was so pretty," Marigold had been tortured into saying once.

Old Grandmother smiled.

"Clementine Lawrence was a beauty, my dear. Not an insignificant little thing like—like her sister up there in Harmony."

But Marigold felt sure Old Grandmother had started to say "like your mother," and she hated Clementine and her hands and her fadeless white lily more poisonously than ever.

Grief? Sorrow? Why, her heart nearly broke when her dear grey kitten had died. She had never known before that anything *she* loved could die. "Has yesterday gone to heaven, Mother?" she had sobbed the next day.

"I—I suppose so," said Mother.

"Then I don't want to go to heaven," Marigold had cried stormily. "I never want to meet that dreadful day again."

"You'll probably have to meet far harder days than that," had been Young Grandmother's comforting remark.

As for fear, had she not always known it? One of her very earliest memories was of being shut up in the dim shuttered parlor because she had spilled some of her jam pudding on Young Grandmother's best tablecloth. How such a little bit of pudding could have spread itself over so much territory she could not understand. But into the parlour she went—a terrible room with its queer streaky lights and shadows. And as she huddled against the door in the gloom she saw a dreadful thing. To the day of her death Marigold believed it happened. All the chairs in the room suddenly began dancing around the table in a circle headed by the big horsehair rocking-chair. And every time the rocking-chair galloped past her it bowed to her with awful, exaggerated politeness. Marigold screamed so wildly that they came and took her out—disgusted that she could not endure so easy a punishment.

"That's the Winthrop coming out in her," said Young Grandmother nastily.

The Lesleys and Blaisdells had more pluck. Marigold never told what had frightened her. She knew they would not believe her. But it was to be years before she could go into the parlour without a shudder, and she would have died rather than sit in that horsehair rocking-chair.

She had never been quite so vindictive over anything as over the affair of the Skinner doll. That had happened last August. May Kemp's mother had come up to clean the apple-barn, and May had come with her. May and Marigold had played happily for awhile in the playhouse in the square of currant-bushes—a beautiful playhouse in that you could sit in it and eat ruby-hued fruit off your own walls—and then May had said she would give one of her eyes to see the famous Skinner doll. Marigold had gone bravely into the orchard room to ask Old Grandmother if May might come in and see it. She found Old Grandmother asleep—really asleep, not pretending as she sometimes did. Marigold was turning away when her eyes fell on Alicia. Somehow Alicia looked so lovely and appealing—as if she were *asking* for a little fun. Impulsively Marigold ran to the glass case, opened the door and took Alicia out. She even slipped the shoe out of the hand that had held it for years, and put it on the waiting foot.

"Ain't you the bold one?" said May admiringly, when Marigold appeared among the red currants with Alicia in her arms.

But Marigold did not feel so bold when Salome, terrible and regal in her new plum-coloured drugget and starched white apron, had appeared before them and haled her into Old Grandmother's room.

"I should have known she was too quiet," said Salome. "There was the two of 'em—with HER on a chair for a throne, offering HER red currants on lettuce leaves and kissing HER hands. And a crown of flowers on HER head. And both HER boots on. You could 'a' kocked me down with a feather. HER, that's never been out o' that glass case since I came to Cloud o' Spruce."

"Why did you do such a naughty thing?" said Old Grandmother snappily.

"She—she wanted to be loved so much," sobbed Marigold. "Nobody has loved her for so long."

"You might wait till I'm dead before meddling with her. She will be yours then to 'love' all you want to."

"But you will live forever," cried Marigold. "Lazarre says so. And I didn't hurt her one bit."

"You might have broken her to fragments."

"Oh, no, no, I couldn't hurt her by loving her."

"I'm not so sure of that," muttered Old Grandmother, who was constantly saying things Marigold was to understand twenty years later.

But Old Grandmother was very angry, and she decreed that Marigold was to have her meals alone in the kitchen for three days. Marigold resented this bitterly. There seemed to be something especially degrading about it. This was one of the times when it was just as well God had arranged it so that nobody knew what you thought.

That night when Marigold went to bed she was determined she would not say all her prayers. Not the part about blessing Old Grandmother. "Bless Mother and Young Grandmother and Salome." Marigold got up then and got into bed, having carefully placed her two shoes close together under the bed so that they wouldn't be lonesome. She did that every night. She couldn't have slept a wink if those shoes had been far apart, missing each other all night.

But she couldn't sleep to-night. In vain she tried to. In vain she counted sheep jumping over a wall. They *wouldn't* jump. They turned back at the wall and made faces at her— a bad girl who wouldn't pray for her old grandmother. Marigold stubbornly fought her Lesley conscience for an hour; then she got out of bed, knelt down and said, "Please bless Mother and Young Grandmother and Salome and everybody who needs a blessing."

Surely that took in Old Grandmother. Surely she could go to sleep now. But just as surely she couldn't. This time she surrendered after half an hour's fight. "Please bless Mother and Young Grandmother and Salome—and you can bless Old Grandmother if you like."

There now. She wouldn't yield another inch.

Fifteen minutes later Marigold was out of bed again.

"Please bless Mother and Young Grandmother and Salome and Old Grandmother for Jesus' sake, amen."

The sheep jumped now. Faster and faster and faster—they were like a long flowing white stream—Marigold was asleep.

7

The stars were coming out. Marigold loved to watch them—though the first time she had seen stars to realise them she had been terribly frightened. She had wakened up as Mother stepped out of Uncle Klon's car when he had brought them home from a visit in South Harmony. She had looked up through the darkness and shrieked.

"Oh, Mother, the sky has burned up and nothing but the sparks are left."

How they had all laughed and how ashamed she had been. But now Uncle Klon had taught her things about them and she knew the names of Betelguese and Rigel, Saiph and Alnita better than she could pronounce them. Oh, spring was a lovely time, when the harbour was a quivering, shimmering reach of blue and the orchard was sprinkled with violets and the nights were like a web of starlight.

But all the seasons were lovely. Summer, when strawberries were red on the hill-field and the rain was so sweet in the wild rose cups, and the faint sweetness of new-mown hay was everywhere, and the full moon made such pretty dapples under the orchard trees, and the great fields of daisies across the harbour were white as snow.

Of all the seasons Marigold loved autumn best. Then the Gaffer Wind of her favourite fairy-tale blew his trumpet over the harbour and the glossy black crows sat in rows on the fences, and the yellow leaves began to fall from the aspens at the green gate, and there was the silk of frost on the orchard grass in the mornings. In the evenings there was a nice reek of burning leaves from Lazarre's bonfires and the ploughed fields on the hill gleamed redly against the dark spruces. And some night you went to bed in a drab dull world and wakened up to see a white miraculous one. Winter had touched it in the darkness and transformed it.

Marigold loved winter, too, with the mysterious silence of its moonlit snow-fields and the spell of its stormy skies. And the big black cats creeping mysteriously through the twilit glades where the shadows of the trees were lovelier than the trees themselves, while the haystacks in Mr. Donkin's yard looked like a group of humpy old men with white hair. The pasture-fields which had been green and gold in June were cold and white, with ghost-flowers sticking up above the snow. Marigold always felt so sorry for those dead flowerstalks. She wanted to whisper to them, "Spring will come."

The winter mornings were int'resting because they had breakfast by candlelight. The winter evenings were dear when the wind howled outside, determined to get into Cloud of Spruce. It clawed at the doors—shrieked at the windows—gave Marigold delicious little thrills. But it never got in. It was so nice to sit in the warm bright room with the cats toasting their furry flanks before the fire and the pleasant purr of Salome's spinning-wheel in the kitchen. And then to bed in the little room off Mother's, with sweet, sleepy kisses, to snuggle down in soft, creamy blankets and hear the storm outside. Yes, the world *was* a lovely place to be alive in, even if the devil did occasionally carry off people who swore.

CHAPTER IV

Marigold Goes A-visiting

1

Marigold, for the first time in her small life, was going on what she called a "real" visit. That is, she was going to Uncle Paul's to stay all night, without Mother or Young Grandmother. In this fact its "realness" consisted for Marigold. Visiting with Grandmother was int'resting and visiting with Mother int'resting *and* pleasant, but to go somewhere on your own like this made you feel old and adventurous.

Besides, she had never been at Uncle Paul's, and there were things there she wanted to see. There was a "watergarden," which was a hobby of Uncle Paul's and much talked of in the clan. Marigold hadn't the least idea what a "water-garden" was. There was a case of stuffed hummingbirds. And, more int'resting than all else, there was a skeleton in the closet. She had heard Uncle Paul speak of it and hoped madly that she might get a glimpse of it.

Uncle Paul was not an over-the-bear, so was not invested with such romance as they, who lived so near the Hidden Land, were. He lived only at the head of the Bay, but that was six miles away, so it was really "travelling" to go there. She liked Uncle Paul, though she was a little in awe of Aunt Flora; and she liked Frank.

Frank was Uncle Paul's young half-brother. He had curly black hair and "romantic" grey eyes. So Marigold had heard Aunt Nina say. She didn't know what romantic meant, but she liked Frank's eyes. He had a nice, slow smile and a nice, soft drawling voice. Marigold had heard he was going to marry Hilda Wright. Then that he wasn't. Then that he had sold his farm and was going to some mysterious region called "the West." Lazarre told Salome it was because Hilda had jilted him. Marigold didn't know what jilted was, but whatever it was she hated Hilda for doing it to Frank. She had never liked Hilda much anyway, even if she were some distant kind of a cousin by reason of her great-grandmother being a Blaisdell. She was a pale pretty girl with russet hair and a mouth that never pleased Marigold. A stubborn mouth and a bitter mouth. Yet very pleasant when she laughed. Marigold almost liked Hilda when she laughed.

"Dey're too stubborn, dat pair," Lazarre told Salome. "Hilda say Frank he mus' spik first an' Frank he say he be dam if he do."

Marigold was sorry Frank was going West, which, as far as she was concerned, was something "beyond the bourne of time and space," but she looked forward to this visit with him. He would show her the humming-birds and the water-garden, and she believed she could coax him to let her have a peep at the skeleton. And he would take her on his knee and tell her funny stories; perhaps he might even take her for a drive in his new buggy behind his little black mare Jenny. Marigold thought this ever so much more fun than riding in a car.

Of course she was sorry to leave Mother even for a night, and sorry to leave her new kitten. But to go for a real visit! Marigold spent a raptured week looking forward to it and living it in imagination.

2

And it was horrid—horrid. There was nothing nice about it from the very beginning, except the drive to the Head with Uncle Klon and Aunt Marigold, over wood-roads spicy with the fern scent of the warm summer afternoon. As soon as they left her there the horridness began. Marigold did not know that she was homesick, but she knew she was unhappy from her head to her toes and that everything was disappointing. What good was a case of humming-birds if there were no one to talk them over with? Even the water-garden did not interest her, and there were no signs of a skeleton anywhere. As for Frank, he was the worst disappointment of all. He hardly took any notice of her at all. And he was so changed—so gruff and smileless, with a horrible little moustache which looked just like a dab of soot on his upper lip. It was the moustache over which he and Hilda had quarrelled, though nobody knew about it but themselves.

Marigold ate very little supper. She thought every mouthful would choke her. She took only two bites of Aunt Flora's nut cake with whipped cream on top, and Aunt Flora, who had made it on purpose for her, never really forgave her. After supper she went out and leaned forlornly against the gate, looking wistfully up the long red road of mystery that led back home. Oh, if she were only home—with Mother. The west wind stirring in the grasses—the robin-vesper calls—the long tree shadows across a field of wheaten gold—all hurt her now because Mother wasn't here.

"Nothing is ever like what you think it's going to be," she thought dismally.

It was after supper at home now, too. Grandmother would be weaving in the garret—and Salome would be giving the cats their milk—and Mother—Marigold ran in to Aunt Flora.

"Aunt Flora, I must go home right away—please—*please*."

"Nonsense, child," said Aunt Flora stiffly. "Don't take a fit of the fidgets now."

Marigold wondered why she had never noticed before what a great beaky nose Aunt Flora had.

"Oh, *please* take me home," she begged desperately.

"You can't go home to-night," said Aunt Flora impatiently. "The car isn't working right. Don't get lonesome now. I guess you're tired. You'd better go to bed. Frank'll drive you home to-morrow if it doesn't rain. Come now, seven's your bedtime at home, isn't it?"

"Seven's your bedtime at home." At *home*—lying in her own bed, with the light shining from Mother's room—with a delicious golden ball of fluff that curled and purred all over your bed and finally went to sleep on your legs. Marigold couldn't bear it.

"Oh, I want to go home. I want to go home," she sobbed.

"I can't have any nonsense now," said Aunt Flora firmly. Aunt Flora was noted for her admirable firmness with children. "Surely you're not going to be a crybaby. I'll take you up and help you undress."

3

Marigold was lying alone in a huge room in a huge bed that was miles from the floor. She was suddenly half wild with terror and altogether wild with unendurable homesickness. It was dark with a darkness that could be felt. She had never gone to bed in the dark before. Always that friendly light in Mother's room—and sometimes Mother stayed with her till she went to sleep, though Young Grandmother disapproved of that. Marigold had been afraid to ask Aunt Flora to leave the light. Aunt Flora had tucked her in and told her to be a good girl.

"Shut your eyes and go right to sleep, and it will be morning before you know it—and you can go home."

Then she had gone out and shut the door. Aunt Flora flattered herself she knew how to deal with children.

Marigold *couldn't* go to sleep in the dark. And it would be years and *years* before morning came—if it ever did.

"There's nobody here who loves me," she thought passionately.

The black endless hours dragged on. They really were hours, though to Marigold they seemed like centuries. It must surely be nearly morning.

How the wind was wailing round the house! Marigold loved the wind at home, especially at this time of the year when it made her cosy little bed seem cosier. But was this some terrible wind that Lazarre called "de ghos' wind"?

"It blows at de tam of de year when de dead peop' get out of dare grave for a lil' while," he told her.

Was this the time of year? And that man-hole she had seen in the ceiling before Aunt Flora took the light out? Lazarre had told her a dreadful story about seeing a horrible face "wit long hairy ear" looking down at him from a man-hole.

There was a closet in the room. *Was that the closet where the skeleton was?* Suppose the door opened and it fell out. Or walked out. Suppose its bones rattled—Uncle Paul said they did sometimes. What was it she had heard about Uncle Paul keeping a pet rat in the barn? Suppose he brought it into the house at night! Suppose it wandered about! Wasn't that a rat gnawing somewhere?

Would she ever see home again? Suppose mother died before morning. Suppose it rained—rained for a week—and they wouldn't take her home. She knew how Aunt Flora hated to get mud on the new car. And wasn't that thunder?

It was only wagons rumbling across the long bridge over the East River below the house, but Marigold did not know that. She did know she was going to scream—she knew she couldn't live another minute in that strange bed in that dark, haunted room. *What was that?* Queer scratches on the window. Oh—Lazarre's story of the devil coming to carry off a bad child and scratching on the window to get in. Because she hadn't said her prayers. Marigold hadn't said hers. She had been too homesick and miserable to think of them. She couldn't say them now—but she could sit up in bed and scream like a thing demented. And she did.

4

Uncle Paul and Aunt Flora, wakened out of their first sound sleep after a hard day's work, came running in. Marigold stopped screaming when she saw them.

"The child's trembling—she must be cold," said Uncle Paul.

"I'm not cold," said Marigold through her chattering teeth, "but I must go home."

"Now, Marigold, you must be a reasonable little girl," soothed Aunt Flora firmly. "It's eleven o'clock. You can't get home to-night. Would you like some raisins?"

"I want to go home," repeated Marigold.

"Who's raising the Old Harry here?" said Frank, coming in. He had heard Marigold's shrieks when he was getting ready for bed. "Here, sis, is a chocolate mouse for you. Eat it and shut your little trap."

It was a lovely, brown chocolate mouse with soft, creamy insides—the kind of confection the soul of the normal Marigold loved. But now it only suggested Uncle Paul's mythical rat.

"I don't want it—I want to go home."

"Perhaps if you bring her up a kitten," suggested Uncle Paul in desperation.

"I don't want a kitten," wailed Marigold. "I want to go home."

"I'll give you my coloured egg-dish if you'll stay quietly till morning," implored Aunt Flora, casting firmness to the winds.

"I don't want the coloured egg-dish. I want to go home."

"Well, go," said Uncle Paul, finally losing his patience with this exasperating child. "There's plenty of good road."

But Aunt Flora had realised that Marigold was on the verge of hysterics, and to have a hysterical child on her hands was a prospect that made even her firmness quail. She had never approved of Paul's whim of bringing the child here anyhow. This was a Winthrop trick if ever there was one.

"I think Frank had better hitch up and take her home. She may cry herself sick."

"She's a great big baby and I'm ashamed of her," said Uncle Paul crushingly. That speech was to rankle in Marigold's soul for many a day, but at the moment she was only concerned with the fact that Uncle Paul told Frank to go out and hitch up.

"Well, this *is* the limit," said Frank grouchily.

Aunt Flora helped the sobbing Marigold to dress. Uncle Paul was so annoyed that he wouldn't even say good-bye to her. Aunt Flora said it very stiffly. When Mother had kissed Marigold good-bye she had whispered, "When you come home be sure to thank Aunt Flora for the lovely time she has given you." But it did not seem just the right thing to say, so Marigold said nothing.

"Cut out the weeps," ordered Frank as he lifted her into the buggy. "Upon my word, I admire Herod."

Frank was abominably cross. He had had a hard day's work in the harvest-field and was in no mood for a twelve-mile ride, all for the whim of a silly kid. Lord, what nuisances kids were. He was glad he would never have any. Marigold conquered her sobs with an effort. She was going home. Nothing else mattered. Frank sent his black mare spinning along the road and never spoke a word, but Marigold didn't care. She was going home.

Half-way home they turned the corner at the school, and Martin Richard's house was just beyond—a little, old-fashioned white house with a tall Lombardy standing sentinel at either corner, and a tangle of rose-bushes fringing its short lane.

"Why, Frank," cried Marigold, "what's the matter with the house?"

Frank looked—shouted, "My Golly!"—stopped the mare—sprang out of the buggy—tore into the yard—hammered on the door. A window over the door opened—Marigold saw a girl lean out. It was Hilda Wright, who must have been staying all night with her cousin, Jean Richards. Frank saw her, too.

"The house is on fire," he shouted. "Get them up—quick. There's no time to lose."

A wild half-hour followed—a most int'resting half-hour. Luckily Frank's mare had been trained to stand without hitching, and Marigold sat there watching greedily. The house suddenly sparkled with lights. Men rushed out for buckets and ladders. Gigantic grotesque shadows went hurtling over the barns in the lantern-light. Dogs barked their heads off. It was very satisfying while it lasted. The fire was soon put out. The kitchen roof had caught from a spark. But after it was out, Marigold could see Frank and Hilda standing very close together by one of the Lombardies.

Marigold sat in the buggy and enjoyed the sudden swoops of wind. It was not a stormy night after all—it was a windy, starry night. How thick the stars were. Marigold would have liked to count them but she did not dare. Lazarre had told her that if you tried to count the stars you would drop down dead. Suppose—somewhere—a star fell down at your feet. Suppose a lot of them did. Suppose you were chasing stars all over the meadows—over the hills—over the dunes. Till you picked up handfuls of them.

Frank and Hilda came out to the buggy together. Hilda was carrying a little lantern, and the red silk scarf around her head fluttered about her face like a scarlet flame. The bitterness had gone out of her mouth and she was smiling. So was Frank.

"And you've sat here all this time alone without a word. And Jenny not even hitched. Well, you're a plucky little kid after all. I don't wonder you were homesick and scared in that big barn Flora calls a spare room. I'll get you home now in two shakes. Nighty-night, honey."

The "honey" was not for Marigold but for Hilda, who after being kissed, leaned forward and squeezed Marigold's hand.

"I'm *glad* you were homesick," she whispered. "But I hope you won't ever be homesick again."

"I guess Frank won't go West now," whispered Marigold.

"If he does I'll go with him," whispered Hilda. "I'll go to the ends of the earth with him."

"Look here, darling, you'll catch cold," interrupted Frank considerately. "Hop in and finish your beauty sleep. I'll be up to-morrow night. Just now I've got to get this little poppet home. She saved your uncle's house to-night with her monkey didoes, anyway."

Frank was so nice and jolly and funny all the rest of the way home that Marigold was almost sorry when they got there. Every one at Cloud of Spruce was in bed, but Mother was not asleep. She came down at once and hugged Marigold when she heard Frank's story—at least as much as he chose to tell. He said nothing about Hilda, but he gave Marigold a fierce parting hug and put two chocolate mice in her hand.

"Guess you can eat these fellows now without choking," he said.

Marigold, safe in her own dear bed, with her kitten at her feet, ate her mice and fell asleep wondering if Frank were "dam" because he had, after all, spoken first.

CHAPTER V

The Door That Men Call Death

1

After all Old Grandmother did not live out her hundred
years—much to the disappointment of the clan, who all
wanted to be able to brag that one of them had "attained the
century mark." The McAllisters over-the-bay had a cente-
narian aunt and put on airs about it. It was intolerable that
they should go the Lesleys one better in anything when
they were comparative newcomers, only three generations
out from Scotland, when the Lesleys were five.

But Death was not concerned about clan rivalry and
somehow even Old Grandmother's "will to live" could not
carry her so far. She failed rapidly after that ninety-eighth
birthday-party and nobody expected her to get through the
next winter—except Marigold, to whom it had never occurred that Old Grandmother would not go on living forever. But in the spring Old Grandmother rallied amazingly.

"Mebbe she'll make it yet," said Mrs. Kemp to Salome.
Salome shook her head.

"No; she's done. It's the last flicker of the candle. I wish
she *could* live out the century. It's disgusting to think of old
Christine McAllister, who's been deaf and blind and with no
more mind than a baby for ten years, living to be a hundred
and Lesley with all her faculties dying at only ninety-nine."

Marigold in the wash-house doorway caught her breath.
Was Old Grandmother going to *die*—could such a thing
happen? Oh, it couldn't. It *couldn't*. The bottom seemed to
have dropped out of everything for Marigold. Not that she
was conscious of any particular love for Old Grandmother.
But she was one of The Things That Always Have Been.
And when one of The Things That Always Have Been disap-
pear, it is a shock. It makes you feel as if *nothing* could be
depended on.

She had got a little used to the idea by next Saturday, when she went in to say her verses to Old Grandmother. Old Grandmother was propped up on her rosy pillows, knitting furiously on a blue jacket for a new great-grandson at the Coast. Her eyes were as bright and boring as ever.

"Sit down. I can't hear your verses till I've finished counting."

Marigold sat down and looked at the brides. She did not want to look at Clementine's picture but she had to. She couldn't keep her eyes from it. She clenched her small hands and set her teeth. Hateful, hateful Clementine, who had more beautiful hands than Mother. And that endless dreamy smile at the lily—as if nothing else mattered. If she had only had the self-conscious smirk of the other brides, Marigold might not have hated her so much. *They* cared what people thought about them. Clementine didn't. She was so sure of herself—so sure of having Father—so sure of being flawlessly beautiful, she never thought for a moment of anybody's opinion. She *knew* that people couldn't help looking at her and admiring her even though they hated her. Marigold wrenched her eyes away and fastened them on the picture of an angel over Old Grandmother's bed—a radiant being with long white wings and halo of golden curls, soaring easily through sunset skies. *Was* Old Grandmother going to die? And if she did, would she be like that? Marigold had a daring little imagination but it faltered before such a conception.

"What are you thinking of?" demanded Old Grandmother so suddenly and sharply that Marigold spoke out the question in her mind before she could prevent herself.

"Will you be an angel when you die, ma'am?"

Old Granny sighed. "I suppose so. How it will bore me. Who's been telling you I was going to die?"

"Nobody," faltered Marigold, alive to what she had done. "Only—only——"

"Out with it," ordered Old Grandmother.

"Mrs. Kemp said it was a pity you couldn't live to be the hundred when old Chris McAllister did."

"Since when," demanded Old Grandmother in an awful tone, "have the Lesleys been the rivals of the McAllisters? *The McAllisters!* And does anybody suppose that Chris

McAllister has been *living* for the last ten years? Why, she's been deader than I'll be when I've been under the sod for a century! For that matter she never *was* alive. As for dying, I'm not going to die till I get good and ready. For one thing, I'm going to finish this jacket first. What else did Mrs. Kemp say? Not that I care. I'm done with curiosity about life. I'm only curious now about death. Still, she was always an amusing old devil."

"She didn't say much more—only that the Lawson baby couldn't live and Mrs. Gray-over-the-bay had a cancer and Young Sam Marr had appendicitis."

"Cheerful little budget. I dreamed last night I went to heaven and saw Old Sam Marr there and it made me so mad I woke up. The idea of Old Sam Marr in heaven."

Old Grandmother shook her knitting-needle ferociously at a shrinking little bride who seemed utterly lost in the clouds of tulle and satin that swirled around her.

"Why don't you want him in heaven?" asked Marigold.

"If it comes to that I don't know. I never disliked Old Sam. It's only—he couldn't *belong* in heaven. No business there at all."

Marigold had some difficulty in imagining Old Grandmother "belonging" in heaven either.

"You wouldn't want him in—the other place."

"Of course not. Poor old harmless, doddering Sam. Always spewing tobacco-juice over everything. The only thing he had to be proud of was the way he could spit. There really ought to be a betwixt-and-between place. Only," added Granny with a grin, "if there were, most of us would be in it."

She knitted a round of her jacket sleeve before she spoke again. Marigold put in the time hating Clementine.

"I was sorry when Old Sam Marr died, though," said Granny abruptly. "Do you know why? He was the last person alive who could remember me when I was young and handsome."

Marigold looked at Old Grandmother. Could this ugly little old woman ever have been young and pretty? Old Grandmother caught the scepticism in her eyes.

"You don't believe I ever was. Why, child, my hair was red-gold and my arms were the boast of the clan. No Lesley man ever married an ugly woman. Some of us were fools and some shrews, but we never shirked a woman's first duty—to please a man's eyes. To be sure, the Lesley men knew how to pick wives. Come here and let me have a look at you."

Marigold went and stood by the bed. Old Grandmother put a skinny hand under her chin, tilted up her face and looked very searchingly at her.

"Hmm. The Winthrop hair—too pale a gold, but it may darken—the Lesley blue eyes—the Blaisdell ears—too early to say whose nose you have—*my* complexion. Well, thank goodness, I don't think you'll be hard to look at."

Old Grandmother chuckled as she always did when achieving a bit of modern slang. Marigold went out feeling more cheerful. She didn't believe Old Grandmother had any idea of dying.

2

Granny continued to improve. She sat up in bed and knit. She saw everybody who came and chattered to them. She held long pow-wows with Lucifer. She wouldn't let Young Grandmother have her new silk dress made without a high collar. She had Lazarre in and hauled him over the coals because he was said to have been drunk and given his wife a black eye.

"She won't die dese twenty year," said the aggrieved Lazarre. "Dere's only room for wan of dem down dare."

Then Aunt Harriet in Charlottetown gave a party in honour of her husband's sister, and Young Grandmother and Mother were going in Uncle Klon's car. They would not be back before three o'clock that night, but Salome would be there and Old Grandmother was amazingly well and brisk. And then at the last moment Salome was summoned to the deathbed of an aunt in South Harmony. Young Grandmother in her silken magnificence and Mother looking like a slender lily in her green crêpe, with the blossom of her face atop of it, came to the orchard room.

"Of course we can't go now," said Young Gramdmother regretfully. She had wanted to go—the said husband's sister had been a girlhood friend of hers.

"Why can't you go?" snapped Old Grandmother. "I've finished my jacket and I'm going to die at three o'clock to-night, but that isn't any reason why you shouldn't go to the party, is it? Of course you'll go. Don't dare stay home on my account."

Young Grandmother was not much worried over Old Grandmother's prediction. That was just one of her characteristic remarks.

"Do you feel any worse?" she asked perfunctorily.

"When I'm perfectly well there's not much the matter with me," said Old Grandmother cryptically. "There's no earthly sense in your staying home on my account. If I need anything Marigold can get it for me. I hope you ate a good supper. You won't get much at Harriet's. She thinks starving her guests is living the simple life. And she always fills the cups too full on purpose—so there'll be no room for cream. Harriet can make a pitcher of cream go farther than any woman I know."

"*We* are not going there for what we will get to eat," said Young Grandmother majestically.

Old Grandmother chuckled.

"Of course not. Anyhow, you'll *go*. I want to hear all about that party. It'll be amusing. I'd rather be amused than loved now. You take notice whether Grace and Marjory are speaking to each other yet or not. And whether Kathleen Lesley has had her eyebrows plucked. I heard she was going to when she went to New York. And if Louisa has on that awful pink georgette dress with green worms on it—try to see if you can't spill some coffee over it."

"If you think we'd better not go——" began Young Grandmother.

"Marian Blaisdell, if you don't get out of this room instantly I'll throw something at you. There's Klon honking now. You know he doesn't like to wait. Be off, both of you, and send Marigold in. She can sit here and keep me company till her bedtime."

Old Grandmother watched Young Grandmother and Mother out with a curious expression in her old black eyes.

"She hates to think of me dying because she won't be *Young* Grandmother any longer. It's a promotion she's not anxious for," she told Marigold, who had come reluctantly in. "Get your picture book and sit down, child. I want to think for awhile. Later on I've got some things to say to you."

"Yes, ma'am." Marigold always said "Yes, ma'am" to Old Grandmother and "Yes, Grandmother" to Young Grandmother. She sat down obediently but unwillingly. It was a lovely spring evening and Sylvia would be waiting at the Green Gate. They had planned to make a special new kind of magic by the White Fountain that night. And now she would have to spend the whole evening sitting here with Old Grandmother, who wouldn't even talk but lay there with her eyes closed. Was she asleep? If she were, couldn't she, Marigold, run up through the orchard to the Green Gate for a moment to tell Sylvia why she couldn't come. Sylvia mightn't understand otherwise. The Magic Door was open right beside her chair—she could slip through it—be back in a minute.

"Are you asleep, ma'am?" she whispered cautiously.

"Shut up. Of course I'm asleep," snapped Old Grandmother.

Marigold sighed and resigned herself. Dear knows what Sylvia would do. Never come again perhaps. Marigold had never broken tryst with her before. She turned her chair softly around so that her back would be toward Clementine, and looked at the other brides in the crinolines and flower-lined poke bonnets of the sixties, the bustles and polonaises of the eighties, the balloon sleeves and bell skirts of the nineties, the hobbles and huge hats of the tens. Marigold knew nothing of their respective dates, of course. They all belonged to that legendary time before she was born, when people wore all kinds of absurd dresses. The only one who didn't look funny was Clementine, in her lace-shrouded shoulders, her sleek cap of hair and her fadeless, fashionless lily. She came back to Clementine every time—somehow she couldn't help it. It was like a sore tooth you *had* to bite on. But she would not turn round to look at her. She *would* not.

3

"What are you staring at Clementine like that for?" Old Grandmother was sitting erectly up in bed. "Handsome, wasn't she? The handsomest of all the Lesley brides. Such colour—such expression—and the charming gestures of her wonderful hands. It was such a pity——" Old Grandmother stopped abruptly. Marigold felt sure she had meant to say, "It was such a pity she died."

Old Grandmother threw back the blankets and slipped two tiny feet over the edge of the bed.

"Get me my clothes and stockings," she ordered. "There in the top bureau drawer. And the black silk dress hanging in the closet. And the prunella shoes in the blue box. Quick, now."

"You're not going to get up?" gasped Marigold in amazement. She had never seen Old Grandmother up in her life. She hadn't supposed Old Grandmother could get up.

"I'm going to get up and I'm going to take a walk in the orchard," said Old Grandmother. "You just do as I tell you and no back talk. I did what I pleased before you were born or thought of, and I'll do what I please to-night. That's why I made them go to the party. Hop."

Marigold hopped. She brought the clothes and the black dress and the prunella boots and helped Old Grandmother put them on. Not that Old Grandmother required much assistance. She stood up triumphantly, holding to the bed post.

"Bring me my black silk scarf and one of the canes in the old clock. I've walked about this room every night after the rest were in bed—to keep my legs in working order—but I haven't been out of doors for nine years."

Marigold, feeling as if she must be in a dream, brought the cane, and followed Old Grandmother out of The Magic Door and down the shallow steps. Old Grandmother paused and looked around her. The moon was not yet up, though there was silvery brightness behind the spruces on the hill. To the west there was a little streak of soft, dear gold behind the birches. There was a cold clear dew on the grass. The Witch of Endor was shrieking insults at somebody out behind the apple-barn.

Old Grandmother sniffed.

"Oh, the salt tang of the sea! It's good to smell it again. And the apple-blossoms. I had forgotten what spring was like. Is that old stone bench still in the orchard under the cedar-tree? Take me there. I want to see one more moon rise over that cloud of spruce."

Marigold took hold of Old Grandmother's hand and they went into the orchard—a spot Marigold was very fond of. It was such a very delightful and extraordinary old orchard where apple-trees and fir-trees and pine-trees were deliciously mixed up together. Between the trees in the open spaces were flower-beds. Thickets of sweet clover, white and fragrant; clumps of Canterbury-bells, pink and purple. Plots of mint and southernwood. Big blush roses. Perfumed winds blew there. Elves dwelt in the currant bushes. Little Green Folk lived up in the old beech-tree.

There was a queer sort of expectant hush over the orchard as Marigold and Old Grandmother went through it to where the great spreading cedar rose out of a drift of blooming spirea-bushes. Marigold thought it must be because the flowers were watching for the moon to rise.

4

Old Grandmother sank down on the stone bench with a grunt. She sat there silent and motionless for what seemed to Marigold a very long time. The moon rose over the cloud of spruce and the orchard became transfigured. A garden of flowers in moonlight is a strange, enchanted thing with a touch of diablerie, and Marigold, sensitive to every influence, felt its charm long years before she could define it. Nothing was the same as in daylight. She had never been out in the orchard so late as this before. The June lilies held up their cups of snow; the moonlight lay silver white on the stone steps. The perfume of the lilacs came in little puffs on the crystal air; beyond the orchard lay old fields she knew and loved, mysterious misty spaces of moonshine now. Far, far away was the murmur of the sea.

And still Old Grandmother dreamed on. Did she see faces long under the mould bright and vivid again? Were there flying feet, summoning voices, that only she could hear in that old moonlit orchard? What voices were calling to her out of the firs? Marigold felt a funny little prickling along her spine. She was perfectly sure that she and Old Grandmother were not alone in the orchard.

"Well, how have you been since we came out here?" demanded Old Grandmother at last.

"Pretty comf'able," said Marigold, rather startled.

"Good," said Old Grandmother. "It's a good test—the test of silence. If you can sit in silence with any one for half an hour and feel 'comfortable,' you and that person can be friends. If not, friends you'll never be and you needn't waste time trying. I've brought you out here to-night for two reasons, Marigold. The first is to give you some hints about living, which may do you some good and may not. The second was to keep a tryst with the years. We haven't been alone here, child."

No; Marigold had known that. She drew a little closer to Old Grandmother.

"Don't be frightened, child. The ghosts that walk here are friendly, homey ghosts. They wouldn't hurt you. They are of your race and blood. Do you know you look strangely like a child who died seventy years before you were born? My husband's niece. Not a living soul remembers that little creature but me—her beauty—her charm—her wonder. But I remember her. You have her eyes and mouth—and that same air of listening to voices only she could hear. Is that a curse or a blessing I wonder. My children played in this orchard—and then my grandchildren—and my great-grandchildren. Such a lot of small ghosts! To think that in a house where there were once fourteen children there is now nobody but you."

"That isn't my fault," said Marigold, who felt as if Old Grandmother were blaming her.

"It's nobody's fault, just as it was nobody's faul' that your father died of pneumonia before you were born. Cloud of Spruce will be yours some day, Marigold."

"Will it?" Marigold was startled. Such a thing had never occurred to her.

"And you must always love it. Places know when they're loved—just the same as people. I've seen houses whose hearts were actually broken. This House and I have always been good friends. I've always loved it from the day I came here as a bride. I planted most of those trees. You must marry some day, Marigold, and fill those old rooms again. But not too young—not too young. I married at seventeen and I was a grandmother at thirty-six. It was awful. Sometimes it seems to me that I've *always* been a grandmother.

"I *could* have been married at sixteen. But I was determined I wouldn't be married till I had finished knitting my apple-leaf bedspread. Your great-grandfather went off in such a rage I didn't know if he'd ever come back. But he did. He was only a boy himself. Two children—that's what we were. Two young fools. That's what everybody called us. And yet we were wiser then than I am now. We knew things then I don't know now. I've stayed up too late. Don't do that, Marigold—don't live till there's nothing left of life but the Pope's nose. Nobody will be sorry when I die."

Suddenly Marigold gasped.

"*I* will be sorry," she cried—and meant it. Why, it would be terrible. No Old Grandmother at Cloud of Spruce. How could the world go on at all?

"I don't mean that kind of sorriness," said Old Grandmother. "And even you won't be sorry long. Isn't it strange? I was once afraid of Death. He was a foe then—now he is a lover. Do you know, Marigold, it is thirty years since any one called me by my name? Do you know what my name is?"

"No-o," admitted Marigold. It was the first time she had ever realised that Old Grandmother must have a name.

"My name is Edith. Do you know I have an odd fancy I want to hear some one call me that again. Just once. Call me by my name, Marigold."

Marigold gasped again. This was terrible. It was sacrilege. Why, one might almost as well be expected to call God by His name to His face.

"Say anything—anything—with my name in it," said Old Grandmother impatiently.

"I—I don't know what to say,—Edith," stammered Marigold. It sounded dreadful when she had said it. Old Grandmother sighed.

"It's no use. *That* isn't my name—not as you say it. Of course it couldn't be. I should have known better." Suddenly she laughed.

"Marigold, I wish I could be present at my own funeral. Oh, wouldn't it be fun! The whole clan will be here to the last sixth cousin. They'll sit around and say all the usual kind, good, dull things about me instead of the interesting truth. The only true thing they'll say will be that I had a wonderful constitution. That's always said of any Lesley who lives to be over eighty. Marigold——" Old Grandmother's habit of swinging a conversation around by its ears was always startling, "what do you really think about the world?"

Marigold, though taken by surprise, knew exactly what she thought about the world.

"It think it's very int'resting," she said.

Old Grandmother stared at her, then laughed.

"You've hit it. 'Whether there be tongues they shall fail—whether there be prophecies they shall vanish away'—but the pageant of human life goes on. I've never tired watching it. I've lived nearly a century—and when all's said and done there's nothing I'm more thankful for than that I've always found the world and the people in it interesting. Yes, life's been worth living. Marigold, how many little boys are sweet on you?"

"Sweet on me." Marigold didn't understand.

"Haven't you any little beau?" explained Old Grandmother.

Marigold was quite shocked. "Of course not. I'm too small."

"Oh, are you? I had *two* beaux when I was your age. Can you imagine *me* being seven years old and having two little boys sweet on me?"

Marigold looked at Old Grandmother's laughter-filled and moonlight-softened black eyes and for the first time realised that Old Grandmother had not always been old. Why, she might even have been Edith.

"For that matter I had a beau when I was six," said Old Grandmother triumphantly. "Girls were *born* having beaux in my day. Little Jim Somebody—I've forgotten his last name if I ever knew it—walked three miles to buy a stick of candy for me. I was only six, but I knew what that meant. He has been dead for eighty years. And there was Charlie Snaith. He was nine. We always called him Froggy-face. I'll never forget his huge round eyes staring at me as he asked, 'Can I be your beau?' Or how he looked when I giggled and said 'no.' There were a good many 'no's' before I finally said 'yes.'" Old Grandmother laughed reminiscently, with all the delight of a girl in her teens.

"It was Great-Grandfather you first said 'yes' to, wasn't it?" asked Marigold.

Old Grandmother nodded.

"But I had some narrow escapes. I was crazy about Frank Lister when I was fifteen. My folks wouldn't let me have him. He wanted me to run away with him. I've always been sorry I didn't. But then if I had I'd have been sorry for that, too. I was very near taking Bob Clancy—and now all I can remember about him was that he got drunk once and varnished his mother's kitchen with maple-syrup. Joe Benson was in love with me. I had told him I thought he was magnificent. If you tell a certain kind of man he's magnificent you can have him—if you really want that kind of a man. Peter March was a nice fellow. He was thought to be dying of consumption, and he pleaded with me to marry him and give him a year of happiness. Just suppose I had. He got better and lived to be seventy. Never take a risk like that with a live man, Marigold. He married Hilda Stuart. A pretty girl but too self-conscious. And every time Hilda spent more than five cents a week Peter took neuralgia. He always sat ahead of me in church, and I was always tormented with a desire to slap a spot on his bald head that looked like a fly."

"Was Great-Grandfather a handsome man?" asked Marigold.

"Handsome? Handsome? Every one was handsome a hundred years ago. I don't know if he was handsome or not. I only know he was my man from the moment I first set eyes on him. It was at a dinner-party. He was there with Janet Churchill. She thought she had him hooked. She always hated me. I had gold slippers on that night that were too tight for me. I kicked them off under the table for a bit of ease. Never found one of them again. I knew Janet was responsible for it. But I got even with her. I took her beau. It wasn't hard. She was a black velvet beauty of a girl—far prettier than I was—but she kept all her goods in the show-window. Where there is no mystery there is no romance. Remember that, Marigold."

"Did you and Great-Grandfather live here when you were married?"

"Yes. He built Cloud of Spruce and brought me here. We were quite happy. Of course we quarrelled now and then. And once he swore at me. I just swore back at him. It horrified him so he never set me such a bad example again. The worst quarrel we ever had was when he spilled soup over my purple silk dress. I always believed he did it on purpose because he didn't like the dress. He has been dead up there in South Harmony graveyard for forty years, but if he were here now I'd like to slap his face for that dress."

"How did you get even with him?" asked Marigold, knowing very well Old Grandmother *had* got even.

Old Grandmother laughed until she had hardly enough breath left to speak.

"I told him that since he had ruined my dress I'd go to church next Sunday in my petticoat. And I *did*."

"Oh, Grandmother." Marigold thought this was going too far.

"Oh, I wore a long silk coat over it. He never knew till we were in our pew. When I sat down the coat fell open in front and he saw the petticoat—a bright Paddy-green it was. Oh, his face—I can see it yet."

Old Grandmother rocked herself to and fro on the stone bench in a convulsion of mirth.

"I pulled the coat together. But I don't think your great-grandfather got much good of *that* sermon. When it was over he took me by the arm and marched me down the aisle and out to our buggy. No hanging round to talk gossip that day. He never spoke all the way home—sat there with his mouth primmed up. In fact he never said a word about it at all—but he never could bear green the rest of his life. And it was my color. But the next time I got a green dress he gave our fat old washerwoman a dress off the same piece. So of course I couldn't wear the dress, and I never dared get green again. After all, it took a clever person to get the better of your great-grandfather in the long run. But that was the only serious quarrel we ever had, though we used to squabble for a few years over the bread. He wanted the slices cut thick and I wanted them thin. It spoiled a lot of meals for us."

"Why couldn't you have each cut them to suit yourselves?"

Old Grandmother chuckled.

"No, no. That would have been giving in on a trifle. It's harder to do that than give in on something big. Of course we worked it out like that after we had so many children the question was to get enough bread for the family, thick or thin. But to the end of his life there were times when he would snort when I cut a lovely thin paper-like slice, and times when I honestly couldn't help sniffing when he carved off one an inch thick."

"*I* like bread thin," said Marigold, sympathising with Old Grandmother.

"But if you marry a man who likes it thick—and I know now that every proper man does—let him have it thick from the start. Don't stick on trifles, Marigold. The slices of bread didn't worry me when your great-grandfather fell in love with his second cousin, Mary Lesley. She always tried to flirt with every male creature in sight. Simply couldn't leave the men alone. She wasn't handsome but she carried herself like a queen, so people thought she was one. It's a useful trick, Marigold. You might remember it. But don't flirt. Either you hurt yourself or you hurt some one else."

"Didn't *you* flirt?" asked Marigold slyly.

"Yes. That's why I'm telling you not to. For the rest—take what God sends you. That was a bad time while it lasted. But he came back. They generally come back if you have sense enough to keep still and wait—as I had, glory be. The only time I broke loose was the night of Charlie Blaisdell's wedding. Alec sat in a corner and talked to Mary all the evening. I flew out of the house and walked the six miles home in a thin evening dress and satin shoes. It was in March. It should have killed me, of course—but here I am at ninety-nine tough and tasty. And Alec never missed me! Thought I'd gone home with Abe Lesley's crowd. Oh, well, he came to his senses when Mary dropped him for something fresher. But I can't say I was ever very fond of Mary Lesley after that. She was a mischief-maker, anyhow, always blowing old jealousies into a flame for the fun of it.

"I got on very well with the rest of the clan, though my in-laws were mostly very stupid, poor things. Alec's mother didn't approve of us having such a big family. She said it kept Alec's nose to the grindstone. I had twins twice just to spite her, but we got on very well for all that. And Alec's brother Sam was a terrible bore. Nothing ever happened to him. He never even fell in love. Died when he was sixty, in his sleep. It used to make me mad to see any one wasting life like that. Paul was a black sheep. Always got drunk on every solemn or awful occasion. Got drunk at Ruth Lesley's wedding—she was married from here—and upset two stands of bees over there by the apple-barn just as the bridal party came out here to the orchard to be married. That was the liveliest wedding I was ever at. Never shall I forget old Minister Wood flying up those steps pursued by bees. Talk about ghosts!"

Old Grandmother laughed until she had to wipe the tears from her eyes.

"Poor Ruth. She was so stung up she looked like a bride with the smallpox. Oh, well, she had only about half a brain, anyway. She always threw her arms about her husband in public when she wanted to ask him some small favor. How red and furious he got! And he always refused. You'd have thought she'd have learned sense in time. Some women never do. Be sure you have some sense, Marigold, when it comes to handling the men."

"Tell me some more stories, Grandmother," entreated Marigold.

"Child, I could tell you stories all night. This orchard is full of them. Up there by the scabby apple-tree Bess Lesley swooned because Alexander McKay asked her to marry him too suddenly. People 'swooned' in my day—'fainted' in your grandmother's. Now they don't do either. But what a lot of fun they miss. Alexander thought Bess was dead—that he'd killed her with his abruptness. We found him on his knees by her, tearing his hair and shrieking blue murder. He thought I was a brute because I threw a dipperful of water over her. She came to very quickly—her curls were only paper ones—and such a looking creature as she was, with them hanging limp about her face and a complexion like a tallow candle. But she had a wonderful figure. It seems to

me the girls look like sticks nowadays. Alexander clasped
her in his arms and implored her to forgive him. She forgave him—and married him—but she never forgave me.
Talking of ghosts—they had a haunted door in their house.
Always found open no matter how it was shut and locked."

"Do you really believe that, Grandmother?"

"Of course. Always believe things like that. If you don't
believe things you'll never have any fun. The more things
you can believe the more interesting life is, as you say yourself. Too much incredulity makes it a poor thing. As for the
ghosts, we had another haunted house in the clan—Garth
Lesley's-over-the-bay. It was haunted by a white cat!"

"Why?"

"Nobody knew. But there it was. The Garth Lesleys were
rather proud of it. Lots of people saw it. *I* saw it. At least, I
saw a white cat washing its face on the stairs."

"But was it the ghost cat?"

"Oh, there you go again. I prefer to believe it was. Otherwise I could never say I'd seen a real ghost. Over there in
that corner where the three pines are, Hilary and Kate
Lesley agreed to tell each other what they really thought of
each other. They thought it would be fun—but they never
'spoke' again. Kate was engaged at one time to her third
cousin, Ben Lesley-over-the-bay. It was broken off and later
she found her photograph in his mother's album adorned
with horns and a moustache. There was a terrible family
row over that. In the tail of the day she married Dave
Ridley. A harmless creature—only he *would* eat the icing
off his wife's piece of cake whenever they went anywhere to
tea. Kate didn't seem to mind—she hated icing—but I always wanted to choke him with gobs of icing until he had
enough of it for once. Ben's sister Laura was jilted by Turner
Reed. He married Josie Lesley and when they appeared out
in church the first Sunday Laura Lesley went too, in the
dress that was to have been her wedding one, and sat down
on the other side of Ben. Alec said she should have been
tarred and feathered, but I tell you I liked her spunk.
There's a piece of that very dress in my silk log-cabin quilt in
the green chest in the garret. You are to have it—and my
pearl ring. Your great-grandfather found the pearl in an
oyster the day we were engaged and had it set for me. It was

reckoned worth five hundred dollars, I've left it to you in my will so none of the others can raise a rumpus or do you out of it. Edith-over-the-bay has had her eye on it for years. Thinks she should have it because she was my first namesake. She owes me more than her name if she but knew it. She wouldn't exist at all if it hadn't been for me. *I* made the match between her father and mother. I was quite a matchmaker in my time. They really didn't want to marry each other a bit but they were just as happy as if they had. All the same, Marigold, don't ever let any one make a match for *you*."

Old Grandmother was silent for a few moments, thinking over, maybe, more old, forgotten loves of the clan. The wind swayed the trees and the shadows danced madly. *Were* they only shadows——?

"Annabel Lesley and I used to sit under the syrup appletree over there and talk," said Old Grandmother—in a different voice. A gentle, tender voice. "I loved Annabel. She was the only one of the Lesley clan I really loved. A sweet woman. The only woman I ever knew who would keep secrets. A woman who would really burn a letter if you asked her to. It was safe to empty your soul out to her. Learn to keep a secret, Marigold. And she was just. Learn to be just, Marigold. The hardest thing in the world is to be just. I never was just. It was so much easier to be generous."

"I could sit here all night and hear you tell about those people," whispered Marigold.

Old Grandmother sighed. "Once I could have stayed up all night—talking—dancing—and then laugh in the sunrise. But you can't do those things at ninety-nine. I must leave my ghosts and go in. After all they were a pretty decent lot. We've never had a real scandal in the clan. Unless that old affair about Adela's husband and the arsenic could be called one. You'll notice when Adela's books are spoken of, she's 'our cousin.' But when the porridge mystery comes up she's 'a third cousin.' Not that I ever believed she did it. Marigold, will you forgive me for all the pills I've made you take?"

"Oh, they were good for me," protested Marigold.

Old Grandmother chuckled.

"Those are the things we have to be forgiven for. But I don't ask you to forgive me for all the Bible verses I made you learn. You'll be grateful to me for them some day. It's amazing what beautiful things there are in the Bible. 'When all the morning stars sang together.' And that speech of Ruth's to Naomi. Only it always enraged me, too, because no daughter-in-law of mine would ever have said the like to *me*. Ah, well, they're all gone now except Marian. It's time—it's high time for me to go, too."

Marigold felt it was such a pity Old Grandmother had to die just when she had got really acquainted with her. And besides Marigold had something on her conscience.

"Grandmother," she whispered, "I—I've made faces at you when you weren't looking."

Old Grandmother touched Marigold's little round cheek with the tip of her finger.

"Are you so sure I didn't see your faces? I did—often. They weren't quite as impish as the ones I made at your age. I'm glad I've lived long enough for you to remember me, little Marigold. I'm leaving off—you're beginning. Live joyously, little child. Never mind the old traditions. Traditions don't matter in a day when queens have their pictures in magazine advertisements. But play the game of life according to the rules. You might as well, because you can't cheat life in the end.

"And don't think too much about what people will say. For years I wanted to do something but I was prevented by the thought of what my cousin Evelina would say. At last I did it. And she said, 'I really didn't think Edith had so much spunk in her.' Do anything you want to, Marigold—as long as you can go to your looking-glass afterwards and look yourself in the face. The oracle has spoken. And after all, is it any use? You'll make your own mistakes and learn from them as we all do. Hand me my cane, child. I'm glad I came out. I haven't had a laugh for years till to-night when I thought of poor Minister Wood and the bees."

"Why, I've heard you laugh often, Grandmother," said Marigold, wonderingly.

"Cackling over the mistakes of poor humanity isn't laughing," said Old Grandmother. She rose easily to her feet and walked through the orchard, leaning very lightly on her cane. At the gate she paused and looked back, waving a kiss to the invisible presences behind her. The moonlight made jewels of her eyes. The black scarf wound tightly round her head looked like a cap of sleek black hair. Suddenly the years were bridged. She was Edith—Edith of the gold slippers and the Paddy-green petticoat. Before she thought, Marigold cried out,

"Oh—Edith—I know what you looked like now."

"That had the right sound," said Old Grandmother. "You've given me a moment of youth, Marigold. And now I'm old again and tired—very tired. Help me up the steps."

5

"Can I help you undress?"

"No, I'm not going to die in a nightdress." Old Grandmother climbed on the bed and pulled the puff over her. "And I'm going to smash one tradition to bits. I'm not going to die in the spare room. But I'm hungry. I think I'd like an egg fried in butter. But you can't do it. Isn't that pathetic? Me wanting a fried egg on my very deathbed and not able to get it."

Old Grandmother chuckled again—her old satiric chuckle. The Edith of the orchard had gone back to the shadows of a lost century.

"Go and bring me a glass of milk and a roll—one of Salome's rolls. She makes the best rolls in the world. You can tell her so after I'm gone. I wouldn't give her the satisfaction of telling it as long as I am alive."

Marigold flew to the kitchen, elate with a secret purpose. She was going to fry Old Grandmother an egg. She had never fried an egg, but she had watched Salome do it for Lazarre a hundred times. And she did it—beautifully. When she went back to the orchard room she carried the gold-and-white circle on Old Grandmother's own particular plate, with one of Salome's crisp golden-brown rolls.

"Well, of all the children!" said Old Grandmother. She sat up against her pillows and ate her egg with a relish. "It's got just the flavour it should have. You have the real Lesley touch. We always know by grace and not by law just how big a pinch to put in. Now bring Lucifer to me. I have things to tell that cat. And you must go to bed. It's twelve o'clock."

"Should I leave you, ma'am?"

Marigold took no stock in Old Grandmother's remarks about dying. That was just Old Grandmother's way of talking. Dying people didn't go roaming in orchards or eat eggs fried in butter. But perhaps she ought to stay with her till Mother and Young Grandmother came home.

"Of course you must leave me. I'm all right—and will be all right. There's no earthly reason why you should stay here. Turn the light low and leave the water on the table here."

Marigold brought Lucifer, warm and black from his nest in the woodshed, and filled Old Grandmother's glass.

"Would you like anything more?"

"Nothing you can get me. I'd like a drink of the dandelion wine Alec's sister Eliza used to make. Nobody could make wine like her. Dead these sixty years—but I can taste it yet—like liquid sunlight. Off with you, now."

Marigold left Old Grandmother sipping ghostly dandelion wine of the vintage of the sixties, with Lucifer purring blackly beside her. Young Grandmother and Mother found her there when they came in at three o'clock. Lucifer was asleep, but Old Grandmother lay very still with a strange, wise little smile on her face, as if she had attained to the ultimate wisdom and was laughing still but in no unkindly fashion at all blind suppositions and perplexities.

"I shall never forgive myself," cried Young Grandmother—*Young* Grandmother no longer.

6

The blinds were drawn. The doors were purple-bowed. The Lesleys came and went decorously. A terrible, abysmal loneliness engulfed Marigold.

And then she suddenly ceased to believe Old Grandmother was dead. That was not Old Grandmother—that little ivory-white creature in the big flower-banked casket. *That* was not the Edith of the old orchard. *She* was living and laughing still—if not in the orchard then somewhere else. Even in heaven—which must and would become an entirely different place the moment Old Grandmother arrived there.

CHAPTER VI

The Power of the Dog

1

Marigold wakened one September morning earlier than her wont, when all the eastern sky was abloom with the sunrise, because she was going to school that day. She did not know whether she was glad or sorry, but she did know she was very much interested—and a little frightened. And she was determined she would not show she was frightened. For one thing she was sure Old Grandmother would have scorned her for being frightened; and Old Grandmother dead had somehow become a more potent influence in Marigold's life than Old Grandmother living. For another thing, Marigold had always felt that Mother was a little bit disappointed in her that night at Uncle Paul's. Of course that was ages ago when she was a mere child of six. She was seven now, and it would never do to show you were frightened.

She lay happily in her bed, her two little silver-golden braids with their curling ends lying over her pillows, looking out of the window beside her. She loved that window because she could see the orchard from it and the cloud of spruce. She could lie in bed and watch the tops of the spruces tossing in the morning wind. Always when she wakened up, there they were dark against the blue. Always when she went to sleep they were weaving magic with the moonlight or the stars. And she loved the other window of her room because she could see the harbour from it and across the harbour to a misty blue cloud behind which was her dear Hidden Land.

Marigold was sure nobody in the world had such a dear little room as hers—a room, too, that could only be entered through Mother's. That made her feel so safe always. Because night, even when you were seven, was a strange though beautiful thing. Who knew what went on outside in the darkness? Strange uncanny beasts were abroad, as Marigold had good reason to know, having seen them. Perhaps the trees moved about and talked to one another. That pine which was always stretching out its arms to the maple might go across the orchard and put them around her. Those two old spruce crones, with the apple-barn between them in daytime, got their heads together at night. The little row of birches along Mr. Donkin's line-fence danced in and out everywhere. Perhaps that slim little beech in the spruce copse behind the barn, who kept herself to herself and was considered very stuck-up by the spruces, escaped from them for awhile and forgot her airs and graces in a romp with her own kind. And the hemlock schoolma'ams, with a final grim fingershake at terrified little boys, stalked at large, shaking their fingers at everything. Oh, the things they did were int'resting beyond any doubt, but Marigold was just as glad none of them could come walking up the stairs into her room without Mother catching them.

The air was tremulous with elfin music. Oh, it was certainly a lovely world—especially that part of it which you entered through The Magic Door and the Green Gate. To other people this part of the world was only the orchard and the "big spruce-bush" on the hill. They knew nothing of the wonderful things there. But you could find those wonderful things only if you went through The Magic Door and the Green Gate. And said The Rhyme. The Rhyme was a very important part of the magic, too. Sylvia would not come unless you said The Rhyme.

Grandmother—who was neither Young nor Old now but just Grandmother—did not approve of Sylvia. She could not understand why Mother permitted Sylvia at all. It was absurd and outrageous and unchristian.

"I could understand such devotion to a flesh-and-blood playmate," said Grandmother coldly. "But this nonsensical imaginary creature is beyond me. It's worse than nonsense. It is positively wicked."

"Almost all lonely children have these imaginary playmates," pleaded Lorraine. "I had. And Leander had. He often told me about them. He had three chums when he was a little boy. He called them Mr. Ponk and Mr. Urt and

Mr. Jiggles. Mr. Ponk lived in the well and Mr. Urt in the old hollow poplar-tree and Mr. Jiggles 'just roamed round!'"

"Leander never told *me* about them," said Grandmother, almost unbelievingly.

"I've often heard you tell as a joke that one day when he was six he came running in out of breath and exclaimed, 'Oh Mother, I was chased up the road by a *pretending bull* and I ran without hope.'"

"Yes; and I scolded him well for it and sent him to bed without his supper," said Grandmother righteously. "For one thing he had been told not to run like that on a hot day and for another I had no more use for pretendings then than I have now."

"I don't wonder he never told you about Mr. Ponk & Co.," thought Lorraine. But she did not say it. One did not say those things to Grandmother.

"It is not so much Sylvia herself I object to," went on Grandmother, "as all the things Marigold tells us about their adventures. She seems actually to believe in them. That 'dance of fairies' they saw. Fairies! That's why she's afraid to sleep in the dark. Mark well my words, Lorraine, it will teach her to lie and deceive. You should put your foot down on this at once and tell her plainly there is no such a creature as this Sylvia and that you will not allow this self-deception to go on."

"I *can't* tell her that," protested Lorraine. "You remember how she fretted when her Sunday-school teacher told her that her dead kitten had no soul. Why, she made herself ill for a week."

"I was almost ill for a week after that fright she gave me the morning she slipped out of bed and went off up the hill to play with Sylvia at sunrise, when you were in town," said Grandmother severely. "Never shall I forget my feelings when I went into her room in the morning and found her bed empty. And just after that kidnapping case in New Brunswick, too."

"Of course she shouldn't have done that," admitted Lorraine. "She and Sylvia had made a plan to go across to the big hill and 'catch the sun' when it came up behind it."

Grandmother sniffed.

"You talk as if you believed in Sylvia's existence yourself, Lorraine. The whole thing is unnatural. There's something wrong about a child who wants to be alone so much. Really, I think she is bewitched. Remember the day of the Sunday-school picnic? Marigold didn't want to go to it. Said she'd rather play with Sylvia. *That* was unnatural. And the other night when she said her prayers she asked God to bless Mother and Grandmother and Sylvia. I was shocked. And that story she came home with last week—how they had seen three enormous elephants marching along the spruce hill and drinking by moonlight at the White Fountain—by which I suppose she meant the spring."

"But that *may* have been true," protested Lorraine timidly. "You know that was the very time the elephants escaped from the circus in Charlottetown and were found in South Harmony."

"If three elephants paraded through Harmony somebody would likely have seen them besides Marigold. No; she made the whole thing up. And the long and short of it is, Lorraine, I tell you plainly that if you let your child go on like this people will think she is not all there."

This was very terrible—to Mother as well as Grandmother. It was a very disgraceful thing to have a child who was not all there. But still Mother was unwilling to destroy Marigold's beautiful dream-world.

"She told us the other day," continued Grandmother, "that Sylvia told her 'God was a very nice-looking old gentleman.' Fancy your child learning things like that from a playmate."

"*You* talk now as if *you* thought Sylvia was real," said Lorraine mischievously. But Grandmother ignored her.

"It is a good thing Marigold will soon be going to school. She will forget this Sylvia riff-raff when it opens."

The school was half a mile away and Grandmother was to drive Marigold there the first day. It seemed to Marigold that they never would get off, but Cloud of Spruce was never in a hurry. At last they really were on the road. Marigold had on her new blue dress, and her lunch was packed in a little basket. Salome had filled it generously with lovely heart-shaped sandwiches and cookies cut in animal shapes, and Mother had slipped in some of her favourite jelly in a little broken-handled cream jug of robin's-egg blue, which Marigold had always loved in spite of its broken handle—or because of it. She was sure it felt it.

It was September and the day was true September. Marigold enjoyed the drive, in spite of certain queer feelings born of the suspicion that Mother was crying behind the waxberry-bush back at Cloud of Spruce,—until she saw The Dog. After that she enjoyed it no more. The Dog was sitting on the steps of old Mr. Plaxton's little house and when he saw them he tore down to the gate and along the fields inside the fence, barking madly. He was a fairly large dog, with short, tawny hair, ears that stuck straight up, and a tail with a black spot on the end of it. Marigold was sure he would tear her limb from limb if he could catch her. And she would have to go to school alone in the future.

She rather enjoyed the day in school, however, in spite of some alarming, sniggering small boys whom Marigold decidedly did not like. It was quite delightful to be made a fuss over, and the big girls made such a fuss over her. They quarrelled as to whom she would sit with and finally settled the matter by drawing straws. Lazarre called and took her home when school came out, and there was no sign of The Dog. So Marigold felt quite happy and thought school was very nice.

2

The next day it was not quite so nice. This time Mother walked to school with her and at first it was lovely. There was no dog at Mr. Plaxton's gate but on the other side of the road was the Widow Turner's great flock of geese and goslings with a huge gander who ran to the road and hissed at them through the fence. Marigold would not tell Mother that the geese frightened her and very soon she forgot about them. After all, a gander was not a dog; and it was delightful to be walking along that beautiful road with Mother. Marigold probably forgot everything she learned in school that day, but she never forgot the tricks of the winding road, the gay companies of goldenrod in the field corners, the way the fir-trees hung over the bend, the long waves going over Mr. Donkin's field of wheat, and the white young clouds sailing adventurously over the harbour. The road ran up the red hill, and the rain in the night had washed all the dust from the rounded clumps of spice fern along the edges.

Then they crossed a brook, not on the plank bridge but on a dear little bridge of stones, where they could see the pearl-crested eddies around the dripping grasses; and then came a dear bit of wood where balsam boughs made music and all the little violet-shadows were stippled with sunlight, and they walked on a fairy path near the fence, over sheets of lovely moss, almost up to the green corner where the white schoolhouse stood. Marigold would have been perfectly happy if she could have forgotten The Dog and the gander.

No, school wasn't quite so nice that day. The big girls did not take much notice of her. There was another new pupil, with amazing red-gold, bobbed curls, and they were all agog over her.

The teacher made Marigold sit with a little girl named Sarah Miller, whom she did not know and did not like; and a hateful boy across the aisle chewed gum and grinned at her alternately. When he chewed his ears waggled, and when he grinned at her his face was that of an unholy imp. He came up to her at recess, and Marigold turned her back upon him. Plainly this Lesley puss must have her claws clipped at once.

"You'd better get your mammy to bring you to school every day," he jeered. "If she don't, old Plaxton's dog'll eat you. That dog has et three people."

"Et them!" In spite of herself Marigold could not help turning round. The Dog had such a terrible fascination for her.

"Body and bones, I'll tell the world. One of them was a little girl about your age. Dogs always know when folks are afraid of them."

Marigold had a queer, sick, cold feeling. But she thought Old Grandmother would have made short work of this impudent boy.

"Do you suppose," she said cuttingly, "that *I* am afraid of a thousand dogs?"

"You talk big like all the Lesleys," retorted her tormentor. "But just you wait till that dog gets his teeth in your shin and you'll sing a different tune, Miss High-and-Mighty."

Marigold did not feel very high-and-mighty. And when she asked Sarah Miller if geese ever bit and Sarah said,

"Yes. Our old gander flew at me and knocked me down one day and bit me," Marigold felt that life was really too difficult. How was she ever to get home? There were no other children going her way. Mr. Donkin had no children nor Mr. Plaxton nor Mr. Ross nor the Widow Turner. Lazarre's children and Phidime's went to the French School "over east," where Marigold had so long ago dreamed the Hidden Land was.

Then Uncle Klon came along and took her home in the car. The gander hissed at them and The Dog flew down to the gate and howled his head off at them. He was really a very noisy Dog. Marigold did not say a word of her fears to Uncle Klon. She couldn't bear that he should think her a coward either. She talked the matter over with Lucifer, who had no opinion of dogs at all.

"Not that I have ever had anything to do with them," he admitted. "But I've heard that a dog insulted one of my ancestors."

When Marigold said her prayers that night she prayed most earnestly that The Dog might not be there the next morning.

3

Mother wanted to take her to school again but Grandmother said,

"There is no use in pampering her like that. She may as well get used to going alone, first as last. There's nothing on the road to hurt her."

"There are motor-cars."

"There are very seldom motor-cars on this road so early in the morning. Besides, they'll be there to-morrow just the same as to-day. Marigold must learn to walk on the side of the road and never cross it."

Marigold was not afraid of motor-cars. She loved to see them go purring past in the violet dusk, with their great golden moons of eyes, and sometimes turning in at the gate, making strange magic with their shifting light on trees and flowers. Even in daylight they were int'resting. But tawny dogs as big as lions and emormous hissing ganders were quite another thing. She had not slept all night for thinking of them. Suppose there wasn't any God! Old Cousin Malcolm-over-the-bay said there wasn't. *Suppose* The Dog should be there? *Suppose* the gate should be open. *Suppose* he could jump over the fence. *Suppose* he "et" her up, body and bones. Nobody would ever know what became of her. She remembered a horrible tale Lazarre had told her of a dog that flew at some one's throat and tore out the "juggler" vein. *Suppose* he tore out her "juggler" vein.

She said her prayers that morning very earnestly. And in spite of her terror she did not forget to put on her green dress, though she didn't like it, because it was its turn and mustn't feel neglected. She tried to eat some breakfast. She went out to the road, that had suddenly stretched to miles and miles, all filled with terror for her, with her lunch-basket and her little quaking heart.

"You're not frightened to go alone, darling?" said Mother, kissing her good-bye.

"Oh, no," lied Marigold gallantly. Mother must not know—must not even suspect.

"And I won't—I *won't* be frightened," she whispered defiantly to the world. "I'll *make* it true. I'm *sure* God will not let The Dog be there. I'm *quite* sure."

"Cheer up," said Lucifer on the gate post, blinking his topaz eyes at her. "A dog is only a dog. Bristle up your tail and spit at him. Any one can bark through a fence."

There was no delight in the road that day for Marigold, though the fir-trees blew gaily together on the windy hill and Mr. Donkin's calves stood in a ferny corner and looked at her with elfin mischief in their soft dark eyes. As she drew near Mr. Plaxton's house she could see The Dog sitting on the steps. Marigold grew cold all over, but she came on. Old Grandmother, she was sure, would have gone on. The Dog rushed down to the gate and tore along the fence and barked. Most furiously. *Did he know she was afraid of him?* It seemed a year to Marigold before she left him behind. She felt rather sickish all day in school and couldn't eat her lunch. And her spirit was bitter within her. God hadn't answered her prayer. Very likely old Cousin Malcolm was right. Of course he was right. Marigold went home past The Dog in a godless world, where only Terror reigned supreme.

4

For a week Marigold lived in that world and tasted its horror to the full. But she would have died before she admitted her cowardice to Mother or Grandmother. She might have told it to Aunt Marigold, but Aunt Marigold was away. She could not play with Sylvia, and a new batch of kittens left her cold. And every day that Dog rushed down to the gate and pursued her beside the fence with Barks. Marigold saw everything connected with The Dog in capitals. Some day—Marigold knew it—he would jump the fence.

One rainy day she felt sure he would not be there, but he was. Noisier than ever.

"I wish you were dead," Marigold whispered passionately. But she could not pray that he would die, though once she tried to. Even a dog has some rights, she felt. She still prayed—though she did not think it a bit of use.

And then one day The Dog did jump the fence.

5

"The child is getting frightfully thin and pale," worried Mother. "She hardly eats any breakfast. I'm sure that long walk to school is too much for her."

"I walked two and a half miles to school when I was her age," said Grandmother, who was worried, too, but wouldn't give in. "How is she to get to school if she doesn't walk? She can't be taken every day."

"She has nightmares—something Marigold never had before," persisted Mother. "Last night she screamed dreadfully that 'it' had caught her. And do you notice how little she laughs?"

"I notice she doesn't go traipsing up the hill after Sylvia any more and that's so much to the good," said Grandmother in a tone of satisfaction. "I'll tell her she mustn't go tearing round with the children at school, tiring herself out. That's what's the matter with her."

There was no need of such a command. Marigold was so quiet at school that the other children thought her stupid and the teacher thought her a model—though a little dull. She couldn't seem to remember half she was told. How could she when she didn't hear it, being wrapped up in dread of the walk home past The Dog? The terrible thing was that it wasn't getting any easier—harder if anything. Marigold felt that she couldn't go on being brave forever. Some day she would break down and confess everything, and everybody would know what a coward she was.

The Dog was at the steps as usual and as usual ran and barked. But Marigold was suddenly confronted with a new terror. The Widow Turner's geese were out on the road! They spread all over the road, and as she drew near, the big gander flew at her with huge outstretched wings, hissing furiously. Marigold dropped book and lunch-box, and screamed.

At that The Dog jumped the fence. He appeared to fly over it without effort. And just when Marigold expected to be devoured at a gulp or feel his teeth at her "juggler" vein, she saw him hurl himself at the gander. The outraged gander turned tail and ran as never gander ran before, towards the hole in the fence where he had escaped. The Dog chivied all the rest of the flock through after him and then leaped victoriously back to Marigold. His impact nearly knocked her off her feet, but the next moment she knew she was not a bit afraid. The Dog was capering around her in an ecstasy of friendliness, stopping every moment or so to yap out his good intentions. Why, he was really only an overgrown pup. And all his barking and tearing had just been sheer neighbourliness. No wonder God hadn't answered her prayer.

As Marigold walked on The Dog trotted cockily along beside her, occasionally licking her hand or lifting his adoring dog face with a delighted yelp. He seemed to be the happiest Dog in the world just to be with her. He went right to the school with her and that night when she went home, no longer a bit afraid, she went right up to the gate and kissed him through the bars.

"I'm so sorry I hated you and prayed that you wouldn't be here," she told him.

"What's a little hatred between friends?" said The Dog. "That gander shan't give you any more sass. *I'll* see to that, Lovely."

Marigold's laughter rang again through Cloud of Spruce that evening. The world was once more a nice, smiling place where everybody was happy. She ate a hearty supper and then she was off up the hill to Sylvia—which didn't please Grandmother so well. After that she scurried off to school early in the morning so that she could have a little time to play with The Dog, who having found he could jump the fence when he had to, jumped it every morning and evening just to be petted by Marigold and fed little snacks from her basket.

Marigold felt a certain sweetness of victory because she had never told any one how frightened she was. It seemed to her that she had redeemed herself from some taint of disgrace that had clung to her ever since the night at Uncle Paul's. But now that she was frightened no longer she told Mother, because she couldn't bear to have secrets from Mother. Lorraine was secretly horror-stricken when she realised what a long-drawn-out agony this small creature had been enduring in silence and solitude.

"I don't think you were a coward at all, dearest. You were very brave to go right on when you were so afraid—and keep going on."

"If I could have picked my mother I'd have picked you," whispered Marigold. Everything was beautiful again and every wind of the world was a friend.

"Didn't I tell you," purred Lucifer.

"I shall always like cats a *little* better than dogs," said Marigold, "but Mr. Plaxton's Dog is a Beautiful Dog."

"There ain't no such animal," Lucifer had the last word.

CHAPTER VII

Lost Laughter

1

Marigold woke up on a Saturday morning in June with stars of delight in her eyes. She thought it the loveliest thing that Sylvia's birthday should be in June. And they were going to have a birthday-picnic in the spruce-bush by the little spring with its untrampled edges—in a banquet-hall with tall spruces for columns. With little frosted cakes—some with "M" on them in pink icing and some with "S." And one gorgeous big cake with both "M" and "S" on it, intertwined, with a drift of cocoanut over everything. Mother had made it specially for Sylvia's birthday. Mother was such a brick. Grandmother, now—but Marigold was not going to think of Grandmother and her attitude in regard to Sylvia, on this wonderful morning of dawn-rosy meadows and sky-ey lures, of white young cherry-trees and winds dancing over the hills.

"Spring is *such* an exciting time," thought Marigold blissfully, as she sprang out of bed and began to dress.

Grandmother and Mother had already begun breakfast—Grandmother, very stately and dignified as usual, with silvery hair and sharp steel-blue eyes, was looking displeased. She disapproved of this birthday picnic as much as she disapproved of Sylvia. She had so confidently expected that Marigold would get over this Sylvia-nonsense when she went to school. But Marigold had been going to school for a year and seemed more besotted on Sylvia than ever.

"We'll have to tell her to-day that you're going to the sanitarium to-morrow," said Grandmother.

"Oh, not to-day," implored Lorraine. "Let her have one more happy day. Not till the morning."

Lorraine had taken a bad cold in March and it "hung on." Aunt Marigold said there was nothing serious as yet but advised a couple of months in the sanitarium. She frightened Grandmother and Lorraine a good deal more than the latter's condition justified, but Aunt Marigold was wise in her day and generation. She knew Lorraine was tired out and run down. She knew she needed a real rest and that she would never get it at Cloud of Spruce or visiting among her relatives. And she knew she would never leave Marigold unless she were thoroughly frightened. So Aunt Marigold did it thoroughly.

"You are going in the afternoon to-morrow. That will give her very little time to get used to it."

"Oh, but not to-day," pleaded Mother. Grandmother yielded. You couldn't refuse the request of a woman who was going to the sanitarium next day, even if you did think it remarkably silly. And then Marigold came running in with her little wild-rose face all alight, and began to eat her porridge out of the dear little blue bowl she loved. Real porridge. Grandmother insisted on that. No imaginary porridges called "cereals" for Grandmother.

"Isn't it lovely that Sylvia's birthday is in June?" she said. "And she's just eight years old, too. Isn't that 'strornary? Why, it makes us pretty near twins, doesn't it, Mother? We're going to have such an elegant time to-day. After the picnic we're going to find that echo that lives 'way, 'way back in the hilly land."

"Don't you go so far away that you can't get back in time for dinner," said Grandmother. "You were late last Saturday."

Marigold looked rather scornfully at Grandmother. Didn't Grandmother understand that when you went through The Magic Door you stepped straight into fairyland, where there was no such thing as time?

"I think I'll be a little scared to go so far back," said Marigold confidentially to Mother. Marigold never minded admitting she was scared since the day of The Dog—The Dog that now, alas, belonged only to the beautiful far-off past. In the winter Mr. Plaxton had sold him to a man who lived over the bay. And Marigold, who had once wished he was dead, walked past Mr. Plaxton's door every school morning with an aching lump in her throat, hating Mr. Plaxton and missing woefully that friendly eager catapult of barks that had always hurled itself over the fence at her. God had answered her prayer after all—rather late, she thought very bitterly.

"I see one has to be careful what one prays for," was her opinion.

"But Sylvia won't be scared. Sylvia isn't afraid of anything. Why——" Marigold cast about for some statement to show how very brave Sylvia was—"why, she'd just as soon call the minister John as not, if she wanted to."

"You see," telegraphed Grandmother's steel-blue eyes. But Mother only laughed.

"What jam do you want in your tarts, dear? Plum or gooseberry?"

Marigold liked gooseberry best, but—— "Oh, plum, Mother. Sylvia likes plum."

The lunch-basket was made up and Marigold trotted happily into the orchard room—and trotted back again.

"Please, where is the key of the orchard door?" she said.

"It's upstairs on my bureau," said Grandmother. "Go out of the side door."

Marigold looked reproachfully at Grandmother, wondering if when *she* got to be over seventy years old she would be so stupid.

"You know I *have* to go through the orchard door, Grandmother. It's a Magic Door. None of the others are."

"Run upstairs and get the key for yourself, dear," said mother gently.

Grandmother sniffed, but looked rather pleased. An idea had just come to her.

Marigold, happily unconscious of Grandmother's idea, got the key and went through The Magic Door into The Land Where Wishes Come True—which unimaginative people called the old orchard. You went through the orchard and up the stone steps until you came to the Green Gate, about which grew the seven slim poplars that always turned into nymphs when she and Sylvia played there. Marigold opened the gate—shut her eyes—said The Rhyme—opened them. Yes, there was Sylvia with her floating dark hair and her dreamy eyes, her snow-white hands and feet among the fine, fair shadows of the poplars. Marigold sprang forward with a cry of joy.

"To think I once thought you were a plum-blossom bough!" she laughed.

2

Grandmother did not carry out her idea as soon as Mother had gone away. That would have been cruel and Grandmother was never cruel—intentionally. She must wait until Marigold recovered from the grief of Mother's going. At first Marigold thought she could never get over it. She was shocked the first day she laughed. She had not expected to be able to laugh again until Mother came home. But Sylvia did say such funny things. And a letter came from Mother every day—such a dear, jolly, understanding letter. Then——

"Grandmother, please, can I have the key of The Magic Door?" asked Marigold one morning.

Grandmother looked at her with cold eyes.

"I have locked that door and it is to remain locked," she said deliberately. "I find that I often forget to lock it at night, and that is very dangerous."

"But, Grandmother," exclaimed Marigold, "I *must* have the key. You *know* I can't see Sylvia unless I go that way."

"Then you must get along without seeing her," said Grandmother immovably.

Marigold did not plead or coax. She knew quite well that no pleading would avail with Grandmother—who had been "one of the stubborn Blaisdells," as Salome said, before she married into the Lesley clan. But she went away with eyes that were stripped of laughter. Grandmother gazed after her triumphantly. This would put an end to all nonsense.

It did. Marigold made one effort to find Sylvia. She went out through the hall door, up the orchard and through the Green Gate. She shut her eyes—said The Rhyme—opened them.

There was no Sylvia.

Marigold crept back to the house—a pathetic, defeated little figure.

For a week Marigold moped—so Grandmother termed it. Grandmother was very good to her. She let her help cook—Salome being away on one of her rare vacations—

shell lovely walnuts with kinkly meats, seed raisins, slice citron peel; even—oh, bliss of happier days!—beat eggs. But Marigold seemed interested in nothing. She sat about a great deal in a big chair on the veranda, looking out on the harbour, with a smileless little face.

One night Grandmother discovered that Marigold had gone to bed without saying her prayers. Horrified, Grandmother made Marigold get right up and say them. But when Marigold got into bed again she looked at Grandmother with sad, defiant eyes.

"My soul didn't pray a bit," she said.

When another week had passed, Grandmother began to worry about Marigold. All was not well with the child. She was growing thin and pale.

"It's the heat," said Grandmother. "If it would only get cooler she would be all right."

Grandmother would not even let herself look at the idea that Marigold was fretting for Sylvia. It was absurd to suppose that a child would become ill because of the imaginary loss of an imaginary playmate.

She went into Harmony and bought Marigold a magnificent doll—almost as big and beautiful as Alicia. Marigold thanked her, played with it a little, then laid it aside.

"Why don't you like your doll?" asked Grandmother severely.

"It's a very nice doll," said Marigold listlessly. "But it isn't alive. Sylvia was."

It was the first time she had spoken of Sylvia. Grandmother's brow grew dark.

"You are a very ungrateful little girl," said Grandmother.

Marigold sighed. She was sorry Grandmother thought her ungrateful. But she did not really care very much. When you are horribly tired you can't care very much about anything. There was no joy in waking up any longer. The bluebells in the orchard had no message for her and she had forgotten the language of the roses. The days seemed endless and the nights—the lonely, black, dreadful nights when the windows rattled so terribly and the wind sang and sobbed so lonesomely in the tree-tops around Cloud of Spruce—worse than endless. There was nothing then but a great, empty, aching loneliness. No sweet medicine of

Mother's kisses. No Sylvia. But one night Marigold heard distant music.

"I think it is Sylvia singing on the hill," she said, when Grandmother asked her sharply what she was listening to.

Grandmother was vexed with herself that she couldn't help recalling that silly old superstition of Salome's that angels sing to children about to die. But Grandmother was really alarmed by now. The child was going to skin and bone. She hadn't laughed for a month. The house seemed haunted by her sad little face. What was to be done? Lorraine must not be worried.

Grandmother got Marigold a lovely new dress of silvery silk and a necklace of beautiful pale green beads. Nobody in the whole Lesley clan had such a beautiful necklace. Marigold put it on and thanked Grandmother dutifully, and went away and sat on her chair on the veranda. Grandmother gave Marigold her own way about everything—except the one thing that really mattered. But Grandmother did not for a moment suppose *that* mattered at all. And she certainly wasn't going to give in about a thing that didn't matter.

Marigold pined and paled more visibly every day. Grandmother was at her wit's end.

"If only Horace's wife was home," she said helplessly.

But Uncle Klon and Aunt Marigold were far away at the Coast, so Dr. Moorhouse was called in—very secretly so that no rumour of it might reach Lorraine—and Dr. Moorhouse couldn't find anything wrong with the child. A little run down. The weather was hot. Plenty of sleep, food and fresh air. He left some pills for her: Marigold took them as obediently for Grandmother as for Old Grandmother, but she grew no better.

"I'll soon be sleeping in the spare room, won't I, Grandmother?" she said one night.

Grandmother's old face grew suddenly older. The spare room!

"Don't be foolish, dear," she said very gently. "You are not going to die. You'll soon be all right."

"I don't want to be all right," said Marigold. "When I die I can go through The Magic Door without any key."

Grandmother could not sleep that night. She recalled what Great-Aunt Elizabeth had once said of Marigold.

"She is too glad to live. Such gladness is not of earth."

But then, Aunt Elizabeth had always been an old pessimist. Always predicting somebody's death. Of course she hit it once in a while, but not a tenth of her predictions ever came true. There was no need to worry over Marigold. The child had always been perfectly healthy. Though not exactly robust. Rather too sensitive—like Lorraine. The weather was so hot. As soon as it cooled, her appetite would come back. But still Grandmother could not sleep. She decided that if Marigold did not soon begin to improve, Lorraine would have to be sent for.

3

Dr. Adam Clow, professor of psychology in a famous university, was talking over family folk-lore with Grandmother, on the veranda of Cloud of Spruce, looking out into a blue dimness that was the harbour but which to him, just now, was a fair, uncharted land where he might find all his lost Aprils. Only the loveliest of muted sounds were heard—the faint whisper of friendly trees, the half-heard, half-felt moan of the surf, the airiest sigh of wind. Down the road the witching lilt of some invisible musician who was playing a fiddle at Lazarre's.

And the purr of black cats humped up on the steps—cats who must have been at Cloud of Spruce forever and would be there forever, changeless, ageless creatures that they were. What did the world look like to a cat, speculated Dr. Clow? Know what he might about psychology he did not know that.

Dr. Clow was a very old friend of Grandmother's, and this visit was a great event to her. There was nobody on earth for whose opinion she had such respect as she had for Adam's. He was one of the few people left to call her Marian—to remember her as "one of the handsome Blaisdell girls."

Adam Clow was that rare thing—a handsome old man, having lived a good life so long that he was very full of the beauty of the spirit. His dark eyes were still softly luminous and his thin, delicately cut, finely wrinkled face rather dreamy and remote. But his smile was vivid and youthful and his mouth showed strength and tenderness and humour.

He came once every year to hear the fir-trees whispering on the hills of home. Here where all his race and all his friends, save Marian Blaisdell, had vanished—here was still "home." Here still on purple evenings and starlit midnights and white dawns the little waves murmured and sighed on the harbour shore. And of all those who had once listened to them with him was left only Marian Blaisdell—handsome Marian, who had a certain queen's loveliness about her still. With her he could talk about charming vanished households and the laughing girls of long ago and old summers so sweet they could not wholly die. He shuddered when he thought of a recent evening spent with a former schoolmate who prided herself on keeping up with the times and talked to him the whole time about eugenics and chromosomes and the growing menace of the feeble-minded. Dr. Adam Clow thanked his stars for a vine-hung veranda and a woman who had grown old gracefully.

"Oh, well, I haven't got to wheel-chairs and gruel yet," said Grandmother complacently.

They talked of the old days and the new days, and watched the moon rising over the old fields they knew. And Dr. Clow told her all the jokes he could think of. He was the only person in the world who dared tell jokes to Grandmother. And finally Grandmother—proud, reserved Grandmother—found herself telling him all about Marigold—who was asleep in her little room with tears still gemming her lashes. She had not taken any int'rest in Dr. Clow. He was Grandmother's meat and, like Grandmother, must long since have forgotten the way to fairyland.

Grandmother *had* to tell somebody. Adam's coming seemed providential. She had always found it easy to tell things to him—always, until now. To her amazement, she found it incredibly hard to tell Adam Clow that she had locked The Magic Door.

"She doesn't seem to *want* to get better," she concluded helplessly.

"'A wounded spirit who can bear'?" quoted Adam Clow softly.

"I don't understand," said Grandmother in a hurt tone. "I—I think I've been very kind to Marigold."

"And *I* think," said Adam Clow rather sternly, "that she is dying of a broken heart."

Grandmother began to say "Bosh," and stopped. One didn't say bosh to doctors of psychology.

"You don't really mean to say you think she has got so ill because she can't see that Sylvia of hers any more? Or imagines she can't?"

Dr. Clow put his slender finger-tips together.

"I think I might talk a great deal of wise jargon about a neurosis caused by a suppressed desire for her playmate," he said. "But I won't. I simply advise you to give her the key of The Magic Door."

"But—Adam!" Grandmother could not give in so easily. "Is it *right* to encourage her in those pretenses—those falsehoods——"

"They are not falsehoods. They are truths to her. She sees things invisible to us. She is a queen in the lovely Kingdom of Make-Believe. She is not trying to deceive anybody. She has the wonderful gift of creation in an unusual degree. It is such a pity that she will lose it as she grows older—that she will have to forego its wonder and live, like us, in the light of common day. Has this never occurred to you, Marian?"

No, it hadn't. But—Grandmother gave a little sigh—of surrender. Dr. Clow stood up.

"I must be going. We have sat up terribly late for old folks."

"I'm sorry you have to walk to Harmony," said Grandmother. "Our horse is too lame to drive just now—and Horace is away—so his car——"

"I don't like a car after dark. In a car you can never feel the charm of the soft enfolding night. I want to walk. It keeps me limber. Well, it's good-bye for another year. I must go back to-morrow and begin work. And if I have to slip off this 'robe of flesh' before next summer I'll save up my jokes to tell you in eternity. After all, there's nothing quite so satisfying as an old friendship, is there, Marian? As for Marigold—the earth has grown very old for us, Marian.

Let us be thankful it is still young and full of magic for Marigold."

4

The next morning after breakfast Grandmother silently laid the key of the orchard door by Marigold's blue bowl. Marigold lifted incredulous eyes.

"Oh, Grandmother! May I—may I?"

"Yes," said Grandmother curtly. In spite of Adam's fine phrases she did not relish defeat by this puss of a Marigold. And there was Lucifer cocking an insolent yellow eye at her, as if he were hugely amused over the whole affair.

Marigold stood still for a moment, transfigured. Her face was as blithe as the day. It was as if a little shower of joy had rained down upon her out of the sky. She flew through the orchard room—through The Magic Door—through the blue-eye grass of the orchard as if there were some Atalanta wizardry in her feet. Through the Green Gate. For another moment she stood, almost afraid. Suppose Sylvia—— Then she shut her eyes and said her Rhyme.

5

Grandmother stood in The Magic Door at twilight. There was a pale moon-glow behind the cloud of spruce. There was a dance of great plumy boughs in the western wind. And there was a sound not heard in the orchard for a long time—the sound of Marigold's laughter as she waved good-night to Sylvia over the Green Gate.

CHAPTER VIII

"It"

1

Mother was home—pink-cheeked and rested and well—and Marigold was going to Blue Water Beach to stay from Friday evening to Sunday night. In other words, a week-end, though that expression had not yet penetrated to Cloud of Spruce. And Marigold was delighted for several good reasons. The best reason was that she would see Nancy—fascinating Nancy of the brown eyes and russet hair; and not only see her but play with her—play with Nancy's beautiful set of dishes kept in the little square box-cupboard in the wall, with the glass door, and not only play with her but sleep with her two whole nights in her fascinating little room, where there was a dressing-table with a lovely frill of sheer white muslin over a pink lining, and a turquoise blue jug and basin with fluted edges, and peacocks on the wallpaper. They would talk delicious little secrets which nobody in the world but their small selves knew. Aunt Stasia's house was near a railroad, and it was such thrilly fun to watch the lighted trains go by in the night, like great dragons breathing smoke and fire.

Then there was to be a party on Saturday afternoon at Lily Johnson's, just across the road from Aunt Stasia's, to which Marigold was invited, and she had the loveliest new dress for it.

Moreover, Blue Water Beach was in that realm of magic "over the bay," where at sunset there were dim old shores of faded gold and dusk. Who knew but that some time she might actually get down to Blue Water Point and see what was beyond it—the Hidden Land, which she had longed all her life to see? She had never dared to ask any one what was beyond Blue Water Point for fear she should be told that there were only the same red coves and headlands and blue

99

silk water that there were on this side of it. Surely there must be something more than that if one could only reach that far purple misty outpost of the "fairylands forlorn" Aunt Marigold talked about. As long as Marigold didn't *know* there wasn't, she could still dream that dear dream.

In the third place, she wanted to wipe out the memory of that old disgrace three years ago, when she had behaved so terribly at Uncle Paul's. Uncle Paul always ragged her about it every time he saw her, and Aunt Flora had never really forgiven her. To be sure, they had to admit that if Marigold had been the good and proper child she should have been, Martin Richard's house would have burned down and Frank Lesley and Hilda Wright would probably never have married each other. Still, Marigold knew she had behaved badly and she burned for a chance to redeem herself.

Standing on the veranda of Cloud of Spruce, Marigold could see three houses in a row over the bay. Three little white dots only six miles away as the crow flew, but nearly fifteen when you had to drive around the Head of the Bay. Though there was a delightful possibility that Uncle Klon just back from the Coast would have his new motor-boat in time to run her over Friday evening.

The middle dot was Aunt Stasia's house—an int'resting house—an unexpected kind of house; like one of those houses in dreams where you are forever discovering new, fascinating rooms; a house where there was red flannel in the glass lamps; a house with a delightful, uncared-for garden where gnarled old apple-trees bent over plots of old-fashioned flowers—thickets of sweet clover, white and fragrant, beds of mint and southernwood, honeysuckles and blush roses; and where there was an old mossy path running up to the ivy-grown front door. Oh, Blue Water Beach was a charming spot, and Marigold couldn't eat or sleep properly for a week because of looking forward to her week-end there.

Of course, this world being as it is, there were one or two small flies in her ointment. Aunt Stasia herself, now. Marigold always felt a little frightened of Aunt Stasia—who wasn't really an aunt but only a cousin. Aunt Stasia of the tragic, wrinkled face, where nothing was left of her traditional beauty but her large dark eyes. Aunt Stasia who always wore black and a widow's veil and never, never smiled. Marigold supposed you couldn't smile if, just a few minutes after you had been married, your husband had been killed by a flash of lightning. But Marigold sometimes wondered, supposing such a thing happened to *her*, if she wouldn't *have* to smile now and then—after years and years had passed, of course. There were so many things in the world to smile at.

Then, too, Aunt Stasia was—fussy. In spite of her romantic and tragic airs, Aunt Stasia was *very* fussy. A crumb on the carpet unfitted her for the day. A fly on the ceiling sent her to bed with a headache. If you got a spot on the tablecloth, Aunt Stasia looked at you as if you had broken all the Ten at once. Marigold knew she would have to be exceedingly proper and perfect at Blue Water Beach if she did not want to smirch the honour of Cloud of Spruce. She liked gentle, kitteny Cousin Teresa better. Cousin Teresa was Aunt Stasia's sister, but she was never called Aunt. There was nothing auntish about her. When Aunt Stasia wasn't around Cousin Teresa could be just like a little girl herself. But then Aunt Stasia mostly was around.

Also, Beulah. Beulah and Nancy were sisters, Aunt Stasia's nieces—real nieces. The children of her dead sister. But whereas Marigold loved Nancy next to Sylvia, she did not like Beulah at all. Not at all. Not the least little bit. Beulah, she thought in her secret soul, was a mean, spiteful little cat. It was Beulah who had once deliberately pushed her into a bush of stick-tights; Beulah who had told her that Mother was disappointed because she wasn't a boy. Marigold had never dared ask Mother about it for fear it was the truth, but it rankled bitterly along with her hatred of Clementine.

2

Marigold was sent from Cloud of Spruce spick and span, with her new dress and her best nightgown in her bag. She arrived at Blue Water Beach spick and span, just in time for supper, to which they at once sat down. Aunt Stasia had welcomed her kindly, though with the usual remote, haunting sound of tears in her voice. Cousin Teresa had kissed and purred; Nancy had given her an ecstatic hug; even Beulah had shaken hands in her superior way and proffered a peck on the cheek.

Marigold was hungry and the supper looked simply gorgeous. There were raspberries in generous blue saucers, and when Aunt Stasia had given her enough cream Cousin Teresa gave her a little more. Nancy was smiling happily and significantly at her across the table, as if to say, "Just wait till we get to bed. I've *heaps* to tell you."

Altogether, in spite of Beulah and Aunt Stasia and the terrible spotlessness of everything, Marigold was rapturously happy. Too happy. The gods didn't like it.

Then—it happened.

Marigold was sitting just where a burst of evening sunshine shone straight down on her shining pale gold hair, with its milk-white parting. Suddenly Aunt Stasia bent forward and looked with awful intentness at Marigold's head. An expression of profound horror came into her eyes. She gasped and looked again. Then looked at Teresa, bent forward and whispered agitatedly in her ear.

"*Im*-possible," said Cousin Teresa.

"See for yourself," said Aunt Stasia.

Cousin Teresa rose and came around the table to the petrified Marigold, who was just realising that something perfectly awful must have happened, but couldn't imagine what. She was so agitated that she slopped her tea over in the saucer. *That* was a terrible break.

"Oh, dear me," wailed Cousin Teresa. "*What* can we do. What *can* we do?"

Cousin Teresa did something. Marigold felt a light touch on her head. Cousin Teresa dashed out of the room and came back a moment later looking ready to faint.

"Do you suppose—there are any more?" demanded Aunt Stasia hollowly.

"I don't *see* any more," said Cousin Teresa.

Beulah was snickering. Nancy was wirelessing sympathy.

"What is the matter with me?" cried Marigold.

No attention was paid to her.

"Is there—a *comb*—in the house?" asked Cousin Teresa in a low, shamed voice.

Aunt Stasia shook her head forcibly. "No—never was. There has never been any need of one here, thank heaven."

Marigold was hopelessly bewildered. No comb at Blue Water Beach? Why, there was an abundance of them—one in every bedroom and one in the kitchen.

"I've a comb of my own in my bag," she said with spirit.

Aunt Stasia looked at her.

"A comb? Do you mean to say that they sent you here—*knowing*——"

"It isn't that kind of a comb," whispered Cousin Teresa. "Oh, Stasia, what can we do?"

"Do. Well, we must keep her away from Nancy and Beulah at all events. Take her up to the spare room, Teresa, until we have consulted over the matter. Run along with Teresa, child—at once. And mind you don't go near the bed. Sit on the hassock by the window. If you haven't finished your supper, take a piece of cake and a cooky with you."

Marigold did not want cake or cooky. She wanted to know what was the matter with her. She dared not ask Aunt Stasia but she indignantly demanded of Cousin Teresa on the stairs what she had done to be put away like this with such scorn and contumely. Marigold didn't use those words but she felt them.

"Hush," said Cousin Teresa nervously, as if the walls around had ears. "The less said about IT the better. Of course, I don't suppose it is your fault. But it's simply terrible."

3

Marigold found herself alone in the spare room. Humiliated—frightened—and a little angry. For all the Lesleys had a bit of temper, and this was no way to treat a visitor. What a hateful grin she had seen on Beulah's face as Cousin Teresa walked her out of the room! She went to the dim mirror and scrutinised her countenance carefully and as much of her sleek head as she could see. Nothing was wrong apparently. Yet that look of horror in Aunt Stasia's eyes!

She must have some terrible disease. Yes, that must be it. Leprosy was an awful thing. Suppose she had leprosy—or smallpox. Or that dreadful thing Uncle Klon flippantly called T. B.? *What* was it she had heard "ran" in the Lesleys. Agatha Lesley had died of it. Something about the heart. But *this* had to do with the head evidently. She wondered if and how soon it would prove fatal. She thought pathetically that she was very young to die. Oh, she must get home right away if she had anything dreadful. Charming Blue Water Beach was now simply a place to get out of as soon as possible. Poor Mother, how terribly she would feel——

Marigold was suddenly aware that Aunt Stasia and Cousin Teresa were talking together in the parlour below the spare room. There was a little grating in the floor under the window, where a small "heat hole" penetrated the parlour ceiling. Marigold had been trained not to eavesdrop. But there were, she felt, exceptions to every rule. She *must* find out what was the matter with her head. Deliberately she lay down on the rag carpet and laid her ear to the grating. She found she could hear tolerably well, save at such times as Aunt Stasia dropped her voice in a fresh access of horror, leaving tantalising gaps which might hold who knew what of ghastly revelation.

"We can't let her go to the party," said Aunt Stasia. "What if any one were to see—what *we* saw. I don't believe such a thing has ever happened to a Lesley before."

"Oh, yes—once—to Charlotte Lesley when she went to school."

Now, Charlotte Lesley was dead. Marigold shuddered. Of course, Charlotte had died of IT.

"And Dan," continued Cousin Teresa. "Remember Dan?"

"A boy is different. And besides, you know how Dan turned out," said Aunt Stasia.

How had Dan turned out? Marigold felt as if she would give anything to know.

"Such a disgrace," Cousin Teresa was wailing when Marigold could hear again. "Her hair will have to be shingled to the bone. I suppose we *could* get a—comb."

"I will not be seen buying a comb," said Aunt Stasia decidedly.

"And where is she to sleep?" moaned Cousin Teresa. "We can't take her home to-night. In the spare room?"

"No—no. She can't sleep *there*. I'd never feel sure of the bed again. We must put her in Annabel's room."

"But Annabel died there," objected Cousin Teresa.

"Marigold doesn't know that," said Aunt Stasia.

Oh, but Marigold did—now. Not that it mattered to her how many people had died in Annabel's room. But she would not be able to sleep with Nancy. This was a far more bitter disappointment than not going to the party.

"There was only *one*," Cousin Teresa was saying hopefully, when their voices became audible again.

"There are sure to be more of them," said Aunt Stasia darkly.

Them! Marigold had a flash of awful illumination.

Germs, of course. Those mysterious, terrible things she had heard Aunt Marigold speak of. She was—what was it? Oh, yes—a germ-carrier. Germs that perhaps she would never be able to get rid of. She must be an outcast all her life! Horror fell over her small face like a frost.

Aunt Stasia and Cousin Teresa were going out of the parlour. Marigold got up and crept pathetically to the window, feeling as if it were years since she had left home that afternoon, so happy and light-hearted, never dreaming of IT. Away out beyond the harbour, a little lonely ship was drifting over the edge of the world. The lonely red road wound past Blue Water Beach in the twilight. A lonely black wind was blowing. Marigold always felt that winds had colour— and this one was certainly black. Everything was black. No party—no night of soul-satisfying exchange of thought with Nancy. Nothing but—germs.

4

Marigold slept—or did not sleep—in Annabel's room, where there was a man-hole in the ceiling with a black, spooky look. But she never thought of being frightened. What were spooks and devils and things generally compared to the horror of IT. The rain began to pour down—the fir-boughs tapped against the windows. The blankets, which

Cousin Teresa had thoughtfully put on because the June night was cold, simply reeked of mothballs. If she were only in her own bed at home between fragrant sheets. Marigold thought the night would never end.

In the morning she had her breakfast at a little table by herself in the corner of the kitchen. Once Nancy slipped in and snuggled down beside her. "I don't care if you have got—them—I love you just the same," said Nancy loyally.

"Nancy Walker! you come right out of there," said Beulah's sharp voice from the door. "Aunt Stasia said you weren't to go near her."

Nancy went out, crying.

"Oh, I'm so sorry for you," said Beulah, before she turned away.

The malice of Beulah's smile was hard to bear and the pity of Beulah bit deep. Marigold went dismally back to Annabel's room—where the bed had already been stripped to the bones. She could see Cousin Teresa busy over tubs in the wash-house. Nancy was carrying a great sheaf of mauve and gold irises across the road to Johnson's, to help decorate for the party.

Away over the harbour was a soft blur that was Cloud of Spruce—dear Cloud of Spruce—dear home. If she were only there! But Aunt Stasia had told her they could not take her home until after the party. A fog was creeping up to Blue Water Beach. It crept on and on—it blotted out the harbour—it blotted out the distant shore of Cloud of Spruce—it blotted out the world. She was alone in the universe with her terrible, mysterious shame. Poor Marigold's Lesley spirit failed her at last. She broke down and cried.

Aunt Teresa drove her home that evening. Again she was coming home from a visit in disgrace. And when they reached Cloud of Spruce, Mother was away. Thinking Marigold would not be home till Sunday evening, she had gone to South Harmony for a visit. Marigold felt she simply could not bear it.

Cousin Teresa whispered mysteriously to Grandmother. "Impossible," cried Grandmother peevishly.

"We found one," said Cousin Teresa positively.

One what? Oh, if Marigold only knew *what*!

"Only one." Grandmother's tone implied that Stasia had made a great deal of fuss over a trifle. Grandmother herself would have made enough fuss about IT if *she* had discovered it. But when Stasia made the fuss that was a cat of a different stripe.

"Have you—a comb?" whispered Cousin Teresa.

Grandmother nodded haughtily. She took Marigold upstairs to her room and gave her head a merciless combing with an odd little kind of comb such as Marigold had never seen before. Then she brought her down again.

"No results," she said crisply. "I believe Stasia simply imagined it."

"I saw IT myself," said Cousin Teresa, a trifle shrewishly. She drove away a little offended. Marigold sat down disconsolately on the veranda steps. She dared not ask Grandmother anything. Grandmother was annoyed and when Grandmother was annoyed she was very aloof. Moreover, she had contrived to make Marigold feel that she was in some terrible disgrace—that she had done something no Lesley ever should do. Ane yet what she had done or how she was responsible, Marigold hadn't the slightest idea. Oh, if Mother were only home!

Then Aunt Marigold came—almost as good as Mother—almost as gentle and tender and understanding. She had been talking with Grandmother.

"So you've been and gone and got into a scrape, Marigold," she said, laughing. "Never mind, precious. There seems to have been only one."

"One what?" demanded Marigold passionately. She simply could not stand this hideous suspense and ignorance any longer. "Aunt Marigold—please—please do tell me what is the matter with my head?"

Aunt Marigold stared.

"Marigold, you dear funny thing, do you mean you don't know?"

Marigold nodded, her eyes like wet pansies.

"And I've just *got* to know," she said desperately.

Aunt Marigold explained.

"It's apt to happen to any child who goes to a public school," she concluded comfortingly.

"Pshaw, is *that* all?" said Marigold. "I guess I got IT when I changed hats with that new girl day before yesterday."

She was so happy she could have cried for joy. Had there then ever been such a starry sky? Such a dear misty, new moon? Such dancing northern lights over the harbour? Down the road Lazarre's dog and Phidime's dog were talking about their feelings at the top of their voices. And Sylvia up in the cloud of spruce. It was too late to go to her to-night, but she would be there in the morning. Marigold blew an airy kiss to the hill. No germs. No leprosy. Aunt Stasia had made all this fuss about so small a matter. Marigold thought bitterly of the party, the unworn dress, the lost two nights with dear Nancy.

"Aunt Stasia is——" began Aunt Marigold. Then she suddenly snapped her lips together. After all, there was such a thing as clan loyalty, especially in the hearing of the rising generation.

"An old fool," said Marigold, sweetly and distinctly.

CHAPTER IX

A Lesley Christmas

1

It was a Lesley tradition to celebrate Christmas by a royal reunion, and this year it was the turn of Cloud of Spruce. This was the first time it had happened in Marigold's memory, and she was full of delighted anticipation. At heart a thorough clansman, she loved, without knowing she loved, all the old clan customs and beliefs and follies and wisdoms as immutable as law of Mede and Persian. They were all part of that int'resting world where she lived and moved and had her being—a world which could never be dull for Marigold, who possessed the talismanic power of flinging something glamorous over the most commonplace fact of life. As Aunt Marigold said, Marigold saw the soul of things as well as the things themselves.

There were weeks of preparation in which Marigold revelled. Grandmother and Mother and Salome worked like slaves, cleaning Cloud of Spruce from attic to cellar. The last week was given over to cooking. Such things as were concocted in that house! Such weighings and measurings and mixings! Mother thought they were really being too lavish, but for once Grandmother counted no cost.

"I have seen many things come into fashion and go out of fashion but a good meal abides," she said oracularly.

Marigold thrilled with bliss because she was permitted to help. It was such fun to beat egg-whites until you could hold the bowl upside down, and dig the kinkly meats out of the walnuts. Grandmother made a big panful of Devonshire clotted cream. Mother made the mince pies that would be taken in with a sprig of holly stuck in them—piping hot, for lukewarm mince pies were an abomination at Cloud of Spruce. And there was a pound cake that required thirty-two eggs—an extravagance known at Cloud of Spruce only

109

when there was a "reunion." Salome baked a whole box of
what she called "hop-and-go-fetch-its"—dear, humpy little
cakes with raisins in them and icing over the tops and pink
candies over that. Marigold knew what the hop-and-go-
fetch-its were for. Just for "pieces" for herself and all the
children who came.

Besides, Marigold had her recitation to learn. It was one
of the Christmas reunion customs to have a "programme" of
speeches and songs and recitations in the parlour after dinner, while the hostesses were cleaning up and washing the
dishes. Aunt Marigold had found a cute little recitation for
Marigold, and Mother had trained her in the appropriate
gestures and inflections. It was to be her first performance
of the kind, and Marigold was very anxious to do well. She
was not in the least afraid that she wouldn't. She knew her
"piece" so perfectly that she could have recited it standing
on her head, and every gesture came pat to the word, end-
ing with the graceful little "curtsey" Mother was at such
pains to teach her. Beulah would be there and Marigold was
sure that curtsey would finish *her* completely.

2

Finally the great day of the feast came. Outside it was a grey
squally day, filling the little empty nests in the maple-trees
full of snow and surrounding the sad black harbour with
meadows of white. But inside there was gaiety and Christmas magic in the very air. The bannisters were garlanded
with greenery, the windows hung with crimson rings. The
big sideboard was a delectable mountain of good things.
The cream was whipped for the banana cake; the kitchen
range was singing a lyric of beech and maple; and Salome
was purring with importance. The spare room bed really
looked too beautiful to be slept in. Grandmother's new pillow slips with crocheted lace six inches deep were on the
pillows and Mother had sewed little flat bags of lavender
inside them. The Christmas-tree in the hall was covered
with lovely red and gold and blue and silver bubbles, such
as fairies must have blown. Every one was dresed up—
Mother in her brown velvet with little amber earrings

against her white neck, Grandmother in her best black silk with a wonderful crêpy purple shawl which was kept in perfumed tissue paper in the lower drawer of the spare room bureau all the year round, save only for big clan affairs like this. Even Lucifer had a new scarlet silk neck-bow, which he considered mere vanity and vexation of spirit.

So far Christmas-Day had been flawless for Marigold. She had got lovely presents from everybody; even Lazarre had given her a near-silver mouse with a blue velvet pincushion erupting from its back. Marigold secretly thought it rather awful. It looked as if the mouse wasn't—healthy. But she wouldn't have hurt Lazarre's feelings for the world by letting him suspect this. Again Marigold was disposed to thank goodness people did not know what you thought.

3

It was such fun to watch the arrivals from the window in Salome's room, where she had her shelf of potted plants. The ivies and petunias fell down in a green screen behind which Marigold could peep without being seen—or being caught at it by Grandmother, who thought "peeking" at visitors extremely bad manners. Bad manners it might be, but it was too int'resting to give up. The folks getting out of the cars and buggies and cutters—for all three were in use today—would have been amazed by the things Marigold, whom they still thought of as a mere baby, knew about them.

There was Uncle Peter's Pete, who had poured whiskey into his aunt's dandelion wine and set her drunk. How solemn and stupid he looked, not at all like a boy who would do such a trick. But you could never tell. And Aunt Katherine, who—so Uncle Klon had said—was a witch and turned herself into a grey cat at night. Marigold no longer believed that but she liked to play with the idea. Aunt Katherine certainly looked like a grey cat in her grey coat trimmed with grey fur; but her rosy smiling face was not properly witch-like. Only Uncle Klon said they were the worst kind of witches—the kind that didn't look like witches.

Uncle Mark and Uncle Jerry were coming up the walk together. At some former Christmas feast they had quarrelled and Uncle Mark had pulled Uncle Jerry's nose. It was years before they spoke. But they seemed on good terms now. Even Old Aunt Kitty, who was really only a distant third cousin, was coming with Uncle Jarvis and Aunt Marcia. Aunt Kitty, whose bonnet had fallen off one day when she was sitting in the front pew of the old Harmony church gallery, peering over the railing to see who was sitting below. Aunt Kitty had nearly pitched after the bonnet herself in her frantic effort to grab it and had only been saved by old Mr. Peasely catching hold of her skirt. It had been a gay, wild bonnet of ostrich plumes and flowers, and its descent had made something of a sensation, especially since, by some impish trick of chance, it had landed squarely on Elder Beamish's bald head as neatly as if it had been fitted on. The Beamishes and the Kittys—Marigold couldn't remember Aunt Kitty's family name—had never been good friends and this incident didn't help matters any. Aunt Kitty looked decorous enough now as she hobbled up the walk leaning on her cane, but she had been a wild old girl at one time, Uncle Klon said.

Aunty Clo was coming, too—who really was an aunt of sorts, though Marigold never could get her placed. She did not like Aunty Clo and neither did Uncle Klon, who vowed she was certainly very much too ugly to live. "She is really lovable under her skin," Aunt Marigold had said, fresh from a reading of Kipling. "Then for heaven's sake, tell her to take her skin off," Uncle Klon had retorted.

Uncle Archibald's Martin and his wife Jenny. They were a by-word for their terrible quarrels, but Aunt Marigold declared they loved each other between times enough to make up for it. Martin had left his car at the gate and she saw him stop Jenny and kiss her under the Scotch pine. Before dinner was over they were calling each other awful names across the table and scandalising the whole clan. But as Marigold listened to the amazing epithets she thought of that long kiss under the pine and wondered if a kiss like that wasn't worth a lot of hard names.

Aunt Sybilla, who "went in for spiritualism." Marigold didn't know what spiritualism was but had a vague idea that it had to do with liquor. Still, Aunt Sybilla didn't look like *that*.

Uncle Charlie, whose laughter boomed over the whole garden, and Garnet Lesley, who would come to a bad end—so every one said. It was int'resting to speculate concerning that bad end. George Lesley, who was going to be married to Mary Patterson. Marigold liked George. "I wish he would wait till I grow up," she thought. "I believe he would like me better than Mary, because there is no fun in her. There is a good deal in me when my conscience doesn't bother me."

Gloomy Uncle Jarvis, with his fierce black beard, who never read any book but the Bible and was always "talking religion" to every one within five minutes of meeting them. Aunt Honora—who *must* have had her face screwed up one time when the wind changed and who had taken a vow never to marry—"quite unnecessarily," Uncle Klon said. Uncle Obadiah, whose great ears stuck out like flaps. Uncle Dan, who had a glass eye and thought nobody knew of it. And last of all Uncle Milton and Aunt Charlotte and Aunt Nora. Thirty years before Uncle Milton had jilted Aunt Nora and when he married Aunt Charlotte, Aunt Nora had decked herself out in widow's weeds and gone to the wedding! And now here they were coming up the walk together, chatting amiably about the weather and their rheumatism. It was very int'resting, looking down on them like this when they couldn't see her, but Marigold paid for her fun when the time came to go in to the parlour and speak to everybody. It was a dreadful ordeal and she shrank back against Mother.

"You must learn to go into a room without thinking every one is staring at you," said Grandmother.

"But they *do* stare," shuddered Marigold. "They're all looking at me to see how much I've grown since the last time or who I look like now. And Aunt Josephine will say I'm not as tall for my age as Gwennie. You know she will."

"It won't kill you if she does," said Grandmother.

"You must act like a lady," whispered Mother.

"Don't be a coward," said Old Grandmother from a faraway moonlit orchard.

It was Old Grandmother who did the trick. Marigold went through the ordeal of handshaking with her head up and her cheeks so crimson that even Aunt Josephine thought her complexion much better. The "big" dinner was in the orchard room, and any one looking at the table would have known that the good old days when nobody bothered about balanced rations had not yet wholly passed at Cloud of Spruce. But Marigold and all the other small fry had theirs in the dining-room.

Marigold rejoiced over this. She never really enjoyed a meal in the orchard room, because she was so busy hating Clementine. They were catered to by Salome, who saw that they all had plenty of dressing and a piece of banana cake besides pudding. Even Uncle Peter's Pete, who had been known to say he wished a fellow could eat two Christmas dinners at once, was satisfied. So everything was beautiful until dinner was over and the "programme" under way in the parlour. And then Marigold crashed down to defeat and not even Old Grandmother's shade could help her.

She got up to say her recitation—and not one word could she remember of it. She stood there before thousands— more or less—of faces, and could not even recall the title. It was all Uncle Peter's Pete's fault, so Marigold always vowed. Just before her name was called he had whispered into the back of her neck, "You haven't washed behind your ears." Marigold knew that territory *had* been washed—Salome had seen to that—but it rattled her nevertheless. And now she stood dazed, frantic, coming out with goose-flesh all over her body. If Mother had been there just to say the first line—Marigold knew she could go on if she could just re-member the first line. But Mother was out helping with the dishes. And there was Pete grinning and Beulah gleefully contemptuous and Nancy squirming in sympathy.

Marigold shut her eyes in a desperate effort to forget every one and straightway saw the most astounding things. Aunt Emma's big cameo brooch with Uncle Ned's hair in it expanded to gigantic size, and Aunt Emma fastened to it— Uncle Jerry with a long nose pulled out like the elephant's child—Uncle Peter's Pete's aunt dancing drunkenly after dandelion wine—Aunt Katherine, a grey cat riding on a broomstick—Aunt Kitty falling headlong after her bonnet—Aunty Clo with her skin off—Uncle Obadiah, just a pair of enormous ears with a tiny manikin between them— Uncle Dan with just one huge eye winking at her all the time—

Dizzy Marigold opened her eyes to come back to reality from that fantastic world into which she had been plunged. But still she could not get that first line.

"Come, come, have you got a bone in your throat?" said Uncle Paul.

"Cat's got her tongue," giggled Uncle Peter's Pete.

"Bit off more than you can chew, eh," said Uncle Charlie, good-naturedly.

Beulah giggled. Flesh and blood could bear no more. Marigold rushed from the room—flew upstairs—tore through Mother's room—slammed shut her door and hurled herself on her bed in an agony of shame and humiliation.

She huddled there all the rest of the afternoon. Mother and Grandmother and Salome were too busy to think about her. Nancy searched but could not find her. Marigold wept in her pillows and wondered what they were saying about her. I don't know if it would have comforted her any had she known they were not thinking about her at all. What was a tragedy to her was only a passing incident to them.

In the rose and purple twilight they went away. Marigold lay and listened to the cars snorting and the sleighbells jingling and then to a tired little lonely motherless wind sobbing itself to sleep in the vines—a wind that had made a fool of itself in the great family of Winds and daren't lift its voice above a whisper.

To Marigold came some one who had never lost the knack of looking at the world through a child's eyes.

"Oh, Aunty Marigold, I've dis-dis-graced myself and— all—the Lesleys," sobbed Marigold.

"Oh, no, darling. There's no disgrace in a little stage fright. We all have it. The first time *I* tried to recite in public my tongue clove to the roof of my mouth and I snivelled—yes, snivelled, and my father had to come up and carry me down from the platform. *You* got away on your own legs at least."

Marigold could not stop crying all at once, but she sat up and blew her nose.

"Oh, Aunty Marigold—really?"

"Yes, really. Father said to me, 'I am disappointed in you,' and I said, 'I wouldn't care for that if I wasn't disappointed in myself.'"

"That's how I feel, too," whispered Marigold. "And then Beulah——"

"Never mind the Beulahs. You'll find heaps of them in life. The only thing to do is ignore them. Beulah would make an excellent mouse-trap, but if she tried for a hundred years she couldn't look as sweet and pretty as you did, standing up there with your puzzled blue eyes. And when you screwed them shut——"

"Oh, I saw such funny things, Aunt Marigold," cried Marigold, bursting into a peal of laughter. Aunt Marigold's little bit of artful flattery was a pick-me-up. It was true poor Beulah was very plain. Oh, how nice to be with some one who just understood and loved. Nothing seemed so disgraceful any more. A truce to vain regrets. She'd show them another time. And here was Lucifer and Salome with a plate of hop-and-go-fetch-its.

"I saved 'em for you," said Salome. "Uncle Peter's Pete was bound to have them but I Peted him. He'll not try to sneak into my pantry again in a hurry."

"I suppose I can take off this absurd ribbon now," said Lucifer, his very whiskers vibrating with indignation. "A dog doesn't mind making an ass of himself, but a cat has his feelings."

CHAPTER X

The Bobbing of Marigold

1

"Sylvia has bobbed her hair," said Marigold rebelliously.

Grandmother sniffed, as Grandmother was apt to sniff at the mention of Sylvia—though since the day of Dr. Clow's visit she had never referred to her, and the key of The Magic Door was always in the lock. But she only said,

"Well, *you're* not going to have yours bobbed, so you can make up your small mind to that. In after years you will thank me for it."

Marigold didn't look or feel very thankful just then. *Everybody* had bobbed hair. Nancy and Beulah—who laughed at her long "tails"—and all the girls in school and even Mrs. Donkin's scared-looking little "home girl" across the road. But she, Marigold Lesley of Cloud of Spruce, had to be hopelessly old-fashioned because Grandmother so decreed. Mother would have been willing for the bob, though she might cry in secret about it. Mother had always been so proud of Marigold's silken fleece. But Grandmother! Marigold knew it was hopeless.

"I don't know if we should do it," said Grandmother—not alluding to bobbed hair. "She has never been left alone before. Suppose something should happen."

"Nothing ever happens here," said Marigold pessimistically and untruthfully. Things happened right along—int'resting things and beautiful things. But this was Marigold's blue day. She could not go with Grandmother and Mother and Salome to Great-Aunt Jean's golden wedding because Aunt Jean's grandchildren had measles. Marigold did so want to see a golden wedding.

"You can get what you like for supper," said Grandmother. "But remember you are not to touch the chocolate cake. That is for the missionary tea to-morrow. Nor cut any of my Killarney roses. I want them to decorate my table."

"Have a good time, honey-child," whispered Mother. "Why not ask Sylvia down to tea with you? There are doughnuts in the cellar crock and plenty of hop-and-go-fetch-its."

But Marigold did not brighten to this. For the first time she felt a vague discontent with Sylvia, her fairy-playmate of three dream-years.

"I *almost* wish I had a real little girl to play with," she said, as she stood at the gate, watching Grandmother and Mother and Salome drive off up the road—all packed tightly in the buggy. Poor Mother, as Marigold knew, had to sit on the narrow edge of nothing.

2

Perhaps this *was* a Magic Day. Perhaps the dark mind of the Witch of Endor, sitting on the gate post, brewed up some kind of spell. Who knows? At all events, when Marigold turned to look down the other road—the road that ran along the harbour shore to the big Summer Hotel by the dunes—there was the wished-for little girl standing by her very elbow and grinning at her.

Marigold stared in amazement. She had never seen the girl before or any one just like her. The stranger was about her own age—possibly a year older. With ivory outlines, a wide red mouth, long narrow green eyes and little dark eyebrows like wings. Bareheaded, with blue-black hair. Beautifully bobbed, as Marigold instantly perceived with a sigh. She wore an odd, smart green dress with touches of scarlet embroidery and she had wonderful slim white hands—very beautiful and very white. Marigold glanced involuntarily at her own sunburned litte paws—and felt ashamed. But— the stranger had *bare knees*. Marigold had never seen this fashion before and she was as much horrified as Grandmother herself could have been.

Who could this girl be? She had appeared so suddenly, so uncannily. She looked different in every way from the Harmony little girls.

"Who are you?" she asked abruptly, before she realised that such a question was probably bad manners.

The stranger grinned.

"I'm me," she said.

Marigold turned haughtily away. A Lesley of Cloud of Spruce was not going to be made fun of by any little nobody from nowhere.

But the girl in green whirled about on tip-toes till she was in front of Marigold once more.

"I'm Princess Varvara," she said. "I'm staying at the hotel down there with Aunt Clara. My uncle is the Duke of Cavendish and Governor-General of Canada. He is visiting the Island and to-day they all went down to visit Cavendish, because it was called after my uncle's great-great-grandfather. All except Aunt Clara and me. She had a headache and they wouldn't take me because there are measles in Cavendish. I was so mad I ran away. I wanted to give Aunt Clara the scare of her life. She's mild and gentle as a kitten but, oh, such a darned tyrant. I can't call my soul my own. So when she went to bed with her headache I just slipped off when Olga was waiting on her. I'm going to do as I like for one day, anyhow. I'm fed up with being looked after. What's the matter?"

"You are telling me a lot of fibs," said Marigold. "You are not a princess. There are no princesses in Prince Edward Island. And you wouldn't be dressed like that if you were a princess."

Varvara laughed. There was some trick about her laugh. It made you want to laugh too. Marigold had hard work to keep from laughing. But she wouldn't laugh. You couldn't laugh when anybody was trying to deceive you with such yarns.

"She must be one of the Americans down at the hotel," thought Marigold. "And she thinks it fun to fool a silly little down-easter like me if she can. But she *can't*! Imagine a princess having bare knees! Just like Lazarre's kids."

"How do you think a princess should be dressed?" demanded Varvara. "In a crown and a velvet robe. You're silly. I *am* a Princess. My father was a Russian Prince and he was killed in The Terror. Mother is English. A sister of the Duke's. We live in England now, but I came out to Canada with Aunt Clara to visit Uncle."

"I'm not a bad hand at making up things myself," said Marigold. She had an impulse to tell this girl all about Sylvia.

Varvara shrugged her shoulders.

"All right. You needn't believe me if you don't want to. All I want is somebody to play with. You'll do nicely. What is your name?"

"Marigold Lesley."

"How old are you?"

"Ten. How old are *you*?" Marigold was determined that the questions should not be all on one side.

"Oh, I'm just the right age. Come, ask me in. I want to see where you live. Will your mother let us play together?"

"Mother and Grandmother have gone to Aunt Jean's golden wedding," explained Marigold. "And Salome was invited, too, because her mother was a friend of Aunt Jean's. So I'm all alone."

The stranger suddenly threw her arms about Marigold and kissed her rapturously on both cheeks.

"How splendid. Let's have a good time. Let's be as bad as we like. Do you know I love you. You are so pretty. Prettier than I am—and I'm the prettiest princess of my age in Europe."

Marigold was shocked. Little girls shouldn't say things like that. Even if you thought them—sometimes, when you had your blue dress on—you shouldn't say them. But Varvara was talking on.

"That sleek, parted gold hair makes you look like a saint in a stained glass window. But why don't you have it bobbed?"

"Grandmother won't let me."

"Cut it off in spite of her."

"You don't know Grandmother," said Marigold.

She couldn't decide whether she really liked this laughing, tantalising creature or not. But she was int'resting— oh, yes, she was int'resting. Something had happened with a vengeance. Would she tell her about Sylvia? And take her up the hill? No, not yet—somehow, not yet. There was the nice little playhouse in the currant-bushes first.

"What a darling spot," cried Varvara. "But how do you play here all by yourself?"

"I pretend I am the Lady Gloriana Fitzgerald, and sit in the parlour and tell my servant what to do."

"Oh, let me be the servant. I think it must be such fun. Now, you tell me what to do. Shall I sweep the floor?"

Marigold had no trouble telling Varvara what to do. She would show this young Yankee, who thought her soft enough to believe any old yarn, just what it was to be Marigold Lesley of Cloud of Spruce.

3

They had a very good time for a while. When they got tired of it they went to see the pigs—Varvara thought them "very droll animals"—and then they went picking raspberries in the bush behind the pig-house. Varvara kept telling wonderful stories. Certainly, thought Marigold, she was a crackerjack at making up. But they suddenly found all their clothes filled with stick-tights, which was decidedly unpleasant.

"What would you think if I said 'damn'?" demanded Varvara explosively.

Marigold didn't say what she would think, but her face said it for her.

"Well, I won't," said Varvara. "I'll just say 'lamb' in the same tone and that will relieve my feelings just the same. What berries are those? Eat some and if they don't kill you I'll take some, too. You know there is a kind of berry—if you eat them you can see fairies and talk to them. I've been looking for them all my life."

"Well, these aren't fairy-berries. They are poisonous," said Marigold. "I *did* eat some once and they made me *awful sick*. The minister prayed for me in church," she concluded importantly.

"When *I* was sick the Archbishop of Canterbury prayed for me," said Varvara.

Marigold wished she had made her minister the moderator of the General Assembly at least.

"Let's go and sit on that seat in the orchard and pick these things out of our clothes," suggested Varvara. "And play 'I see' while we do it. The game is which will see the most wonderful things. *I* see a china cat with diamond whiskers walking over the lawn."

"*I* see a bear with wings," said Marigold, who felt she could see things quite as marvellous as any girl from the States trying to pass herself off as a princess.

"*I* see five angels sitting in that apple-tree."

"*I* see three little grey monkeys on a twisted bough with four moons rising behind them."

Varvara drew her black brows together in a scowl. She didn't like being outseen.

"*I* see the devil squatting over there in your garden, with his tail curled up over his back."

Marigold was annoyed. She felt that *she* couldn't see anything more amazing than that.

"You don't!" she cried. "That—that person never comes into *our* garden."

Varvara laughed scornfully.

"It'd be a more interesting place if he did. Do you know"—confidentially—"I pray for the devil every night."

"Pray for him! *For* him!"

"Yes. I'm so sorry for him. Because he wasn't always a devil you know. If he *had* been I suppose he wouldn't mind it so much. There must be spells when he feels awfully homesick, wishing he could be an angel again. Well, we've got all the stick-tights out. What will we do now?"

Again Marigold thought of introducing her to Sylvia. And again for some occult reason she postponed it.

"Let's go and fire potato-balls. It's great fun."

"I don't know how to fire potato-balls. What are they?"

"I'll show you—little tiny things like small green apples. You stick one on the point of a long switch—and whirl it—so—and the potato ball flies through the air for miles. I hit Lazarre in the face with one last night. My, but he was mad."

"Who is Lazarre?"

"Our French hired boy."

"How many servants have you got?"

"Just Lazarre. Salome isn't really a servant. She is related to us."

"We had fifty before The Terror," said Varvara. "And eight gardeners. Our grounds were a dream. I can just barely remember them. Uncle's are wonderful, too. But I like your little garden, and that house of currant-bushes. Isn't it fun to sit and eat currants off your own walls? Well, where are your potato-balls?"

"Over there in Mr. Donkin's field. We must go up the orchard and along by the fence and——"

"Why not cut straight across?" asked Varvara, waving her hand at Mr. Donkin's creamy green oats.

"There's no path there," said Marigold.

"We'll make a path," said Varvara—and made it. Right through the oats. Marigold followed her, though she knew she shouldn't, praying that Mr. Donkin wouldn't see them.

Varvara thought firing potato-balls the best sport ever. In her excitement she fell half-a-dozen times over potato-plants and got her dress in a fearful state in the wet clay a morning shower had left. And the potato-ball juice stained her face and hands till she looked more like a beggar-maid than a princess.

"I never was real dirty in my life before. It's nice," she said complacently.

4

Varvara insisted on helping Marigold to get supper, though Marigold would have preferred being alone. Company did not help to get supper at Cloud of Spruce. But Varvara was out to do as she liked and she did it. She helped set the table, remarking,

"That cup is just like one Aunt Clara used to have. Her husband bit a piece out of it one day when he was in a tantrum."

Marigold knew by this alone that Varvara was no princess. Princess's uncles could never do things like *that*. Why, Phidime had done that once—bit a piece right out of his wife's much prized cut-glass tumbler. The only one she had. A lady she had worked for had given it to her.

Varvara even went to the spare room with Marigold to get the fruit-cake. Marigold decided that for company she must cut some fruit-cake. Grandmother always did. And it was kept in a box under the spare room bed—the sleek, smooth terrible spare room bed where so many people had died. The fruit-cake had always been kept there, ever since Grandmother's children were small and the spare room the only place they dared not go to look for it.

"Oh!" squealed Varvara. "Is that a feather bed? A *real* feather bed?"

"Yes."

Varvara took one wild leap and landed squarely in the middle of it, bounding up and down in ecstasy right on Grandmother's famous spread of filet crochet.

"I've always wanted to see what a feather bed was like. I didn't think there were any left in the world."

Marigold was horrified. That sacred spare room bed! *What* would Grandmother say.

"Every dead person in our family except Old Grandmother has died in that bed," she said.

Varvara turned pale and hastily slid off the bed.

"Why didn't you tell me that before I jumped on it, you little whelp?" she cried excitedly.

"I'm not a little whelp," said Marigold.

"Of course you're not." There was another wild hug and kiss. Marigold emerged from it somewhat discomposed. The Lesleys were not so emotional.

But when Varvara saw the chocolate cake in the pantry, she must have *that* for supper. She must.

"We can't," said Marigold. "Grandmother said I wasn't to touch it."

Varvara stamped her feet.

"I don't care what your grandmother said. I *will* have it. I'm keen on chocolate cake. And they never let me have more than two tiny pieces. Just put that cake right on the table. At once."

"We are not going to have that cake," said Marigold. There was no one by to see it, but at that instant she looked like a pocket-edition of Grandmother. "There is the fruit-cake and the date loaf and the hop-and-go-fetch-its."

"I don't want your hop-and-go-what-do-you-call-'ems. Once and for all, are we going to have this cake?"

"Once and for all we're *not*."

Varvara clenched her hands.

"If I were my grandmother I'd order you to be knouted to death——"

"If I were *my* grandmother I'd turn you over my knees and spank you," said Marigold intrepidly.

Varvara at once grew calm—deadly, stonily calm.

"If you don't let me have that chocolate cake for my supper I'll go out and climb what you call the apple-barn roof and jump down."

"You can't scare me with that," said Marigold scornfully.

Varvara turned without another word and marched out. Marigold followed her a little uneasily. Of course she was only bluffing. She wouldn't do *that*. Why, it would kill her. Even this wild creature couldn't do a thing like that.

Varvara was running nimbly up the ladder. In another second she was on the flat top of the gambrel roof.

"*Now*, will you let me have the chocolate cake?" she cried.

"No," said Marigold resolutely.

Varvara jumped. Marigold screamed. She shut her eyes in anguish and opened them expecting to see Varvara dead and broken on the stones of the path below. What she saw was Varvara hanging, shrieking on the pine-tree by the apple-barn. Her dress had billowed out and caught on the stub of a lopped branch.

Marigold ran to her frantically.

"Oh, you can have the chocolate cake—you can have *anything*."

"How am I to get down?" moaned Varvara, whose temper and determination had evaporated between heaven and earth.

"I'll bring up the step-ladder. I think you can reach it," gasped Marigold.

Varvara managed to escape by the grace of the step-ladder, though she tore her dress woefully in the process.

"I always do just what I say I'll do," she remarked coolly.

"Just look at your dress," shivered Marigold.

"I am more important than my dress," said Varvara loftily.

Marigold was trembling in every limb as she went back to the pantry. Suppose Varvara really had fallen on those stones. Grandmother had said those girls from the States would do *anything*. Marigold believed it.

"Just look how beautifully I've decorated the table," said Varvara proudly.

Marigold looked. Grandmother's Killarney roses were drooping artistically in the big green basket. Oh, yes, artistically. Varvara had the knack.

"Grandmother told me I wasn't to pick any of those roses," wailed Marigold.

"Well, you didn't, did you, you darling donkey? Tell her *I* did it."

5

The real quarrel did not come until after supper. They had had quite a jolly supper. Varvara was so funny and interesting and said such dreadful things about the picture of Queen Victoria on the dining-room wall.

"Doesn't she look like somebody's old cook with a lace curtain on her head?"

It was really a terrible chromo, originally sent out as a "supplement" with a Montreal paper and framed in hundreds of houses all over the loyal Island. It represented the good queen with a broad blue ribbon across her breast and a crown on her head filled with diamonds, the least of which was as big as a walnut. From the crown descended the aforesaid lace curtain around the face and bust of the queen, and what wasn't lace curtain was diamonds—on ears and throat and breast and hand and arm. Marigold had always had much the same opinion as Varvara about it and had once expressed it. Only once. Grandmother had looked at her as if she had committed *lese-majeste* and said,

"*That is Queen Victoria*," as if Marigold hadn't known it.

But Marigold wasn't going to have girls from the States coming in and making fun of the royal family.

"I don't think you have any business to talk like that of *our* queen," she said haughtily.

"Silly—she was Mother's aunt," retorted Varvara. "Mother remembers her well. She wasn't a bit handsome, but I'm sure she never looked like *that*. If that's where you get your ideas of a princess's dress from I don't wonder you don't think I'm one. Marigold, this chocolate cake is simply topping."

Varvara ate about half of the chocolate cake and paid it a compliment with every piece. Well, reflected Marigold complacently, certainly Cloud of Spruce cookery was good enough for anybody even if she had been the princess she pretended to be. Varvara certainly was—nice. One couldn't help liking her. Marigold decided that after the dishes were washed she would take Varvara through The Magic Door and the Green Gate and introduce her to Sylvia.

But when she went out to the garden after washing the dishes she found Varvara tormenting her toad—her own pet toad who lived under the yellow rose-bush and knew her. Marigold was certain he knew her. And here was this abominable girl poking him with a sharp stick that must hurt him terribly.

"You stop that!" she cried.

"I won't—it's fun," retorted Varvara. "I'm going to kill it—poke it to death."

Marigold darted forward and wrenched the stick out of Varvara's hand. She broke it in three pieces and confronted her self-invited guest in a true Lesleyan anger.

"You shall not hurt my toad," she said superbly. "I don't care what you threaten—not one bit. You can jump off the apple-barn or down the well or go and throw yourself into the harbour. But you shan't kill my toad, Miss *Princess!*"

The derision that Marigold contrived to put into that "princess" is untransferable to paper. Varvara suddenly was in a most terrible temper. She was almost like an animal in her rage. She bared her teeth and dilated her eyes. Her very hair seemed to bristle.

"Pig! Louse! Flea!" she snarled. "Moon-calf! Beast!" Oh, the venom she contrived to put into her epithets. "You'd make God laugh! Cry-baby! Snivelling thing!"

Marigold *was* crying, but it was with rage. Russian princesses, real or pretended, had no monopoly of temper.

"You have the face of a monkey," Marigold cried.

"I'll—pull—your—ears—out—by—the—roots," said Varvara, with a horrible kind of deliberate devilishness.

She hurled herself against Marigold. She pulled Marigold's hair and she slapped Marigold's face. Marigold had never been so manhandled in her life. She, Marigold Lesley. She struck out blindly and found Varvara's nose. She gave it a fierce, sudden tweak. Varvara emitted a malignant yowl and tore herself loose.

"You—you—do you think you can use me like this—*me?*"

"Haven't I done it?" said Marigold triumphantly.

Varvara looked around. On a garden seat lay Grandmother's shears. With a yell like a demon she pounced on them. Before Marigold could run or stir there was a sudden fierce click—another—and Marigold's two pale gold braids were dangling limply in Varvara's beautiful hand.

"Oh!" shrieked Marigold, clapping her hands to her shorn head.

Suddenly Varvara laughed. Her brief insanity had passed. She dropped the shears and the golden tresses and flung her arms around Marigold.

"Let's kiss and make up. Mustn't let a little thing like this spoil a whole day. Say you forgive me, darlingest."

"Darlingest" said it dazedly. She didn't want to—but she did. This wild girl of laughter and jest had a hundred faults and the one great virtue of charm. She would always be forgiven anything.

But Marigold, in spite of her shorn tresses, was almost glad to see Grandmother and Mother driving into the yard.

"Why? What?" began Grandmother, staring at Marigold's head.

"I did it," interposed the ragged, flushed, juice-stained Varvara resolutely. "You are not to blame her for it. It was all my doings. I did it because I was furious, but I'm glad. You'll have to let her have it trimmed decently now. And *I* ate the chocolate cake and picked the roses and jumped on the feather bed. She is not to be scolded at all for it. Remember that."

Grandmother made an involuntary step forward. The Princess Varvara had the narrowest escape of her royal life.

"Who are you?" demanded Grandmother.

Varvara told her as she had told Marigold. With this difference. She was believed. Grandmother knew all about the

Vice-Regal visit to Prince Edward Island, and she had seen Varvara's picture in the Charlottetown *Patriot*.

Grandmother set her lips together. One couldn't, of course, scold a grand-niece of Queen Victoria and the daughter of a Russian Prince. One couldn't. But, oh, if one only could!

An automobile stopped at the gate. A young man and an elderly lady got out of it and came up the walk. A very fine, tall, stately lady, with diamonds winking on her fingers. Her hair snow-white, her face long, her nose long. She could never have been beautiful but she was not under any necessity of being beautiful.

"There's Aunt Clara and Lord Percy," whispered Varvara to Marigold. "I can see she's mad all over—and there's so much of her to get mad. Won't I get a roasting!"

Marigold stiffened in horror. A dreadful conviction came over her that Varvara really was the princess she had claimed to be.

And she had pulled her nose!

The wonderful, great lady walked past Varvara without even looking at her—without looking at anything, indeed. Yet one felt she saw everything and took in the whole situation even to Varvara's muddy dangling rags and dirty face.

"I am sorry," she said to Grandmother, "that my naughty little runaway niece should have given you so much trouble."

"She has not been any trouble to *us*," said Grandmother graciously, as one queen to another. "I am very sorry I was not at home this afternoon"—combining truth with courtesy to a remarkable degree.

The great lady turned to Varvara.

"Come, my dear," she said softly and sweetly.

Varvara disregarded her for a moment. She sprang past her and embraced Marigold tempestuously.

"If you were sugar I'd eat you up. Promise me you'll always love me—even if you never see me again. Promise—as long as grass grows and water runs. Promise."

"I will—oh, I will," gasped Marigold sincerely. It was very odd, but in spite of everything she felt that she did and would love Varvara devotedly.

"I've had such a *satisfying* time to-day," said Varvara.
"They can't take *that* from me. I really didn't mean to kill
your old toad. And you've got your hair bobbed. You can
thank me and God for that."

She danced off to the gate, ignoring Lady Clara but
throwing an airy kiss to Grandmother. "Laugh, Marigold,
laugh," she called imperiously from the car. "I like to leave
people laughing."

Marigold managed the ghost of a laugh, after which Varvara deliberately turned a complete double somersault before everybody and hopped into the back seat. Lord Percy
smiled at Mother. Mother was a very pretty woman.

"An incorrigible little demon," he said.

6

"I think," said Grandmother quite quietly when she had
heard the whole tale, "that princesses are rather too stren-
uous playmates for you. Perhaps, after all, your imaginary
Sylvia is really a better companion."

Marigold thought so too. She ran happily through the
dreamy peace of the orchard to meet the twilight that was
creeping out of the spruce-grove. Back to Sylvia, her com-
rade of star-shine and moon-mist, who did not pull hair and
slap—or provoke pulling and slapping—Sylvia, who was
waiting for her in the shadows beyond the Green Gate. She
was very well satisfied with Sylvia again. It was just as
Grandmother had said. Princesses were too—too—what
was it? Too *it*, anyhow.

She was glad she hadn't told her about Sylvia. She was
glad she hadn't shown her the dear fat grey kittens in the
apple-barn. Who knew but Varvara would have held them
up by their tails? And though she felt sure she could never
forget Princess Varvara—the tang of her—the magic of her
mirth and storms—there was a queer, bitter little regret far
down in her soul.

She had been used to pretend "Suppose a Princess
dropped in to tea." And it *had* happened—and she hadn't
known it. Besides Varvara wasn't a bit like a Princess. The

way she had gobbled things down at supper. Marigold was the poorer for a lost illusion.

Meanwhile down in Cloud of Spruce Mother was putting away Marigold's golden braids and crying over them. Grandmother was girding an apron on with a stern countenance, to make another chocolate cake, late as it was. Salome was counting the hop-and-go-fetch-its and wondering how two children could ever have eaten so many in one afternoon. Marigold's appetite was never very extensive.

"I'll bet that princess will have stomach-ache to-night if she never had it before," she thought vindictively. And Lucifer and the Witch of Endor were talking over the general cussedness of things under the milk bench.

"Take it from me," Lucifer was saying, "princesses aren't what they used to be in the good old days."

CHAPTER XI

A Counsel of Perfection

1

There was really only one creature in the world whom Marigold hated—apart from Clementine, who couldn't be said to be in the world. And that creature was Gwendolen Vincent Lesley—in the family Bible and on the lips of Aunt Josephine. Everywhere else she was Gwennie, the daughter of "Uncle" Luther Lesley, who lived away down east at Rush Hill. She was a second cousin of Marigold's and Marigold had never seen her. Nevertheless she hated her, in her up-rising and her down-sitting, by night and by day, Sundays as well as week-days. And the cause of this hatred was Aunt Josephine.

Aunt Josephine, who was really a second cousin, was a tall severe lady with a pronounced chin and stabbing black eyes which Marigold always felt must see to her very bones—X-ray eyes, Uncle Klon called them. She lived in Charlottetown, when she was home—which wasn't often. Aunt Josephine was an old maid; not a bachelor girl or a single woman but a genuine dyed-in-the-wool old maid. Lazarre added that she "lived on" her relations; by which cannibalish statement he meant that Aunt Josephine was fonder of visiting round than of staying home. She was especially fond of Cloud of Spruce and came as often as she decently could, and every time she came she praised Gwendolen Vincent Lesley to the skies. But she never praised Marigold.

The very first time she had ever seen Marigold she had said, looking at her scrutinisingly,

"Well, you have your father's nose beyond any doubt."

Marigold had never known that her father's nose had been his worst point, but she knew Aunt Josephine was not being complimentary.

132

"Gwendolen Lesley has such a beautiful little nose," continued Aunt Josphine, who had just come from a visit to Luther's. "Purely Grecian. But *then* everything about *her* is beautiful. I have never in all my life seen such a lovely child. And her disposition is as charming as her face. She is very clever, too, and led her class of twenty in school last term. She showed me the picture of an angel in her favourite book of Bible stories and said, 'That is my model, Aunty.'"

Who wouldn't hate Gwendolen after that? And that was only the beginning. All through that visit and every succeeding visit Aunt Josephine prated about the inexhaustible perfections of Gwendolen Vincent, in season and out of season.

Gwendolen, it appeared, was so conscientious that she wrote down every day all the time she had spent in idleness and prayed over it. She had never, it seemed, given any one a moment's worry since she was born. She had taken the honour diploma for Sabbath-school attendance—Aunt Josephine never said "Sunday"—every year since she had begun going.

"She is *such* a spiritual child," said Aunt Josephine.

"Would she jump if you stuck a pin in her?" asked Marigold.

Grandmother frowned and Mother looked shocked—with a glint of unlawful, unLesleyan amusement behind the shock—and Aunt Josephine looked coldly at her.

"Gwendolen is *never* pert," she rebuked.

It also transpired that Gwendolen always repeated hymns to herself before going to sleep. Marigold, who spent *her* pre-sleep hours in an orgy of wonderful imagery adventures, felt miserably how far short she fell of Gwendolen Vincent. And Gwendolen always ate just what was put before her and *never* ate too much.

"I never saw a child so free from greediness," said Aunt Josephine.

Marigold wondered uneasily if Aunt Josephine had noticed her taking that third tart.

And with all this Gwendolen, it appeared, was "sensible." Sensible! Marigold knew what that meant. Somebody who would use roses to make soup of if she could.

Gwendolen had never had her hair bobbed.

"And she has such wonderful, luxuriant, thick, long, shining, glossy curls," said Aunt Josephine, who would have added some more adjectives to the curls if she could have thought of them.

Grandmother, who did not approve of bobbed hair, looked scornfully at Marigold's sleek, cropped head. Marigold, who had never before known a pang of jealousy in regard to a living creature, was rent with its anguish now. Oh, how she hated this paragon of a Gwendolen Vincent Lesley—this angelic and spiritual being, who took honour diplomas and led her class but who yet—Marigold clutched avidly at the recollection of the note Gwennie had written her at Christmas—didn't appear to know that "sapphire" shouldn't be spelled "saffire."

Gwendolen Vincent was "tidy." She was brave—"not afraid of thunderstorms," said Aunt Josephine when Marigold cowered in Mother's lap during a terrible one. She always did *exactly* what she was told—"See that, Marigold," said Grandmother. She never slammed doors—Marigold had just slammed one. She was a wonderful cook for her age. She was never late for meals—"See that, Marigold," said Mother. She never mislaid anything. She always cleaned her teeth after *every* meal. She never used slang. She never interrupted. She never made grammatical errors. She had perfect teeth—Marigold's eye-teeth were just a wee bit too prominent. She was never tomboyish—Marigold had been swinging on a gate. She never was too curious about anything—Marigold had been asking questions. She always was early to bed and early to rise because she knew it was the way and the only way to be healthy and wealthy and wise.

"I don't believe *that*," said Marigold rudely. "Phidime gets up at five o'clock every morning of his life and he's the poorest man in Harmony."

And then it appeared that Gwendolen never answered back.

Once and once only did Marigold, for a fleeting moment, think she might like Gwendolen in spite of her goodness. It was when Aunt Josephine told how Gwendolen had once got up in the middle of the night and gone downstairs *in the dark* to let in a poor, cold, miserable pussy-cat crying on the doorstep. But the next minute Aunt Josephine was describing how careful Gwendolen was to keep her nails clean—looking at Marigold's as she talked.

"Gwendolen has such lovely white half-moons at the base of her nails."

Now, Marigold had no half-moons.

"In short"—though it never really was in short with Aunt Josephine—"Gwendolen is a perfect little lady."

Somehow that phrase got under Marigold's skin as nothing else had done.

"I'm fed up with this," she reflected furiously. It was the first time she had ever dared to use this new expression even in thought. Grandmother and Mother merely got rather tired of things. But rather tired was too mild to express her feelings towards the perfect little lady. And under it all that persistent stabbing ache of jealousy. Marigold would have liked as well as any one else to have a clan reputation of being a perfect lady.

And now Gwendolen was coming to Cloud of Spruce for a visit. Luther had written Grandmother that he wanted his little girl to visit Harmony and get acquainted with all her relatives. Especially did he want her to know Cloud of Spruce, where he had had such jolly times when a boy. Grandmother screwed up her lips a bit over the reference to "jolly times"—she remembered some of them—but she wrote back a very cordial invitation.

Aunt Josephine, who was just completing a visit, said she hoped, if Gwendolen came up for the mooted visit, Marigold would learn from her how a really nice little girl should behave. If Marigold had not been there Grandmother would have bristled up and said that Marigold was a pretty well-behaved child on the whole and her friends reasonably satisfied with her. She would probably have added that Luther Lesley had been a devil of a fellow when he was young and Annie Vincent was the biggest tomboy on the Island before she was married. And that it was curious, to say the least of it, that the pair of them should have produced so saintly an offspring.

But Marigold *was* there, so Grandmother had to look at her sternly and say, "I hope so too."

Marigold did not know that when she had betaken her wounded spirit to the gay ranks of rosy hollyhocks beside the grey-green apple-barn for solace, Grandmother remarked to Mother,

"Thank mercy *that* is over. We won't have another infliction of the old fool for at least three months."

"Aunt Josephine 'likes cats in their place,'" said Lucifer. "*I* know the breed."

2

And then Gwendolen Vincent Lesley came. Marigold got up early the day she was expected, in order to have everything in perfect readiness for the task of entertaining a thorough lady. She was going to be as proper and angelic and spiritual as Gwendolen if it killed her. It was hard to have Mother say pleadingly, "Now, *please* see if you can behave nicely when Gwennie is here," as if she never behaved nicely when Gwennie wasn't there. For a moment Marigold felt an unholy desire that the very first thing she might do would be to scoop up a handful of mud and throw it at the visitor. But that passed. No, she was going to be good—not commonly good, not ordinarily good, but fearfully, extraordinarily, angelically good.

They met. Gwendolen stiffly put out a slender immaculate hand. Marigold glanced apprehensively at her own nails—thank goodness they were clean, even if they had no half-moons. And oh, Gwendolen *was* just as beautiful—and just as ladylike—and just as faultless as Aunt Josephine had painted her. Not one comforting, consoling defect anywhere.

There were the famous nut-brown curls falling around her delicate, spiritual face—there were the large, mild, dewy blue eyes and the exquisitely arched brows—there were the pearly teeth and the straight Grecian nose, the rosebud mouth, the shell-pink ears that lay back so nicely against her head, the cherubic expression, the sweet voice—very sweet. Marigold wondered if it was jealousy that made her think it was a little *too* sweet.

Marigold could have forgiven Gwendolen her beauty but she couldn't forgive her her hopeless perfection of conduct and manners. They had a ghastly week of it. They didn't, as Uncle Klon would have expressed it, click worth a cent in spite of the determined spirituality of both. And oh, how good they both were. Grandmother began to think there might be something in a good example after all.

And they bored each other nearly to death.

Marigold felt forlornly that they *might* have had such a good time if Gwendolen wasn't so horribly proper and if she hadn't to live up to her. Swinging in the apple-barn—housekeeping among the currant-bushes—rollicking in the old grey hay-barn full of cats—prowling about the spruce wood—wading in the brook—gathering mussels down by the shore—making nonsense rhymes—talking sleepy little secrets after they went to bed. But there were no secrets to talk over—nice girls didn't have secrets. And of course Gwendolen was occupied—presumably—repeating hymns.

Once there was a terrible thunderstorm. Marigold was determined she would not show how frightened she was. Gwendolen remarked calmly that the lightning kept her from going to sleep and covered her head with the bed-clothes. Marigold wouldn't do that—Gwendolen might think *she* was doing it because she was terrified. Mother came to the door and said, "Darling, are you frightened?"

"No, not a bit," answered Marigold gallantly, hoping that the bed-clothes would keep Gwendolen from noticing how her voice was shaking.

"Aren't thunderstorms jolly?" asked Gwendolen in the morning.

"Aren't they?" answered Marigold most enthusiastically.

It was Gwendolen's beautiful table-manners that were hardest to emulate. This had always been one of Marigold's weak points. She was always in such a hurry to get through and be at something. But now she liked to linger at the table as long as possible. There would be all the less time to spend in Gwendolen's dull company, cudgelling her brains for some amusement that would be proper and spiritual. Gwendolen ate slowly, used her knife and fork with the strictest propriety, apparently enjoyed crusts, said "Excuse me" whenever indicated, and asked, "May I have the butter if you please, Aunt Lorraine?" where Marigold would have polished it off in two words, "Butter, mums?" And oh, but she would have loved Gwendolen if the latter had ever spilled one drop of gravy on the tablecloth!

One night they went to church with Grandmother to hear a missionary speak. Marigold hadn't wanted to go especially, but Gwendolen was so eager for it that Grandmother took them along, though she did not approve of small girls going out to night meetings. Marigold enjoyed the walk to the church—enjoyed it so much that she had an uneasy feeling that it wasn't spiritual to enjoy things to such an extent. But the white young clouds sailing over the moonlit sky were so dear—the shadows of the spruces on the road so fascinating—the sheep so pearly-white in the silver fields—the whole dear, fragrant summer night so friendly and lovesome. But when she said timidly to Gwendolen,

"Isn't the world lovely after dark?" Gwendolen only said starchily,

"I don't worry so much about the heathen in summer when it's warm, but oh, what *do* they do in cold weather?"

Marigold had never worried about the heathen at all, though she faithfully put a tenth of her little allowance every month in a mite-box for them. Again she felt bitterly her inferiority to Gwendolen Vincent and loved her none the better for it.

But it was that night she prayed,

"Please make me pretty good but not quite as good as Gwen, because she never seems to have any fun."

"Those two children get on beautifully," said Grandmother. "They've never had the slightest quarrel. I really never expected that the visit would go off half so well."

Mother agreed—it was better to agree with Grandmother—but she had a queer conviction that the children weren't getting on at all. Though she couldn't have given the slightest reason for it.

3

Came a morning when Grandmother and Mother had to go into Harmony village. Grandmother was getting a new black satin made and Mother had a date with the dentist. They would be away most of the forenoon and Salome had been summoned away by the illness of a relative, but Gwendolen was so good and Marigold so much improved that they did not feel any special anxiety over leaving them alone. But just before they drove away Grandmother said to them,

"Now mind you, don't either of you stick your head between the bars of the gate."

Nobody to this day knows why Grandmother said that. Marigold believes it was simply predestination. Nobody ever *had* stuck her head between the bars of the gate and it had been there for ten years. A substantial gate of slender criss-cross iron bars. No flimsy wire gates for Cloud of Spruce. It had never occurred to Marigold to stick her head between the bars of the gate. Nor did it occur to her now.

But as soon as Grandmother and Mother had disappeared from sight down the road Gwendolen the model, who had been strangely silent all the morning, said deliberately,

"I *am* gong to stick my head through the bars of the gate."

Marigold couldn't believe her ears. After what Grandmother had said! The good, so-obedient Gwendolen!

"I'm not going to be bossed by an old woman any longer."

She marched down the steps and down the walk, followed by the suddenly alarmed Marigold.

"Oh, don't—don't, please, Gwennie," she begged. "I'm sure it isn't safe—the squares are so small. What if you couldn't get it out again?"

For answer, Gwendolen stuck her head through one of the oblong spaces between the bars. Pushed her head through to be exact—and it was a tight squeeze.

"There!" she said triumphantly, her mop of curls falling forward over her face and confirming a wild suspicion Marigold had felt at the breakfast-table—that Gwendolen had not washed behind her ears that morning.

"Oh, take it out—please, Gwennie," begged Marigold.

"I'll take it out when I please, Miss Prunes-and-prisms. I'm so sick of being good that I'm going to be just as bad as I want to be after this. I don't care how shocked you will be. You just watch the next thing I do."

Marigold's world seemed to spin around her. Before it grew steady again she heard Gwendolen give a frantic little yowl.

"Oh, I can't get my head out," she cried. "I can't—get—my—head—out."

Nor could she. The thick mop of curls falling forward made just the difference of getting in and getting out. Pull—writhe—twist—squirm as she might, she could not free herself. Marigold, in a panic, climbed over the gate and tried to push the head back—with no results save yelps of anguish from Gwendolen, who, if she were hurt as badly as she sounded, was very badly hurt indeed.

Gwendolen was certainly very uncomfortable. The unnatural position made her back and legs ache frightfully. She declared that the blood was running into her head and she would die. Marigold, shaking in the grip of this new terror, murmured faintly,

"Will it—do—any good—to pray?"

"Pray—pray. If you went for the blacksmith it would do more good than all the prayers in the world, you sickening, pious little cat!" said the spiritual Gwendolen.

The blacksmith! Phidime Gautier. Marigold went cold all over. She was in mortal dread of Phidime, who was a dead shot with tobacco-juice and not the least particular about his targets. She had never really believed the legend about the baby, but the impression of it was still in possession of her feelings. Phidime was very gruff and quick-tempered and never "stood for any kids" hanging round his shop. Marigold felt that she could never have the courage to go to Phidime.

"Oh, don't you think if I took you round the waist and pulled hard I could pull you out?" she gasped.

"Yes, and pull my head clean off," snapped Gwendolen. She gave another agonised squirm but to no effect, except that she nearly scraped one of her ears off. Suddenly she began shrieking like a maniac. "I can't stand this another minute—I can't," she gasped between shrieks. "Oh—I'm dying—I'm dying."

Marigold dared hesitate no longer. She tore off down the road like a mad thing. As she went the wild howls of Gwendolen Vincent could be heard faintly and more faintly. Was Gwennie dead? Or just yelled out?

"Hey, left a pie in the oven?" shouted Uncle Jed Clark as she spun by him.

Marigold answered not. To reach the blacksmith shop, to gasp out her tale, took all the breath she had.

"For de love of all de saints," said Phidime. He killed a nail on the floor with a squirt of tobacco-juice and hunted out a file very deliberately. Phidime had never seen any reason why he should hurry. And Gwennie might be dead!

Eventually the file was found, and he started up the road like the grim black ogre of fairy-tales. Gwendolen was not dead. She was still shrieking.

"Here now, stop dat yelling," said Phidime unsympathetically.

It took some time to file the bar and Phidime was not overly gentle. But at last it was done and Gwendolen Vincent was free, considerably rumpled and dishevelled, with a head that felt as if it were three sizes larger than ordinarily.

"Don't you go for do dat fool t'ing any more again," said Phidime warningly.

Gwendolen looked up at him and said spitefully,

"Old devil-face!"

Marigold nearly dropped in her tracks. Ladylike? Spiritual? Not to speak of commonly grateful?

"You keep dat sassy tongue of yours in your haid," said Phidime blackly as he turned away. Gwendolen stuck her tongue out at him.

Marigold was feeling a bit shrewish after her terror. She looked at Gwendolen and uttered the four most unpopular words in the world.

"I told you so," said Marigold.

"Oh, shut your head!"

This was indecent. "Shut your mouth" was an old friend—Marigold had often heard the boys at school using it—but "shut you head" was an interloper.

"I don't care if you *are* shocked, Miss Prim," said Gwendolen. "I'm through with trying to be as good as you. Nobody could be. I don't care *what* Aunt Josephine says."

"Aunt—Jo-seph-ine!"

"Yes, Aunt Jo-seph-ine! She does nothing all the time she is at Rush Hill but sing your praises."

"Mine!" gasped Marigold.

"Yes. She just held you up as a perfect model—always telling me how good you were! I knew I'd hate you—and I didn't want to come here for a visit—I like to go somewhere where something's happening all the time—but Father made me. And I made up my mind I'd be just as ladylike as you. Such a week!"

"Aunt Josephine told me *you* were a model—a perfect lady. *I*'ve been trying to be as good as you," gasped Marigold.

They looked at each other for a moment—and understood. Gwendolen began to laugh.

"I just couldn't stand it a day longer. That's why I stuck my head in the gate."

"Aunt Josephine told me you said hymns before you went to sleep—and took an angel for your model—and——"

"I was just stuffing Aunt Josephine. My, but it was easy to pull her leg."

Which was wicked of course. But in proportion to the wickedness did Marigold's sudden and new-born affection for Gwendolen Vincent increase.

"She made me so mad praising you. I wanted to show her you weren't the only saint in the world."

"Did you really want to hear that missionary?" asked Marigold.

"I sure did. Wanted to hear if he'd tell any cannibal yarns so's we could make a game of them when I went back to Rush Hill," said Gwennie promptly.

Which was wickeder still. But oh, how Marigold loved Gwennie.

"We've wasted a week," she said mournfully.

"Never mind. We'll make up for it this week," said Gwendolen Vincent ominously.

Grandmother can't understand it to this day. She never forgot that second week.

"One of your deep ones, that," Salome always said afterwards, whenever any one mentioned the name of Gwendolen Vincent.

"You can't always tell a saint by the cut of his jib," remarked Lucifer, who had never felt that his tail was safe in spite of Gwendolen's saintliness.

CHAPTER XII

Marigold Entertains

1

"No more fat for me. I've nearly died eating fat this week," was Gwendolen's declaration of independence that night at supper. Grandmother, who hadn't noticed the gate yet—Phidime had wired it up rather cleverly—wondered what had happened to her.

"You should eat the fat *with* the lean," she said severely.

Gwennie stuck out her tongue at Grandmother. It gave Marigold a shock to realise that anybody could do that and live. Grandmother actually said nothing. What was there to say? But she reflected that Annie Vincent's child possibly ran truer to form than they had supposed after all. Grandmother would never have admitted it, but she was almost as tired of Gwennie's perfection as Marigold was. So she pretended not to see the grimace.

Grandmother had to pretend blindness a good many times in the days that followed, rather than outrage hospitality and incur Annie Vincent's eternal wrath by spanking her offspring or sending her home with a flea in her ear. The famed serenity of Cloud of Spruce was smashed to smithereens. A day without a thrill was a lost day for Gwennie.

Marigold enjoyed it—with reservations. Gwennie cared nothing for story-books or kittens and knew nothing whatever about the dryads that lived in the beech clump or the wind spirits that came up the harbour on stormy nights. Marigold would never have dreamed of telling her about Sylvia or taking her along the secret paths of her enchanted groves. But still Gwennie was a good little scout. There was always something doing when she was about, and she *was* funny. She was always "taking off" some one. She could imitate anyone to perfection. It was very amusing—though you

143

always had a little uneasy feeling that the minute your back
was turned she might be imitating *you*. Grandmother really
was very cross the day Gwennie spilled soup over Mrs. Dr.
Emsley's silk dress at the dinner-table because she was
"taking off" the old doctor's way of eating soup and sending
poor Marigold into convulsions of unholy mirth.

Of course fun was all right. But Gwennie laughed at so
many things Marigold had been taught to hold sacred, and
giggled when she should be reverent. It was awful to go to
church with her. She said such funny things about everybody and it was so wicked to laugh in church, even silently.
Yet laugh Marigold sometimes had to till the pew shook and
Grandmother glared at her.

But Marigold would not allow Gwennie to baptise the
kittens. Gwen thought it would be "such fun" and had the
bowl of water and everything ready. She was to be the minister and Marigold was to hold the kittens.

But Marigold had put her foot down firmly. No kittens
were going to be baptised and that was that.

"Grandmother wouldn't allow it," said Marigold.

"I don't care a hang for Grandmother," said Gwennie.
"*I* do."

"You're just afraid of her," said Gwennie contemptuously.
"Do have some spunk."

"I've lots of spunk," retorted Marigold. "And it isn't because I'm afraid of her that I won't have the kittens baptised. It just isn't right."

"Do you know," said Gwennie, "what I do at home when
Father or Mother won't let me do things. I just sit down and
yell at the top of my voice till they give in."

"You couldn't yell Grandmother out," said Marigold
proudly.

Gwennie sulked all the evening and Marigold felt badly
because she really liked Gwennie very much. But there
were some things that simply were not done and baptising
kittens was one of them. Gwennie announced in the morning that she would forgive Marigold.

"I don't want to be forgiven. I haven't done anything
wrong," retorted Marigold. "I *won't* be forgiven."

"I *will* forgive you. You can't prevent me," said Gwennie
virtuously. "And now let's arrange for something different to

happen to-day. I'm tired of everything we've been doing. Look here, was there ever a day in your life you did *everything* you wanted to?"

Marigold reflected. "No."

"Well, let's do everything we want to to-day. Every single thing."

"Everything *you* want or everything *I* want?" queried Marigold significantly.

"Everything *I* want," declared Gwennie. "I'm the visitor, so you *ought* to let me do as I want. Now, come on, don't be a 'fraid-cat. I won't ask you to baptise kittens. We'll leave the holy things out since you're so squeamish. I'll tell you what I *am* going to do. I'm dying to taste some of that blueberry wine. I asked your grandmother yesterday for some but she said it wasn't good for little girls. That's all in my eye. I'm just going to get a bottle out right now and open it. We'll take a glass apiece and put the bottle back. Nobody'll ever know."

Marigold knew quite well this wasn't right. But it was a different kind of wrongness from the kitten-project. And she knew that Gwennie would do it whether it was right or not; and Marigold had a secret hankering to see what blueberry wine was like. They would never give her any of it, which she thought very mean. Grandmother's blueberry wine was famous, and when evening callers came they were always treated to blueberry wine with their cake.

Grandmother and Mother and Salome were all far up in the orchard picking the August apples. It was a good chance and, as Gwennie said, likely nobody would miss the two glassfuls if they put the bottle away back on the pantry shelf in the dark corner.

The dining-room was cool and shadowy. It had been newly papered in the spring, and Mother had just put up the new cream net curtains that waved softly in the August breezes. Grandmother's beautiful bluebird centrepiece, which Aunt Dorothy had sent her all the way from Vancouver, was on the table under the bowl of purple delphiniums. Hanging over a chair was Salome's freshly laundered blue and white print dress.

Marigold lingered to whisper something to the delphiniums, while Gwennie popped into the pantry and came out with a bottle.

"The cork is wired down," she said. "I'll have to run out to the apple-barn and get the pliers. You wait here and if you hear any one coming pop the bottle back into the pantry."

Nobody came and Marigold watched the bottle with its beautiful purplish-red glow. At last she was going to know what blueberry wine was like. It was really rather jolly to have some one round who dared fly in Grandmother's face.

Gwennie saw nobody but Lazarre on her trip to the apple-barn. Lazarre, whose opinion of Gwennie's ancestry was sulphurous, knew something was in the wind.

"Dat kid she always look special lak de angel w'en she plannin' some devil-work," he muttered. But he said nothing. If three women couldn't look after her it was none of his business.

"I've brought a corkscrew, too," said Gwennie, twisting the wire deftly around with the pliers.

As it happened, there was no need of the corkscrew. None whatever.

Gwennie and Marigold hardly knew what had happened. There had been a noise like a gun-shot—and they were standing in the middle of the dining-room looking wildly at each other. There was not much blueberry wine left in that bottle. The rest of it was on the ceiling—on the walls—on the new curtains—on Salome's dress—on the blue bird centrepiece—on Gwennie's face—on Marigold's pretty pink linen dress! Gwennie had learned something she had never known before about blueberry wine. And if thrills were what she was after, she had had enough in one moment to last several weeks.

For an instant she stood in dismay. Then she seized Marigold's hand. "Come quick," she hissed, "get that dress off—get something on—hurry."

Marigold let herself be whisked upstairs. What dreadful thing had happened? Blueberry stains never came out, she had heard Salome say. But Gwennie gave her no time to think. The stained dress was dragged off and thrown into the closet—Marigold's old tan one was thrown over her head—Gwennie wiped the blueberry wine off her face with one of Mother's towels. There were some spots on her dress, too, but that did not matter.

"Come," she said imperiously, snatching Marigold's hand.

"Where are we going?" gasped Marigold as they tore down the road.

"*Anywhere*. We've got to vamoose until they get over that dining-room. They'd kill us if they saw us when they see *it*. We'll stay away till evening. Their fit will be over by then and maybe we'll get off with whole hides. But I'd like to be a fly on the ceiling when Grandmother sees that room."

"We can't stay away all day. We've nothing to eat," groaned Marigold.

"We'll eat berries and roots—and things," said Gwennie. "We'll be Gipsies and live in the woods. Come to think of it, it will be fun."

"Will you take a drive," said a voice above them.

It was Mr. Abel Derusha, the Weed Man, on his double-seated wagon, bareheaded as always, with his dog Buttons beside him!

2

The Weed Man was one of the few romantic personages the country around the harbour could boast. He lived somewhere up at the Head but was well known all over the surrounding communities—at least people thought they knew him well, whereas perhaps nobody really knew him at all.

In his youth Abel Derusha had gone to college and studied for the ministry. Then that was given up. There was a heresy hunt and the result was that Abel Derusha came home, lived at the Head with his old-maid sister Tabby and set up his weed-wagon. Soon he was known as the "Weed Man." In summer he drove all over the Island gathering medicinal plants and herbs and selling them and the decoctions he made from them. He made only a pittance by it. But he and Tabby had enough to live on, and Abel Derusha's weed-fad was little more than an excuse to live in the open. Marigold thought him very "int'resting" and often felt that it would be a delightful thing to drive about with him on his red wagon. She always felt the strange charm of his personality though she knew little of his history—just what she had heard Salome say to Mrs. Kemp one day.

"Abel Derusha always took things easy. Never seemed to worry over trials and disappointments as most folks do. Seems to me that as long as he can wander over the country hunting weeds and talking to that old red dog of his as if it was a human being he don't care how the world wags on. Didn't even worry when they put him out of the ministry. Said God was in the woods as well as any church. He favours his mother's people, the Courteloes. Sort of shiftless and dreamy. All born with hang-nails on their heels. The Derushas were all ashamed of him. 'Tisn't the way to get on in the world."

No, good and worthy Salome. It is not the way to get on in your world, but there may be other worlds where getting on is estimated by different standards, and Abel Derusha lived in one of these—a world far beyond the ken of the thrifty Harbour farmers. Marigold knew that world, though she knew it didn't do to live in it *all* the time as Abel did. Though you were very happy there. Abel Derusha was the happiest person she knew.

He had a face so short it positively looked square, a long, rippling, silky red beard and an odd, spiky, truculent moustache that didn't seem to belong to the beard at all. There was no doubt he was ugly, but Marigold had always thought it was a nice kind of ugliness. He had beautiful clear blue eyes that told he had kept the child-heart. The red squirrels would come to him in the woods and he called all the dogs in the country by their first name. When he came to Cloud of Spruce—which he did not always do, being "pernickety" in regard to his ports of call—he sat in his red wagon and talked with Lazarre and Salome and Mother and Grandmother by the hour, if they would linger to talk with him, though he would never enter the house. After he had gone Lazarre would shrug his shoulders and say contemptuously,

"Dat man, he's crack." Whereat Salome would inform Lazarre, by way of standing by her race, that Abel Derusha had forgotten more than he, the said Lazarre, ever knew. He had promised once to take Marigold for a drive with him and Marigold hankered after it, though she knew she would never be let go. And now here she and Gwennie were out to do as they liked for a whole day and here was the Weed Man offering them a drive.

"Sure," said Gwennie promptly. But Marigold, in spite of her secret wishes, hung back.

"Where are you going?"

"Anywhere—anywhere," said Abel easily. "I'm just poking along to-day—just poking along, thinking how I'd have made the world if I *had* made it. And if you two small skeesicks want to come along why just come."

"But they wouldn't know what had happened to us at home," said Marigold doubtfully.

"They'll know what has happened to the dining-room," giggled Gwen. "Come on now, Marigold. Be a sport."

"Marigold's right," said the Weed Man. "Doesn't do to worry folks who worry. *I* never worry myself. Here's Jim Donkin coming along. I'll ask him to drop over to Cloud of Spruce and tell the folks you've come for a day with me. We'll get our dinners somewhere along the road and we'll go home to my place for supper, and I'll bring you back in the evening. How's that?"

Nobody but the Weed Man would have proposed such a plan. But Abel didn't see any reason if the girls wanted a drive why they shouldn't have it on a day God had made specially for people who wanted to be out. Gwennie had quite made up her mind to go and Marigold couldn't help thinking it would be very int'resting.

So Jim Donkin was asked to take the word to Cloud of Spruce, and Marigold and Gwennie were in the back seat of the red wagon, amid fragrant bundles of Abel's harvest, bowling along the road, quite delighted with themselves. Marigold resolved to forget the catastrophe of the blueberry wine. It had been Gwen's doings, anyway. They wouldn't kill Gwen because she was a visitor and meanwhile here was a whole golden day, with the very air seeming alive, flung into their laps as a gift. Perhaps Marigold had a spice of Uncle Klon's wanderlust in her. At any rate the prospect of driving about with the Weed Man filled her with secret delight. She had always known she would like the Weed Man.

"What road are you going to take?" demanded Gwen.

"Whatever road pleases me," said the Weed Man, looking disdainfully at a car that passed. "Look at that critter insulting the daylight. I've no use at all for them. Nor your aeroplanes. If God had meant us to fly He'd have given us wings."

"Did God mean you to drive this poor old horse when He gave you legs?" said Gwen pertly.

"Yes, when He gave him four legs to my two," was the retort. Abel was so well pleased with himself that he chuckled for a mile. Then he turned into a red side road, narrow and woodsy, with daisies blowing by the longer fences, little pole-gates under the spruces, stone dykes overgrown with things he loved to rifle, looping brooks and grassy fields girdled by woods. It was all very dear and remote and lovely and the Weed Man told them tales of every kink and turn, talking sometimes like the educated man he really was and sometimes lapsing into the vernacular of his childhood.

There was one lovely, gruesome tale of a hollow where a murdered woman's body had been found; and at a certain corner of the road a "go-preacher" had been stoned.

"What did they stone him for?" asked Gwen.

"For preaching the truth—or what he believed the truth, anyhow. They always do that if you preach the truth—stone you or crucify you."

"You meant to be a preacher once yourself, didn't you?" Gwen was possessed of a questioning devil.

"The preaching was Tabby's idea. I never wanted to myself—not enough to tell lies for it anyhow. See that house in the hollow. There was a man lived there who used to say his prayers every morning and then get up and kick his wife."

"Why did he kick her?"

"Ah, that's the point, now. Nobody ever knew. Mebbe 'twas just his way of saying 'amen.'"

"He wouldn't have kicked me twice," said Gwen.

"I believe you." The Weed Man grinned at her over his shoulder. "Here's the old Malloy place. Used to be a leprechaun living there—the Malloys brought him out from Ireland among their bits of furniture, 'twas said. Guess 'twas true. Never heard of any native leprechauns in Prince Edward Island."

"What is a leprechaun?" asked Marigold who had a thrill at the name.

"A liddle dwarf fairy dressed in red with a peaky cap. If you could seè him and keep on seeing him he'd lead you to a pot of buried gold. Jimmy Malloy saw him once but he tuk his eyes off him for a second and the liddle fellow vanished. Howsomever, Jimmy could always wiggle his ears after that. He got that much out of it."

"What good did wiggling his ears do him?"

"Very few can do it. *I* can. Look."

"Oh, will you show me how to do that?" cried Gwennie.

"'Tisn't an accomplishment—it's a gift," said the Weed Man solemnly. "Tom Squirely lives over there. Always bragging he doesn't owe a cent. Good reason why. Nobody would lend him one."

"I heard Lazarre say the same thing about you," said Gwen impudently. "If you live in glass houses you shouldn't throw stones."

"Why not now? Somebody'll be sure to throw a stone at your house whether or no, so you might as well have your fun, too. C. C. Vessey lives on that hill. Not a bad feller—not so mean as his dad. When old Vessey's wife died she was buried with a little gold brooch unbeknown to him. When he found it out he went one night to the graveyard and opened up the grave and casket to get that brooch. Here, wait you a minute. I've got to run in and see Captain Simons for a second. He wanted me to bring him a south-west wind to-day. I have to tell him I couldn't bring it to-day but I'll send him one to-morrow."

"Do you suppose he really sells the winds?" whispered Marigold.

"No," scornfully. "I see through your Weed Man. His head isn't screwed on very tight. But he's good fun and his stories are great. I don't believe that leprechaun yarn though."

"Don't you now?" said the Weed Man, returning creepily from behind, though they had never seen him leave the house, and looking at Gwennie compassionately. "What a lot you're going to miss if you don't believe things. Now, I just drive round believing everything and such fun às I have."

"Lazarre says you're lazy," commented Gwen.

"No, no, not lazy. Just contented. I'm the biggest toad in my own puddle, so it don't worry me none if there's bigger toads in other puddles. I'm king of myself. Now look-a-here. Suppose we call and see old Granny Phin. I haven't seen her for a long while. And maybe she'll let Lily give us a bite of dinner."

Gwen and Marigold surveyed rather dubiously the little house before which the Weed Man was stopping. It was a tumbledown little place with too many brown paper window-panes. The gate hung by one hinge, the yard was overgrown with Scotch thistle and tansy, and even at a distance the old woman who sat on the crazy veranda did not seem attractive.

"I don't like the look of the place much," whispered Gwen. "Hope we don't catch the itch."

"What is that?"

"Marigold, don't you know *anything*?"

Marigold thought gloatingly of certain things she *did* know—lovely things—things Gwennie never would or could know. But she only said,

"I don't know what *that* is."

"Then pray heaven you never *do* know," said Gwen importantly. "*I* know. Caught it from a kid going to school who lived in just such a place as this. Ugh! Lard and sulphur till you could die."

"Come on, now, and don't you be whispering to each other," said the Weed Man. "Granny Phin won't like that. You don't want to get on the rough side of *her* tongue. She's eighty-seven years old, but she's every inch alive."

3

Physically, Granny Phin was hardly every inch alive, for she could not walk alone, having, as she told her visitors later, "paralattics of the hips." But, mentally, her strength had not abated. She was of striking appearance, with snow-white hair in elf-locks around her dead-white face and flashing greenish-blue eyes. She still possessed all her teeth, but they were discoloured and fang-like and when she drew back her lips in a smile she was certainly a rather wolf-like old dame. She wore a frilled widow's cap tied tightly under her chin, a red calico blouse, and a voluminous skirt of red-and-black checked homespun, and was evidently addicted to bare feet. She liked to sit on the veranda, where she could scream maledictions and shake her long black stick at any persons or objects that incurred her dislike or displeasure. Marigold had heard of Granny Phin, but she had never expected to see her. Curiosity mingled with her trepidation as she followed the Weed Man up the path. What a difference there was in old women, she thought, comparing Old Grandmother and Grandmother to this crone.

"Well, this *is* a treat," said Granny Phin.

"It's a warm day, Mistress Phin," said the Weed Man.

"Ye'll be in a warmer place ere long, no doubt," retorted Granny, "and I'll sit in my high seat in heaven and laugh at yez. Hev ye forgot the last time ye was here that dog o' yourn bit me?"

"Yes, and the poor liddle brute has been ill almost ever since," said the Weed Man rather sternly. "He's only just got well. Don't let me see you letting him bite you again."

"The devil himself can't get the better of yer tongue," chuckled Granny admiringly. "Well, come up, come up. Lucky for you I'm in a good humour to-day. I've had such fun watching old Doc Ramsay's funeral go past. Ten years ago to-day he told me I'd only a year to live. Interduce yer family, please."

"Miss Marigold Lesley of Cloud of Spruce—Miss Gwennie Lesley of Rush Hill."

"Cloud o' Spruce folk, eh? I worked at Cloud o' Spruce in my young days. The old lady was a bigotty one. Yer Aunt Adela was there that summer. She looked like an angel, but they do be saying she p'isened her man."

"She isn't our Aunt Adela. She's only a third cousin," said Gwen. "And she didn't poison her husband."

"Well, well, take it easy. Half the husbands in the world ought to be p'isened, anyhow. I had four so I ought to know something of the breed. Sit down all of yez on the floor of the veranda and let yer feet hang down, till dinner's ready. That's what ye've come for, I reckon. Lily—Lily."

In response to Granny's yells a tall, thin, slatternly woman with a sullen face showed herself for a moment in the doorway.

"Company for dinner, Lily—quality folks from Cloud o' Spruce. Put on a tablecloth and bring out the frog pie. And mind ye brew some skeewiddle tea. And send T. B. out to talk to the girls."

"Lily's peeved to-day," grinned Granny as Lily disappeared without a word. "I boxed her ears this morning 'cause she left the soap in the water."

"And her past sixty. Come, come," protested the Weed Man.

"I believe ye. Ye'd think she could have larned sense in sixty years," said Granny, choosing to misunderstand him. "But some folks never larn sense. Yerself now—ye was a young fool once and now ye're an old one. Sad that. T. B., come here and entertain the young ladies."

T. B. came rather sulkily and squatted down by Gwennie. He was a shock-headed urchin with his grandmother's wicked green eyes. Marigold took little notice of him. She was absorbed in awful visions of frog pie. And *what* was skeewiddle tea? It sounded worse than frog pie because she hadn't the least idea what it was. But Gwennie, who had a flair for all kinds of boys, was soon quite at home, bandying slang with Timothy Benjamin Phin—T. B. for short. T. B. soon learned that there were "no flies on her," even if she were one of those "bigotty Lesleys," and also no great need to be overfussy as to what he said. When a plain "damn" slipped out Gwen only giggled.

"Oh, T. B., aren't you afraid you'll go to the bad place if you say such words?"

"Nix on that," contemptuously. "*I* don't believe there's any heaven or hell. When you die there's an end of you."

"Wouldn't you like to go on living?"

"Nope. There's no fun in it," said the youthful misanthrope. "And heaven's a dull place from all the accounts I've heard."

"You've never been there or you wouldn't call it dull," said Marigold suddenly.

"Have *you* been there?"

Marigold thought of the Hidden Land and the spruce hill and Sylvia.

"Yes," she said.

T. B. looked at her. This Marigold-girl was not as pretty as the Gwen one and there wasn't as much "go" in her; but there was something that made T. B. rather cautious, so instead of saying what he would have said to Gwen, he merely remarked politely,

"You're lying."

"Mind yer manners," Granny suddenly shot at T. B. from her conversation with the Weed Man. "Don't ye let me catch ye calling ladies liars."

"Oh, give your face a rest," retorted T. B.

"No shrimp sauce if ye please," said Granny.

T. B. shrugged his shoulders and turned to Gwen.

"She was picking on Aunt Lily all day 'cause Aunt Lily left the soap in the wash-pan. She used to smack her, but *I* stopped that. I wasn't going to have Granny abuse Aunt Lily."

"How did you stop her?" queried Gwen.

"The last time she smacked Aunt Lily I went up to her and bit her," said T. B. coolly.

"You ought to bite her oftener, if that will stop her," giggled Gwen.

"There ain't nothing else worth standing up to her for," grinned T. B. "Granny's tough biting. No, I let her alone and she lets me alone—mostly. She gave me a jaw last week when I got drunk."

"Apple-sauce. You never," scoffed Gwen.

T. B. *had*—as a sort of experiment, it appeared.

"Jest wanted to see what it was like. And it was awful disppointing. I jest went to sleep. Could do that without getting drunk. No fear of my getting jagged again. No kick in it. Nothing *is* ever like what you expect it to be in this world. It's a dull old hole."

"'Tisn't," interjected Granny again. "It's an int'resting world. Vi'lent int'resting."

Marigold felt there was one thing she had in common with Granny at least. In a sense Marigold was enjoying herself. All this was a glimpse into a kind of life she had never known existed, but it was int'resting—"vi'lent int'resting," as Granny said.

Granny and the Weed Man appeared to be enjoying themselves, too, in spite of an occasional passage-at-arms.

"Going to the Baptist church, are yez?" snarled Granny. "Well, if ye do yer dog'll go to heaven afore ye do. Catch *me* going to a Baptist church. I'm a Episcopalian—always was and always will be, world without end, amen."

"I don't believe you ever saw the inside of an Episcopalian church in your life," taunted the Weed Man.

"Yah, I'd tweak yer nose for that if I could reach it," retorted Granny. "Go to yer Baptist church—go to yer Baptist church. Ye son of a monkey-faced rabbit. And I'll sit here and imagine yez all being fried."

She suddenly turned to Marigold.

"If this Weed Man was as rich as he's poor he'd be riding over the heads of all of us. I tell you the real pride of this man is rildic'lous."

"Dinner's ready," Aunt Lily called sulkily from inside.

"Come and help me in," said Granny, reaching briskly for her black stick. "All that keeps me alive is the little bit I eat."

Before the Weed Man could go gallantly to her assistance a shining new car, filled with gaily dressed people, suddenly swung in at the gate and stopped in front of the veranda. The driver bent from the car to make some request, but Granny, crouched like an old tigress, did not allow him to utter a word. She caught up the nearest missile—which happened to be a plate filled with gravy and bacon scraps—from the bench beside her and hurled it at him. It missed his face by a hair's breadth and landed squarely, gravy and all, in a fashionable lady's silken lap. Granny Phin followed this up by a series of fearsome yells and maledictions of which the mildest were, "May all yer pittaties be rotten" and "May ye always be looking for something and never finding it" and—finally, "May ye all have the seven-year itch. I'll pray for it, that I will."

The half-dazed driver backed his car out of the gate and broke all speed-limits down the road. Gwen was squealing with delight, the Weed Man was grinning and Marigold was trying hard to feel shocked.

Granny was in high good humour.

"My, but that did me good. I kin hold up my end of a row yit. Ye could tell by the look of that fellow his grandfather hanged himself in the horse-stable. Come to dinner, all of yez. If we'd known ye were comin' we'd a killed the old rooster. It's time he was used anyway. But there's always frog pie, hey? Now for the frog pie."

To Marigold's relief and Gwen's disappointment there was no frog pie. Indeed, there wasn't much of anything but fried ham and potatoes with some blueberry jam—which suggested rather dismal recollections to Marigold. The dinner was a dull affair, for Aunt Lily was still sulky, Granny was busy gobbling and the Weed Man was silent. It was one of his peculiarities that he seldom talked inside any house.

"Can't think or talk right with walls round me—never could," he had told Salome once.

After dinner the Weed Man paid for their meal with a bottle of liniment for Granny's "paralattics," and Granny bade them a friendly good-bye.

"It's sorry I am that ye're goin' instead o' comin'," she said graciously.

She pulled Marigold so close to her that Marigold had a horrible idea that Granny Phin was going to kiss her. If *that* happened Marigold knew she would never be the same girl again. But Granny only whispered,

"She's a bit purtier than you, but I like *you* best—ye look like a bit o' spring."

Which was a nicer compliment than one would have expected old Granny Phin to pay.

4

Their afternoon drive led along the winding shore of a little river running into the Head of the Bay. Far down was the blue, beckoning harbour and beyond it the sunny dunes and the misty gulf. The Weed Man shook his whip at it mournfully.

"One poetry has vanished fron the gulf forever," he said, more to himself than to the girls. "When I was a boy that gulf there would be dotted with white sails on a day like this. Now there's nothing but gasoline boats and they're not on speaking terms with romance at all. Romance is vanishing—romance is vanishing out of our world."

He shook his head gloomily. But Marigold, looking on the world with the eyes of youth, saw romance eveywhere. As for Gwennie she was not concerned with romance or the lack of it but only with her stomach.

"Gee, I'm hungry," she said. "I didn't get half enough at the Phins's. Where'll we have supper?"

"Down at my place," said the Weed Man. "We're going there now. Tabby'll have a bite for us. After supper I'll take you home—if the weather keeps good-humoured. Those weather-gaws aren't out for nothing. It'll rain cats and dogs to-morrow."

Marigold wondered what weather-gaws were—and then forgot in thinking how interesting it would be if it really rained cats and dogs. Little silk-eared kittens everywhere by the basketful—loads of darling pudgy puppies.

The Weed Man's "place" was at the end of a wood road far down by the red harbour shore. He did not like to have his fellow-mortals too close to him. The little white-washed house seemed to be cuddled down among shrubs and blossoms. There were trees everywhere—the Weed Man would never have any cut down—and four blinking, topaz-eyed kittens in a row on the window-sill, all looking as if they had been cut out of black velvet by the same pattern.

"Cloud o' Spruce breed," said the Weed Man as he lifted the girls down. "Your Old Grandmother gave me the great-grandmother of them. You are very welcome to my poor house, young ladies. Here, Tabby, we've company for supper. Bring along a glass o' water apiece."

"Goodness, aren't we going to have anything for supper but a glass of water?" whispered Gwen.

But Marigold was taken up with Tabby Derusha, about whom she had heard her elders talking. She was not, so Salome said, "all there." She was reported to go Abel one better in the matter of heresy, for she didn't believe in God at all. She laughed a great deal and seldom went from home.

Tabby was very stout and wore a dress of bright red-and-white striped material. Her face was round and blank but her red hair was abundant and beautiful, and she had her brother's kind, childlike blue eyes. She laughed pleasantly at the girls as she brought them the water.

"Down with it—every drop," ordered the Weed Man. "Every one who comes into my house has to drink a full glass of water first thing. People never drink half enough water. If they did they wouldn't have to pay as many doctors' bills. Drink, I say."

Marigold was not in the least thirsty and she found the second half of the generous tumbler hard to "down." Gwennie drank half of hers.

"Finish," said the Weed Man sternly.

"There, then," said Gwennie, and threw the rest of her water in the Weed Man's face.

"Oh, Gwennie!" cried Marigold reproachfully. Miss Tabby laughed. The Weed Man stood quite still, looking comical enough with the water dripping from his whiskers.

"That'll save me washing my face," he said—and it was all he did say.

"How *does* Gwennie do such things and get away with it?" wondered Marigold. "Is it because she's so pretty?"

She was ashamed of Gwennie's manners. Perhaps Gwen was a little ashamed of herself—if shame were possible to her—for she behaved beautifully at the table—making only one break, when she asked Tabby curiously if it were true she didn't believe in God.

"As long as I can laugh at things I can get along without God," said Tabby mysteriously. "When I can't laugh I'll have to believe in Him."

They had a good supper with plenty of Tabby's applecake and cinnamon-buns and raisin-bread and the Weed Man's stories in between. But when he came in after supper and said the rain was very near and they must wait till morning to go home, it was not so very pleasant.

"Oh, we *must* go home," cried Marigold. "Please, please take us home, Mr. Derusha."

"I can't drive you home and then drive back fourteen miles in a rainstorm. I am content with my allotted portion but I am poor—I can't afford a buggy. And my umbrella's full of holes. You're all right here. Your folks know where you are and won't worry. They know we're clean. Your

Grandmother was rained in here one night herself seven years ago. You go right to bed and sleep, and morning'll be here 'fore you know it."

5

"I know I won't sleep a wink in this horrid place," said Gwen snappily, looking scornfully around the tiny bedroom and seeing only the bare uneven floor with its round, braided rug, the cheap little bureau with its cracked mirror, the chipped pitcher and bowl, the stained and cracked ceiling, the old-fashioned knitted lace that trimmed the pillow slips. Marigold saw these things, too, but she saw something else—the view of the harbour through the little window, splendid in the savage sunset of approaching storm. Marigold was tired and rather inclined to think that doing everything you wanted wasn't such fun after all; but under the spell of an outlook like that, the sense of romance and adventure persisted. Why couldn't Gwen make the best of things? She had been grumbling ever since supper. She wasn't such a sport after all.

"If the wind changes, your face will always look like that."

"Oh, don't try to be smart," snapped Gwen. "Old Abel should have taken us home. He promised to. I'm scared to death to sleep in the same house with Tabby Derusha. Any one can see she's cracked. She might come in and smother us with a pillow."

Marigold was a little frightened of Tabby herself—now that it was dark. But all she said was,

"I do hope Salome won't forget to give the cats their strippings."

"I do hope there aren't any bed-bugs in this bed," said Gwen, looking at it with disfavour. "It looks like it."

"Oh, no, I'm sure there isn't. Everything is so clean," said Marigold. "Let's just say our prayer and get into bed."

"I wonder you aren't afraid to say your prayers after that lie you told T. B. to-day about having been in Heaven," said Gwen—who was tired and out of sorts and determined to wreak it on somebody.

"It wasn't a lie—it wasn't—oh, you don't understand," cried Marigold. "It was Sylvia——"

She stopped short. She had never told Gwennie about Sylvia. Gwen had somehow got an inkling that Marigold had some secret connected with the spruce wood and teased her to tell it at intervals. She pounced on Marigold's inadvertent sentence.

"Sylvia! You've some secret about Sylvia, whoever she is. You're mean and dirty not to tell me. Friends always tell each other secrets."

"Not some kinds of secrets. I'm *not* going to tell you about Sylvia, and you needn't coax. I guess I have a right to my own secrets."

Gwen threw one of her boots at the wall.

"All right then. Keep it to yourself. Do you think I want to know your horrid secrets? I *do* know one of them, anyhow. You're jealous of Clementine Lawrence."

Marigold coloured hotly. How on earth had Gwennie found that out? She had never mentioned Clementine to her.

"Oh-h-h!" Gwennie chuckled maliciously. She had to torment somebody as an outlet to her nerves, and Marigold was the only one handy. "You didn't think I knew that. You can't hide things from *me*. Gee, how sour you looked when I praised her picture! Fancy being jealous of a dead woman you never saw! It is the funniest thing I ever heard of."

Marigold writhed. The worst of it was it was *true*. She seemed to hate Clementine more bitterly every day of her life. She wished she could stop it. It was a torture when she thought of it. And it was torture to think that Gwennie had stumbled on it.

"Of course," went on Gwen, "the first Mrs. Leander was ever so much handsomer than your mother. Of course your father would love her best. Ma says widowers just marry the second time for a housekeeper. I could just stand and look at Clementine's picture for hours. When I grow up I'm going to have mine taken just like that, looking at a lily, with my hair done the same way. I'm never going to have *my* hair bobbed. It's *common*."

"The Princess Varvara had *hers* bobbed," retorted Marigold.

"Russian princesses don't count."

"She is a grand-niece of Queen Victoria."

"So *she* said. You needn't put on any airs with me, Marigold Lesley, because you had a princess visiting you. I'm a—a—Democrat."

"You're not. It's only in the States there are Democrats."

"Well, it's something that doesn't take stock in kings and queens, anyway. I forget the right word. And as for politics, do you know I'm going to be a Tory after this. Sir John Carter is ever so much better looking than our Liberal man."

"You *can't* be a To—Conservative," cried Marigold, outraged at this topsy-turvy idea. "Why—why—you were *born* a Grit."

"You'll see if I can't. Well——" Gwen had got her clothes off and wriggled into one of the rather skimpy little cotton nightgowns Tabby had unearthed from somewhere for them, "now for prayers. I'm awful tired of saying the same old prayer. I'm going to invent a new one of my own."

"Do you think it's—safe?" asked Marigold dubiously. When you were a stranger in a strange land wouldn't it be best to stick to the tried and tested in prayers as well as politics.

"Why not? But I know what I'll do. I'm going to say *your* prayer—the one your Aunt Marigold made up for you."

"You shan't," cried Marigold. "That's my very own special prayer."

"Selfish pig," said Gwennie.

Marigold said no more. Perhaps it *was* selfish. And anyway Gwennie would say it if she wanted to. She knew her Gwennie. But she also knew her own dear prayer would be spoiled for her forever if that imp from Rush Hill said it.

Gwennie knelt down with one eye on Marigold. And at the last moment she relented. Gwen wasn't such a bad sort after all. But having said that she was going to invent a new prayer it was up to her to invent one. She wouldn't back down altogether, but Gwen suddenly discovered that it was not such an easy thing to invent a prayer.

"Dear God," she said slowly, "please—please—oh, please never let me have moles like Tabby Derusha's. And never mind about the daily bread—I'm sure to have lots of that—but please give me lots of pudding and cake and jam. And please bless all the folks who deserve it."

"There, that's done," she announced, hopping into bed.

"I'm sure God will think that a funny prayer," said Marigold.

"Well, don't you suppose He wants a little amusement sometimes?" demanded Gwennie. "Anyway, it's my own prayer. It isn't one somebody else made up for me. Gee, Marigold, what if there should be a nest of mice in this bed? There's a chaff tick."

What gruesome things Gwennie did think of. They had blown out their lamp and it was very dark. They were fourteen miles from home. The raindrops began to thud against the little windows. *Was* Tabby Derusha "cracked."

"Abel sent in some apples for you."

Gwennie, to use her own expression, let out a yelp. Tabby was standing by their bed. How could she have got there without their hearing her? Certainly it was eerie. And when she had gone out again they did not dare eat the apples for fear there were worms in them.

"What's that snuffing at the door?" whispered Gwen. "Do you s'pose it's old Abel Derusha turned into a wolf?"

"It's only Buttons," scoffed Marigold. But she was glad when a sudden snore proclaimed that Gwen had fallen asleep. Before she went to sleep herself Tabby Derusha came in again—silently as a shadow, with a little candle this time. She bent over the bed. Marigold, cold with sudden terror, kept her eyes shut and held her breath. Were they going to be killed? Smothered with pillows?

"Dear little children," said Tabby Derusha, lifting one of Gwen's lovely curls gently. "Hair soft as silk—sweet little faces—pretty little dears."

There was a touch soft as a rose-leaf on Marigold's cheek. Tabby gloated over them for a few minutes longer. Then she was gone, as noiselessly as she had come. But Marigold was no longer afraid. She felt as safe and as much at home as if she were in her own blue room at Cloud of Spruce. After all, it had been an int'resting day. And Gwen was all right. She hadn't stolen her prayer. Marigold said it over again under her breath—the beautiful little prayer she loved because it *was* so beautiful and because Aunt Marigold had made it up for her—and went to sleep.

6

"I didn't sleep a wink the whole night," vowed Gwen.

"Never mind, here's a new morning—such a lovely new morning," said Marigold.

'The rain was over. The southwest wind the Weed Man had promised Captain Simons was blowing. The clouds were racing before it. Down on the beach the water was purring in little blue ripples. The sky in the east was all rosy silver. The grass was green and wet on the high red cliffs. Over the harbour hung a milky mist. Then the rising sun rent it apart and made a rainbow of it. A vessel came sailing through it over a glistening path. Never, thought Marigold, had the world seemed so lovely.

"What are you doing?" said Gwen, struggling impatiently into her clothes, much annoyed because Buttons had got in after all and slept on her dress.

"I—I think—I'm praying," said Marigold dreamily.

7

Uncle Klon came for them in his car before breakfast was over.

"Are they very mad at Cloud of Spruce?" asked Gwennie. Rather soberly for her. She did not like Uncle Klon. He was always too many for her.

"There's a special Providence for children and idiots," said Uncle Klon gently. "Jim Donkin forgot to give the message till late last night and they were so relieved to find out where you had gone, that the dining-room rather sank into the background. You'd better not look again on blueberry wine when it is purple, Miss Gwen."

"It's a good thing we're too big to be spanked," whispered Gwen, when she saw Grandmother's face.

"I believe you," said Lucifer.

CHAPTER XIII

A Ghost Is Laid

1

That affair of the blueberry wine was certainly a bad business. There was some secret talk at Cloud of Spruce of sending Gwennie home after it. But nothing came of it, and Gwennie never even knew it had been mooted. It would never do to offend Luther and Annie, Grandmother concluded, though for her part she couldn't understand Josephine. But the real reason was that they all liked Gwennie in spite of—or maybe because of—her deviltries. "An amusing compound of mischief and precocity," said Uncle Klon, who liked to be amused.

"A darn leetle minx," said Lazarre, but he ran his legs off for her. "A child of Beelzebub," said Salome, but kept the old stone cooky-jar full of hop-and-go-fetch-its for Gwennie. Gwennie might be saintly or devilish as the humour took her, but she was not a bit stuck-up about her looks and she had Annie Vincent's kind, ungrudging heart and Luther Lesley's utter inability to hold any spite. As for Marigold, she and Gwennie had some terrible spats, but they had so much fun between that the fights didn't greatly matter. Though Gwennie had a poisonous little tongue when she got mad and said some things that rankled—especially about Clementine.

Clementine's picture had been left on the orchard room wall when most of Old Grandmother's faded brides had been packed away in the oblivion of the garret. There she hung in the green gloom, with her ivory-white face, her sleek braided flow of hair, her pale beautiful hands and her long-lashed eyes forever entreating the lily. Marigold felt she would not have hated Clementine so much if she had looked squarely and a little arrogantly at you like the other brides—if you could have met her eyes and defied them.

But that averted, indifferent gaze, as if you didn't matter at all—as if what you felt or thought didn't matter at all. Oh, for the others Clementine Lesley might be dead, but for Marigold she was torturingly alive and she knew Father had only married Mother for a housekeeper. All his love belonged to that disdainful Lady of the Lily. And Gwennie, suspecting this secret wound in Marigold's soul, turned the barb in it occasionally by singing the praises of Clementine's picture.

The only faint comfort Marigold had was a hope that if Clementine had lived to be old she might have become enormously fat like her mother up at Harmony village. A good many Lawrences lived in or about Harmony and none of them, it was whispered, cared very much for Lorraine, though they were always painfully polite to her. Marigold knew this, as she knew so many things older folk never dreamed of her knowing, and always felt whenever old Mrs. Lawrence's eye rested on her that she had no right to exist. If she could only have believed thoroughly that Clementine would have looked like her mother when she grew old she would not have been jealous of her.

For old Mrs. Lawrence was a funny old dame, and one is never jealous of funny people.

Mrs. Lawrence was very proud of her resemblance to Queen Victoria and dressed up to it. She had three chins, a bosom like a sheep and a harmless, if irritating, habit of shedding hairpins wherever she went. Her favourite adjective was "Christian," and she had a very decided dislike to being reminded that she was either fat or old. She constantly wore a brooch with Clementine's hair in it and when she talked of her daughter—as she did very often—she snuffled. In spite of this, Mrs. Lawrence had many good qualities and was a decent old soul enough, as Uncle Klon said.

But Marigold saw only her defects and foibles because that was all she wanted to see in Clementine's mother; and it rejoiced her when Uncle Klon poked fun at Mrs. Lawrence's pet peculiarity of saving all her children's boots. It was said she had a roomful of them—every boot or shoe that her family of four had ever worn from their first little slipper up. Which did nobody any harm and need not have given

Marigold such fierce pleasure. But when was jealousy ever reasonable?

2

Uncle Peter's son Royal had married and brought his bride home to Harmony. She was said to be unusually pretty, and even Aunt Josephine had said she was the most exquisite bride she had ever seen. There had been the usual clan jollifications in her honour, and now Uncle Klon and Aunt Marigold were giving a party for her—a "fancy dress" dance where all the young fry were to be masked. It sounded very int'resting to Marigold and very provocative to Gwennie as they listened to Mother and Grandmother talking it over at the supper-table. Both wished intensely that they could see that party. But both knew that they must go right to bed as soon as Mother and Grandmother had gone.

"And be good little girls," said Grandmother warningly.

"There's no fun in being a good little girl," said Gwennie, with a pout at Grandmother. "I don't see why we can't go to that party, too."

"You were not invited," said Mother.

"You are not old enough to go to parties," said Grandmother.

"Your day is coming," comforted Salome.

Uncle Klon came out from Harmony for them in his car— already dressed in his fancy costume—a great, flowered-velvet coat that had belonged to some Great-great across the sea, a real sword, and a powdered wig. With lace ruffles at wrist and breast. Mother and Grandmother were not wearing fancy dress, but Grandmother was very splendid in velvet and Mother very pretty in brown brocade and pearls. And Marigold felt delightfully that it was just like a bit out of a story, and she wished she could go up the hill and tell Sylvia about it. She had never even seen Sylvia since Gwennie came, and there were times when she was consumed with longing for her. But she never went up the hill. Gwennie simply must not find out about Sylvia.

"Run on in, kidlets, and go to bed now," said Uncle Klon, grinning rather maliciously, because he knew perfectly well how they hated it.

"Don't call me '*kidlet*,'" flashed Gwen.

After the car had purred off in the twilight, she sat down on the veranda steps and would not say a word. Such a visitation of silence was rare with Gwennie, but Marigold rather welcomed it. She was glad to sit and dream in the lovely twilight, while Lucifer skulked like a black demon among the flower-beds.

It was not the Lucifer of Old Grandmother's days. That Lucifer had gone where good cats go. But there had been another Lucifer to step into his four shoes, looking so exactly like him that in a few weeks it seemed just the same old Lucifer. There had been a procession of Lucifers and Witches for generations at Cloud of Spruce, all looking so much alike that Phidime and Lazarre thought they were one and the same and concluded they were the Old Lady's devils.

Salome, after milking, came along.

"I'm going to bed," she said. "I've got a headache. And it's time you went, too. There's lemonade and cookies for you in the pantry."

"Lemonade and cookies," said Gwennie scornfully, after Salome had gone in, leaving a couple of minxes at large in Cloud of Spruce. "Lemonade and cookies! And they are having all kinds of ices and salads and cakes at the party."

"There's no use thinking about that," said Marigold with a sigh. "It's 9 o'clock. We might as well go to bed."

"Bed! *I'm* going to the party."

Marigold stared.

"The party? But you can't."

"Maybe I can't. But I will. I've been thinking it all out. We'll just *go*. It's only a mile in—we can easily walk it. We must be dressed up ourselves so that if any one sees us they'll think we belong to the party. There's heaps of things in those chests in the garret and I'll make masks. We won't go in the house—just peep in at the windows and see all the dresses and the fun."

So far had evil communications corrupted good manners that Marigold felt no qualms of conscience at all. It would certainly be int'resting. And she was quite wild to see that "exquisite bride" and all the wonderful costumes. Uncle Peter's Pete, she had heard, was going as a devil. The only thing that gave her to think was whether they could really get away with it.

"What if Grandmother catches us?" she said.

"A fig for your grandmother. She won't—and if she does, what then? She can't kill us. Have some gizzard."

Marigold had lots of "gizzard" and in ten minutes they were in the garret tiptoeing cautiously lest Salome hear them in the retreat of her kitchen chamber. The garret was rather a spooky place by candlelight, and Marigold had never been there after dark before.

Great bunches of dried herbs hung from the nails in the rafters, together with bundles of goose-wings, hanks of yarns and various discarded coats. Grandmother's big loom, where she still wove homespun blankets, was before the window. An old, old piano was in one corner and there was some legend of a ghostly lady who played on it by times. And there was a chest under the eaves filled with silken dresses in which gay girls had danced years ago. Marigold had never seen the contents of that chest, but Gwennie seemed to know all about them. She must have been rummaging, Marigold thought. Gwennie *had*—one rainy day when nobody knew where she was—and she knew what was in the big chest, but she did not know—and neither did Marigold—that the little gown of misty green crêpe with tiny daisies sprinkled over it and a satin girdle with a rhinestone buckle in it, which was lying in a box on the top of the contents of the chest, had been a dress of Clementine's. Marigold knew that Clementine had been buried in her wedding-dress and that old Mrs. Lawrence had taken away the rest of her pretty gowns. But this one had been overlooked; perhaps Mrs. Lawrence did not know it still existed. The first Mrs. Leander had her own reasons for keeping it and it had remained in the box in which she had placed it all those years.

"Here's the very thing for you," said Gwen. "*I'm* going as a fortune-teller, with this scarlet cloak and hood and the pack of cards. They're all here together—somebody must have worn them once to a fancy ball."

Marigold fingered the emerald satin of the girdle lovingly. She adored satin.

"But I can't wear this," she objected. "It's miles too big for me."

"Put it on," ordered Gwen. "I can fix it for you. I'm a crackerjack at that. Ma says I'm a born dressmaker. Let's go down to our room. Salome'll hear us creaking about up here."

Marigold put on the daisy dress, with its pretty, short sleeves of lace and its round low neck. Oh, it *was* pretty even if it were old-fashioned and wrinkled. Marigold was tall for her ten years and Clementine had been small and slight; still the dress was too long—and loose. But resourceful Gwennie, with a paper of safety-pins, worked marvels. The skirt was looped up at intervals all around and the pins hidden under clusters of daisies Gwen got off an old hat and which matched the daisies in the dress admirably.

"Now get your good slippers and pink silk stockings," commanded Gwen, sprinkling her own cloak and the green dress lavishly with Mother's violet water. "I've got to make our masks."

Which she proceeded to do, slashing ruthlessly into Old Grandmother's widow "fall" of stiff black crêpe. Then she put on her own red stockings and fixed up a "wand" for herself out of an old umbrella handle with a silvery Christmas-tree ball at the end and a Japanese snake of scarlet paper wreathed around the handle. Nobody could deny that Gwen was past mistress in her own particular brand of magic, and Marigold was lost in admiration of her cleverness. A few minutes later two black-faced figures, one in green and one in red, slipped silently out of Cloud of Spruce and fled along the dark Harmony road, while Salome slept the sleep of the just in the kitchen chamber and Lucifer told the Witch of Endor that he'd be condemned if he ever let that young demon from Rush Hill walk him about the yard on his hind legs again.

3

Marigold, who was never frightened in the dark if she had any one with her, enjoyed the walk to the village. It was a fairy night, with eerie pixie voices in the bracken. Why were the clouds racing across the moonlit sky in such a hurry? To what mysterious sky-tryst were they hastening? An occasional rabbit frisked across the moonlit road. Marigold was half sorry when they reached the village.

Luckily Uncle Klon's house was in the outskirts, so they had no need of traversing the streets. They slipped up the side lane, squirmed through a gap in the privet hedge, boldly walked across the lawn and found themselves at the window of the big room where the dancing was going on. It was open and the blind was up, and they had a full view of the inside.

Marigold caught her breath with delight. Oh, it was fairyland. It was like a little glimpse into another world. For the second time in her life Marigold thought it might be really quite nice to be grown up. She remembered the first time. Long ago, when she had been only six, curled up on the ottoman in the spare room, watching an eighteen-year-old cousin dressing for a dance. When would she be like that? Not for twelve years. She groaned aloud.

"What's the matter, Sugar-pie? Sick?"

"No. It's only—it takes so long to grow up," sighed Marigold.

"Not so long as you think," remarked Grandmother, passing through the hall.

And now again, for a moment, Marigold felt that it really took too long to grow up.

The room was rosily lighted by a gay enormous Chinese lantern hung from the ceiling. The floor was filled with dancers in the most wonderful dresses. There was gaiety in the very air. Lovely low laughter was everywhere, drifting out over the lawn in front and the flower-garden behind. Aunt Marigold's dog was howling heart-brokenly to the music in his kennel. Such flowers—such lights—such music—such dresses. Most of the younger guests were masked but few of the older ones were, and Marigold liked best to watch them because she knew them. There was Aunt Anne, in grey lace over amber silk—Marigold had never seen Aunt Anne so magnificent before! Cousin Jen, with a diamond wreath in her hair, and Cousin Barbara, who always had runs in her stockings, and Cousin Madge, who was the best dancer in the Lesley clan. Her very slippers would have danced by themselves the night through. Aunt Emma, who still wore her hair pompadour and old Uncle Percy, whose wife had her hair bobbed three months before he ever noticed it. Old Uncle Nathaniel, with his great shock of grey hair reaching to his shoulders and looking, so Uncle Klon was wont to say, like a lion that had eaten a Christian who disagreed with him. And, sitting maskless by Aunt Marigold in the palm corner, a creature so lovely, in her gown of pale pink chiffon embroidered with silver, with her hair folded about her head like a golden hood, that Marigold felt at once that this was the "exquisite bride." *Exquisite* was the word. Marigold could hardly drag her eyes from her. It had been worth it all, just to see her.

Mother was dancing—actually dancing—and Grandmother was sitting by the wall, looking as if she didn't think much of fox-trots and tangos. Beside her, a stately old dowager in mauve satin, with hair arranged a la Victoria, and a cameo brooch with Clementine's hair in it. The sight of Mrs. Lawrence spoiled things for Marigold. She was quite ready to turn away when Gwen said,

"We've seen all we can see here. Let's take a sneak around to the dining-room and have a look at the supper."

But the dining-room blinds were down and they could see nothing.

"We'll go right in and see it," said Gwen.

"Oh, do you think it's safe?"

"Of course, it's safe. Look at all the rigs here. We'll never be noticed. I'm going to see all that's to be seen, you bet."

In they went. As Gwen said, nobody noticed them. The supper-table proved such a dream that they hung over it breathlessly. Never in her life had Marigold seen such *pretty* eats—such dainty cakes and cakelets, such wonderful striped sandwiches, such beautiful dishes. Cloud of Spruce could put up a solid banquet, but this alluring daintiness was something new. Gwen perceived sourly that there was no chance of "swiping" anything—there were too many waitresses around, so, after they had looked their fill, she pulled Marigold grumpily away.

"Let's take a peep at the other room again and get out."

Hitherto all had gone well. They were reckless with success. Boldly they crossed the hall and boldly they stood in

the doorway of the dancing-room. The floor was not so
crowded now. The August night was warm and many of the
dancers had gone out to the moonlit lawn. More of the old
folks were sitting around the room. Mrs. Lawrence was
more Queen-Victorian than ever as she languidly plied a
hugh ostrich fan of the vintage of the nineties. Old Uncle
Percy was down at the end of the hall telephoning, and
shouting at the top of his voice as usual. Marigold thought of
the clan story about him and snickered.

"What is that racket?" a caller in Uncle Percy's office had
once asked.

"Oh, that's only old Mr. Lesley talking to his wife down in
Montague," the junior partner had replied.

"Well, why doesn't he phone her instead of yelling across
the Island like that?" said the caller.

Gwen turned to see why Marigold was shaking with
laughter. Then the end of the world came. Gwen stepped
on a small ball that somehow happened to be lying under
the fringe of the portière, shot wildly into the room and fell
with a curdling scream. As she felt herself shooting she
grabbed Marigold—who did not fall but went staggering
across the room on the slippery floor and there sat neatly
down at the very feet of old Mrs. Lawrence, who had just
begun to tell Grandmother how many times she had had
the flu.

The next moment Mrs. Lawrence was all but in hysterics,
and the room was full. Marigold had scrambled to her feet
and was standing there dazedly, but Gwen was still
sprawled on the floor. It was Uncle Klon who picked her up
and stripped the mask from her face.

"I knew it was you." He stood her beside Marigold, from
whose face some one else had removed the mask.

"Oh, Marigold," cried Mother in horror. But old Mrs.
Lawrence was still the centre of attraction. Until she could
be revived and calmed nobody had any time to spare for
Gwen and Marigold.

"Clementine's dress—Clementine's dress," Mrs. Lawrence was shrieking and sobbing. "The dress—she wore—
when she came—in to tell me she had just—promised to
marry—Leander Lesley. I didn't think—you'd let—your
daughter—insult me so—Lorraine."

"Oh, I had nothing to do with it—truly I hadn't," almost sobbed Mother.

"My heart broke—when Clementine died—and now to have it brought up like this—*here*——" people made out between Mrs. Lawrence's yoops. "Oh—I shouldn't—have come. I had a presentiment—one of my dark—forebodings came to me."

"Calm yourself, Mrs. Lawrence—here, try a sip of water," said Aunt Marigold.

"Calm—myself! It's—enough—to kill me. We all—die—sudden—unexpected—death— Oh, Lorraine—Lorraine—you took her place—but your daughter—might have left—her dress—her sacred—little—dress—alone."

"Oh, I didn't know," cried Marigold. She wanted to cry—but cry she would not before all those people. Had not Old Grandmother once said that a Lesley should never cry before the world? Yet it was plain to be seen she had involved Mother in some terrible disgrace. All the sense of mystery and romance had fled. She felt that she and Gwennie were only naughty, silly children who had been ignominiously found out.

Mrs. Lawrence yooped more wildly than ever.

"You'd better have her carried upstairs," said Aunt Marigold. "She really has a weak heart—I'm afraid——"

"Oh, Clementine—Clementine," wailed Mrs. Lawrence. "To think—of the dress—you wore—being *here*. That—dreadful—child—Lorraine—how could you——"

Gwen, who had hitherto been rather dazed and sobered by the suddenness of the catastrophe, now wrenched her shoulder from Uncle Klon's restraining hand and sprang forward.

"Shut your face, you old screech-owl," she said furiously. "You've been told Aunt Lorraine had nothing to do with it. Neither had Marigold. It was me found that mouldy old dress and made Marigold put it on. Now, get that through your dippy old head and stop making a fuss over nothing. Oh, glare—glare! You'd like to boil me in oil and pick my bones, but I don't care *that* that for you, you fat old *cow*."

And Gwen snapped her fingers under outraged Queen Victoria's very nose.

Mrs. Lawrence, finding some one else could make more noise than she could, ceased yooping. She got on her feet, scattering a shower of hairpins on the floor, with the noted Carberry temper sticking out of every kink and curve of her abundant figure, and assisted by Aunt Marigold and Uncle Percy, moved slowly to the stairs.

"One must—make allowances—of course," she sobbed, "for the things—children will do. I am—glad—it wasn't your fault—Lorraine. I didn't—think—I had—deserved that—of you."

"Dear Mrs. Lawrence, don't be angry," implored Lorraine.

"Angry—oh, no. I'm not angry—I'm only—heart-broken. If God——"

"You might as well leave God out of it," said Gwen.

"Gwen, keep quiet," said Uncle Klon furiously.

Whereupon Gwen threw back her head and yelled loud and long.

Everybody was now in the room or the hall, or crowding up to the windows outside. Marigold felt as if everyone in the world were staring at her.

"Could you run us home, Horace?" said Grandmother wearily. "I'm tired—and this has about finished me. Do you want to stay for supper, Lorraine?"

"No—oh, no," said Lorraine, struggling to keep back her tears.

In the back seat of the car Marigold cried for sorrow and Gwen howled for vexation of spirit. But Uncle Klon laughed so uproariously that Grandmother said nervously:

"Horace, *do* pay attention to your steering. I don't see how you can laugh. It's been simply a terrible affair. If it had been any one but old Mrs. Lawrence!"

"Good for her," said Uncle Klon. "I don't believe any one ever told her the truth about herself before. It was priceless."

Gwen stopped sniffling and pricked up her ears. After all, there *was* something nice about Uncle Klon.

"But it *must* have been a shock to see Clementine's dress suddenly come before her like that," said Grandmother. What was the matter with Grandmother's voice? Grandmother couldn't be laughing—she *couldn't*. But was she trying *not* to laugh? "You know, Horace, she really worshipped Clementine——"

"Clementine was a good little scout," said Uncle Klon. "I always liked her. It was to her credit that she wasn't spoiled by such a silly old mother."

"She was a pretty thing," said Grandmother. "I remember her in that dress. People raved about her skin and her hands."

"Clem certainly had pretty hands. It was a pity she had such huge feet," said Uncle Klon.

"She couldn't help her big feet," rebuked Grandmother.

"Of course not. But they were certainly—generous," laughed Uncle Klon. "No wonder the old lady kept all her boots. Too much good leather to waste. Clem had only one quarrel in her life that she never made up. The quarrel with Emmy Carberry. Emmy was going to marry a man neither the Carberrys nor the Lawrences approved of. 'I wouldn't be in your shoes for the world, Emmy,' said Clem solemnly."

"'Don't worry, Clem darling' said Emmy, sticking out a foot in her little Number Two's beside poor Clem's brogans. 'You could never get into them.' Of course, Clem never forgave her."

Just then in a twinkle something happened to poor, crushed, weeping Marigold in the back seat. The spirit of jealousy departed from her forever—at least as far as Clementine was concerned. *Clementine had big feet*. And Mother had feet that even Uncle Klon thought perfection. Oh—Marigold smiled through her tears in the darkness—oh, she could afford to pity Clementine.

"Give me a good reason why I shouldn't take the hide off you," said Uncle Klon as he lifted Gwen from the car.

"I made you laugh," said Gwen saucily.

"You shameless young hussy," said Uncle Klon.

Grandmother said nothing. Of what use was it saying anything to Gwen? Of what use was it trying to drown fish? And she was going home the next evening. Besides, in her secret soul, Grandmother was not sorry that Caroline Lawrence had got her "come uppance" at last.

"Well, this is the end of Wednesday. Now for Thursday. But they might have given us a bite to eat," grumbled Gwen as she rolled into bed. "I wish I'd swiped that little plate of striped sandwiches. But did you ever see anything so funny as that old dragon yowling? Didn't I shut her up! I hope the devil flies away with her before morning. After all I'm glad I'm going home to-morrow night, Marigold. I like you better than I ever dreamed I'd do after Aunt Jo's sickening praises. But your grandmother gets my goat."

"Aren't you going to say your prayers?" reminded Marigold.

"No use waking God up at this hour of the night," said Gwen drowsily.

She was sleeping like a lamb before Marigold had finished her prayers. Marigold was very very thankful and told God so. Not exactly that Clementine had big feet, of course, but that the horrible feeling of hatred and jealousy had gone completely out of her little heart. It was *so* comfortable.

Mother gave Marigold a little scolding in the morning.

"Mrs. Lawrence might have died of heart-failure. Think how you would have felt. As it is, we heard this morning that she cried all night—cried *violently*," Mother added, fearing that Marigold was not just alive to the awfulness of what she had done.

"Never you worry," said Salome. "It served old Madam right. Her and her old boots. Thinking she's like Queen Victoria. But all the same, I'm thankful that limb of Satan is going home to-night. I should really like to have a few minutes' peace. I feel as if I'd been run through a meat-chopper these three weeks. Heaven help the clan when *she* grows up."

"Amen," said Lucifer with an emphatic whisk of his tail.

Gwennie went home that evening.

"Now maybe we can call our souls our own again," said Salome. And yet she did not say it very briskly. Nor did she snub Lazarre when he remarked mournfully,

"By gosh, you t'ink somebody was die in de house."

The lost serenity of Cloud of Spruce had returned to it, only slightly rippled next day by the arrival of an inky postcard from Gwen, addressed to Grandmother.

"I forgot to tell you that I dropped one of your best silver spoons through a crack in the apple-barn floor day before yesterday. I think you can get it easily if you crawl under the barn."

Marigold missed her badly for two days and in a lesser degree for the third. But after all, it was very nice to be alone with Sylvia again. Laughter and frolics were good things, but one didn't want to laugh and frolic *all* the time. She was like one tasting the beauty of quiet after days of boisterous, stimulating wind. The velvet faces of the pansies were waiting for her in the twilight and her own intimate, beloved trees welcomed her once more to their fraternity. When she shut the little Green Gate behind her she went into a different world—where one could be happy and have beautiful hours without being noisy all the time. She turned and looked down on the old vine-hung house and the harbour beyond. There was no sound in the great quiet world but the song of the wind. And there were soft, dewy shadows in every green meadow-nook of Mr. Donkin's farm.

"If I could have picked my place to be born, I'd have picked Cloud of Spruce," she whispered, holding out her arms as if she wanted to put them around the house—this beautiful old place that so many hands had made and so many hearts had loved.

And Clementine's ghost was forever laid. The next time she went to the graveyard she stole over and put a little flower on Clementine's grave—poor pretty Clementine. She no longer felt that she wanted to push her away from Father's side. And she knew now that Father hadn't married Mother just for a housekeeper. For she had told Mother the whole story, and Mother had laughed a little and cried a little.

"*I* was never jealous of Clementine. They were children. He did love her very dearly. But to me he gave the love of his manhood. I *know*."

So Marigold had no further grudge against Clementine's picture. She could look at it calmly and agree that it was very beautiful. But once she gave herself the satisfaction of remarking to it,

"It's a good thing your feet don't show."

CHAPTER XIV

Bitterness of Soul

1

"Here's a new morning," said Marigold blithe as the day. Somehow she was unusually happy that autumn-tinted morning as she went to school. She always felt as if she had wings on a day like this. She loved October—loved it well in its first crimson pomp, when frosted leaves hung like a flame and the asters along the road were like pale purple songs; and even better in its later quiet of brown autumnal fields and the shadowy interfoldings of the hills over the bay; with its evenings full of the nice smell of burning leaves in Lazarre's bonfires and all its apples to be picked and stored in the apple-barn, until such time as it grew too cold and they must be put away in barrels in the cellar.

A group of girls tittered a little as Marigold passed them on the playground. She did not mind very much. Marigold was, in truth, rather a lonely creature in school. She had never "made up" with any of the girls particularly, and with the new seats that held only one there was not the olden chance for intimacies. Not one of them went her way home. She did not quarrel with them and she played games with them at noon-hour and recess, but in some mysterious way she was not of them and they faintly resented it. "Stuck-up," they called her; though Marigold was not in the least stuck-up.

The sense of cleavage deepened as she grew older, instead of disappearing. Sometimes Marigold felt wistfully that it would be nice to have a real chum, of the kind you read about in books—not a fitful visitor like Varvara or Gwennie, bringing a wild whirl of colour into your life and then vanishing as completely as if they had never existed. But she could not find her in Harmony school. And being of a nature that could not compromise with second best when

179

best was denied Marigold made no lesser friendships. There was always Sylvia—though Sylvia was not *quite* as real as she had once seemed. The old magic still worked but it was not quite so magical now.

This morning Marigold felt something new in the school atmosphere. It was not her imagination that the girls whispered and looked at her—with much of curiosity and a little malice. Marigold felt it all through the forenoon and at recess, but no one said anything in particular to her until noon-hour. Then, as her class sat in a circle among the fern-smothered spruce-stumps on the banks of the brook below the schoolhouse the barrage opened.

"How do you like Mr. Thompson, Marigold?" asked Em Stanton with a giggle.

Marigold wondered why upon earth Mr. Thompson's name was dragged into it. He was the new minister who had come to Harmony in the spring. Marigold was not as yet vitally interested in new ministers. It had been a rather exciting time for the older folks. It would be hard to fill old Mr. Henry's place—Mr. Henry who had filled the pulpit of Harmony church for thirty years and was "a saint if ever there was one."

"He used to make me weep six times every Sunday," sighed Miss Amelia Martin. "I hoped my time would come before his. I've always felt he would be such a lovely man to bury you."

"Oh, Lord," Aunt Kitty Standish had prayed at the first Aid meeting after his retirement, "Oh, Lord, send us as good a minister as Mr. Henry—but, oh, Lord, you can't do it."

Nobody thought Mr. Thompson as good but he seemed the best of the candidates.

"He's a good preacher," said Salome, "but it's a pity he's a widower. He'll marry in the congregation and that'll spoil him." Adding, however, by way of a comforting afterthought, "But I'm glad they've picked him. I like a comfortable-looking minister."

Mr. Thompson had one daughter about Marigold's age—round and rosy little Jane Thompson, who went, however, to the village school, the church and manse being there, so that Marigold saw little of her save in Sunday school, where

they were in the same class. Jane always knew her golden
text and memory-verses and cathechism-questions perfectly well—one would expect a minister's daughter to do
that. But it didn't make her any the more int'resting, Marigold thought. As for Mr. Thompson, she liked him when
she thought about him at all—which was, to tell the truth,
only when he called at Cloud of Spruce. She liked the jolly,
unministerial twinkle in his eye especially. Now, why
should Em Stanton be so suddenly interested in her feelings towards Mr. Thompson? A disagreeable little sensation
came over Marigold—as if a faint chill wind had blown over
the secret places of her soul.

"I like Mr. Thompson very well," she said stiffly.

Em gave another irritating snigger and exchanged
glances with the other girls.

"That is a good thing," she said significantly.

They expected Marigold to ask why it was a good thing,
but she would not. She bit a dainty little crescent out of a
hop-and-go-fetch-it and chewed it remotely.

"How will you like him for a stepfather?" said Velma
Church slyly.

That particular hop-and-go-fetch-it was never eaten.
Marigold laid it down in her box and stared at Velma.

"Didn't you *know?*"

"Know what?" said Marigold through pale lips.

"That your mother is going to marry him?"

Marigold wondered what had happened to her—or to the
world. Had somebody slapped her in the face? Had the sun
been blotted out of the sky?

"I don't—believe it——" she said helplessly.

"Everybody says so," said Em triumphantly. "We thought
you knew, of course. It's funny your mother hasn't told you.
Why, he spends half his time at Cloud of Spruce."

This was, of course, an exaggeration. But Marigold suddenly remembered with horror that Mr. Thompson had
made a great many calls lately. Of course Grandmother had
had a slight attack of bronchitis; but a dreadful conviction
assailed her that Mr. Henry had never called so often, even
when Salome had pneumonia. She stared miserably at Em.

"They're to be married before spring, *I* heard," said
Fanny Collins. "Your mother was in Summerside the other

day helping him pick paper for the manse. Aunt Lindy saw them."

"My, won't *your* nose be out of joint," said Sally McLean.

"You'll have to be Marigold Thompson after the wedding," said Lula Nelson.

"They'll send you to a boarding-school, true's you live," said Dot Church.

None of these jabs produced any sign of life in Marigold. She sat as one stunned. Oh, if she could only be alone—far, far away from these hateful girls—to face this!

"Ma says your mother isn't a bit suitable for a minister's wife," said Velma.

"Too dressy and extravagant," added Em.

"Aunt Beth says his first wife was the finest woman that ever lived," said Pet Dixon.

"It's a wonder your mother would marry a bluenose," said Janet Irving.

"I guess she has a hard enough time with the old lady," said Pet.

"Ma says Mrs. Leander has perked up amazing this fall," said Lula.

The school-bell rang and the ring of malicious faces melted away. Marigold followed them slowly into the school. Her feet were like lead and her spirit that had "flown on feathers" in the morning was heavier still. The world had all at once got so very dark. Oh, *could* it be true? It couldn't—Marigold had another awful recollection.

"Mrs. Lesley's engaged," Salome had said gently one day the preceding week, as she had shut the door in the face of a too-persistent insurance-man.

Oh, yes, it must be true.

"Salome," said Marigold that evening, "do you think God ever does things out of spite?"

"Just listen to her," said Salome. "You mustn't ask such wicked questions. That's as bad as anything Gwen Lesley could say."

"I'm sorry," said Marigold with more persistence, "but *does* He?"

"Of course not," said Salome. "It's the Old Gentleman that's spiteful. What's the matter with you? You don't look just right. Have you got a cold?"

Marigold felt that a cold had got her. She was cold and sick to the core of her soul. Everything had been torn out of her little life at once. And not a word could she say to Mother about it.

2

Marigold had thought she was done forever with jealousy when she discovered the truth about Clementine's feet. And now she was in the grip of a jealousy tenfold worse. *That* had been merely a ghostly vexation of the soul. *This* was a burning torment of the heart. Perhaps Marigold was never more bitterly unhappy in all her life than she was during the two months following that day by the brook. Everything fed her suspicion and jealousy. She was filled with hate. She could not enjoy anything because she was hating Mr. Thompson so much. She even hated poor, innocent little Jane Thompson. Would Jane call Mother "mother?" If she did!

November came in, with its dark, dull twilights that made Marigold feel grown up and old—with its mournful winds rustling the dead leaves on its cold, desolate, moonless nights—with its wintry song of old grey fields and the sorrowful grey ghosts of the goldenrod in the fence corners. And Mr. Thompson's motor-lights burning cheerfully at the gate in so many of its chill evenings. Marigold felt that it was going to be November forever. "To-morrow" had once been a word of magic to her. Now "to-morrow" would only be more cruel than to-day.

But it was a torturing satisfaction to hate Mr. Thompson. She felt sure she had always hated him. Lucifer certainly had—and cats *knew*. You couldn't hoodwink Lucifer. Nothing about him pleased Marigold any more. She remembered what Lazarre had once said about another Frenchman who had done something that reflected on his race.

"But you surely don't want to see him hanged," protested Salome.

"No—no—oh, no, course we not lak to see heem hang," acknowledged Lazarre, "but we lak to see heem *destroyed*."

That exactly expressed Marigold's feelings towards Mr. Thompson. She would not want to see him hanged but she would cheerfully have had him "destroyed." It was a certain ephemeral satisfaction to name the big dead Scotch thistle behind the apple-barn "Rev. Mr. Thompson" and cut it down and burn it. She looked at him drinking his tea and wished there were poison in the cup. Not enough to kill him—oh, no, just enough to make him awfully sick and disgusted with the idea of marrying any one. Once, when he grew angry over what some one in the church had done and pounded the table, Marigold had said under her breath to Mother, "See what a husband you'll have!"

She wished she could refuse to go to church but she could not do that, so she sat there scowling blackly at him. When he came to the house she was the very incarnation of disdain. And he never noticed it! To be disdainful and not have it noticed was unendurable. Half the time he couldn't even remember her name and called her Daffodil. Once he grew fatherly and tried to stroke her hair. "I'm not a cat," said Marigold rudely, jerking away. She had to beg his pardon for that. Cloud of Spruce couldn't imagine why Marigold had taken such a scunner to the minister.

"He preaches such lovely sermons," said Salome reproachfully. "He can draw tears to my eyes."

"So can onions," said Marigold savagely.

And yet when Em Stanton told her that Stanton *père* said Mr. Thompson was a shallow-pated creature Marigold flashed pale lightning at her. This would never do. If Mother were really going to marry him he must be defended.

"Oh, all right," said Em, walking off. "I didn't know you liked him. I didn't suppose any one could like a bluenose."

"He isn't a bluenose," said Marigold, who hadn't the slightest idea what a bluenose was.

"He *is*. Your Uncle Klon told me so himself the day he picked me up on the road. We met the minister in his car and your Uncle Klon said, 'Trust a bluenose to bust the speed-limit every time.' And *I* said, 'Is Mr. Thompson a bluenose?' and he said, 'The very bluest of them.' So there now!"

"But what is a bluenose?" demanded Marigold wildly. She *must* know the worst.

"Well, I'm not sure but I *think* it is a dope-fiend," said Em cautiously. "I asked Vera Church and she said she thought that's what it was. It's a terrible thing. They see hidjus faces wherever they look. There's nothing too bad for them to do. And they're that sly. Nobody would ever suspect them at first until they get so they can't hide it. Then they have to be put away."

Put away! What did "put away" mean? But Marigold would ask no more questions of Em. Every question answered seemed to make a bad matter worse. But if Mr. Thompson ever had to be "put away" she wished it might happen before he married Mother.

Things constantly happened that tortured her. Mr. Thompson came more and more often to Cloud of Spruce. He took Mother to Summerside to pick more wallpaper; he came one evening and said to Mother,

"I want to consult you about Jane's adenoids."

Mother took him into the orchard room and closed the door. Marigold haunted the hall outside like an uneasy little ghost. What was going on behind that closed door? *She* had a sore throat, but was Mother troubled over *that*? Not at all. She was wrapped up in Jane's adenoids—whatever they were.

When nothing happened to torture her she tortured herself. Would she have to leave dear Cloud of Spruce when Mother married Mr. Thompson? Or perhaps Mother would leave her all alone there with Grandmother, as Millie Graham's mother had done. And there would be no one to meet her any more when she came from school; or stand at the door in the twilight calling her in to shelter out of the dark; or sit by her bed and talk to her before she went to sleep. Though now her bedtime talks with Mother were not what they had been. Always some veil of strangerhood hung between them.

Lorraine feared her child was growing away from her— growing into the hard Blaisdell reserve perhaps. She could not ask Marigold what had changed her—that would be to admit change. When Aunt Anne wanted Mother to let

Marigold go to her for a visit and Mother consented, Marigold refused almost tearfully—though she had once wanted so much to go. Suppose Mother would get married while she was away? Suppose that was why she wanted her to go to Aunt Anne's? And they wouldn't even have the same name! How terrible it would be to hear people say, "Oh, that is Marigold Lesley—*Mrs. Thompson's* daughter, you know."

They might even call her Marigold Thompson!

Marigold felt she could not bear it. Why, she wouldn't be wanted anywhere. Oh, couldn't something—or somebody—prevent it?

"I wonder if it would do any good to pray about it," she thought wearily and concluded it wouldn't. It would be of no use to pray against a minister, of course. Gwen had said she jumped up and down and screamed until she got her own way. But Marigold could not quite see herself doing that. Just suppose she did. Why the brides in the garret would come rushing down—Clementine would at last look up from her lily—Old Grandmother would jump out of her frame in the orchard room. But still Mother would marry Mr. Thompson. Mother who was looking so pretty and blooming this fall. Before she knew this ghastly thing Marigold had been so pleased when people said, "How well Lorraine is looking." Now it was an insult.

As Christmas grew near, Cloud of Spruce was fairly haunted by Marigold's sad little face. "How thin you're getting, darling," said Mother anxiously.

"Jane Thompson's fat enough," said Marigold pettishly.

Mother smiled. She thought Marigold was a little jealous of the rose-faced Jane. Probably some Josephinian person had been praising Jane too much. Mother thought she understood—and Marigold thought *she* understood. And still the gulf of misunderstanding between them widened and deepened.

Would this be the last Christmas she would ever spend with Mother? The day before Christmas they went to the graveyard as usual. Marigold crushed the holly wreath down on Father's grave with savage intensity. *She* hadn't forgotten him, if Mother had.

"And I'll never call *him* 'Father,'" she sobbed. "Not if they kill me."

3

The Christmas reunion was at Aunt Marcia's that year, and Grandmother could not go because her bronchitis was worse and Mother would not leave her. Marigold was glad. She was in no mood for Christmas reunions.

In the afternoon Salome got Lazarre to hitch up the buggy and drove herself over to the village to see some old friends. She took Marigold with her and Marigold prowled about the streets while Salome gossiped. It was a very mild, still day. The wind had fallen asleep in the spruce woods behind South Harmony and great beautiful flakes were floating softly down. Some impulse she could not resist drew her to the manse. Would Mother soon be living there? Such an ugly square house, with not even a tree about it. And no real garden. Only a little kitchen-plot off to one side. With an old pig rooting in it.

Marigold perceived that the pig was in Mr. Thompson's parsnip-bed. Well, what of it? *She* wasn't going to tell Mr. Thompson. He could look after his own parsnips. She turned and walked deliberately to the main street. Then she turned as deliberately back. If Mother were living in that manse in the spring she must have parsnips. Mother was so fond of parsnips.

Marigold went firmly up the walk and up the steps and to the door. There she stood for a few minutes, apparently turned to stone. The door was open. And the door of a room off the hall was open. An unfurnished room, still littered with the mess paperhangers make but with beautiful walls blossoming in velvety flowers. And Mr. Thompson was standing in this room with Third Cousin Ellice Lesley from Summerside. Marigold knew "Aunt" Ellice very well. A comfortable woman who never counted calories and always wore her hair in smooth glossy ripples just like the wave marks on the sand. Aunt Ellice was not handsome, but as old Mr. McAllister said, she was "a useful wumman—a verra useful wumman." She was also a well-off woman and she wore just now a very smart hat and a rich plush coat with a big red rose pinned to the collar.

And Mr. Thompson was kissing her!

Marigold turned and stole noiselessly away—but not before she had heard Mr. Thompson say,

"Sweetums," and Aunt Ellice say "Honey-boy!"

The pig was still rooting in the parsnips. Let him root—while the minister kissed women he had no business to kiss—women with complexions like tallow candles and ankles like sausages and eyes so shallow that they looked as if they were pasted on their faces. And called them "Sweetums!"

Marigold was so full of indignation for her mother's sake that she would not wait for Salome. She tore homeward through the white flakes to Cloud of Spruce, and found Mother keeping some tryst with the past before a jolly open fire in the orchard room.

"Mother," cried Marigold in breathless fury, "Mr. Thompson's kissing Aunt Ellice—in the manse—*kissing* her."

"Well, why shouldn't he kiss her?" asked Mother amusedly.

"Don't you—*care?*"

"Care? Why should I care? He is going to marry Aunt Ellice in two weeks' time."

Marigold stared. All her life seemed to have been drained out of her body and concentrated in her eyes.

"I—thought—that—*you* were going to marry him, Mother."

"Me! Why, Marigold, whatever put such a silly idea into your head, darling?"

Marigold continued to stare. Great tears slowly formed in her eyes and rolled down her cheeks.

"Marigold—Marigold!" Mother folded her arms about her and drew her to her knee. "Why are you so disappointed because I'm not going to marry Mr. Thompson?"

Disappointed!

"I'm so happy—so happy, Mother," sobbed Marigold. "I was so afraid you *were*."

"And that's why you've been so funny to him. Marigold, why didn't you ask me——"

"I couldn't bear to. I was so afraid you'd say it was true."

Lorraine Lesley cuddled her baby closer. She understood and did not laugh at the torture the little soul had endured.

"Darling, no one who had loved your father could ever love any one else. I've *had* love—and now I have its memory—and *you*. That is enough for me."

"Mother," whispered Marigold, "were you—disappointed because—I wasn't a boy?"

"Never. Not for one minute. I wanted you to be a girl. And so did your father. There hadn't been a little girl at Cloud of Spruce for so long, he said."

Marigold sat very still with her face against her mother's. She knew this was one of the moments that last forever.

4

Mr. Thompson was such a nice man. Such a nice, jolly, friendly man. She hoped that pig hadn't eaten *all* his parsnips. She was dreadfully sorry for him because he wasn't going to get Mother, but Aunt Ellice would do very well. She was so useful. A minister's wife should be useful. And Jane was a darling. How jolly it was not to hate anybody any more. Life and she were good friends again.

It had stopped snowing. A big round silvery moon was floating up over a snowy hill. The little hollow in Mr. Donkin's field that would be a pool, blue-flagged, in summer, was a round white dimple, as if some giantess had pressed her finger down. The orchard was full of fine, faint blue shadows on the snow. It was a lovely world and life was beautiful. The paper that day had said a king's son had been born in Europe and a millionaire's son in Montreal. A far more interesting event which the paper had not chronicled, was that the Witch of Endor had three lovely kittens in the apple-barn. And to-morrow she would go up the hill and tryst again with Sylvia.

CHAPTER XV

One Clear Call

1

I am afraid that if Marigold could have defined her state of mind when her mother told her she must go to the missionary meeting in the church that evening, she would have said she was bored with the prospect. For a little girl who had three fourth cousins in the foreign-mission field it must be confessed that Marigold was shamefully indifferent to missionary work in general.

She had planned to spend the evening with Sylvia and she didn't want to exchange Sylvia's alluring company for a dull, stupid, poky, old missionary meeting. The adjectives are Marigold's, not mine, and if you blame her for them, please remember that very few lasses of eleven, outside of memoirs, have any very clear ideas of the heathen in their blindness. For Marigold, foreign missions were something that grown-ups and ministers naturally took to but which were far removed from her sphere of thought and action. So she didn't see why she should be dragged out to hear a foreign missionary speak. She had heard one the night she went with Gwennie—a queer, sun-burned spectacled man, tremendously in earnest but dreadfully dull. And Marigold considered she had had enough of it. But Grandmother could not go out after night because of her rheumatism and Salome had a sore foot; and Mother, for some strange reason, was set on going. It seemed that the speaker of the evening was a lady and an old schoolmate of hers. She wanted Marigold for company. Marigold would have done anything and gone anywhere for Mother—even to a missionary meeting. So she trotted resignedly along the pleasant, star-lit road with Mother and thought mainly about the new dress of apricot georgette that Mother, in spite of Grandmother's pursed lips, had promised her for Willa Rogers's birthday-party.

Marigold got her first shock when the missionary rose to speak. Could that wonderful creature be a missionary? Marigold had never seen any one so entrancingly beautiful in her life. What strange, deep, dark, appealing eyes! What cheek of creamy pallor despite India's suns! What a crown of burnished, red-gold hair! What exquisite out-reaching hands that seemed to draw you magnetically whither they would! What a haunting voice, full of pathos and unnameable charm! And what a lovely, lovely white dress with a pale, seraphic-blue girdle hanging to the hem of it!

Dr. Violet Meriwether had not been speaking for ten minutes before Marigold was longing through all her soul to be a foreign missionary, with the uttermost ends of the earth for her inheritance The only thing that surprised her was that there was no visible halo around Dr. Violet's head.

Oh, what a thrilling address! Marigold had a moment of amazed wonder at herself for ever supposing foreign missions were poky before she was swept out on that flood-tide of eloquence to a realm she had never known existed—a realm in which self-sacrifice and child-widows and India's coral strand were all blended together into something indescribably fascinating and appealing. Nay, more than appealing—demanding. Before Dr. Violet was half through her address Marigold Lesley, entranced in the old Lesley pew, was dedicating her life to foreign missions.

It was a sudden conversion but a very thorough one. Already Marigold felt that she was cut off forever from her old life—her old companions—her old dreams. *She* was not the silly, wicked little girl who had come unwillingly to the missionary meeting an hour ago, thinking of apricot dresses and fairy playmates on the hill. Not she. Consecrated. Set apart. All the rest of her life to follow that shining, upward path of service Dr. Violet Meriwether pointed out. Some day she, too, might be Dr. Marigold Lesley. Think of it. She had sometimes wondered whom she would like to resemble when she grew up. Mother? But Mother was "put upon." Everybody bossed her. But she had no longer any doubt. She wanted to be exactly like Dr. Violet Meriwether.

She hated Em Church for giggling behind her. She looked with scornful contempt at Elder MacLeod's four grown-up daughters. Why weren't *they* in the foreign-mission field? She almost died of shame when she sneezed rapidly three times in succession just when Dr. Violet was making her most impassioned appeal to the young girls. Was there not *one* in this church to-night who would answer, "Here Am I" to the "one-clear call"? And Marigold, who longed to spring to her feet and say it, could only sneeze until the great moment was passed and Dr. Meriwether had sat down.

Mr. Thompson followed with a few words. He lacked entirely the fascination of Dr. Meriwether, but one of his sentences struck burningly across Marigold's thrilled soul. A foreign missionary, he said, must be calm, serene, patient, tactful, self-reliant, resourceful and deeply religious. Marigold remembered every one of his adjectives. It was something of a large order but Marigold in her uplift had no doubt she could fill it eventually. And she would begin at once to prepare herself for her life-work. At once. She went down the aisle as if she trod on air. Oh, how wicked and foolish she had been before this wonderful night! But now her face was—what had been Dr. Meriwether's phase—"set towards the heights"—distant, shining heights of service and sacrifice. Marigold shivered in ecstasy.

Tommy Blair was going down the opposite aisle. Marigold had hated Tommy Blair bitterly ever since the day he had written across the front page of her reader in his sprawling, inky hand,

"This book is one thing, my fist is another. If you steal the one, you'll feel the other."

But she must forgive him—a missionary must forgive everybody. She smiled at him so radiantly across the church that Tommy Blair went out and told his cronies that Marigold Lesley was "gone" on him.

2

Marigold could not tell her mother of her great resolve. It would make poor Mother feel so badly. If Father had been alive, it would be different. But she was all Mother had. That was where part of the self-sacrifice lay. As for telling Grandmother, Marigold never dreamed of it. But she plunged at once with all her might into the preparation for her life-work. Grandmother and Mother knew there was something in the wind, though they couldn't imagine what. I do not know if they considered Marigold calm, serene, patient, tactful, etc., but I do know they thought her very funny.

"Whatever it is I suppose it will run its course," said Grandmother resignedly, out of her experience. But Mother was secretly a little bit worried. Something must be the matter when Marigold said she would rather not have a new apricot dress—her old one was quite good enough. And she didn't even want to go to Willa's party—only Grandmother insisted because the Rogerses would be offended. Marigold went under protest and condescended to the other little girls, pitying them for the dull, commonplace lives before them. Pitying Algie Rogers too. Every one knew his mother had vowed he should be a minister when he wanted furiously to be a carpenter. How different from her high, self-elected lot.

"My, but ain't Marigold Lesley getting stuck-up," Willa Rogers said.

Marigold laid aside the tiny diamond ring Aunt Marigold had given her on her last birthday. Consecrated people should not, she felt, wear diamond rings. Uncle Klon offered to get her one of the new striped silk parasols she had craved, but Marigold thanked him firmly and serenely and would he please give her a concordance instead. Uncle Klon chuckled and gave it to her. He did not know what particular magic Marigold was making now, but he knew she was getting a tremendous lot of satisfaction out of it.

She was. It was positive rapture to refuse the new ribbon hat-streamers for which her soul had once longed and wear her old hat to Cousin Nellie's wedding. Once Marigold had been interested in weddings. Who knew—when one grew up——? But that was past. She must never ever think of being married. Marigold was nothing if not thorough. Naught but counsels of perfection for her. She washed dishes and beat eggs and weeded her garden rapt as a saint.

She gave up reading everything except missionary literature. She pored over the missionary books from the Sunday-school library—especially one fascinating little fat

brown volume, the biography of a missionary who had
"prepared" herself from the age of six. Marigold felt she had
lost many precious years. But she would do her best to
catch up. She rose at five o'clock—once—to read the Bible
and pray. *That* would sound well in a memoir. The said missionary had arisen at five o'clock every morning of her life
from her sixth birthday. But said missionary did not have a
Grandmother. That made all the difference.

The only thing that really hurt very badly was giving up
Sylvia. At first Marigold felt that she could not—could
not—do this. But she must. Sacrifice was not really sacrifice
unless it hurt you. Dr. Violet had said so. She explained it
all tearfully to Sylvia. Was it only fancy or did a mocking
elfin-rill of laughter follow her down the orchard from the
cloud of spruce? It almost seemed as if Sylvia didn't think
she meant it.

Marigold tried to fill up the resulting gap in her life by
imagining herself being carried about on the backs of elephants and rescuing child-widows from burning, at the risk
of her life. To be sure, Dr. Violet had not said anything
about riding on elephants—she had even mentioned a pro-
saic motor-car—and Mr. Thompson said widows were no
longer burned. But no doubt something just as dreadful was
done to them. Marigold stifled her longing for Sylvia in rescuing them by the dozen. Oh, I fancy Uncle Klon was right.

Marigold had some moments of agonised wonder if she
would ever be able to pray in public. She tried to make a
small beginning by saying "Amen" under her breath whenever Mr. Thompson said anything in his prayers that ap-
pealed to her. And it was very hard to decide where she
would go as a missionary. She shuddered for days between
Japanese earthquakes and Indian snakes. Until she got a
book about the lepers in India. The lepers carried the day.
They must be attended to, snakes or no snakes. She would
be a missionary to the lepers. And meanwhile Grandmother was horribly cross because Marigold had forgotten
to water the geraniums. She couldn't explain to Grandmother that she had forgotten because she was bringing an
Indian village through a famine. But she was calm and serene under Grandmother's disapproval. Very.

3

For two or three weeks this was all very well and satisfying. Then Marigold yearned for what Alexander the Great would have called more worlds to conquer and Dr. Violet Meriwether might have termed a wider field of service. The heroine of the memoirs was always visiting some one who was sick or in trouble and working wonders of consolation. Marigold felt she should do the same. But whom to visit? There was nobody sick or in trouble—that Marigold knew of—near Cloud of Spruce just then. Unless it might be Mrs. Delagarde. The thought of her came to Marigold like an inspiration. Mrs. Delagarde of the black robes and the sad, sad face. Who never went anywhere but wandered about in her big garden all day long in South Harmony.

Marigold had heard some one say that Mrs. Delagarde was a "little off." She did not know what that meant exactly but she felt sure any one with that sorrowful face was in need of comforting. She would go to see her and—and—what? Read the Bible to her as the Lady of the Memoirs had done? Marigold could not see herself doing that. But she would just go to see her—and perhaps the way would be opened up. In the Memoirs a way was always opened up. Marigold slipped up to her room before she went, and said a little special prayer. A very earnest, sincere little prayer, in spite of the fact that it was couched largely in the language of the Memoirs. Then she stole away through the fragrant evening.

Marigold had a moment of panic when she found herself really inside Mrs. Delagarde's gate facing a grim house that looked black against the sunset. But a missionary must be self-reliant. A missionary must not give way to panic. With a gallant smile Marigold marched down the aisle of daffodils to where Mrs. Delagarde was standing among the pale gold of lemon lilies in the shadows, with an amber sky and dark hills behind her, staring unseeingly before her with her large, strange agate-grey eyes.

Mrs. Delagarde surprised Marigold. Her whole sad face lighted up with a wonderful radiance of joy. She stepped forward and held out her hands. Marigold was to be haunted for weeks by those long pale hands held out in supplication.

"Delight—Delight—you have come back to me——" she said.

Marigold let Mrs. Delagarde take her hands—put her arms round her—press her lips to her forehead. She suddenly felt very queer—and frightened. There was something about Mrs. Delagarde—and she was being drawn into the house. What was Mrs. Delagarde saying—in that quick, strange, passionate voice of hers, that wasn't like any voice Marigold knew?

"I've often seen you walking before me—with your face turned away. You'd never wait for me. But now you have come back, Delight. So you must have forgiven me. Have you forgiven me, Delight?"

"Oh—yes—yes." Marigold would have said "yes" to any question. She did not know what she was saying. She was no brave missionary—no ambitious candidate for Memoirs—she was only a very badly frightened little girl— shut up in a strange house with a strange—a very strange woman.

Again that wonderful flash of joy crossed Mrs. Delagarde's face.

"Come up to your room, Delight. It is all ready for you. I have kept it all ready. I knew you would come back to me sometime—when I had been punished enough. So I have kept it ready for you."

Marigold was being drawn up the stairs by that insistent arm—across the hall—into a room. A large, shadowy room with four great windows. And in the midst a huge white bed with something lying on it. Marigold felt a prickling in the roots of her hair—— Was it—was it——?

"There is your big doll, Delight," said Mrs. Delagarde, laughing a little wildly. "I've kept it for you, you see. Take it up and play with it. I want to see you play, Delight. It's so long since I have seen you play. And your dresses are all in the closet for you. See."

She opened the closet-door and Marigold saw them—rows of dainty dresses hanging there, awfully like Bluebeard's wives in a picture-book she had.

Marigold found her voice—a shaky, panicky voice.

"Please may I go home now?" she gasped. "I—I think Mother will be wanting me. It's—getting late."

A look of alarm crossed Mrs. Delagarde's pale face—followed by a look of cunning.

"But you *are* home, Delight. You are my child—though you have left me so long. Oh, it was cruel to leave me so long. But I will not scold you—— I will never scold you again. Now you have come back. You must never leave me again. Never. I am going to find your father and tell him you have come back. I have never spoken to him since you went away—but I will speak now. Oh, Delight, Delight!"

Marigold eluded the outstretched arms.

"Please, please let me go," she entreated desperately. "I'm not your little Delight—really I'm not—my name is Marigold Lesley. Please, dear Mrs. Delagarde, let me go home."

"You are still angry with me," said Mrs. Delagarde sorrowfully. "That is why you talk so. Of course you are Delight. Don't you think I know your golden hair? But you are angry with me because I whipped you that day before you went away. I will never do that again, Delight. You need not be afraid of me, darling. Tell me again that you forgive me, sweetest—tell me again that you forgive me."

"Oh, I do—I do." If only Mrs. Delagarde would let her out! But Mrs. Delagarde knelt down by her entreatingly.

"Oh, we will be so happy now that you have come back, Delight. Kiss me—kiss me. You have turned your face away from me so long, my golden-haired Delight."

Her voice was so appealing that Marigold, in spite of her terror, could not refuse. She bent forward and kissed Mrs. Delagarde—then found herself seized in a wild embrace and smothered with hungry kisses.

Marigold tore herself from the encircling arms and darted towards the door. But Mrs. Delagarde caught her as she reached it—pushed her aside with a strange little laugh and slipped out. Marigold heard the key turn in the lock.

She was a prisoner in the house of a crazy woman. She knew now. *That* was what people meant when they called Mrs. Delagarde "a little off."

What could she do? Nothing. Nobody knew where she was. Alone in this horrible, big, darkening room with the shrouded windows. With those dreadful dresses of dead Delight hanging in the closet. With that terrible doll lying on the bed like a dead thing. With a huge, black bearskin muff on a little stand by the bed. What wild tale had Lazarre once told her about those big, old-fashioned bearskin muffs? That they were really witches and went out on moonlit nights and danced in the snow. There was a moon to-night—already its faint radiance was stealing into the room—suppose the muff began to dance around the room before her!

Marigold stifled the scream that rose to her lips. It might bring Mrs. Delagarde back. Nothing would be so dreadful as that—not even a bewitched bearskin muff. She was afraid even to move—but she managed to tiptoe to window after window. They were all nailed down—every one of them. Anyway, all of them opened on a steep bare wall. No chance of escape there. And through one she saw the home-light at Cloud of Spruce. Had they missed her? Were they searching for her? But they would never think of coming here.

She sat down in an old cretonne-covered wing-chair by the window—as far as possible from the bed and the muff. She sat there through the whole of the chilly, incredible, everlasting night. Nobody came. At first there was only a dreadful stillness. There did not seem to be a sound in the whole earth. The wind rose and the moonlight went out and the windows rattled unceasingly. And she was sure the muff moved. And the dresses in the closet surely stirred. Twice she heard footsteps in the hall.

Morning came—a cloudy morning with a blood-red sunrise sky. The windows all looked out on green widespread fields. There was no way in which she could attract attention. No way of escape. She would die here of starvation, and Mother would never know what had become of her. Again and again she heard footsteps passing along the hall—again and again she held her breath with fear lest they pause at the door. She suffered with thirst as the day wore on but she felt no hunger. A queer, numb resignation was stealing over her. Perhaps she would die very soon—but that no longer seemed terrible. The only terrible thing was that Mrs. Delagarde might come back.

Evening again—moonlight again—wind again—a snarling, quarrelsome wind that worried a vine at the window and sent a queer shadow flying across the room to the bearksin muff. It seemed to move—it *was* moving—Marigold suddenly went to pieces. She shrieked madly—she flew across the room—she tugged frantically at the locked door. It opened so suddenly that she nearly fell over backward. She did not pause to reflect that it could never have been locked at all, in spite of the turned key—she was past thinking or reflecting. She fled across the hall—down the stairs—out—out into freedom. She never stopped running till she stumbled into the hall at Cloud of Spruce—a hall full of wild, excited people, amid which she caught one glimpse of Mother's white anguished face before—for the first time in her life—she fainted.

"Good God," said Uncle Klon. "Here she is."

4

It was next day and Marigold was in bed with Mother sitting by her bedside and Grandmother coming in and out trying to look disapproving but too relieved and thankful to make a success of it. The whole story had been told—and much more. Marigold knew all about Mrs. Delagarde now—poor Mrs. Delagarde, who had lost her only little child a year ago, and had not been right in her mind ever since. Who had sat for hours by her little girl's side entreating her to speak to her once more—just one word. Who could not forget for a moment that she had whipped Delight the day before her sudden illness. Who had never forgiven her husband because he had been away when Delight took ill and there was no one to go for the doctor through the storm.

"The poor unhappy lady is greatly to be pitied," Mother said. "But, oh, darling, what a terrible time you have had."

"Some of the rest of us have had a terrible time, too," said Grandmother grimly. "Mrs. Donkin was sure she saw you at dusk in an automobile with two strange-looking men. And Toff LeClerc's boat is missing and we thought you had floated out into the channel in it. The whole country has been combed for you, miss."

"I'm afraid I'm not fit to be a missionary, Mother," sobbed Marigold when Grandmother had gone out. "I wasn't brave—or resourceful—or serene—or anything."

Mother cuddled her—compassionate, tender, understanding.

"It's a very fine, splendid thing to be a missionary, dear, and if, when you grow up, you feel called to that particular form of service nobody will try to hinder you. But the best way to prepare for it is just to learn all you can and get a good education and live as happily and pleasantly as a small girl can, meanwhile. Dr. Violet Meriwether was the jolliest little tomboy in the world when we were girls together—a perfect mischief and madcap."

Aunt Marigold made her namesake stay in bed for a week. On the day Marigold was allowed to get up Mother came in smiling.

"After all, your missionary effort seems to have done some good, Marigold. Mrs. Delagarde's doctor says she is very much better. She has ceased to talk about Delight and she has forgiven her husband. Dr. Ryan says she is quite rational in many ways and he thinks if she is taken away for a complete change of scene and association she will recover completely. He says she told him she was 'forgiven' and this conviction seems to have cured some sick spot in her soul."

"Humph," said Grandmother—rather gently, however.

"Isn't it funny she never came back to the room?" said Marigold.

"She probably forgot all about you the minute you were out of her sight."

"I was so afraid she would. I thought I heard her outside all the time. That was why I never dared go near the door. And it wasn't locked at all—though I *know* I heard the key turn."

"I suppose it didn't turn all the way. Keys sometimes stick like that."

"Wasn't it silly to think I was locked in when I might have got out right away? I guess I've been silly right through. But——"

Marigold sighed. After having been consecrated and set apart for three weeks it was somewhat flat and savourless to come back to ordinary, memoirless life.

But visions of a new apricot dress were again flickering alluringly before her eyes. And Sylvia was on the hill—a forgiving Sylvia, who made no difference at all because of her brief defection.

CHAPTER XVI

One of Us

1

"I'm going travelling to-morrow. It makes me feel very important," Marigold told Sylvia one evening.

Hitherto Marigold had not done a great deal of visiting. Grandmother disapproved of it and Mother seldom dared to disagree with Grandmother. Besides Marigold herself had no great hankering to visit—by which she meant going away from home by herself to stay overnight. Only twice had she done it before—to Uncle Paul's and to Aunt Stasia's, and neither "visit" had been much of a success. Marigold still tingled with shame and resentment whenever she thought of "IT." She vowed she would never go to Aunt Stasia's again.

But, of course, it was different at Aunt Anne's. Marigold loved Aunt Anne best of all her aunts. So when Aunt Anne came one day to Cloud of Spruce and said:

"I want to borrow Marigold for awhile," Marigold was very glad that Grandmother raised no objections.

Grandmother thought it was time the child was seeing something of the world. She had her head stuffed too full of nonsense, like that Sylvia business. Despite Dr. Adam Clow—who came no more to Cloud of Spruce, having fared forth on an adventurous journey beyond our bourne of time and space—Grandmother thought it was hanging on too long. What might be tolerated at eight was inexcusable at eleven. Anne and Charles were sensible people—though Anne was too indulgent. Grandmother expected Marigold to come home with her digestion ruined for life.

But Marigold went to Aunt Anne's with no cloud over her golden anticipations. Aunt Anne was a twinkly-eyed lady who was always saying, "I must go and see if there is anything nice in the pantry." You couldn't help adoring an aunty like that. It may be that Grandmother's fears were not altogether unfounded.

But she had to content herself with exacting a promise from Anne that Marigold must eat porridge every morning—real oatmeal porridge. If that were done, Grandmother felt that the rest of the day might be trusted to take care of itself.

So Marigold went to Broad Acres and loved it at first sight. An old grey homestead right down by the sea—the real, wonderful sea, not merely the calm, land-locked harbour. Built on a little point of land running out into a pond, with a steep fir-clad hill behind it and slender silver birch-trees all over it. With an old thorn-hedge the slips of which had been brought out from the Old Country—that mysterious land across the ocean where the Lesley clan had its roots. Enclosing a garden even more wonderful and fascinating than the garden at home—for a garden by the sea has in it something no inland garden can ever have. An old stone dyke between the house and the hill, with gorgeous hollyhocks flaunting over it. And a dear little six-sided room in "the tower," where you could lie at night and watch the stars twinkling through the fir-boughs. All this, with an uncle who knew a joke when he saw it and an aunty who let you alone so beautifully made Broad Acres just the spot for a vacation-visit.

And at first—Mats. Mats lived on the next farm and had been christened Martha. But she had lived that down. She was a fat, jolly little soul with round grey eyes, notorious freckles, luxuriant unbobbed sugar-brown curls, a face meant for laughter, and a generous mother who made enchanting pies. For a week she and Marigold had "no end of fun" together and got into no more mischief than two normal small girls should with no grandmothers around. And the soul of Marigold was knit into the soul of Mats and all was harmony and joy—until Paula came. Came and took immediate possession of the centre of the stage, as is the way of the Paulas.

2

It happened at Sunday-school. All the Lesleys were Presbyterians—of course—but the Presbyterian church over-the-bay was three miles away, so Marigold was sent to Sunday-school in the little white Baptist church on the other side of the pond, with the spruce-trees crowding all around it. Marigold loved it. She thought it seemed like a nice, friendly little church. She wore her pretty new green dress, with its little embroidered collar, and her smart little white hat with its green bow. *And* kid gloves—new kid gloves—*real* kid gloves. Mats, who knew no jealousy, was puffed up with pride over having for a chum a girl who wore real kid gloves. All the other little girls in Sunday-school cast envious glances at her and Marigold.

All but one. That one was sitting by herself on a bench, reading her Bible. And when Marigold and Mats sat down beside her that one got up and moved away—not contemptuously or proudly, but as some consecrated soul might remove itself automatically and unconsciously from the contamination of worldly contact.

"Well, I never," said Mats. "Aren't we good enough to sit beside you, Paula Pengelly?"

Paula turned and looked at them—or rather at Marigold. Mats she seemed entirely to ignore. Marigold looked back at her, spellbound from the start. She saw a girl, perhaps a year older than herself, slight as a reed, with large, glowing hazel eyes in a small, pale-brown face. A braid of long, straight, silky, dark-brown hair fell over each shoulder. Her cheek-bones were high and her lips thin and red. She was hatless and shabbily dressed and the Bible she clasped dramatically against her breast in her very long, very slender hands seemed to have been a Bible a great many years. She was not pretty but there was Something in her face. "Int'resting" was hardly a strong enough word and Marigold had not yet picked up "fascinating." She could not help looking at this Paula. There was—something—in her eyes that made you suddenly feel she saw things invisible to others—things you wanted ardently to see, too. A look that made Marigold think of a picture over Aunt Marigold's desk—the look of a white saint in ecstasy.

"No," said Paula, in an intense, dramatic way that made Marigold shiver deliciously, "you are *not*. You are not Christians. You are children of wrath."

"We ain't," cried Mats indignantly. But Marigold felt that they might be. Somehow one believed what Paula said. And she did not want to be a child of wrath. She wanted to be like Paula. She fairly ached with her desire for it.

"We're just as good as you," continued Mats.

"Goodness isn't enough, wretched child," answered Paula. "Hold your peace."

"What does she mean?" whispered Mats as Paula turned away. Whispered it rather fearfully. *Was* she a wretched child? She had never thought so, but Paul Pengelly *made* you believe things.

"She means hold your yap," said another girl passing. "Paula's 'got religion,' didn't you know?—like her father." Whatever it was that Paula had, Marigold felt she wanted it too. All through Sunday-school she yearned for it as she watched Paula's saintly little profile under that prim, straight hair. Grandmother and Mother were Christians, of course. But they never made her feel as Paula had done. At one time Marigold had believed Gwennie was very saintly. But Gwennie's supposed goodness only aggravated her. *This* was different. Marigold stayed for church that day because Mats was a Baptist, and Paula sat opposite them in a side seat. All through the waiting time before service Paula read her Bible. When the service began she fixed her eyes un-winkingly on the top of one of the little oriel windows. Oh, thought Marigold passionately, to be saintly and wonderful like that! She felt religious and sorrowful herself. It was a beautiful feeling. She had never felt anything quite like it before, not even when listening to Dr. Violet Meriwether. Once Paula looked from the window and right at her—with those compelling, mystical eyes. They said "Come" and Marigold felt that she must go—to the world's end and further.

When church was out Paula came straight up to Marigold.

"Do you want to come with me on the way of the cross?" she asked solemnly and dramatically. Paula had the knack of making every scene in which she took part dramatic—which was probably a large part of her fascination. And she had a little way of saying things, as if she could have said so much more and didn't. One yearned to discover the mystery of what she didn't say.

"If you do, meet me under the lone pine-tree at the head of the pond to-morrow."

"Can Mats come too?" asked Marigold loyally.

Paula flung Mats a condescending glance.

"Do *you* want to go to Heaven?"

"Y-e-es—but not for a long time yet," stammered Mats uncomfortably.

"You see." Paula looked eloquently at Marigold. "She's not One of Us. I knew *you* were the moment I saw you."

"I am," cried Mats, who couldn't bear to be left out of anything. "And of course I want to go to heaven."

"Then you must be a saint." Paula was inexorable. "Only saints go to heaven."

"But—do you have any fun?" wailed Mats.

"*Fun!* We are saving our souls. Would you," demanded Paula hollowly, "rather have fun and go to—to—a place too dreadful to speak of?"

"No—no." Mats was quite subdued and willing—temporarily—to do and surrender everything.

"To-morrow then—at nine o'clock—under the lone pine," said Paula.

The very tone of her voice as she uttered "lone pine" gave you a thrilling sense of mystery and consecration. Marigold and Mats went home, the former expectant and excited, the latter very dubious.

"Paula's always got some bee in her bonnet," she grumbled. "Last summer she read a book called *Rob Roy,* and she made all us girls call ourselves a clan and have a chieftain and wear thistles and tartans. Of course *she* was chieftain. But there was some fun in that. I don't believe this religious game will be as good."

"But it's not a game," Marigold was shocked.

"Maybe not. But you don't know Paula Pengelly."

Marigold felt she did—better than Mats—better than anybody. She longed for Monday and the lone pine.

"Old Pengelly's her father," said Mats. "He used to be a minister long ago—but he did something dreadful and they put him out. I think he used to get drunk. He's——" Mats tapped her forehead with a significant gesture, as she had

seen her elders do. "He preaches a lot yet, though in barns
and places like that. I'm scared to death of him but lots of
people say he's a real good man and very badly used. They
live in that little house on the other side of the pond. Paula's
aunt keeps house for them. Her mother is long since dead.
Some people say she has Indian blood in her. She's never
decently dressed—all cobbled together with safety pins,
Ma says. Are you really going to the head of the pond to-
morrow?"

"Of course."

"Well," Mats sighed, "I s'pose I'll have to go too. But I
guess our good times are over."

3

Monday and the lone pine came though Marigold thought
they never would. She told Aunt Anne and Uncle Charlie at
the breakfast-table where she was going, and Uncle Charlie
looked questioningly at Aunt Anne. As Marigold went out,
he asked,

"What is that young devil in petticoats up to now?"

Marigold thought he was referring to her and wondered
what on earth she had done to be called a young devil. Her
conduct had really been very blameless. But she forgot all
such minor problems when they reached the lone pine.
Paula was awaiting them there—still rapt, still ecstatic. She
had not, so she informed them, slept a wink all night.

"I couldn't—thinking of all the people in the world who
are going to be—*lost*."

Marigold immediately felt it was dreadful of her to have
slept so soundly. She and Mats sat down, as commanded,
on the grass. Paula gave a harangue, mainly compounded of
scraps of her father's theology. But Marigold did not know
that, and she thought Paula more wonderful than ever. Mats
merely felt uncomfortable. Paula hadn't even told them to
sit in the shade. All very fine if you had the Lesley pink-
and-white or the Pengelly brown. But when you hadn't!
Right here in the boiling sun! It must be admitted, I am
afraid, that Mats just then was much more concerned with
her freckles than with her soul.

"And now," concluded Paula with tragic earnestness, "both of you ask yourselves this question, 'Am I a child of God or of the devil?'"

Mats thought it was horrid to be confronted with such a problem.

"Of course I'm not a child of the devil," she said indignantly.

But Marigold was all at sea. Under the spell of Paula's eloquence she did not know what her ancestry ought to be.

"What'll—we do—about it—if we are?" she asked unsteadily.

"Repent. Repent of your sins."

"Oh, I haven't any sins to repent of," said Mats, relieved.

"You can never go to heaven if you haven't committed sins, because you can't repent of them and be forgiven," said Paula inexorably.

This new kind of theology dumbfounded Mats. While she was wrestling with it, Paula's mesmeric eyes were on Marigold.

"What would—you call sins?" Marigold asked timidly.

"Have you ever read stories that weren't true?" demanded Paula.

"Ye-es—and——" Marigold was seized with the torturing delight of confession, "and—made them up—too."

"Do you mean to say you've *lied*?"

"Oh, no. Not lies. Not lies. I mean——"

"They must be lies if they weren't true."

"Well—perhaps. And I've thought of—things—when Uncle Charlie was having family prayers."

"What things?" said Paula relentlessly.

"I—I thought of a door in a picture on the wall—I thought of opening it—and going in—seeing what was inside—what people lived there——"

Paula waved her hand. After all what did it matter if Marigold did think of queer things while Charlie Marshall was praying? What did *his* prayers matter? Paula was after things that mattered.

"Have you ever eaten meat?"

"Why—yes—is that——"

"It's wicked—very wicked. To sacrifice life to your appetites. Oh, shame!"

Shame, indeed!

Marigold writhed with it. It was intolerable to have Paula looking at her in such scorn. Paula saw the shame and promptly assuaged it.

"Never mind. You didn't know. I've et meat—too—till last spring. I had an awful rash. I knew it was a judgment because I'd done something wrong. I knew it was eating meat—Father said so. He said the finger of God had touched me. So I vowed I'd never eat any more. Oh, how my conscience vexed me. It was awful how I suffered."

There was real anguish in Paula's voice. She stood, a flaming, fascinating figure under the old pine—a young priestess, inspired, devoted. Marigold felt she would follow her to the stake.

"What are we going to do about it?" said that detestable practical Mats.

"We are going to form a society for saving our souls and the world," said Paula. "I've thought it all out. We'll call ourselves the Lighted Lamps. Don't you think that's a spendid name? I'll be head of it and you must do just as I tell you. We will live such beautiful lives that everybody will admire us and want to join us. We will be just as good every day as we are on Sunday"—here Mats emitted a "marvellous grisly groan"—"but we will be very exclusive. No one can come in who is not ready to be a martyr."

"But what are we to *do*?" said Mats with a sigh. She must go where Marigold went, but her chubby personality had no heritage of martyrdom.

Paula allowed herself to sit down.

"First, we must *never* eat anything more than is absolutely necessary. No meat—no pudding—no cake——"

"Oh, I have to eat *some*," cried Marigold sorrowfully. "Aunty would think I was sick or something and send me home."

"Well, then, there must be no second helpings," said Paula inexorably. They pledged themselves—Marigold thinking guiltily of the delicious little strawberry shortcakes Aunt Anne had said she was going to make for dinner.

"We must never read or tell anything that isn't strictly true. Never *pretend* anything"—Marigold gave a gasp but recovered herself gallantly—"never wear any jewelry—and *never* play silly games."

"Can't we play at all?" implored Mats.

"Play. In a world where we must prepare for eternity? *You* can play if you like but *I* shall not."

"What will we do if we can't play?" asked Marigold humbly.

"Work. The world is full of work waiting to be done."

"I always help Aunt Anne every way I can. But when I get through what can I do?"

"Meditate. But we'll find lots to do when we get going. Now, Mats, if you're coming in on this, come with all your soul. You *must* sacrifice. You have to be miserable or you can't be good. You mustn't forget for *one* moment that you're a sinner. You can't be both religious and happy in this world of sin and woe. We must live up to our name. And every time our light goes out we must do penance."

"How?" Mats again.

"Oh, lots of ways. *I* put some burrs next my skin yesterday because I only *wanted* a second helping at dinner. And kneel on peas. And *fast*. I fast often—and do you know, girls, when I fast I hear *voices* calling me by name." Paula's face took on a strange, unearthly radiance that completed Marigold's subjugation. "And I know it is angels calling me to my life's work—singling me out—setting me apart."

Mats had a hazy idea that it was going to be pretty hard to live up to Paula. But she meant to get to the bottom of things. "You've told us what we mustn't do. Now tell us what we must do."

"We must visit sick people——"

"I hate sick people," muttered Mats rebelliously, while Marigold thought with a shudder of her experience with Mrs. Delagarde. Paula, she felt, would not have been a bit frightened of Mrs. Delagarde.

"And read the Bible every day and say our prayers night and morning——"

"I don't see any use in saying prayers in the morning. I ain't scared in daytime," protested Mats.

Paula tried to ignore her and addressed herself to Marigold—who, as she felt instinctively, was a devotee of promise. You could never make anything of Mats—always chattering like a silly little parrot—but this new girl was after her own heart.

"We must hand out tracts—Father has stacks of them—and ask people if they're Christians—you can ask your father's hired man, Mats."

"He'd leave if I did and Father'd kill me," said Mats uncomfortably.

"Well, we're organised," said Paula. "Repeat after me, 'Lighted lamps we are and lighted lamps we will be as long as grass grows and water runs.'"

"Ow," whimpered Mats. But she repeated the vow glibly, comforted by recollections of other vows with the same implication of eternity which had proved to be of time when Paula grew tired of them.

"And now," concluded Paula, "I'll lead in prayer"—which she did, so beautifully and fervently, with her pale hands clasped and her eyes fixed on the sky, that Marigold's soul was uplifted and even Mats was impressed.

"There may be some fun in this after all," she reflected. "But I wish Paula would repent in winter. That's the best time for repenting."

4

As the days went on, Mats grimly concluded that there wasn't much fun in it. She was with them but not of them. As she had foreseen, it was very hard to live up to Paula. At least, for her, Marigold didn't seem to find it hard. Marigold, who went about with stars in her eyes, so unnaturally good that Aunt Anne was worried. Good on the outside, at least. Marigold knew she was full of sin inside because Paula told her so. Marigold was by now wholly in the power of this pale brown girl and thought her the most wonderful saintly creature that ever lived. She grieved constantly because she fell so far short of her. Paula fasted so much—as that wan, rapt face and those purple-ringed eyes testified eloquently. Marigold couldn't fast because of unsympathetic relatives. She could only refuse second helpings and "pieces" and writhe in bitterness when she heard Paula say loftily,

"*I* haven't touched a morsel of food since yesterday morning."

Neither could she hand out little time-yellowed tracts at church as Paula did every Sunday and as Mats flatly refused to do at all.

"You can amuse yourselves by being miserable if you want to," said Uncle Charlie, "but I'm not going to have you making a nuisance of yourself as Paula Pengelly does."

Paula a nuisance! That self-sacrificing little saint who was positively happy in wearing a shabby, faded dress to church and who knew whole chapters of the Bible by heart. Not the int'resting ones, either, but the—the—dull ones like those in Numbers and Leviticus. Who wouldn't play games—not even jackstones, though she was crazy about them—because it was wrong. Who cried all night about her sins, when she, Marigold, could only squeeze out a few tears and then fall ignominiously asleep. Who never laughed—there was no place in religion for laughter, not even with an Uncle Charlie forever saying things that nearly made you die. Who *never* did anything she liked to do because if you liked a thing it was a sure sign it was wrong. Marigold was furious with Uncle Charlie.

"It's lovely here at Aunt Anne's," she sighed. "But it's so hard to be religious. I suppose it's easier at Paula's. Her father doesn't hinder her."

Marigold knew Paula's father by this time. She had been to have tea with Paula and stay all night with her—a great privilege which Aunt Anne did not properly appreciate.

Paula lived in a little grey house on the other side of the pond. A tired little house that looked as if it were on the point of lying down. Inside, the blinds were very crooked and the furniture very dusty. There was nothing for supper but nuts, apples, brown bread and some stale, sweet crackers. But that did not matter, for Marigold could not have eaten anyhow, she was in such awe of Mr. Pengelly—a tall old man with long grey hair, a wonderful grey beard, a great hawk nose and eyes that shone in his lined face like a cat's in the dark. He never spoke a word to her or any one. Paula told her it was because he had one of vows of silence on.

"Sometimes he never says a word for a whole week," said Paula proudly. "He is such a good man. Once Aunt Em made a pudding for dinner Christmas—a *little* pudding—and Father grabbed it from the pot and hurled it out of doors. But even *he* isn't as good as Great-Uncle Josiah was. *He* let his nails grow till they were as long as birds' claws, just to please God."

Marigold couldn't help wondering what particular pleasure Uncle Josiah's nails would give God, but she crushed back the thought rigidly as a sin.

They slept in a stuffy little hall-bedroom that had shabby, faded pink curtains and a broken pane, and was lighted by a lamp that seemed never to have been cleaned.

The head of the funny little old wooden bedstead was just against the rattling window.

"The snow drifts in on my pillow in winter," said Paula, the fires of martyrdom burning in her eyes as she knelt on peas to say her prayers.

The rain beat against the panes. Marigold half wished she were back in the tower room at Broad Acres. This was not one of the nights Paula lay awake to worry over her sins. She slept like a log. She *snored*. Marigold did the lying-awake.

Breakfast. No salt in the porridge. Paula had burned the toast. The tablecloth was dirty. And Marigold had a chipped cup. Then she drank avidly. This was certainly a good chance to do something for penance. Penance for certain thoughts she had been thinking. But not about Paula. Paula, in spite of the snores, still shone amid all her shabby surroundings like a star far above the soil and mist of earth—a star for worship and reverence. Marigold worshipped and reverenced. She was strangely happy in all her renunciations and denials. She would give up anything rather than face Paula's scornful smile. It was all the reward she wanted when Paula said graciously, as a priestess might stoop to approve the acolyte,

"I knew, as soon as I saw you, that you were One of Us."

Aunt Anne and Uncle Charlie couldn't understand it.

"That Pengelly imp seems to have a power to bewitch the other girls," grumbled Uncle Charlie. "Marigold is absolutely infatuated with her and her kididoes. But there's one thing—if this keeps on after she goes home, old Madam Lesley will make short work of it."

5

Marigold spent a considerable part of her time doing penance in various small ways for various small misdemeanours. It was not always easy to find a penance to do—something Aunt Anne would let you do. No fasting or kneeling on peas for Aunt Anne. And even when Marigold and Paula between them—Mats bluntly declined to have anything to do with penances—hit on a workable penance, Marigold was apt to discover that she rather liked it—it was int'resting—and Paula had said,

"Just as soon as you like doing a thing it isn't penance of course."

But one "penance" was an experience that always stood out clearly in Marigold's memory. At its first conception it looked like a real penance. She had fallen from grace terribly—she and Mats, if Mats could ever have been considered in a state of grace by Paula's standards. She had been invited to supper at Mats's; and she couldn't resist that supper.

Mats's mother was a notable cook and she had four different kinds of cake. And, alas, every one was a kind of which Marigold was particularly fond. Banana cake with whipped cream—strawberry shortcake—date layer-cake—jelly-roll cake. Marigold took a piece of each and *two* pieces of the shortcake. She *knew* she was doing wrong—from Mother's point of view as well as Paula's; but with Mats gobbling industriously by her side and Mats's mother saying reproachfully,

"You haven't eaten *anything*, child,"

What was one to do?

And after supper she and Mats had got a big fashion-book and picked out the dresses they'd have when they grew up; and filled their cup of iniquity to overflowing by "boxing" the bed of the hired man in the kitchen loft. At that, he probably slept better than Marigold, who was sick all night and had horrible dreams. Which might have been thought a sufficient penance. But Paula had a different opinion.

Marigold's conscience gave her no rest until she had confessed everything to Paula.

"You are a Pharisee," said Paula sorrowfully.

"Oh, I'm *not*," wailed Marigold. "It was just——"

Then she stopped. No, she was *not* going to say, "Mats and her mother just *made* me eat."

That wasn't altogether true. She had been very willing to eat and she must bear her own iniquities. But had she lost caste forever in Paula's eyes? Would she no longer be considered One of Us?

"You've been very wicked," said Paula. "Your lamp has almost gone out and you must do a specially hard penance to atone."

Marigold sighed with relief. So she was not to be cast off. Of course she would do a penance. But what penance—at once severe enough and practicable. Paula thought of it.

"You're afraid of being alone in the dark. Sleep out all night on the roof of the veranda. *That* will be a real penance."

It certainly would. How real, Marigold knew too well. It was true that she was afraid of being alone in the dark. She was never afraid in the dark if any one was with her, but to be alone in it was terrible. She was becoming very ashamed of this terror. Grandmother said severely that a girl of eleven should not be such a baby and Marigold was sure that Old Grandmother would have scorned her for a coward. But so far she had not been able to conquer her dread of it. And the thought of spending the night *alone* on the veranda roof appalled her. Nevertheless she agreed to do it.

It was easy enough from one point of view. There was a door in her little tower-room opening on the veranda roof and there was a little iron bedstead on it. All Marigold had to do was to slip out of bed as soon as everybody was asleep and drag her bedclothes and mattress out.

She did it—in a cold perspiration—and crept into bed trembling from head to foot.

"I *won't* be scared of you," she gasped gallantly to 'the night.

But she was. She felt all the primitive, unreasoning fear known to the childhood of the race. The awe of the dark and the shadowy—the shrinking from some unseen menace lurking in the gloom. The night seemed creeping down through the spruce wood behind the house like a living—but not human—thing to pounce on her. Darkness all about her—around—above—below. And in that darkness—what?

She wanted to cover up her head but she would not. That would be shirking part of the penance. She lay there and looked up at the sky—that terrible ocean of stars which Uncle Klon had told her were suns, millions of millions of millions of miles away. There did not seem to be a sound in the whole earth. It was waiting—waiting—for *what*? Suppose every one in the world was dead! Suppose she was the only person left alive in that terrible silence!

Then—she could not have told whether it was hours or minutes later—something changed. All at once. She was no longer frightened. She sat up and looked about her. On a world of velvet and shadow and stars. The boughs of the spruces tossed in a sudden wind against the sky. The gulf waters were silver under the rising moon. The trees were whispering in the garden like old friends. The fern scents of a warm summer night drifted down from the hill.

"Why—I like the dark," Marigold whispered to herself. "It's nice—and kind—and friendly. I never thought it could be so beautiful."

She stretched out her arms to it. It seemed a Presence, hovering, loving, enfolding. She lay down again in its shadow and surrendered herself utterly to its charm, letting her thoughts run out into it far beyond the Milky Way. She did not want to sleep—but after a time she slept. And wakened in the pale, windless morning just as a new dawn came creeping across Broad Acres. The dreamy dunes along the shore were lilac and blue and gold. Above her were high and lovely clouds just touched by sunrise. Below in the garden the dews were silver in the hearts of unblown roses. Uncle Charlie's sheep in the brook pasture looked amazingly white and pearly and plump in the misty morning light. The world had a look Marigold had never seen it wear before—an expectant, untouched look as if it were a morning in Eden. She sighed with delight. A mystic happiness possessed her.

Paula was over soon after breakfast to find out if Marigold really had stuck it out on the veranda all night.

"You look too happy about it," she said reproachfully.

"It *was* a penance for a little while at first and then I enjoyed it," said Marigold honestly.

"You enjoy too many things," said Paula despairingly. "A penance isn't a penance if you *enjoy* it."

"I can't help liking things and I'm glad I do," said Marigold in a sudden accession of common sense. "It makes life so much more int'resting."

6

Marigold was going to the post-office to mail a letter for Aunt Anne. It was a lovely afternoon. Never had the world seemed so beautiful, in spite of the hundreds of millions of sinful people living in it. When she passed Mats's gate, Mats was playing by herself at jackstones under the big apple-tree. Mats had backslidden sadly of late and had returned to her wallowing in jackstones—thereby proving conclusively that she was not One of Us. She beckoned a gay invitation to Marigold, but Marigold shook her head and walked righteously on.

A little further down there was a sharp turn in the red road and Miss Lula Jacobs's little white house was in the angle. And Miss Lula's famous delphiniums were holding up their gleaming blue torches by the white paling. Marigold stopped for a moment to admire them. She would have gone in, for she and Miss Lula were very good friends, but she knew Miss Lula was not home, being in fact at Broad Acres with Aunt Anne at that very moment.

Marigold could see the pantry-window through the delphinium-stalks. And she saw something else. A dark-brown head popped out of the window, looked around, then disappeared. The next moment Paula Pengelly slipped nimbly over the sill to the ground and marched off through the spruce-bush behind Miss Lula's house. And Paula held in her hands a cake—a whole cake—which she was devouring in rapid mouthfuls.

Marigold stood as if turned to stone, in that terrible moment of disillusion. That was the cake Miss Lula had made for the Ladies' Aid social on the morrow—a very special cake with nut and raisin filling and caramel icing. She had heard Miss Lula telling Aunt Anne all about it just before she came away.

And Paula had stolen it!

Paula the Lighted Lamp—Paula the consecrated, Paula the rigid devotee of fasts and self-immolation, Paula the hearer of unearthly voices. Paula had stolen it and was gobbling it up all by herself.

Marigold went on to the post-office, torn between the anguish of disillusionment and the anger of the disillusioned. Nothing was quite the same—never could be again, she thought gloomily. The sun was not so bright, the sky so blue, the flowers so flowery. The west wind, purring in the grass, and the mad merry dance of the aspen-leaves hurt her.

An ideal had been shattered. She had believed so in Paula. She had believed in her vigils and her denials. Marigold thought bitterly of all those untaken second helpings.

Mats was not in when Marigold returned, but Marigold went home to Broad Acres and played jackstones by herself. And let herself go in a mad orgy of pretending, after all these weeks when, swallowed up in a passion of sacrifice, she had not even allowed herself to think of her world of fancy. Also she remembered with considerable satisfaction that Aunt Anne was making an apple-cake for supper.

Paula found her there and looked at her reproachfully—with purple-ringed eyes which, Marigold reflected scornfully, certainly did not come from fasting this time. Indigestion more likely.

"Is this how you, the possessor of an immortal soul, are wasting your precious time?" she asked rebukingly.

"Never mind my soul," cried Marigold stormily. "Just you think of poor Miss Lula's cake."

Paula bounced up, her pale face for once crimson.

"What do you mean?" she cried.

"I saw you," said Marigold.

"Do you want your nose pulled?" shrieked Paula.

"Try it," said Marigold superbly.

Suddenly Paula collapsed on the grey stone and burst into tears.

"You needn't make—such a fuss—over a trifle," she sobbed.

"Trifle. You *stole* it."

"I—I was so hungry for a piece of cake. I *never* get any— Father won't let Aunt Em make any. Nothing but porridge and nuts for breakfast and dinner and supper, day in and day out. And that cake looked so scrumptious. You'd have taken it yourself. Miss Lula has heaps of them. She *loves* making cake."

Marigold looked at Paula, all the anger and contempt gone out of her eyes. Little sinning, human Paula, like herself. Marigold no longer worshipped her but she suddenly loved her.

"Never mind," she said softly. "I—guess I understand. But—I can't be a Lighted Lamp any longer, Paula."

Paula wiped away her tears briskly.

"Don't know's I care. I was getting awfully tired of being so religious, anyhow."

"I—I think we didn't go the right way about being religious," said Marigold timidly. "Aunt Marigold says religion is just loving God and people and things."

"Maybe," said Paula—going down on her knees—but not to pray. "Anyhow I got all the cake I wanted for *once*. Let's have a game of jacks before Mats shows up. She always spoils everything with her jabber. She isn't really One of Us."

CHAPTER XVII

Not by Bread Alone

1

Salome had gone to Charlottetown for the day—rather unwillingly, for she had had a horrible dream of fourteen people coming to supper and nothing in the house for them to eat but cold boiled potatoes.

"And there's more truth than poetry in *that*, ma'am," she said, "for there isn't a thing baked except the raisin-bread. I assure you I don't dream dreams like that for nothing. And there's the Witch of Endor polishing her face out by the apple-barn."

It was an inflexible Cloud of Spruce tradition that there must always be cake in the pantry—fresh, flawless cake— lest unexpected company come to tea. No company had ever found Cloud of Spruce cakeless. Grandmother and Mother would both have died of horror on the spot if such a thing had happened. Kingdoms of Europe might rise and fall—famines might ravage India and revolutions sweep China—Liberals and Conservatives, Republicans and Democrats might crash down to defeat, but so long as cake-box and cooky-jar were filled there was balm in Gilead.

Yet this unthinkable thing had actually occurred. The evening before three car-loads of visitors had come out from Summerside and found cake in the pantry—but left none. No wonder Salome was upset.

"*I* have made cake before now," said Grandmother rather sarcastically. Every once in so long Salome had to be snubbed. "And so has Mrs. Leander."

When Grandmother called Lorraine Mrs. Leander before Salome, Salome knew she was snubbed.

"I am well aware," she said with meek stateliness, "that I am not the only cook at Cloud of Spruce. I merely thought, ma'am, that seeing it was my duty to keep the pantry well

filled, I ought not to neglect it for the sake of my own pleasure. *I* am not like my sister-in-law Rose John, ma'am. *She*
hasn't any sense of shame. When unexpected company
comes to tea she just runs out and borrows a cake from a
neighbour. Whatever John saw in *her* enough to marry her I
have never been able to imagine."

"Go and enjoy your holiday, Salome," said Lorraine
kindly, knowing that if Salome once fairly embarked on the
delinquencies of Rose John there was no telling when she
would stop. "You deserve it. Grandmother and I will soon
fill up the pantry."

Alas! Mother had got only as far as getting out her mix-
ing-bowl when Uncle Jack's Jim arrived. ". . . bloody with
spurring, fiery red with haste,"—or the modern equivalent
for it. Great-Uncle William Lesley was dying at the Head of
the Bay, or thought he was. And he wanted to see Grandmother and Leander's wife. They must lose no time if they
were to get there before he died.

It was a tragedy.

"I have never," said Grandmother in a tone of anguish as
she tied on her bonnet, "gone away from home and left absolutely *no* cake in the house."

"Surely no one will come to-day," moaned Mother,
equally wretched. Really, it was a most inconvenient time
for Great-Uncle to die.

"Don't forget to feed the cats," Grandmother told Marigold. "And mind you don't go wandering in Mr. Donkin's
hill pasture. He's turned his ox in there."

"That's not his ox," said Marigold. "That's his old red
bull."

Grandmother would have died before she would have
said the word "bull" aloud. She drove away with Uncle
Jack's Jim, sadly wondering what the young people of this
generation were coming to. Apart from that she did not
worry over leaving Marigold alone. Marigold was eleven
now and tall for her age. One year she had been measured
by the rose-bush—the next by the blue-bells. This year she
was as tall as the phlox.

She liked being alone very well once in a while. It was
quite important being in charge of Cloud of Spruce. She
swept the kitchen, and got dinner for herself and Lazarre;

she fed the cats and washed the dishes and wrote a letter to Paula.

Then the end of the world came. A car stopped at the gate; seven people descended therefrom and marched in past the platoons of hollyhocks with the air of people coming to stay. Marigold, staring aghast through the window, recognised them. She had met them all two weeks ago at a clan-funeral, where Grandmother had proffered them all a warm invitation to Cloud of Spruce. Second-Cousin Marcus Carter, his wife and son and daughter from Los Angeles; Second-Cousin Olivia Peake from Vancouver; *and* Third-Cousin Dr. Palmer of Knox College, Toronto, with *his* wife.

And there was no cake at Cloud of Spruce!

Marigold accepted the situation. In that moment she had decided what she would do.

As graciously as Mother herself could have done, she welcomed the guests at the door.

"Aunt Marian and Lorraine away? Then I don't suppose we'll stay," exclaimed Cousin Marcella Carter, who had a long thin face, a long thin nose, and a long thin mouth.

"You must stay for supper of course," said Marigold resolutely.

"Have you got anything good for us to eat?" asked Cousin Marcus with a chuckle. He had a square face with a spiky moustache and bristly white eyebrows. Marigold thought she did not like him and was glad she did not have to call him "uncle."

"I know the Cloud of Spruce pantry is always well supplied," said Mrs. Dr. Palmer, smiling. In her smooth grey silk dress she looked, Marigold decided, just like a nice sleek grey cat.

"Well, give us something that will stick to our ribs," said Cousin Marcus. "We've had dinner at a place—I won't say where—but there was heaps of style and precious little comfort."

"Marcus," said Cousin Marcella rebukingly.

"Fact. And now, Marigold, I'll give you a quarter for a kiss."

Cousin Marcus was quite genial. A joke was his idea of being kind and friendly. But Marigold did not know this and she resented it. Lifting her head as she had seen Varvara do, she said freezingly,

"I don't sell my kisses."

The visitors laughed. Jack Carter said,

"She's saving her kisses for *me*, Dad."

There was another laugh. Marigold shot a furious glance at Jack. She did not like boys—any boys. And she at once hated Jack. He was about thirteen with a fat moon-face, straight whitish hair parted in the middle, staring china-blue eyes and spectacles. Under ordinary circumstances Marigold could and would have annihilated him with ease and pleasure. She had not sparred with Tommy Blair four years without learning how to handle the sex. But a Cloud of Spruce hostess must not show discourtesy to any guest.

"She's got a nice mouth for kissing, anyhow," said Cousin Marcus more genially than ever.

2

Marigold left her guests in the orchard room and flew to the pantry. She was breathless with excitement, but she knew exactly what was to be done. There was plenty of cold boiled chicken and ham left over from the previous day; the Cloud of Spruce jam-pots were full as always. Cream galore for whipping. But hot biscuits—there *must* be hot biscuits—and cake!

If Marigold had been asked if she could cook she might have answered like canny Great-Uncle Malcolm when asked if he could play the violin. "He couldna' say. He had never tried."

Marigold had never tried. She could boil potatoes—and fry eggs—but further than that her culinary accomplishments as yet did not go. But she was going to try now. She had the Cloud of Spruce cook-book and she had helped Salome and Mother scores of times, looking forward with delight to the time when she would be allowed to do it off her own bat.

She clasped floury hands over the cake-bowl.

"Oh, dear God, I think I can manage the biscuits but You *must* help me with the cake."

Then she proceeded to mix, measure and beat. To make matters worse, Jack appeared. Jack was not happy unless he was teasing somebody. He proceeded to tease Marigold, not having any idea that it was a dangerous pastime, even when protected by Cloud of Spruce custom.

"I'm a terrible fellow," he declared. "I throw dead cats into wells. S'pose I throw *yours*?"

"I'll get Lazarre to call the new pig after you," said Marigold scornfully, and cracked an egg with violence.

Jack stared. What kind of girl was this?

"I'm just over the measles," he said. "Black measles. Ever had measles?"

"No."

"Mumps?"

"No."

"I've had mumps and whooping cough and scarlet fever and chicken pox and pneumonia. I'm a wow to have things. *You* ever had any of them?"

"No."

"Did you ever have *anything*?" Jack was plainly contemptuous.

"Yes," said Marigold, suddenly recalling some of Aunt Marigold's diagnoses. "I've had urticaria."

Jack stared again—but more respectfully.

"Golly. Is it bad?"

"Incurable," said Marigold mendaciously. "You never get over it."

Jack edged away.

"Is it catching?"

"*You* couldn't catch it." There was that in Marigold's tone Jack didn't like. Did this puling girl think she had something he couldn't have?

"Look here," he said furiously, "you give yourself airs that don't belong to you. And your nose is crooked. See!"

Marigold crimsoned to the tip of the offending nose. But tradition held. She spared Jack's life.

"But if I ever meet you away from Cloud of Spruce I'll ask you who put your ears on for you," she thought as she measured the baking-powder.

"What are you thinking of?" queried Jack, resenting her silence.

"I'm imagining how you'll look in your coffin," answered Marigold deliberately.

This gave Jack to think. Was it safe to be alone with a girl who could imagine such things? But to leave her, was to confess defeat.

"In five minutes by that clock I'm going to kiss you," he said with a fiendish grin.

Marigold shuddered and shut her eyes.

"If you do I'll tell everybody at supper what a sweet-looking baby you were."

That got under Jack's skin. He wished he was well out of the pantry and the presence of this exasperating creature. He shifted to a new point of attack.

"My, but I'm sorry for the man you're going to marry."

Marigold cast tradition to the winds.

"Oh, never mind," she said. "Your wife will be able to sympathise with him."

"Don't waste your breath now," drawled Jack.

"It's *my* breath."

"Think you're smart, don't you?"

"I don't think it, I know it," retorted Marigold, beating her cake-batter terrifically.

"After all, you're only a female," said Jack insolently.

"I heard you pinned a dishcloth to a minister's coat once," said Marigold.

But the minute she said it she knew she had made a mistake. He was proud of it.

"What are you two young divvils up to?" demanded Cousin Marcus, peering in at the door. "Oh, fond of the boys I see, Marigold. Come alone, Jack. Lazarre is going to show us the apple-orchard."

Jack, as relieved to be rid of Marigold as she was to be rid of him, vanished. Marigold breathed a sigh of thanksgiving. Oh, would her cake be all right? That wretched boy had bothered her so. *Had* she put in the baking-powder?

The cake was a gorgeous success. Marigold was a Lesley, and besides there was Providence—or Luck. It was a delicious feathery concoction with whipped cream and golden orange crescents on it—*the* special company-cake of Cloud of Spruce. And Marigold had just as good fortune with her biscuits. Then she set the table with the hemstitched cloth and Grandmother's best Coalport. Every domestic rite of Cloud of Spruce was properly performed. The ham was sliced in thin pink slices, the chicken platter was parsley-fringed, the white cake-basket with the china roses round it was brought out, the water in the tumblers was ice-cold.

3

Marigold sat behind the tea-cups facing the ordeal before her, a gallant and smiling hostess. She could feel her pulses beating to her fingertips. If only her hands would not tremble! She steadied her legs by twisting them around the rungs of the chair. Cousin Marcus did what in him lay to rattle her by conjuring her not to fill the cups so full of tea that there wasn't room for cream—as mean Aunt Harriet always did—and Dr. Palmer helped the chicken so lavishly that she broke out into a cold perspiration lest there shouldn't be enough to go round. Mrs. Dr. Palmer took cream and no sugar and Dr. Palmer took sugar and no cream and Cousin Marcella took neither and Cousin Marcus took both. Cousin Olivia took cambric tea. It was very difficult to remember everything, but she thoroughly enjoyed asking Jack how he took his. It seemed to put him in his place for once. Eventually everybody got something to drink and the chicken *did* go round.

Jack kept quiet for awhile, being fully occupied with gorging. But just as it had dawned on Marigold that the supper was almost over and had gone very well, Jack said,

"Say, Marigold, *you can cook*. If you'll promise to have my slippers warm for me every night when I come home, I'll come back and marry you when I grow up."

"I wouldn't marry you——"

"Oh, come, come now, my duck," said Jack, with an irritating snigger, "wait till you're asked."

"So you were courting in the pantry," chuckled Cousin Marcus.

Jack grinned like a Chessy cat.

"Marigold has such a nice little way of cuddling in your arms, Dad."

He hadn't really meant to say it, but it suddenly struck him as a very clever thing to say.

Marigold positively came out in goose-flesh.

"I haven't—I mean—*you* couldn't know it if I had."

"You're beginning young," said Cousin Marcus solemnly, pretending to shake his head over the doings of modern youth.

Marigold had a stroke of diabolical inspiration.

"*Johnsy* is telling his dreams," she said coolly.

That "Johnsy" was what Jack would have called "a mean wallop." He dared not open his mouth again at the table and did not recover his impudence until they were leaving.

"Isn't that a lovely moon?" said Marigold softly, more to herself than to any one, as she stood by the car.

"You should see the moons we have in Los Angeles," he boasted.

"What do you really think of him?" said Uncle Marcus in a pig's whisper, giving Marigold a poke in the ribs.

Marigold remembered that Salome had once said that Rose John had once said that if there was one thing more than another that lent spice to life, it was tormenting the men.

"I think Johnsy isn't really half as big a fool as he looks," she said condescendingly.

Cousin Marcus roared with laughter. "You've said a mouthful!" he exclaimed. Jack was crimson with rage. The car rolled away and Marigold stood by the gate, victress.

"I don't know how it is some girls like boys," she said.

4

When Grandmother and Mother came home—slightly annoyed, though they did not know it, that Great-Uncle William Lesley had been so inconsiderate as not to have died after all the bother but had rallied surprisingly—they had already heard the news, having met Cousin Marcus's car on the road.

"Marigold, *did you make the cake*? Cousin Marcella said she wanted the recipe of our cake."

"Yes," said Marigold.

Grandmother sighed with relief.

"Thank goodness. When I heard there was cake I thought you must have borrowed it from Mrs. Donkin—like Rose John. You didn't forget to put the pickles on."

"No. I put pickles and chow both."

"And you didn't—you're sure you didn't—slop any tea over in the saucers."

"I'm sure."

Mother hugged Marigold in the blue room upstairs.

"Darling, you're a brick! Grandmother and I felt *dreadful* until we found out there was cake."

CHAPTER XVIII

Red Ink or——?

1

Marigold thought the world a charming place at all times but especially in September, when the hills were blue and the great wheat-fields along the harbour-shore warm gold and the glens of autumn full of shimmering leaves. Marigold always felt that there was something in the fall that *belonged* to her and her alone if she could only find it, and this secret quest made of September and October months of magic.

To be sure there was generally school in September. But not this September for Marigold. She had not been quite herself through the August heat, so Mother and Grandmother and Aunt Marigold, who remembered that she was an M.D. in her own right when Uncle Klon let her remember it, advised that she be kept out of school for some weeks longer.

Then Aunt Irene Winthrop wrote to Mother and asked her to let Marigold visit her and Uncle Maurice. Aunt Irene was Mother's sister, and the Winthrops and the Lesleys were none too fond of each other. Grandmother rather grimly said she thought Marigold would be just as well at home.

"We let her visit Aunt Anne last year," said Mother. "I suppose Irene thinks it is her turn now."

Mother was too timid—or too good a diplomat—to say that she thought Marigold should visit her mother's people as well as her father's. But Grandmother understood it that way and offered no further objection. So Marigold went to Uncle Maurice and Aunt Irene at Owl's Hill. A name that fascinated Marigold. Any name with a hill in it was beautiful and Owl's Hill was magical.

Uncle Maurice and Aunt Irene were secretly a little afraid that Marigold might be lonesome and homesick. But

229

Marigold never thought of such a thing. She liked Owl's Hill tremendously. Such a romantic spot on a high sloping hill with a little tree-smothered village snuggling at its foot and above it woods where at night sounded laughter that was merry but not human, while other hills lay beyond like green wave after wave. Uncle Maurice's face was so red and beaming that Marigold felt he made fine weather out of the gloomiest day. And Aunt Irene was like Mother. Only she laughed more, not being a widow. And having no Grandmother living with her.

There was a long letter to be written every night to Mother, in which Marigold told her everything that happened during the day. She always went down the lane to put it in the mail-box herself every morning. And there was Amy Josephs, of the chubby, agreeable brown face, next door, to play with. Amy was the daughter of Uncle Maurice's brother, so a cousin of sorts if you like. Amy made a fairly satisfactorily playmate who really seemed to have a dim conception of what Marigold meant when she talked of the laughter of bluebells and daisies, and they had good fun together.

Amy's two village chums came up the hill to play with them. Marigold liked them fairly well also. Not one of the three was anything like as good a playmate as Sylvia but Marigold carefully concealed this thought because she was beginning to feel that it was a bit queer that she should like an imaginary playmate better than real ones. But there it was.

One of Amy's chums was a very fat little girl with a most romantic name—June Page. A fair girl with hair so flaxen that beside it Marigold's shone like spun gold. Caroline Chrysler was a missionary's daughter. Sent home from India. Caroline, apart from her insistence on the fact that she was going to be a missionary, too—had been "consecrated to it in her cradle"—was quite a nice girl. It wasn't her fault that she was dark and sallow—perhaps not her fault that she wouldn't be called Carrie. Too frivolous for a consecrated. Marigold, who had once believed herself consecrated, too, could not be too hard on Caroline's poses. So they all got on very well, each having her own private opinion of the others, and every new dawn that broke across the autumn up-land, ushered in a day full of interest and delight.

Even Sundays. Marigold loved going down to church Sunday evenings with Aunt Irene and Amy. They always went down across the fields to the road. Aunt Irene always carried a little lantern because, though it was only crisp steel-blue twilight when they left, it was dark long before they reached the church. The lantern cast such fascinating shivery, giant shadows. They went along the edge of the sheep-pasture. Marigold loved the cool grass under her feet and the soft eerie sighs in the trees, the sweet wild odours of the wandering winds and the elfin laugh of the hidden brook down under the balsam-boughs. There was a smell of aftermath clover in the air and the Milky Way was over-head. All around were misty stars over the harvest-fields. One really felt too happy for Sunday.

Aunt Irene never talked much and Amy and Marigold talked in whispers.

"I wonder if Hip Price will be in church to-night," said Amy.

"Who is Hip Price?" asked Marigold.

"He's the minister's son. His real name is Howard In-graham Price, but he never gets anything but Hip—from his initials. He's awfully clever. I never," vowed Amy, speak-ing out of her tremendous experience of eleven and a half years, "met any one who knew so much. And he's so brave. He saved a little girl from drowning once, at the risk of his life."

"When?"

"Oh, before he came here. They only moved to this church last spring. He says he can lick his weight in wild-cats. And he took the diploma for learning the whole Shorter Catechism by heart."

Marigold felt rather bored with this prodigy.

"What does he look like?"

"He's handsome. His eyes are just like an archangel's," said Amy fervently.

"How do you know? Did you ever see an archangel's eyes?" demanded Marigold relentlessly.

2

The choir was singing *Joy to the World*, and Marigold was
thinking of "Tidal, king of nations," in the chapter the minister had just read. That phrase always fascinated her whenever she heard it. There was something so mysterious about
it. Tidal, king of nations, was so much grander than just
Tidal, king of one little country. Splendid. Triumphal. An
entrancing figure of royalty ruling over hundreds of subject
peoples. And just then Marigold saw Hip and thought no
more forever of Tidal, king of nations.

He was sitting right across from her in the corner seat,
staring at her. He continued to stare at her. Marigold felt
that glance on her inescapably. She tried to look away—she
fought against looking back—but in the end *her* eyes always
returned to the corner seat to find *his* eyes still intent on
her. Eyes can say so much in a second. Marigold felt very
queer.

And, oh, he *was* handsome. Just like the slim princeling
of fairy-tales. Brown curls shining in the lamplight. Cheeks
rose-red under golden-tan. Dark-blue, romantic eyes. She
felt that she would die of shame and humiliation when an
old lady behind her suddenly held a peppermint out to her
over the back of the seat. Marigold had to take it—and
could not help looking at Hip as she did it. She could not—
would not—did not eat it, but she felt as if Hip must see it
all the time, moist and sticky in her warm, unwilling hand,
and despise her for a baby who had to be kept good in
church with peppermints. Marigold, to her dying day,
never quite forgave Aunt Lucy Bates, who thought she had
done a kind act to Lorraine Winthrop's little girl.

Marigold found her legs were trembling when she got
up for the last hymn. Her face was burning under Hip's
seemingly mesmerised eyes. She was sure every living soul
in the church must notice him.

One at least had. Marigold met Caroline on the porch,
going out, and it seemed to her that Caroline was a bit cool.

"Did you see Hip Price?" asked Caroline.

"Hip Price?" Marigold was not without the feminine knack of protective coloration. "Who is he?"

"That boy in the corner seat. I saw him staring at you. He always stares like that at a new girl."

"Sly thing," thought Marigold—not meaning Hip.

Amy did not go back with them. She was staying all night with June. So Marigold walked home alone with Aunt Irene. Not altogether alone.

On the other side of the road, until they reached the pasture gate, stalked a slender figure with a smart cap worn a bit rakishly on the back of its head. The figure whistled *The Long, Long Trail*. Marigold knew that it was Hip Price and she also knew that the manse was away on the other side of the church. It is terrific what damsels of eleven do know sometimes. But she was—almost—glad when they left the road and started up over the fields.

As they walked along Marigold was not thinking of the charm of starlit evening or the wind in the trees or the pixy lantern-shadows. I shall not tell you what she was thinking of. I will only state that next day she scorched a panful of cookies she had been left to watch because she was thinking of the same thing. Aunt Irene was annoyed. A Cloud of Spruce Lesley was supposed never to be careless. But Marigold with shining eyes and a dreamy smile lingering on her lips, did not worry about the cookies at all.

3

During the following three weeks life was a thing of rainbows for our Marigold. She had a delightful secret—a secret that nobody knew. Even when she wrote "everything" to Mother she did not tell her about Hip Price. Though she put an extra row of kisses in to make up for it.

The morning after that memorable Sunday evening, when Marigold went down to the end of the lane to mail Mother's letter, she found a letter in the box addressed to herself. Marigold trembled again—a delicious trembling. She sat down among the goldenrod under a friendly little spruce-tree and read it. It was a very wonderful epistle. Ask Marigold. To be told she was beautiful! Once in awhile she had heard a hint that she was pretty. But beautiful! And what did it matter that he spelled "angel" angle? Angel really was a very tricky word. *Anybody* might spell it wrong. Besides, doesn't everybody know that it doesn't make a mite of difference how a love-letter is spelled? He signed himself "fondestly yours" with lots of flourishes and curlicues. And there was a little x for a P. S.

Marigold's cheeks were so rosy when she went back to the house that Aunt Irene thought the child was picking up wonderfully. Marigold slept that night with Hip's letter under her pillow. And found another in the mailbox the next morning! In which he asked her if she were going to June Page's party Thursday evening and would she wear the blue dress she had worn to church? Would she? She had been wondering which of her two "good" dresses became her most and had been dangerously near selecting the green. And he wrote, "When the moon rises to-night think of me and I'll think of you." Marigold hunted out the time of moonrise in the almanac. Really, the moons of Owl's Hill were wonderful. Cloud of Spruce never had such moons. And would any other boy she knew ever think of saying a thing like that? Not in a thousand years.

Hip cornered her off at the party and asked her why she hadn't answered his letters. Marigold didn't think she could without Aunt Irene knowing.

"But you don't mind my writing them?" asked Hip softly—tenderly. Looking at her as if his very life depended on her answer. Marigold, dyed in blushes, confessed she didn't. Whereupon Hip surveyed the room with the air of a conqueror. When called upon to recite he gave "Casabianca" in ringing tones, standing all beautiful and brave as the immortal hero. A horrible thought suddenly arose in Marigold's mind. Did he *know* he was all beautiful and brave. She strangled and buried the hateful intruder instantly.

Hip was certainly captivating. He said such smart up-to-date things like "attaboy" and "apple-sauce" and "I'll tell the world!"—looking at Marigold to see if she admired his smartness. And he walked home with her—not exactly from the house. He joined her on the road, having dashed across lots. And at the gate of Owl's Hill lane he took her hand and kissed it. Marigold had read of young knights doing that but that it should happen to *her*!

It was thrilling to hear of all the deeds of high emprise Hip had done. That he had once saved a little girl from being burned to death—Amy must have got it twisted—that he often climbed to the very top of telegraph-poles—that he had once stopped a team of runaway horses by his own unaided prowess—that he would, on occasion, really relish a fight with blood-maddened tigers. As for sea-serpents, take Hip's word for it, they ate out of his hand.

"I don't believe he's done all the wonderful things he's always talking about," Amy said scornfully once.

Marigold knew what *that* meant. Just sheer jealousy. And of course it was also jealousy that led Caroline to say that Hip had bitten his sister when he was four years old and left open old Mr. Simon's gate on purpose so that the pigs could get into the garden. Marigold did not believe a word of it.

She had such a funny feeling when other people pronounced his name. It was thrilling to go to church and listen to Mr. Price preaching. *His* father. Marigold hated old Tom Ainsworth for sleeping in church. And there was one almost painfully rapturous day when she and Amy were invited to the manse to tea. To eat a meal at the same table with Hip was something in the nature of a rite, with the big maple rustling outside the window on which, Hip told her, he had cut their intertwined initials. How bitterly she resented it when his mother told him to keep his elbow off the table and not talk with his mouth full!

And every morning that romantic journey to the mailbox to find a letter—a delightful letter. There were times when Marigold felt, though she would not admit it even to herself, that she really liked Hip's letters much better than Hip himself.

In one he told her she was his Little Queen. And he had written that especial sentence in red ink—or—was it?—could it be—Marigold had heard of such things. She pitied every other girl, especially the consecrated Caroline, and thought of Hip every time the moon rose or didn't rise.

"You are so different from everybody else," Hip told her. Clever Hip.

4

The course of true love even at eleven never runs smooth. There came a dreadful day when she and Hip almost quarrelled. Marigold had been told a certain shameful little secret by Netta Caroll about Em Dawes. Em Dawes was living with an aunt down in the village because her father and mother were divorced, true's you live. Netta had heard it over in Halifax and cross your heart you were never to tell a word of it. Marigold promised solemnly she would never tell. And then Hip, with his uncanny nose for secrets, discovered that Marigold had one and coaxed her to tell him.

Marigold wanted to tell him—yearned to tell him—felt her heart must really break if she didn't tell him. But there was her solemn promise. Lesleys did not break their solemn promises. It was a custom of their caste. Hip grew angry when he found her so unexpectedly unmalleable, and when anger gave him nothing—except perhaps the look in Marigold's face—he became sad and reproachful. She didn't like him a bit, of course, when she wouldn't tell him what she and Netta had been whispering about that time.

"If you don't tell me," said Hip earnestly, "I'll go and drown myself. When you see me lying dead you'll wish you'd told me."

Hip rather overreached himself there, because Marigold didn't believe at all that there was the slightest fear of his drowning himself. She stuck gallantly to her determination not to tell, despite his pleadings. And then the next afternoon, when it became known that Hip Price had disappeared and could not be found anywhere, though everybody in the community was madly searching for him, Marigold thought she must die. *Had* Hip actually drowned himself because he thought she did not like him? *Had* he? The dread was intolerable. How terrible to live all your life remembering that some one had drowned himself because of you! Who could support such a prospect?

"I heard a dog howling under my window last night," sobbed Amy. "Mother says that's a sure sign of death."

"That was only old Lazy Murphy's dog. Surely you don't think *he* knows anything," protested Marigold. She was resentful of Amy's crying. What right had Amy to cry about Hip? She, Marigold, could not cry. Her dread went too deep for tears.

"His mother believes he's kidnapped," said Amy, hunting for a dry spot in her handkerchief. "She's just been going from one fainting fit to another all day. But some say he was seen going down the river in that leaky old boat of Shanty George's. Certain death, Shanty George says it was. Oh, I won't sleep a wink to-night."

Then came Caroline and June, and Caroline and June were also in tears—which did not improve the looks of either of them. Or their tempers, evidently. Caroline was shrewish.

"I don't see what *you*'re crying about, June Page. He wasn't *your* minister's son. You're a Baptist."

"I guess I've as good a right to cry as you," retorted June. "Hip was my friend—my special friend. He thought more of me than of any girl in Owl's Hill. He's told me so *dozens* of times. He told me I was different from anybody he'd ever met. Cry! I will cry. Just you try to stop me."

An unbecoming red flush had risen in Caroline's pale face.

"Did Hip Price really tell you that?" she asked in a queer voice. Marigold, in the background, stood as if turned to the proverbial stone. Amy had put her handkerchief in her pocket.

"Yes, he did. And wrote it. I've had a letter from him every day for weeks."

"So have I," said Caroline.

June in her turn stopped crying and glared at Caroline. "You haven't."

"I have. I can show them to you. And he told *me* I was different from any one he ever knew and that he couldn't help being crazy about me."

"He wrote me that, too," said June.

They looked at each other. No more tears were shed for Hip—nor would be if he were lying forty fathoms deep.

"Did he ever kiss your hand?" demanded Caroline.

June giggled—a giggle that seemed to make everything ugly. "More than that," she said significantly.

Marigold involuntarily brushed something from her hand. The power of thought had returned to her. She was very thankful now that she hadn't been able to cry. There were no stains on her face. Calmly, proudly as any Lesley of them all, she drained her cup of wormwood and gall.

June began to cry again—in self-pity this time. The Pages, Marigold reflected disdainfully, had no pride.

"He called me his Little Queen," she sobbed, "and said I had a crown of golden hair."

To call June Page's hair golden when it was just tow-coloured! And fancy a Little Queen with a nose like a dab of putty! Oh, it was to laugh.

Caroline did not cry. But she looked very limp. She had been also Little-Queened. "And he said my eyes were so sweet and provoking."

To think of those round pale eyes of Caroline's being called sweet and provoking! Oh, of course Hip had left old Simon's gate open and bit his sister—bit her frequently. Not a doubt of it.

"He's just been a regular mean two-faced deceitful little sneak," said June violently, "and I hope he *is* drowned, I do."

"I didn't think a minister's son would do that," said Caroline mournfully. There was something especially terrible about a minister's son doing a thing like that. Whom could one trust if not a minister's son?

"I believe they are the worst sometimes," said June. "Well, you can have him."

"I don't want him!" said Caroline superbly, remembering at last that she was consecrated.

They went away on that note. Amy looked guiltily at Marigold.

"I—I wasn't going to tell *them*," she said, "but I got letters from Hip, too. Lovely letters. I *can't* believe he didn't mean them. Of course he was just fooling *them* but——"

"He was fooling everybody," said Marigold shortly. "And we needn't worry over his being drowned. He'll turn up safe and sound. I'm going home to write to Mother."

Marigold did write to Mother—not telling her *quite* everything, however. But first she burned a packet of schoolboy love-letters. She felt as if she had been mixed up in something very grimy. And she suddenly felt a great longing to be sitting on the old wharf below Cloud of Spruce, watching the boats coming in and feeling the clear, fresh sea-breeze from the dunes blowing in her face. Oh, how she hated and despised Hip Price.

But what was it Old Grandmother had said once?—That it was the hardest thing in the world to be just.

"I guess I was as much to blame as Hip," admitted Marigold candidly.

All that saved her self-respect was the fact that she had not told him The Secret.

5

Hip turned up safe and sound next day. He had gone for a day's ride with Lazy Murphy's son-the-pedlar and Lazy Murphy's horse had taken sick eighteen miles away, in a place where there was no telephone. So Owl's Hill folks gave up searching and Mrs. Price recovered from her fainting fits and Hip came straight up to Owl's Hill to see Marigold. It was rather unfortunate that Hip should have selected that day for appearing out in kilts. He had thin legs.

"Come on for a walk down to the pasture-spring," he whispered.

"No, thank you, Howard."

Hip had never heard that an enchantment is at an end as soon as the enchanter is called by name. But he knew there was something wrong with Marigold, standing there, the very incarnation of disdain.

"What's the matter? You don't look as if you were glad to see me back. And I was thinking of you every minute I was away."

"And about June and Caroline, too?" asked Marigold sweetly, as one who knew her Hip at last.

For the first time since she had known him Hip lost face.

"So they've blabbed," he said. "Why, I was just seeing how much they'd believe. It was different with you—honest—— You've got *them* skinned a mile."

"I think you'd better go home," said Marigold sarcastically. "Your mother may be anxious about you. She might even take a fainting-fit. Good-bye."

Marigold went away stiffly, regally, without a backward glance. Hip had not drowned himself in despair over her lack of confidence, but he was for her not only dead but, as the French would say, very dead.

"He was never very int'resting, anyhow—not even as much as Johnsy," she thought, suddenly clear-sighted.

It seemed years since she had left home. At the end of that long red road were Mother and Sylvia and Cloud of Spruce. She felt clean once more.

"I guess it was only red ink after all," she said.

CHAPTER XIX

How It Came to Pass

1

When Marigold had gone to visit Aunt Anne and then Aunt Irene, something was started. Grandmother gloomily said,

"They'll all be wanting her now," and her prediction was speedily fulfilled. Aunt Marcia wanted her share of Marigold, too.

"If Anne and Irene Winthrop could have her I think I should too. She's never spent a night in my house—my favourite brother's child," she said reproachfully.

So Grandmother with a look of I-told-you-so and Mother with a look of How-can-I-do-without-Marigold again consented rather unwillingly.

"Jarvis is so—odd," said Grandmother to Mother.

Grandmother had very little use for Jarvis Pringle, even if he were her son-in-law. Nobody in the clan had much use for him. He was known to have got up once in the middle of the night to dot an "i" in a letter he had written that evening. As Uncle Klon said, that was carrying things rather too far.

Marigold did not know, as the grown-ups of the clan knew, that he had lived all his life with the shadow of madness hanging over him. She didn't know what Uncle Klon meant when he said Jarvis took the universe too seriously. But she did know she had never seen Uncle Jarvis smile. And when Uncle Jarvis once asked her if she loved God and she had said "yes," she had the oddest feeling that she was really telling a lie, because her God was certainly not the God Uncle Jarvis was inquiring about. And she did know that she didn't like Uncle Jarvis. She loved him, of course— you have to love your relations—but she didn't like him— not one little bit. She always made her small self scarce when he came to visit Cloud of Spruce. She did not know he had the face of a fanatic; but she knew he had a high, narrow, knobby forehead, deep-set, intolerant eyes, austere, merciless mouth, and a probing nose, which he had a horrible habit of pulling. Also a fierce, immense, black beard which he would never even trim because that would have been un-Scriptural and contrary to the will of God.

Uncle Jarvis knew all about the will of God—or thought he did. Nobody could go to heaven who did not believe exactly as he did. He argued, or rather dogmatised, with every one. Marigold was so small a fish that she generally slipped through the meshes of his theological nets and he paid scant attention to her. But she wondered sometimes if Uncle Jarvis would really be contented in heaven. With nobody to frown at. And a dreadful God who hated to see you the least bit happy.

Nevertheless she was pleased at the prospect of another visit. Uncle Jarvis and Aunt Marcia also lived "over the bay," which of course had a magic sound in Marigold's ears. And she loved Aunt Marcia, who had calm, sea-blue eyes and one only doctrine—that "everybody needs a bit of spoiling now and then." Her pies praised her in the gates and she was renowned for a lovely cake called "Upside-down cake," the secret of which nobody else in the clan possessed. Marigold knew she would have a good time with Aunt Marcia. And Uncle Jarvis couldn't be 'round all the time. Grain must be cut and chores done no matter how dreadful the goings-on might be in your household during your absence.

So she went to Yarrow Lane farm, where she found a low-eaved old house under dark spruces and a garden that looked as if God smiled occasionally at least. Aunt Marcia's garden, of course. The only thing in the gardening line Uncle Jarvis concerned himself with was the row of little round, trimmed spruces along the fence of the front yard. Uncle Jarvis really enjoyed pruning them every spring, snipping off all rebellious tips as he would have liked to snip off the holder of every doctrine he didn't agree with.

Marigold had a room with a bed so big she felt lost in it and a small, square window looking out on the silver-tipped waves of the bay. She had the dearest little bowl to eat her porridge out of—it made even porridge taste good. And the Upside-down cake was all fond fancy had painted it.

Uncle Jarvis did not bother her much, though she was always secretly terrified at his gloomy prayers.

"Why," Marigold wondered, "must one groan so when one talks to God?" Her own little prayers were cheerful affairs. But perhaps they oughtn't to be.

The only unpleasant day was Sunday. Uncle Jarvis was almost as bad as the man in another of graceless Uncle Klon's stories—who hung his cat because she caught a mouse on Sunday. When he heard Marigold laugh the first Sunday she was at Yarrow Lane he told her sternly that she must never laugh on Sunday in his house.

"Whatever may be done at godless Cloud of Spruce," his manner seemed to say though his tongue didn't.

2

Marigold was not long at Yarrow Lane before she picked up a chum. By the end of a week she and Bernice Willis had known each other all their lives. Aunt Marcia had rather expected Marigold to chum with Babe Kennedy on the next farm, who lived much nearer than Bernice. And Babe was very ready to be chummed with. But chumship, like kissing, goes by favour. Marigold simply did not like Babe—a pretty little doll, with hair of pale, shining, silky-red; pale green eyes, an inquisitive expression and an irritating little snigger that set Marigold's nerves on edge. She would have none of her. Bernice was the choice of her heart—the first real friend she had ever had—the first real rival to Sylvia.

Bernice lived half a mile away, with an odd old aunt in "the house behind the young spruce wood." The very description intrigued Marigold. The *young* spruce wood—so delightful. What charming things must foregather in a *young* spruce wood. Bernice was ugly but clever. She had uncut mouse-coloured hair and big, friendly grey eyes in a thin, freckled face—a face that seemed meant for laughter, although it was generally a little sad. Her father and mother were both dead and Bernice did not seem to have any rela-

tives in the world except the aforesaid odd old aunt. Lots of
the girls in Ladore—even magical, over-the-bay places have
to have post-office names—didn't like her.

But it happened that she and Marigold talked the same
language—liked the same things. They could both have
supped on a saucer of moonshine and felt no hunger—for a
time, anyhow. They both understood the stories the wind
told. They both liked silk-soft kittens and the little fir woods
that ran venturesomely down to the shore and the dancing
harbour ripples like songs. A bluebird singing on the point
of a picket in the Yarrow Lane thrilled them and an imaginary trip to the moon was all in the evening's work. And
they made every day a gay adventure for themselves.

"You'll find out she isn't as good as you think her," Babe
told Marigold with sinister significance.

But that, Marigold believed, was only Babe's jealousy.

3

Then one night Marigold and Bernice had the supreme
bliss of sleeping together. And not only of sleeping together
but sleeping in the granary-loft—the little white granary
across the small, hollow field carpeted with sheets of green
moss and full of birch-trees. Such a romantic thing.

Aunt Marcia had told Marigold to ask Bernice to stay all
night with her. And soon after Bernice's arrival two loaded
automobiles came out from Charlottetown. The guests must
be put up somehow for the night. The little house was taxed
to its limit. Marigold's room must be commandeered in the
emergency. But what was the matter with sleeping in the
neat little granary-loft this warm September night? Aunt
Marcia would make them up a comfortable bed. If they
wouldn't be afraid!

Afraid! Bernice and Marigold hooted at the idea. They
were all for it at once. So after they had prowled about till
nearly ten—Bernice had gone to bed at eight every night of
her life and Marigold was supposed to go—they went
through the moonlit birches with their nighties under their
arms and a huge piece of apple-pie in their paws. Aunt
Marcia actually let people eat pie at night. Perhaps that ac-

counted for some of Uncle Jarvis's religious gloom. They took a drink from the truly delightful stoned-up spring behind the granary, which Uncle Jarvis called the barn-well, and then mounted the outside granary stairs to the loft. Its bare boards were beautifully white-washed, and Aunt Marcia had made up a bed on the floor and covered it with a charming white quilt that had red "rising suns" all over it. And she had set a lighted candle on a barrel for them, feeling that it would never do to give them a kerosene lamp in the granary.

They bolted the door—more romance—and blew out the candle to have the fun of undressing by moonlight.

It was when they were ready for bed that Marigold made her shocking discovery.

"Now, let's say our prayers and snuggle down for a good jaw," she said. "We can talk just as long as we like to-night and nobody to pound on the wall and tell us to stop."

Bernice turned from the loft window whence she had been gazing rapturously on the glimpse of moonlit bay over the birches.

"I never say any prayers," she announced calmly.

Marigold gasped.

"Why, Bernice Willis, that is wicked. Aren't you afraid God will punish you?"

"There isn't any God," said Bernice, "and I won't pray to any one I don't believe in."

Marigold stared at her. This thing had been *said*—and yet the granary still stood and Bernice still stood, a slim, white sceptic in the moonlight.

"But—but—Bernice, there *must* be a God."

"How do you know?"

"Mother told me," said Marigold, gasping at the first argument that presented itself to her dumbfounded mind.

"She told you there was a Santa Claus, too, didn't she?" asked Bernice relentlessly. "Mind you, I'd like to believe in God. But I can't."

"Why not?" wondered Marigold helplessly.

"Because—because I haven't *anybody*. Nobody but Aunt Harriet—and she's only a half-aunt and she doesn't like me a bit. Father and mother are dead—and she won't even talk to me about them. I had a kitten and it died and she won't let me have another. As for this praying-business, I used to pray. Once when I was so small I can just remember it Aunt Harriet sent me down to the store on an errand. The wind was awful cold. And I knelt right down on the road behind a little spruce-bush and asked God to make the wind warmer before I came out of the store. He *didn't*—it was colder than ever and right in my face. And when my kitten took sick I asked God to make it well. But it died. And then I knew there was no God. Because if there had been He wouldn't have let my kitten die when it was the only thing I had to love. So I never prayed any more. Of course I have to kneel down when Aunt Harriet has family prayers. But I just kneel and make faces at God."

"You just said you didn't believe in Him," cried Marigold.

"Well——" Bernice was not going to be posed, "I just make faces at the idea of Him."

So this, Marigold reflected bitterly, was what Babe Kennedy had meant.

"Besides, look at me," continued Bernice rebelliously. "See how ugly I am. Look at the size of my mouth. Why did God make me ugly? Babe Kennedy says I've got a face like a monkey's."

"You haven't. And think how clever you are," cried Marigold.

"I want to be pretty," said Bernice stubbornly. "Then people might like me. But I don't believe in God and I'm not going to pretend I do."

Marigold got up with a long sigh of adjustment and flung her arms about Bernice.

"Never mind. *I* love you. I love you whether you believe in God or not. I only wish you did. It's—it's so much nicer."

"I won't have *you* long," said Bernice, determinedly pessimistic. "Something'll happen to take you away, too."

"Nothing can happen," Marigold challenged fate. "Oh, of course I'll have to go home when my visit's ended—but we'll write—and I'll get Mother to ask you to Cloud of Spruce. We'll be friends forever."

Bernice shook her head.

"No. Something will happen. You'll see. This is too good to last."

A new fear assailed Marigold.

"Bernice, if you don't believe in God how can you expect to go to heaven?"

"I don't. And I don't want to," Bernice answered defiantly. "Aunt Harriet read about heaven in the Bible. All shut in with walls and gates. I'd hate that."

"But wouldn't it be better than—than——"

"Hell? No. You wouldn't have to pretend you liked hell if you didn't. But I don't believe in either place."

"Bernice, don't you believe in the Bible *at all*?"

"Not one word of it. It's all about God and there isn't any God. It's just a—just a fairy-tale."

Somehow, this seemed more terrible to Marigold than not believing in God. God was far-away and invisible but the Bible was right in your hand, so to speak. She sighed again as she knelt to say her own prayers. It seemed a very lonely performance—with that little sceptic of a Bernice standing rigidly by the window, disbelieving. But Marigold prayed for her very softly. "Please, dear God, make Bernice believe in You. Oh, *please*, make Bernice believe in You."

4

At dinner-time next day Marigold made the mistake of her life. Aunt Marcia asked what she was worrying about. And Marigold confessed that she was—not exactly worrying about Bernice but so sorry for her.

"Because, you see, she doesn't believe in God. And it must be terrible not to believe in God."

"What's that?" Uncle Jarvis shot at her suddenly. "What's that about Bernice Willis not believing in God?"

"She says she doesn't," said Marigold mournfully.

"Poor child," said Aunt Marcia.

"Poor child? Wicked child!" thundered Uncle Jarvis. "If she doesn't believe in God you'll not play with her again, Marigold."

"Oh, Jarvis," protested Aunt Marcia.

"I've said it." Uncle Jarvis stabbed a potato with a fork as if he were spearing an infidel. "Woe to them that are at ease in Zion. We keep the Ten Commandments in *this* house."

"Oh, Jarvis, remember the poor child has no one to teach her really. That queer old——"

"Marcia, be silent. She has had plenty of opportunity in a Christian land to learn that there is a God. Doesn't she go to Sunday-school and church? And Harriet Caine is an earnest Christian woman. There is no doubt that Bernice has been taught the truth. But she is plainly not of the elect and she is too wicked for you to play with. Why, I refused to shake hands with Dr. Clarke because he said he believed there were two Isaiahs. Do you think I'll tolerate infidelity?"

Aunt Marcia knew he was inexorable and Marigold felt he was. She began to cry, though she knew tears would have no influence on Uncle Jarvis.

"Oh, Uncle Jarvis—if Bernice—if Bernice comes to believe there is a God can't I play with her then?"

"Yes, but not till them." Uncle Jarvis gave his nose a frantic tweak and left the table, his black beard fairly bristling with indignation. Uncle Jarvis had one of his headaches that day and so was more than usually theological. Aunt Marcia wanted him to take an aspirin to relieve it but he would not. It was flying in the face of God to take aspirin. If He sent you pain it was for you to endure it.

Aunt Marcia tried to comfort Marigold but could not hold out much hope that Uncle Jarvis would change his mind.

"Oh, if I'd only held my tongue," moaned Marigold.

"It would have been wiser," agreed Aunt Marcia sadly. Thirty years of living with Jarvis Pringle had taught her that.

Marigold never forgot Bernice's sad little face when she told her Uncle Jarvis wouldn't let them play together any longer.

"Didn't I tell you? I knew something would happen," she said, her lips quivering.

"Oh, Bernice, couldn't you—couldn't you—*pretend* you believe in Him?" Marigold's voice faltered. She *knew*, deep in her soul, that this wasn't right—that a friendship so purchased must be poisoned at the core. Bernice knew it, too.

"I can't, Marigold. Not even for you. It wouldn't be any use."

"Oh, Bernice, if you come to find out—sometime—that you do believe in Him after all, you'll tell me, won't you? And then we can be friends again. Promise."

Bernice promised.

"But I won't. Isn't this very thing that's happened a proof? If there was a God He'd know it would make me feel more than ever there wasn't."

The week that followed was a very lonely one for Marigold. She missed Bernice dreadfully—and that hateful Babe was always poking round, triumphing.

"Didn't I tell you. *I* knew ages ago Bernice didn't believe there was a God. I'll bet He'll punish her right smart some of these days."

"She doesn't pronounce sepulchre 'see-pulker,' anyhow," retorted Marigold, thinking of the verse Babe had read in Sunday-school the day before.

Babe reddened.

"I don't believe Miss Jackson knows how to pronounce it herself. You make me *sick,* Marigold Lesley. You're just mad because you've found out your precious Bernice isn't the piece of perfection you thought her."

"I'm not mad," said Marigold calmly. "I'm only sorry for you. It must be so terrible to be *you.*"

Marigold prayed desperately every night for Bernice's conversion—prayed without a bit of faith that her prayer would be answered. She even tried to consult the minister about the matter, the night he came to Yarow Lane for supper.

"Tut, tut, everybody believes in God," he said when Marigold timidly put a suppositious case.

So *that* wasn't much help. Marigold thought wildly of refusing to eat unless Uncle Jarvis let her play with Bernice. But something told her that wouldn't move Uncle Jarvis a hair's breadth. He would only tell Aunt Marcia to send her home.

And, oh, the raspberries were thick on the hill—and there was a basketful of adorable kittens in the old tumbledown barn—Uncle Jarvis was always so busy with theology that he hadn't time to patch up his barns. And it was a shame, so it was, that Bernice must miss all this just because she couldn't believe in God.

5

"I've found out something about Bernice Willis. I've found out something about Bernice Willis," chanted Babe Kennedy triumphantly, rocking on her heels and toes in the door of the granary-loft, grinning like a Cheshire cat.

Marigold looked scornfully over her shoulder from the corner where she was arranging her cupboard of broken dishes.

"What have you found out?"

"I'm not going to tell *you*," crowed Babe. "I'm going to tell Bernice, though. I gave her a hint of it this afternoon at the store but I wasn't going to tell her then—I just gave her something to think of. I'm going right down to her aunt's to tell her as soon as I've taken Mrs. Carter's eggs to her. Oh, it's awful—the awfullest thing you ever heard of. You'll find it out pretty soon. Everybody will. Well, bye-bye. I've got to be off. It's coming up a storm, I guess."

Marigold made one swift bound across the granary, caught Babe by the arm, pulled her with scant regard for her eggs into the loft, slammed and bolted the door and stood with her back to it.

"Now, you just tell me what you mean and no more nonsense about it."

Marigold was not a Lesley for nothing. Babe surrendered. She snapped her thin-lipped, cruel little mouth shut, then opened it.

"Very well then. Bernice Willis's father isn't dead. Never was dead. He's in the penitentiary at Dorchester, for stealing money."

"I—don't believe it."

"It's true—cross my heart. I overheard Mrs. Dr. Keyes from Charlottetown telling Ma all about it. He was in a bank—and he—em—embezzled the money. So he was sent to the pen for twelve years and his wife died of a broken heart—though Mrs. Keyes said it was her extravagance drove him to stealing. And Bernice's Aunt Harriet took her.

She was just a baby—and brought her up to think her father was dead, too."

Marigold wanted to disbelieve it. But it was too hopelessly, horribly, evidently true.

"My, ain't I glad I've never played with Bernice!" gloated Babe. "The daughter of a jail-bird. Just think of her face when I tell her!"

"Oh, Babe——" Marigold stooped to plead with Babe Kennedy piteously, "oh, you're not going to tell her. Please—please don't tell her."

"I will so tell her. It'll bring that pride of hers down. Carrying her head as high as if she came of honest people."

"If you were changed into a toad this minute you'd only look like what you are," cried Marigold passionately.

Babe laughed condescendingly.

"Of course you're sore—after thinking nobody was good enough for you to play with but Bernice. Oh, my, Miss Lesley. You can pull in your horns now, I guess. I'm going to tell Bernice right off. She'd have to know it, anyhow, soon—her father'll soon be out of jail. I'm going to have the fun of telling her first. Think of her face. Now, you just open that door and let me out."

Marigold did as she was ordered. The spirit was clean gone out of her.

This was dreadful—dreadful. No hope now that Bernice would ever believe in God. Marigold felt she could hardly blame her. "Think of her face——" Marigold did think of it—that dear, freckled, sensitive, homely little face—when Babe told her the terrible truth. And of course Babe would tell. Babe did so love to tell ugly things. Hadn't she told Kitty Houseman she was going to die? Hadn't she told the teacher Sally Ford had stolen Jane McKenzie's pencil in school?

"If I could get there and tell Bernice first," said Marigold. "If she *has* to hear it she could stand it better from me. I could go by the Lower road—Mrs. Carter lives on the Upper road and I could get there before Babe. But it's dark—and going to rain——"

Marigold shuddered. She didn't mind being out after dark on a road she knew. But a road she didn't know was different.

She ran down the granary stairs and across the birch field to the Lower road. She *must* get to Bernice first. But, oh, how weird and lonely that Lower road was in the sudden swoops of wind and the sudden gushes of wan moonlight between the clouds. Melancholy dogs were howling to each other across the dark farms. The wind whistled dolefully in the fence corners. *Something*—with red eyes—glared out at her from under a bush. And the trees!

By daylight Marigold was a little sister to all the trees in the world. But trees took on such extraordinary shapes in the dark. A huge lion prowled through John Burnham's field. An enormous, diabolical rooster strutted on the fence. A queer elfish old man leered at her over a gate. A very devil squatted at the turn of the road. The whole walk was full of terrors. Marigold was in a cold reek of perspiration when she reached the house behind the young spruce wood and stumbled into the little kitchen, where Bernice was—fortunately—alone.

"Bernice," gasped Marigold, "Babe's coming to tell you something—something dreadful. I—tried to stop her but I couldn't."

Bernice looked at Marigold with fear in her sad grey eyes.

"I knew she meant something this afternoon. She asked me where my father was buried. I said in Charlottetown. 'Go and see if his grave is there,' she said. What is it? Tell me. I'd rather hear it from you than her."

"Oh, I can't, Bernice—I can't," cried Marigold in agony. "I thought I could—but I can't."

"You *must*," said Bernice.

In the end Marigold told her—haltingly—tearfully. Then buried her face in her hands.

"Oh, I'm so happy," said Bernice.

Marigold pulled her away. Bernice was radiant. Eyes like stars.

"Happy?"

"Yes—oh, don't you see. I've got *somebody* after all. It was so dreadful to think I didn't belong to anybody. And Father'll *need* me so much when he comes out next year. There'll be so much I can do for him. Oh, Marigold—I *do* believe in God now—I'm sorry I ever said I didn't. Of course there's a God. I love Him—and I love everybody in the world. I don't mind a bit how poor and ugly I am now that I have a father to love."

In Marigold's utter confusion of thought only one idea stood out clearly.

"Oh, Bernice—if you do—believe in God—Uncle Jarvis will let us play together again."

"Well, I do declare." Babe Kennedy stood in the doorway. A vicious, disappointed Babe. "So *that* was why you didn't want me to tell—so's you could tell youself."

"Exactly."

Marigold put her arm around Bernice and faced Babe defiantly. "And I *have* told it first. So you can just go home, Miss Meow. Nobody wants you here."

CHAPTER XX

The Punishment of Billy

1

"I have the evil eye," said Billy ominously. "People are scared of me."

"If you are going to talk nonsense we can't be friends," said Marigold coldly. "If you're sensible we can have some fun."

Billy—nobody but Aunt Min ever called him William—looked at this sprite-like Marigold and decided to be sensible. When Aunt Min had told him that Marigold Lesley was coming to Windyside for a week Billy had two reactions.

Firstly, he was mad. He didn't want a girl poking and snooping round. Secondly, he was rather pleased. It would be good fun to tease her and teach her her place. Now came a third. Marigold, sleek of hair, blue of eye, light of foot, found favour in his eyes. As sign and seal that evening, sitting on the granary steps, he told her all his troubles. Marigold listened and sympathised with one side of her mind, and with the other carried on her own small thought-processes. As is the way of womenkind of all ages, whether men knew it or not.

Marigold could not quite understand why Billy detested staying at Aunt Min's so bitterly. For herself she rather liked it. Billy thought Aunt Min too strict to live, but in Marigold's eyes her regimen compared very favourably with Grandmother's. Though Marigold called her Aunt Min, according to the custom of the caste, she was really only a cousin of the Cloud of Spruce Lesleys. But she was a genuine aunt of Billy's, that is to say, she had once been married to a half-brother of his father's. So Marigold and Billy might call themselves cousins of a sort.

This was Marigold's first visit to Aunt Min, and was to be the final one of the autumn. Next week she must go to school again.

Marigold liked Windyside. She liked the big airy house with its rooms full of quaint old furniture. There were so many beautiful things to look at, especially the scores of strange and exquisite Indian shells, brought home by Aunt Min's sailor-husband, and the case of stuffed parrots in the hall, with the model of a full-rigged ship atop of it.

To be sure, Aunt Min was very strict about her diet— which was why Grandmother had been so willing to let her come—and her table was something of the leanest. Aunt Min's temper was a bit uncertain also. She could say sharp things on occasion and had been known to slam doors. But there were compensations. For one thing, Aunt Min always asked her casually how she took her tea. For another, cats. Dozens of adorable animals basking on the window-sills, sunning themselves in the garden walks, and prowling about the barn. A batch of kittens was all in the day's work at Windyside. For once in her life Marigold felt that she had all the cats she wanted.

Now, all the use Billy had for a cat was a target.

Marigold thought Billy very funny to look at. He had a round moon face of pink and white, large china-blue eyes, a shock of fine straight yellow hair and a mouth so wide he seemed to be perpetually grinning. But she rather liked him. He was the first boy she had ever liked.

Hip? No, she had never *liked* Hip. This was entirely different.

She listened sympathetically to his tale of woe. She thought Billy had a case.

Billy, it seemed, had not wanted to come to Aunt Min's at all. His mother was dead and he and his father lived together at a boarding-house, where life was tolerable because of Dad. But Dad had to go to South America on a prolonged business-trip and hence Billy's sojourn with Aunt Min.

"Rotten, I call it," he growled. "I wanted to go to Aunt Nora's. She's a real aunt—Mamma's own sister. Not a half-aunt like Aunt Min. I tell you Aunt Nora's great. Always cuts a pie in six pieces. Aunt Min, 'jever notice, always cuts it in eight. A feller can do as he likes at Aunt Nora's. You haven't gotter sit up on your hind-legs and act real pretty *all* the time there. *She* ain't one of your fussy old things."

"Aunt Min is pretty particular," agreed Marigold, thinking how lovely that little blue glimpse of the harbour was at the end of the orchard aisle.

"Particular! Say, I've gotter wash my face *every* day, and brush my teeth more times 'n you could shake a stick at. And live on health foods. Say, you ought to taste Aunt Nora's raspberry buns."

"They sound good," agreed Marigold, who herself felt certain hankerings after Salome's pantry.

"Just think how splendid it would 'a' been there. I wouldn't have to be respectable for one minute—only on Sundays and then I could 'a' stood it for a change. I could go barefoot—and slide down the pighouse roof—and eat everything that come handy. Hot dogs. There's a hot-dog stand just outside Aunt Nora's gate."

Billy groaned. It was agonising to think of the delights one might enjoy at Aunt Nora's and contrast them with the bitter reality at Aunt Min's.

"Why wouldn't your father let you go to Aunt Nora's?" asked Marigold.

"Search *me*. I think he had some fool notion Aunt Min would be offended. I was to Aunt Nora's last summer and Aunt Min thought it was her turn. Mind you, it isn't because she likes me. She's got some fool idea of doing her duty by Dad. And mind you, she thinks Aunt Nora's is an awful place because Aunt Nora is poor. She thinks I wouldn't be 'happy' there. Happy!"

Billy groaned again.

"I *never* had such a good time as I had at Aunt Nora's. Say, I had to hunt her turkeys up every evening. Roam everywhere I liked and no questions asked so long's I turned up at bedtime with the turks. Here if I go outer the gate it's, 'William, *where* have you been?' and 'William, did you scrape your boots?' Why, the cats here have to wipe their feet afore they go in."

"Now, Billy, *that's* exaggerating," said Marigold rebukingly.

"Well, 'tain't exaggerating to say I don't dast throw a single stone here," said Billy defiantly. "It's aggravating, that's what it is. Millions of cats and not a chance to throw a stone at one of 'em. I *did* throw one first day I was here—gave her

old yellow Tom the thrill of his life—and she jawed at me for
a week and made me read a chapter of the Bible every day.
I'd rather she'd taken it out of my hide. She thinks out so
many different ways of punishing me and I never know what
to expect. And then—'ja hear her?—telling Mrs. Kent what
I looked like when I was a baby? She's always at it. Catch
Aunt Nora telling on a feller like that. Or kissing me good-
night. Aunt Min always does. Thinks it's her 'duty,' I
s'pose."

Billy thrust his hands in his pockets and scowled at the
universe. But he was feeling better. Remained only one
grievance to be discussed. The worst of all.

"I could worry along if it wasn't for Sundays," he said. "I
hate Sunday here—hate it worse'n p'isen."

"Why?"

"'Cause I have to write a snopsis."

"What's a snopsis?"

"Why, you go to church and when you come home you
gotter write out all you can remember of the sermon. And if
you can't remember enough—oh, boy! She says *her* children always done it. She'll make *you* do it, too, next Sunday, I'll bet."

Marigold reflected a bit. She didn't think she would
mind. It might be int'resting—a kind of game in fact. For
one Sunday. But poor Bill had to do it every Sunday.

"Well, never mind," she said soothingly. "Sunday's a long
way off yet. Let's see how much fun we can have before
that."

Decidedly, thought Billy, here was a girl.

2

Sunday might be far off—but Sunday came. After a week
during which Billy forgot to hanker for Aunt Nora's. That
was all very well. But Marigold was going home Tuesday.
Billy would have been torn in pieces by wild horses before
he would have confessed how he hated the thought.

But here was Sunday afternoon—and church. To which
Billy and Marigold must go alone because Aunt Min had

been summoned to Charlottetown to see an old friend who was passing through and could be seen on no other day.

"I'm sorry I can't go to church," she said, "because young Mr. Harvey Nelson is preaching for a call and I'd like to hear him. But it can't be helped. I've left your suppers in the pantry for you. Now be good children. Marigold, you'll see that Billy behaves properly, won't you? Don't forget to pay close attention to the sermon. You must both write out a synopsis of it this evening, and I want to see a better result than last Sunday, Billy."

"A-ha," gloated Billy as Aunt Min went out. "I told you you'd have to do it, too."

Marigold did not resent his gloating. He was really behaving very well, considering she had been told to look after his behaviour. That was too awful of Aunt Min. Why *couldn't* people understand certain perfectly plain, self-evident things?

"Oh, my, ain't we Sundayfied!" chanted Davy Dixon on the fence, as they went down the lane. Davy was freckled and snub-nosed, bareheaded and barefooted. With no more clothes on than decency required. But he did look so jolly and care-free. All the Dixons did. But they were a family Aunt Min detested. She never let Billy and Marigold play with them, though they lived only a cat's walk away through the bush behind Aunt Min's.

"Comin' to the picnic?" asked Davy.

"What picnic?"

"Oh, just the Dixon family picnic," grinned Davy. "This is Mom's and Pop's wedding-day. Twelve years married 'n' ain't sorry for it yit. We're going to take our new car 'n' go to the sand-hills. Got a basket of eats 'd make your eyes stick out. Yum-yum. 'N' mom said to ask youse to come along, too, 'cause she knew your Aunt Min was going away 'n' youse'd be lonesome."

Marigold found herself wishing they could go. At home she liked going to church, but she was sure she wouldn't like going to Windyside church. She didn't like the look of it; a big, bare, wind-beaten, drab-tinted church with a spire as long and sharp as a needle; somehow it was not a friendly church. And she knew nobody there. A drive in a motor-car to the sand-hills sounded very alluring. But of course it was unthinkable.

What was Billy saying?

"I'll go if you'll lend me that book at your place—*The Flying Roll*."

"Bill-*ee*," said Marigold.

"Oh, all right," said Dave. "It belongs to old Aunt Janey but she won't care."

"I'll go," said Billy decidedly. "Coming, Marigold?"

"Oh, please, remember what day this is," implored Marigold, with a wild wish in the back of her mind that she could go. "And what will Aunt Min say?"

"Aunt Min isn't going to know a thing about it. I've got a plan. Aw, come on. We'll have a rip-roaring time."

"Billy, you don't mean it."

"You bet I do. You can go to church if you want to and stick all the afternoon to varnishy seats."

"Gotter make up your mind quick," said Dave. "Lizzie's waiting."

Marigold reflected rapidly. She *couldn't* go alone to a strange church. And it would be so lonesome to stay home. The sand-dunes—the waves—the wind on the sea——

"I'll—go," she said helplessly.

"I knew you'd some gizzard in you. Atta girl," gloated Bill. "Let's scoot back and take off our proud rags. Jes' a minute, Dave."

A few minutes later they were running along the path through a scented field of hay on a short cut to the Dixons. Ordinarily Marigold felt she had wings on a day like this. Now she suddenly felt leaden-footed. But Billy must not suspect it. He would despise her if he found out she really did not care for all this lawlessness.

The Dixons' new car proved to be a very second-hand snub-nosed little Ford, into which they all piled and rattled and bounced down a narrow deep-rutted lane to the sand-dunes. Marigold sat on the knee of Mrs. Dixon, a big, pink, overblown lady who used what even Billy knew to be bad grammar, in a cheerful, excruciating voice. Marigold thought the bones would be shaken out of her before they got to the dunes.

It should have been a wonderful afternoon. Polly Dixon was a pretty, gentle little girl and Marigold liked her. They slid down the sand-hills and made shore pies and dug wells in the sand. They gathered clam-shells and went bathing in a little sand-cove up the shore where the water was like soft, warm, liquid turquoise. They played games with the boys. They laughed and ran and scampered. And under it all Marigold knew perfectly well that she was not having a good time. She was only trying to make herself think she was.

Even the lunch—to which she looked forward a little ashamedly after a week of Aunt Min's diet—was a disappointment. There was plenty of it—but Mrs. Dixon was not a good cook. Marigold ate stale sandwiches, and cookies that reeked of soda, and a piece of mushy lemon-pie. She always believed that she also ate two crickets that had got tangled up in the meringue of the pie. But Billy thought that feed was extra-x. "I wish to goodness I could eat some more but I can't," he sighed, bolting the last morsel of a gorgeous piece of cake whose iced surface was decorated with violent red-and-yellow candies.

3

"Wasn't it jolly?" said Billy, drawing a long unregretful breath as they walked home together through the hayfield.

"Won't it be jolly when Aunt Min asks you to write a synopsis and you can't?" demanded Marigold rather wearily and sarcastically.

Billy grinned.

"I'll just write it. This *Flying Roll* book is full of sermons. I read some dandy ones in it one day down at Dixons' before you came. We'll just write a snopsis of one of them, and Aunt Min will never know the difference."

"*We* won't," cried Marigold. "You can do as you like, but I won't cheat like that."

"Then you'll go and give the whole thing away," said Billy, pale with wrath and fear.

"No-o-o, I won't. I'll just tell Aunt Min I couldn't write a synopsis."

"She'll send you to bed 'thout any supper."

"I don't care," said Marigold pathetically, putting her hand on her stomach. "That lemon-pie was awful."

Billy betook himself to a little room Aunt Min called her library. His opinion was that writing a "snopsis" with the printed sermon before you was a snap. When Aunt Min came home he was ready for her. Marigold said, with a very good imitation of Grandmother Lesley's manner, that she could not write a synopsis.

Aunt Min looked at her for a moment but said nothing. She took Billy's copious sheets with a very grim smile—a smile that speedily changed to a frown.

"Surely—surely Harvey Nelson never preached such stuff as this."

"Why, what's the matter with it?" cried Billy.

"Matter. It's heresy—rank heresy. Why, the man must be a Second Adventist. I never read such doctrines. Well, he'll not get any call to Windyside if I can prevent it. I was in favour of him because he's engaged to Dovie Sinclair and she is a distant relation of mine. But this preposterous sermon is too much."

Aunt Min rustled indignantly out of the room, leaving Billy to reflect on the snares and pitfalls of existence.

"What do you suppose was wrong with it?" he whispered miserably.

"I don't know," said Marigold agitatedly, "but I do know that if Mr. Nelson is engaged to Dovie Sinclair he's *got* to get that call. Dovie is my Sunday-school teacher at home and I won't have her disappointed through our fault."

"Don't you dare snitch on me," cried Billy. "Let things alone. Maybe she'll cool down—or find out from some one else he didn't preach it."

Marigold's face was white and tragic.

"She never will. She'll just say he doesn't preach sound doctrine and she won't explain anything about it. You know Aunt Min. She's got to be told and I'm going to tell her. But you needn't come if you're scared."

"I'm scared but I'm coming. You don't suppose I'm going to leave you to do it all alone?" said Billy staunchly. "Besides it was all my doings. I made you go. If Aunt Min has to be told, she's gotter be told that, too."

No wonder folks liked Billy.

4

Half an hour later Billy and Marigold were sitting on the granary steps. The fatal interview was over and it had not been a pleasant one, to state it mildly.

None the pleasanter for Marigold in that Aunt Min forgave her readily because Billy had led her astray. Perhaps Aunt Min did not want to get in wrong with the Cloud of Spruce people. But all the vials of her wrath were uncorked on Billy's devoted head. She told Billy he had disgraced his name and ordered him to go out and stay out until she had decided on his punishment.

If it had not been for Billy, Marigold would have been feeling very happy. It was so delightful to be good friends with herself again. And—if only one knew what was going to be done to Billy—it was such a perfect evening. Those little golden dells among the sunset hills—that path of moonrise glitter on the harbour over which a ship of dreams might come sailing—those gossiping poplars—the green creaminess of that field of buckwheat-blossom in the shade of the wood—those pines behind the well like big green purring pussy-cats—that sweetest imp-faced kitten purring at her from under the milk-bench—but——

"*What* do you suppose she'll do?" she whispered to Billy. The subject had such a gruesome fascination.

"Oh, likely make me wear a girl's apron for a week," groaned Billy. "She made we wear one for two days the time I put the peanut-shells in Elder Johnny's pocket at prayer-meeting. Say——" Billy began to laugh, "that *was* fun. When he pulled out his hanky in the middle of his prayer the shells flew every which way for a Sunday. One struck the minister on the nose."

Marigold *saw* the picture and laughed satisfyingly. Billy reflected gloomily that she was going home Tuesday. If only she were to be around to help him through whatever Aunt Min would visit on him. To be sure, she had got him into the scrape but he bore her no grudge for that. She was a good little scout.

The moon had come up until she seemed to be resting on the very tip of the tall Lombardy on the hills when Aunt Min came across the yard, a rigid figure of outraged majesty. She looked scornfully at Billy and spoke in a sad, gentle way. When Aunt Min banged doors and looked or spoke sourly or sharply no one worried. But when Aunt Min smiled in that curious sweet fashion and spoke in that low, even tone, then beware. It was the calm before the levin-bolt.

"Do you realise that you have behaved very badly?" she asked.

"Yes'm," gulped Billy.

"I have decided——" Aunt Min paused.

Billy was speaking. *What* fiendish punishment had Aunt Min devised? Marigold slipped a little cold hand of backing into his.

"I don't feel equal to the responsibility of looking after you any longer," resumed Aunt Min more gently than ever, "so I have decided to send you to your Aunt Nora's to-morrow."

CHAPTER XXI

Her Chrism of Womanhood

1

A new magic had fallen over Cloud of Spruce. Grandmother solemnly decreed that Marigold might play with Sidney Guest. Grandmother would not, of course, call him Budge as everybody else did. His mother was a Randolph from Charlottetown, so that he was a quite permissible playmate for a Lesley of Harmony. Mr. Guest had bought Mr. Donkin's farm and so Budge lived right next door to Cloud of Spruce.

He was a "nice-mannered" little boy, so Grandmother said. Rather thin and scrawny as to looks, with sandy hair but fine clear grey eyes. The only thing Grandmother was seriously afraid of was that they might poison themselves in some of their prowls and rambles. Not an ill-founded fear at all. For, in spite of all warnings, they ate or tried to eat nearly everything they came across.

Marigold had never had a real playmate in Harmony before, save for Gwen's hectic three weeks. She did not seem to care for any of the girls in Harmony, and though she wrote fat gossipy letters to Gwen and Paula and Bernice she did not see them very often. Perhaps Sylvia spoiled her for other little girls, as Mother sometimes thought rather anxiously. Mother had always defended Sylvia sympathisingly against a Grandmother who did not understand some things. But sometimes lately she wondered if she had been wise in so doing. It would not be a good thing if the wild secret charm of fairy-playmates spoiled Marigold for the necessary and valuable companionship of her kind. Marigold was twelve. Her golden hair was deepening to warm brown and she had at last learned not to pronounce interesting "int'resting." Surely it was time she was outgrowing Sylvia.

So Lorraine Lesley was glad when, just at the beginning of vacation, the Guests bought the Donkin place and Marigold and Budge took a prompt liking to each other. Marigold was amazed to find herself really liking a boy. She had never liked any of the boys in school. She had liked Billy but she had forgotten him. She had detested Cousin Marcus's Jack. As for Hip Price, he had made her hate all boys for a time. But Budge was different from any boy she had ever known.

For weeks Marigold's existence became one of hair-raising excitement. She did things to win Budge's approval that she had never dreamed of doing. They went trouting up the brook and Marigold was such a sport in regard to worms that Budge thought in his heart—but did not say—that she was almost as good as a boy. They waded under the bridge. They climbed to the ventilator on top of the big Guest barn. They played pirate on an old green boat—the *Daisy Dean*—stranded on the harbour shore, with a black flag made out of Salome's old black silk skirt and decorated with a skull and cross-bones. In it they sailed on amazing voyages hunting for gold and glamour and adventure. They had a password and a secret sign. They fixed up a stove of stones and cooked mussels and potatoes over it.

With Budge, Marigold could explore all the pretty playlands down the harbour where she would never have dared to go alone. They even went as far as that grey misty end of the world known as the harbour's mouth, where the silver-and-lilac sand-dunes stretched in all their wild sweet loveliness of salt-withered grasses and piping sea-winds. Nobody ever knew *that*, or that they had got caught by the tide and had to climb the banks and come home through dripping wet meadows. 'Twas a guilty triumphant secret. And another was the driftwood fire they made on the shore one twilight. They had both been told never to play with fire, but that did not spoil their enjoyment of it one bit. Rather heightened it, I am afraid. This secret forbidden thing had a charm all its own. And some days they fairly lived in the froggy marsh—where a very decent dragon also had his abode and grizzly bears grizzled.

Marigold had a deadly horror of frogs but she never let Budge know it, and she compelled herself to carry a dead snake—on a stick—to win his admiration. She also brought herself to say "Holy cats," but try as she would she could never compass a "darn," which was just as well. Because in his heart Budge did not care for girls who said "darn."

She was never able to learn to whistle on a blade of grass, as he did. But she could do one thing he couldn't do—make the dearest pudding-bags out of the fat live-forever leaves. Budge tried and tried but his thumb pressure was always too heavy, so the balance of respect was kept true. And when Budge sat down on a hot oven door one day, in trousers that needed a patch, Marigold never even asked him how his burns were getting on. By such tact is friendship preserved.

Budge patted Marigold's kitten, Pops, and Marigold loved his dog, Dix. But Sylvia she could not yet share with him. Budge had somehow got the idea that Marigold had some pet mystery connected with the hill of spruce, and sometimes teased her to tell him what it was. But Marigold always refused. Not yet—not yet. She had never, in spite of fleeting temptation, told any of her playmates about Sylvia—not even Bernice. Sylvia was so much her own. Although—Marigold owned it to herself occasionally with a sorrowful sigh—somehow Sylvia wasn't just the same. Not so vivid—so living—so *real*. The change had come about so slowly that Marigold did not yet realise how far her jolly chumship with Budge had replaced that goblin-comradeship of her lonely years. She clung to Sylvia, remembering what Aunt Marigold had said to her one evening as they sat in the orchard.

"Keep your dream, little Marigold, as long as you can. A dream is an immortal thing. Time cannot kill it or age wither it. You may tire of reality but never of dreams."

"It hurts—to wake up, though," said Marigold timidly. "When I come back through the Green Gate I always feel that it's just terrible to think there really isn't any Sylvia— that she's just something I've dreamed."

"The dreamer's joy is worth the dreamer's pain," said Aunt Marigold, knowing that since Marigold had begun to think of Sylvia as a dream the sad awakening was near.

So, almost every day, some time of it, Marigold slipped through The Magic Door and the Green Gate and summoned Sylvia. Sylvia always came—still. But there was a difference.

Marigold would have told Budge about Sylvia if she could have been sure how he would take her. Marigold knew of a side of his nature which made her think he might understand Sylvia. Rarely, Budge gave her glimpses of this side. When they grew tired of prowling and pirating and sat on the wharf watching the ghostly sails of outgoing ships in the twilight, Budge would recite to her shyly the queer little verses of poetry he sometimes made up. Marigold thought they were wonderful. Budge understood, too, the secret thrill that came when you opened a new book. And he was a crackerjack at yarns. She liked his scarlet boy-stories better than her rose-pink and moon-blue girl-fancies. That one of the wolf-skin rug on the Guest parlour floor coming alive and prowling at night with burning eyes. Marigold couldn't sleep when she went to bed for the delicious horror of it. Was it coming across the road now—snuffing through the garden—padding up the stairs? Marigold screamed aloud and Mother came in and said she'd had a nightmare.

2

And then. The Austins bought the old Burnaby place and moved in. Tad Austin was a boy of Budge's age. And Marigold found herself deserted.

"'Tis an old tale and often told."

Tad Austin's parents, for some inscrutable reason, had seen fit to christen him Romney, but he never got anything but Tad. He was really not a bad-looking boy, with a chubby, agreeable brown face, although Marigold, who naturally could see nothing attractive about him, thought that his round, prominent blue eyes looked absurdly like the fat blue plums on the tree by the apple-barn.

The world was suddenly a cold, lonely, empty place for our poor Marigold. Always hitherto she had taken her troubles to her mother. But she couldn't take this—she couldn't. Not even Mother could understand. Certainly Grandmother couldn't. Grandmother, who, passing Marigold sitting disconsolately on the twilight steps, had re-marked humorously,

> "'Don't sigh but send
>   And if he doesn't come let him be hanged.'"

Send, indeed. Marigold would have died the death be-fore she would have made the slightest effort to get Budge back. The cats could have him. She got an enormous satis-faction out of picturing to herself how haughty and implaca-ble she would be if he *did* come back. At least this was how she felt about it at first.

"Perhaps he'll be sorry when I'm dead," thought Mari-gold darkly. But she would show Budge—show every-body—*she* didn't care. She went and made candy and sang like a lark.

But there was nobody to share the candy with when it was made. She gave Lazarre the most of it to take to his children.

Life was a howling wilderness for Marigold the next few weeks. It seemed to her that Budge and Tad literally flaunted their intimacy and fun in her face—though the shameful truth was that they never thought about her at all. They got up a show and all the boys of Harmony could see it for a cent, but no girls. Oh, it was *mean*!

Budge and Tad went fishing up the brooks. Budge and Tad dug for pirate gold. Budge and Tad had a smuggler's rendezvous in the cave Marigold had discovered on the har-bour shore. Budge and Tad had the kitten-hunt in the Guest barn which Marigold and Budge had planned to have in the fulness of time when there should be kittens to hunt.

This was the last straw that broke Marigold's pride. She would so have loved a kitten-hunt with Budge in the great dusky hay-scented old barn.

She must get Budge back. She *must*. Existence was quite impossible without him. But how? What could she do? Marigold knew she must not show her hand too plainly. Instinct told her that. Besides she had a dim old memory of something Old Grandmother had said long, long ago.

"If you run after a man he'll run away. It's instinct. We *have* to run when anything chases us."

Wherefore she, Marigold, would *not* run after Budge. Was there any other way?

"I wonder if it would do any good to pray about it," she thought. Then she decided she couldn't try it anyway.

"I don't want him to come back because God made him come. I want him to come back because he *wants* to."

Like an inspiration came the thought of Sylvia. She would tell him about Sylvia. He had always wanted to know about Sylvia. He might come back then.

It was a fortunate coincidence that Salome asked her to go over to the Guest place on an errand that very afternoon. Budge was sitting on the side door-steps packing fish-worms in a tin can. He grinned at her cheerfully and absently. It had never occurred to Budge that he had treated Marigold shamelessly. She had simply—for the time—ceased to count.

"I have something to tell you," whispered Marigold.

"What is it?" said Budge indifferently.

Marigold sat down beside him and told him all about Sylvia at last. About The Magic Door and the Green Gate and the Land of Butterflies and The Rhyme. She had a curious unpleasant sense of loss and disloyalty as she told it. As if she were losing something that was very precious.

And she had her reward.

"Aw, that sounds awful silly," said Budge.

Marigold went away without another word. She would *never* speak to Budge Guest again. She would *never* have anything to do with *any* boy again. All tarred with the same brush, as Lazarre said. She would go back to Sylvia—darling, neglected Sylvia. Through The Magic Door—up the slope of fern—through the Green Gate. Then The Rhyme.

And no Sylvia!

Marigold stared helplessly around her with a quivering lip. No Sylvia. Sylvia would not come. Would never come again. Marigold felt this as we feel certain things irrevocably. Was it because she had told Budge about her? Or was it because she had suddenly grown too old and wise for fairyland. Were the "ivory gates and golden" of which Mother sometimes sang, closed behind her forever? Marigold flung herself down among the ferns in the bitterest tears she had ever shed—ever would shed, perhaps. Her lovely dream was gone. Who of us is there who has not lost one?

3

It was the next day Budge came back—an indignant Budge, avid to pour out his wrongs to somebody. And that somebody was the disdained and disdainful Marigold, who had vowed afresh the night before that if Budge Guest ever spoke to her again she would treat him with such scorn and contempt that even his thick hide would feel it.

Budge and Tad had fought because their dogs had fought.

"*My* dog won," gulped Budge. "And Tad got mad. He said Dix was only a *mongrel cur.*"

"He's jealous," said Marigold comfortingly. "And he has an awful temper. I heard that long ago from a girl who knew him *well.*"

"*I* dared him to fight *me*, then—and he said he *wouldn't* fight me because I was such a sissy."

"He wouldn't fight you because he knew he'd get licked even worse than his dog did," said Marigold, oh, so scornfully. But the scorn was all for Tad.

"He *wouldn't* fight—but he kept on saying mean things. He said I wore a *nightcap*. Well, I did once, years ago—when I was little but——"

"Everybody wears nightcaps when they're *little*," said Marigold.

"And he said that I was a coward and that I wouldn't walk through the graveyard at night."

"Let's go through it to-night and *show* him," said Marigold eagerly.

"Not to-night," said Budge hastily. "There's a heavy dew. You'd get wet."

Happiness flowed through Marigold like a wave. Budge was thinking of *her* welfare. At least, so she believed.

"He said *his* grandfather had whiskers and mine hadn't. *Should* a grandfather have whiskers?"

"It's ever so much more *aristocratic* not to have them," said Marigold with finality.

"And he said *I* wasn't tattooed and couldn't stand tattooing. He's always been so conceited about that snake his sailor-uncle tattooed on his arm."

"What if he is tattooed?" Marigold wanted to know. She recalled what Grandmother had said about that tattooed snake. "It's a barbaric disfigurement. Didn't *you* say anything to *him*?"

Budge gulped.

"Everything *I* said he said it over again and *laughed*."

"There's something so insulting about *that*," agreed Marigold.

"And he called me a devilish pup."

"*I* wouldn't mind being called a devilish pup," said Marigold, who thought it sounded quite dashing and romantic.

But there was something yet worse to be told.

"He—said—I was *unladylike*."

This was a bit of a poser for Marigold. It would never do to imply that Budge *was* ladylike.

"Why didn't you tell him that he's pop-eyed and that he eats like a rhinoceros?" she inquired calmly.

Budge was at the end of his list of grievances. His anger was ebbing and he had a horrible feeling that he was going to—cry. And back of that a delicious feeling that even if he did Marigold would understand and not despise him. What a brick of a girl she was! Worth a million Tad Austins.

As a matter of fact Budge got off without crying but he never forgot that feeling.

"I'm never going to have anything to do with him again," he said darkly. "Say, do you want one of them grey kittens? If you do I'll bring it over to-morrow."

"Oh, do," said Marigold. "The Witch's are all black this summer."

They sat there for an hour eating nut-sweet apples, entirely satisfied with themselves. To Marigold the tiny roses on the bush by the steps seemed like the notes or echoes of the little song that was singing itself in her heart. All that had once made magic made it again. And she asked Budge if he had told Tad about Sylvia.

"Of course not. That's *your* secret," said Budge, grandly. "And he doesn't know about the password and the secret sign either. That's *our* secret."

When Budge went home it was agreed that he should bring the kitten the next afternoon and that they should go on a quest for the Holy Grail up among the spruces.

"I'll *never* forget to-night," said Marigold. Some lost ecstasy had returned to life.

4

But the next morning it seemed as if the night before had never been. When Marigold had sprung eagerly out of her blue-and-white bed, slipped into her clothes and run liltingly down to the front door—what did she see?

Budge and Tad walking amiably down the road with fishing-poles and worm-cans, while two dogs trotted behind in entire amity.

Marigold stood rigid. She made no response when Budge waved his pole gaily at her and shouted hello. Her heart, so full of joy a moment ago, was lead, heavy and cold.

That was a doleful forenoon. Her new dress of peach silk came home but Marigold was not interested in it. A maiden forsaken and grieved in spirit has no vanity.

But just let Budge Guest come to her again for comfort!

Budge came that afternoon but not in search of comfort. He was cheerful and grinful and he brought an adorable clover-scented kitten with a new pattern of stripes. But Marigold was cold and distant. Very.

"What's biting you?" asked Budge.

"Nothing," said Marigold.

"Look here," expostulated Budge, "I came over to go Grailing with you. But if you don't want to go just say so. Tad wants me to go to the harbour mouth."

For a moment, pride and—something else—struggled fiercely together in Marigold's heart. Something else won.

"Of course I want to go Grail-hunting," she said.

They did not find the Grail but they found one of Grandmother's precious pink-lustre cups which had been lost for two years, ever since a certain Lesley Reunion Picnic had been held on the spruce hill. Found it safe and unharmed in a crevice of the stone dyke. And Grandmother was so pleased that she gave them a whole plateful of hop-and-go-fetch-its to eat—which was symbolic. She would not have given them hop-and-go-fetch-its if it had really been the Grail they found.

5

Budge went home. He had a tryst with Tad for the evening. Marigold sat down on the veranda steps. The little streak of yellow sky above the dark hills over the harbour was very lonely. The sound of breakers tumbling on the far away outer shore was very lonely. She was very lonely—in spite of her jolly afternoon with Budge.

Aunt Marigold coming out, noted Marigold's face and sat down beside her. Aunt Marigold, who had never had any children of her own, knew more mothercraft than many women who had. She had not only the seeing eye but the understanding heart as well. In a short time she had the whole story. If she smiled over it Marigold did not see it.

"You must not expect to have Budge wholly to yourself, dear, as you had Sylvia. Our earthly house of love has many mansions and many tenants. Budge will be always coming back to you. He finds something in your companionship Tad can't give him. He'll come for it, never fear. But you must share him with others. We—women—must always share."

Marigold sat awhile longer after Aunt Marigold had gone away. But she was no longer unhappy. A dreamy smile lingered on her lips. The new kitten purred on her lap. The twilight wrapped her round. Robber winds came down out of the cloud of spruce to rifle spices from the flower-beds in the orchard. There was gold of her namesake flowers all along the dusk of the walk. The stars twinkled through the fir-trees and right and left the harbour range-lights shone like great earth stars. Presently a moon rose and there was a sparkling trail over the harbour like a lady's silken dress.

Yes, she must share Budge. The old magic was gone forever—gone with Sylvia and the Hidden Land and all the dear, sweet fading dreams of childhood. But after all there were compensations. For one thing, she could be as big a coward as she wanted to be. No more hunting snakes and chivying frogs. No more pretending to like horrible things that squirmed. She was no longer a boy's rival. She stood on her own ground.

"And I'll always be here for him to come back to," she thought.

ABOUT THE AUTHOR

L. M. MONTGOMERY's fascinating accounts of the lives and romances of Anne, Emily, and other well-loved characters have achieved long-lasting popularity the world over. Born in 1874 in Prince Edward Island, Canada, Lucy Maud showed an early flair for storytelling. She soon began to have her writing published in papers and magazines, and when she died in Toronto in 1942 she had written more than twenty novels and a large number of short stories. Most of her books are set in Prince Edward Island, which she loved very much and wrote of most beautifully. *Anne of Green Gables*, her most popular work, has been translated into thirty-six languages, made into a film twice, and has had continuing success as a stage play. Lucy Maud Montgomery's early home in Cavendish, P.E.I., where she is buried, is a much-visited historic site.

Special Offer
Buy a Bantam Book
for only 50¢.

Now you can order the exciting books you've been wanting to read straight from Bantam's latest catalog of hundreds of titles. *And* this special offer gives you the opportunity to purchase a Bantam book for only 50¢. Here's how:

By ordering any five books at the regular price per order, you can also choose any other single book listed (up to a $5.95 value) for only 50¢. Some restrictions do apply, so for further details send for Bantam's catalog of titles today.

Just send us your name and address and we'll send you Bantam Book's SHOP AT HOME CATALOG!